SHAMUS

THE EVER-LOST IMMORTAL

Story and Illistrations By:

Zachary Tait Frappier

Pubished By:

For my Grandfather
A crazy man with a heart of gold and purple.

AND A SPECIAL THANKS TO THOSE WHO HELPED ME GET TO THIS POINT.

Prologue

I have seen many familiar eyes Across the face of the earth. Our meetings are always in vastly different locations and periods of time. I know it would be crazy to believe that these are always the same souls, so I refer more to the notion that all the souls I have encountered have roughly gone through similar experiences and heartaches. No matter the point in time, the location on the earth, or the ethnicity that resides where I stood, I've seen the same tortured eyes over and over again. The only caveat is that they are permanently attached to new souls with new stories and personalities.

Being in the profession I am in, I've been able to meet world leaders, street urchins, and everyone else that falls within the man-made class structures. Frankly, I am always excited to be reintroduced to the eyes I've grown to know and cherish. I always look forward to any change to what they may bring, and I'm always looking for a new story to keep me company on my long, lonesome journey. I just wish they were as thrilled to see me as I am to see them. Unfortunately, it seems the people I encounter would prefer to run from me than embrace me as they should. My coming is only natural. There have been people who were overcome with joy to know that I would take their sorrows and illnesses, but most of the souls try to run. Unfortunately, there is no escaping. The most recent encounter I had before everything in my life changed was just a few moments ago.

The most recent encounter I had before everything in my life changed was with someone who thought they could outrun death. The event occurred within a crowded hospital on a warm summer day. I was standing at the end of a guest's room, where a balding man in his late fifties was lying unconscious in his bed. He was clinging to life, being supported by machinery alone. His time was near, hence why I was there. He was surrounded by the people that loved him. The first was a woman who was just about the man's age. I could see that she had graying-blonde hair, and a wedding band indicating she was his wife. Then there were two men who resembled the man in the bed, one of which was in his early thirties, and the other was in his late twenties. They were brothers, his sons. There was also a woman around the same age as the two standing men. In her arms was an infant. These two were his daughter and grandchild. All together, these people formed a family that was gathered together one last time. They were grieving. Suddenly, the light of the outside world that caused the sanitized room to illuminate started to dull as if a large cloud began to block the sun's rays.

As soon as the colors dulled, all these gathered family members vanished, leaving the man in the bed, myself, and the inanimate objects in the room. After watching his family disappear, I looked at a digital alarm clock on a nightstand near the head of the bed. I found that the time had frozen at three thirty-seven. Suddenly, The man began to stir within seconds and sat up in his bed. He looked around the room, and as soon as he saw me, a cloud of yellow light radiated from his torso. To give you a little insight into one of my many abilities, I can see the aura of a human's soul. I can see how they feel as I receive a glimpse into the life they once lived. His name was Matthew Addams, and he was just an average person. He was an accountant, but his eyes told me that they could have been attached to

2

a blue-collar factory worker in their past life. He was admitted to this hospital only a few days prior. At the same time, he was in a critical state due to a terrible motor vehicle accident. Due to the fear in his aura, I could tell that he thought this was not his time to go, but the universe disagreed. Matthew scrambled off the bed and fell to the floor before rushing to the door. Within a second, he pulled it open and entered the hall while shouting for assistance. I slowly followed, and after noticing my pursuit, Matthew began to run down the now vacant hallway. He was sprinting away as fast as he could but began to slow after realizing his surroundings were starting to fade into nothingness. As if he was running toward a void.

Seeing this, he decided to make an about-face to face his demon in the hallway. This choice didn't impact me in the slightest since both of these options would lead to the same place. So, he rushed up to me and tried to attack. I would have congratulated him for being a simple accountant while having the bravery to try and best the darkness of my stature. Still, I am under strict orders to subdue violent souls using extreme measures to ensure compliance. This meant that I was forced to draw my infamous scythe and strike him down. This caused his soul to dissipate into glowing teal particles, fall toward the ground, and become absorbed by the earth. I hate when I am forced to do this, but I have to do what it takes to take my claim.

Yes, the occasional few are overcome with happiness even if there is a somber undertone. Matthew was an exceptional soul trying to fight for his life. Still, typically these souls will become terrified and try to run away. I've always extended a hand to greet the souls I am made to encounter. I am never trying to be hostile, being that the transition they'll be making is one of the hardest they ever faced, but they always run and try to escape. I just find it sad. There is no changing the course of time. Once they see me, it is over for them.

Now, you may be asking why I let them run if it burdens me so much. The answer is that it makes no difference if I take these souls personally or if they leave the earth themselves. It's just a matter of finding them in the void after they get there. Usually, this isn't hard since my abilities force me to keep up. No matter how far they decide to run, I am always a few steps behind. Once I target a soul, we are bound until the soul leaves the mortal earth for good. With that being said, there are exceptions. Sometimes a soul is meant to return to its body, and if I receive the command before I capture the soul, I let them go. Nevertheless, I wish they wouldn't run from me. The souls that embrace me once they lay their gaze upon me are always the best to encounter.

I'm sure you have been able to put together precisely who I am by now, or at least the role I am meant to play, but I need to inform you that I am not a monster. I do not like being labeled as the one that destroys lives. I'm not "the darkness at the end of the road" that many of the living claim that I am. I'm merely a ferryman meant to lead the souls I encounter towards a new life based on their actions within the mortal coil. I understand that no one wants to lose the love of their lives, but they should know that death is inevitable, and they should be happy that I am here to lead them. I am not a monster; I am a savior.

You may be asking, why am I saying all of this? My response would be; in due time, hopefully, all questions will be answered by the end of all of this, but I know others will arise along the way. I need you to know that this is not a story about myself alone. Instead, this story is about how a very important human and I are mysteriously drawn together before facing a supernatural adventure. You see, I've tried to look into the eyes of this one, but their eyes are unlike the others I have seen. At first, I was baffled by his mere existence. His eyes were unlike any others that I've met. There was something about him. I can often see the path a human will take by looking into their eyes; however, the way he is supposed

4

to take appears to be hazed from my vision. I can usually see the exact moment where a soul and I are supposed to cross paths. Still, this one seems like we crossed several times. I am unsure why this is the one that was chosen. So, I will recount the tale that I was made to be part of. Our tragedy of having to experience lies, deceptions, deaths, and resurrections. This is the story of myself and the man known as Shameis Eli.

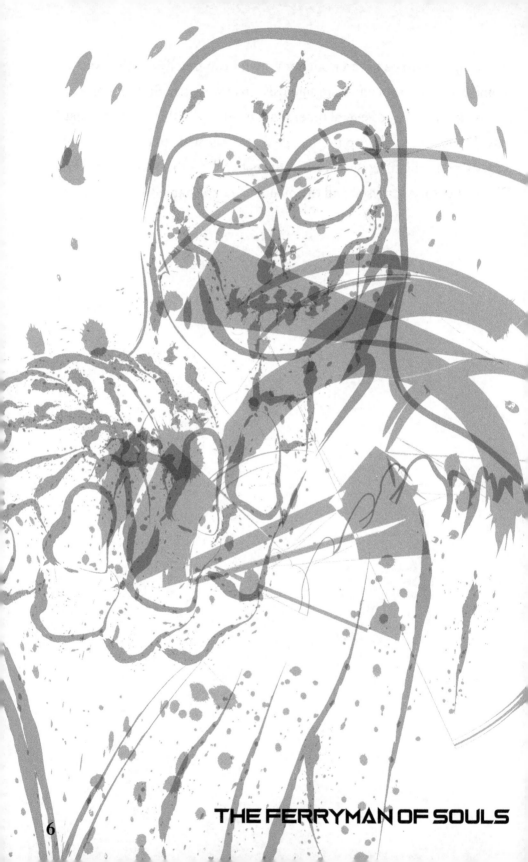

THE FERRYMAN OF SOULS

6

Part One: Decending into Madness

Chapter One

Typically, I am not introduced to a soul until moments before their mortal world passes. Then, as described in my anecdote, I can get to know a person as if I was a long-lasting acquaintance. This is the cruel joke that my existence plays on me. I get to see the life of every human I interact with, just for me to have to take them from this world. At least that's how it was until I was first introduced to Shameis. When I was initially *pulled* to the very first intersection of our lives, the course of my life and what I know of my path shifted. Of course, I didn't realize that things were going to change. I can't see into the future. I just get a feeling of where another soul's path could vaguely lead them. Not my own life, just others. This is necessary for my profession, mainly if the soul is meant to simply have a near-death experience. Anyways, I guess I should start this tale with a sequence of chronological events.

In that first meeting, it was wintertime. I found myself *pulled* to the middle of a two-lane motorway in the dead of night. There was not a pair of headlights or taillights in sight. This specific stretch of road was nearly flat, with no hill or valley within view. There wasn't much to this particular place on the motorway in terms of scenery. It was lined with frost-covered pine trees on either side. It had a couple of snow-covered strips of the earth, one in the middle between the two directions of pavement and one on each side between the motorway and wood lines. The wind was still, and there wasn't a cloud in the sky. This motorway was illuminated by the overhead moonlight that beamed brightly through the night sky. I could feel the frigid pavement underneath my bony feet as I stood in place. It's moments like this that I am thankful that my otherworldly abilities do not allow me to experience pain the way a mortal would. It has been quite a while since I could take in the details of my surroundings for more than a few seconds. I was even able to gaze at the stars for a bit. Based on their placement, I could tell that I was standing in the northwestern hemisphere. Perhaps in the northern section of what is currently known as the United States of America? The Midwest, if I recall correctly. So, as I gazed up at the stars, I understood that this moment was meant to be quiet. The scene was relatively peaceful while serving as a short yet fantastic break from the hecticness of my average day-to-day ongoings.

Shortly after enjoying the silence for a few moments, the faint roar of a motor vehicle pierced the night sky. It was steadily growing with every passing second. I turned toward the distracting noise and was able to see a pair of headlights approaching. Being that the light and noise had just come into range, I could tell the vehicle was nearly ten miles away from where I stood. The pair of lamps were heading toward me on the same strip of concrete I was standing on, so I wasn't going to have to move far for it. I have been in this situation more than a few times. I'm often *pulled* to a location moments before death to take the soul easier. Still, I did find it rather odd that I was brought here more than ten minutes before I was needed. Yes, it was strange, but it has happened before. So I took the opportunity to walk off the pavement onto the cold, white snow piled up on the side of the pavement as dreadful thoughts filled my mind.

8

"Their vehicle is going to hit a patch of black ice, and I'm going to pull their young souls from the wreckage," I muttered. I took a few minutes to walk over to the side, being that I was filled with the sorrow of what was to come on such a blissful night. I made it over to the side and was able to look back to the car with plenty of time to spare before it passed by. "Here we go," I whispered with expectation. I became confused when the vehicle began to pass by without incident while I simply watched. As it passed, I was quickly whisked into the backseat. This was when my slight confusion became full-on astonishment.

The car's interior was much cozier compared to the frigid exterior air. Unlike the exterior, which was illuminated by the moon's light, the interior of this vehicle was rather dark. A computerized screen built into the vehicle's dashboard illuminated the front section. As I inspected it, the monitor suggested that the radio was on and tuned to a station playing holiday music. Still, the speaker system's volume was off, so the car was silent. The radio station's information took up most of the monitor and was positioned directly in the middle. The last thing the monitor displayed, besides a navy background with bubbles of lighter blue, the time and date was centered along the top edge. It was just after midnight on December twenty-fourth.

As I further looked around the illuminated section of the vehicle, I noticed two people were occupying the space. I first looked toward the driver and was able to see a bit of his face as a reflection of the front windshield due to the monitor illuminating him. He was a sharply dressed caucasian male with dark brown hair that bled into an unkept reddish-brown beard. Due to the limited amount of light, the way he was sitting, and the positioning of his attire, it was hard to describe his body type. With my best guess, I would say he stood between five feet and ten inches to six feet and two inches

9

tall while weighing somewhere between one-hundred and ninety to two hundred and ten pounds. I would also guess that he strived to be in peak shape but stopped exercising as much. The person in the passenger seat was a female with fiery red hair and dressed in a pretty red dress. All I could see of her face was the blur that reflected off the passenger window as she stared out of it. From what I could see, I could easily tell she was seven inches shorter that the driver. As I looked over them, I was a but confused as to why they weren't interacting with eachother. I knew I was here to collect one of their souls, but I couldn't tell who I was here for.

We drove for a few miles in complete silence. It was tense. I could tell that an altercation caused these two to be speechless for quite a while. This quietude was nothing like the silence I experienced while on the motorway pavement. Out there, the quiet was quite calming; this is making me anxious. At least it was until the woman turned to the man and asked, "Did you at least have fun?"

"What do you mean?" He replied without breaking his concentration from the road ahead.

"Did you at least have fun?", She asked again.

"'Did I have fun'?" He joked through angrily gritted teeth. "We are driving from my parent's house at eleven fifty-eight on Christmas Eve. No, I did not have fun. They know I don't like doing that. So they gave us the ultimatum of doing what they say or getting out. Who does that?"

"It was only four times," she interjected.

"Whatever. You know I don't like going there. It's almost like those people don't even know who I am or even care about me." He complained.

"We could have at least stuck it out, Shameis. Tomorrow is Christmas." She insisted.

10

"No, Sammie. It's not worth the misery that they put me through." Shameis stated before the conversation died, and the thick tension came back. Once the silence returned, she looked out the window again as he continued to focus on the road. We sat in silence for a little bit longer before Shameis looked into his rearview mirror, presumably to see if there was another vehicle coming up from behind. Listening to arguments has always been awkward for me. I was sitting in the middle of the back seat, and it looked as if he was staring directly at me with his piercing greenish-hazel eyes. The moment we locked eyesight, his aura revealed itself to me, and I couldn't make sense of it. I have never seen an aura that looked like this in all my years. It was as if he was radiating a rainbow. From his tone of voice, I could tell that he was upset, but a person's aura is supposed to match the color of their mood. His, however, was consistently changing color. He only looked at the mirror for a few seconds before looking back at the road, but within a fraction of a second, he looked back up at the mirror with terror in his eyes. He then tried to spin around to look into the backseat causing the vehicle to swerve, then yanked himself forward after feeling his loss of control. Throughout all this, his aura continued to change. There was never a solid red for anger or a yellow for fear, just the varying array of colors that comprised a rainbow.

"What? What's wrong?" Sammie asked in confusion and panic.

"I thought I saw a person in the back seat!" Shameis exclaimed. She quickly turned around to inspect the seat, then slowly turned around to inform him there wasn't anything back here. "I could have sworn I saw something."

"Maybe you're just tired and need a rest. I think I saw a sign that said a rest stop is coming up soon. I need to use the restroom anyway." She suggested, though I felt that I could pick up on something in her voice that made me presume that this suggestion was not for his benefit. I still couldn't see her aura, but I could tell she was playing some sort of game.

"Yeah, you're probably right," Shameis said as he forced himself to focus on the road ahead and tried to avoid the mirror hanging from the inside at the top center of the windshield. This incident caused the three of us to sit in silence for a few more miles until a turn-off came up on the right. Upon exiting the freeway, Shameis drove us into a relatively large and empty row of parking spaces. He then proceeded down the lead way to the row of slots, with the vehicle decreasing in speed until Shameis pulled into one of the many open spaces and brought us to a complete stop. Immediately, Shameis shut off the engine and exited the vehicle as Sammie slowly followed behind.

I think this is a bit obvious, but I need to inform you that I am not supposed to be seen by anyone living. Not a living soul in all of the time has ever been able to see me. Since both Shameis and Sammie could not see while actively looking for me, I assumed that the darkness of the night had begun to play tricks on Shameis's tired eyes. After all, he is a cocktail full of enzymes, testosterone, and emotions. He is only human. Still, I am getting a bit worried. I have duties and obligations that I should be attending to. I need to figure out why I came to be here. Why am I still following these two? Why am I here if neither of them have passed on?

Chapter Two

There have been less than a handful of moments that I can admit to genuinely being confused over a situation. I can practically count them on a single hand. The first and most crucial moment was when I was thrown into the role I now serve. Another that stands out was when I was first clued into what lays beyond the reach of the mortals. Currently, there is what the universe wants me to witness. Near my beginning, I have tried to warn the humans that there is more than what they can see, but I've since learned that the rules placed upon me state I am not allowed to meddle with the affairs of the humans. Therefore, when I am *pulled* to a mortal, I simply collect the soul and depart for the next. I wish I could explain what happens when I am not available to retrieve a soul, but this is the first instance I was allowed to be away from my duties for an extended period of time. Knowing that I am not slacking with my duties, this experience was exciting and nerve-racking. I suppose it is nice to have a connection to a human, as opposed to only seeing one's passing, even if I have absolutely no idea who this person was.

I've been alone for so long, I can't even remember what it is like to have a connection with someone. Although, is it truly a relationship if the other party doesn't know of the other's existence? I guess I've met some souls that would claim it would count. As exciting as this all is, the fact that I have been *pulled* to a mortal's side for this amount of time and have not been able to collect a soul nor be able to leave is quite problematic. I need to get back to my obligations. Thus, I need to figure out why I'm here with these two people.

I felt as if I needed to wait a few seconds before I exited the vehicle to follow the couple. Honestly, I was still processing what had just happened myself. Being in a single location for this amount of time was starting to make me feel uncomfortable since I'm accustomed to whizzing across the earth every few seconds. That is a hard feeling to acclimate to, but a neutral footing starts to feel unnatural once one does. By the time I decided to follow, both Shameis and Sammie entered a building in front of where the vehicle had been parked through a pair of glass doors. As I began my approach, I observed the structures simplistic modern architecture. It's front wall was essentially all glass with a few beams of steel to hold the panels in place. Protruding past the glass wall was a dark-colored, slanted metallic roof that was supported by four decorative stone pillars. They were all spaced out evenly with bushes planted in between the lot of them. Due to the time of year, their foliage had been replaced with snow and ice.

So, I guess it was my turn to go into the structure. Unlike a human having to exit a vehicle, my otherworldly abilities allow me to pass through solid objects with minimal effort. The process of entering the cold exterior air from the cozy interior of the vehicle caused my bones to quiver. As I made my way across the empty lot, the bright neon lights that lingered over the lot caused an uneasy feeling to enter my skull. Yet, Since I have no idea why I am being made to follow such a mundane situation, all I could do was follow the footprints in the snow-dusted lot.

14

The walk from their vehicle to the building took about a minute, but I tried my best to hurry so I could get out of the cold. The path that led to the entrance was freshly covered with a light blanket of snow, with the only imperfections being the footprints left from the dress shoes Shameis was wearing and the high heels belonging to Sammie. I followed the trail that the pair had left, and as I approached the building, the interior grew increasingly transparent. When I eventually reached the glass wall separating the harsh cold of the world from the presumably warm interior of the structure, I could see Shameis laying on a lone wooden bench running perpendicular to the entrance; located in the middle of a large room. The bench was designed without a backrest so that any visitor could engage in rest from either side. Shameis had his right arm draped across his eyes so that the pale yellow light that illuminated the room wouldn't bother him.

I continued to examine the room and noticed a large map pinned to the wall on the left side of the room. The map consisted of Ohio, confirming that we were currently in the United States of America. A small golden sticker in the shape of a star was placed upon it, indicating that we were somewhere in the northwestern part of the state. Then, as expected from such an ordinary place, there were a few doors leading to restrooms and a janitorial closet. The only other things I could see were a few vending machines positioned directly across from the map and a small card rack that held several different pamphlets and brochures that sat across from the building's entrance. After observing the genericness of the room, I placed my hand right on the glass with the intention of going past it but paused to feel the warmth of the room permeating through the glass and into my boney hand. I also noticed the glass was vibrating, as if a frequency from the inside of the room was trying to get out. This vibration was the only aspect that was out of place, as everything seemed relatively updated.

While disregarding the out of place buzz, I pushed my hand forward and phased through the glass; just as I did to exit the vehicle. Once inside, a faint buzzing echoed in my skull, almost as if a bumblebee was hovering around. However, it was as if there was no actual noise. Just the vibration of my skull. I looked around to see what the noise was originating from, but my search was inconclusive. Perhaps it was the lighting system, but typically a buzz would come from an archaic outlet, and this entire station seemed as if it was recently constructed. I would have questioned it more, but that was when I heard a faint conversation leaking from the women's restroom door. Yet another ability I'm cursed with is 'above human hearing', as I require hearing the moment when a heartbeat stops drumming. Being that it was quiet, even for me, I knew there was no way the guy on the bench was able to hear it. So, as anyone wondering why they are being made to experience an event as trivial as this would do, I strolled over to the door to eavesdrop.

"So, everything is going according to our plan?" Questioned a deep male voice. I could tell that whoever this was, I had entered the conversation at a point where he was a bit irritated. I could also hear that he had an accent, unlike the accent Shameis and Sammie share. They have what is referred to as a "General American Accent." It's the generic accent of the United States' midwestern region, which makes sense after learning where we are currently. The man I had just heard sounded like a citizen of a different country, but could speak English fluently as a second language. Based on my travels, the accent may originate from Germany, but there are so many countries and languages that the point of origin is a bit hazy.

The conversation picked up with a woman replying, "Yeah, exactly as ya expected it ta." in a whiny, east coast city dialect. I'm thinking Boston, Pittsburg, or New York. This threw me off a bit since, as I said, Sammie has a Generic American accent. I also do not recall

16

seeing another vehicle, meaning it is unlikely anyone else is here. Perhaps an employee was in the vicinity working a late shift with their car located somewhere else? There is a high probability of that option in this country.

"Good, so you know what to do now? Right, Lillith?" The deep German voice continued to quiz.

"Yeah, I'm supposed ta make that idiot take me onna little vacation or somethin' like that." She answered.

"No!" The voice boomed, causing some static to interfere with the conversation, indicating the male voice was not currently present and was on the opposite end of a communication device. "This needs to go precisely as discussed. There are a few specific options that were picked out. We have been over this several times. You need to get this right." He patronized the east coast accented voice.

"Ya got it Doc," She affirmed as the flush of a toilet covered up the distinct ending tone of the call. Within a matter of seconds, Sammie swung the door open. If I had known she would go straight to the door from the toilet, I would have moved out of the way. Instead, the door sprung at me. This was one of the few moments I'm glad that I do not interact with physical objects. If I were human, it would have knocked me to the ground with the possibility of injury. I'm assuming that the flush was meant to make Shameis think she used the restroom. I genuinely hope that's what it was, as she left the bathroom without washing her hands. I can't tell you how many humans passed due to the indirectness of germs inside public restrooms. If I was human, I would wash whenever I entered a place as filthy as a public restroom.

Nevertheless, after the door passed through me, Sammie and I were now standing face-to-face, and I could finally get a better look at her. Her hair appeared as a fiery orange in this yellow lighting instead of the red I initially observed. Her eyes shimmered a brilliant blue color as if they

17

were made of pure diamond, and she possessed several light freckles that were scattered across her face as thick black eyeliner and ruby red lipstick accented her features. With this eye-to-eye encounter, I could tell that she was the same height as me while wearing her heels. Unfortunately, I couldn't get much other information as she walked right through me and over to Shameis. The feeling of her passing through me was an easy reminder of how alone I am. The thought that I would never again be able to feel human contact saddened me, unlike these two, where she was able to walk up to him and tap him in the middle of his chest. He must not have heard her coming since he was startled by her contact and almost fell from the bench.

"Geez, Sam!" He expressed with exasperation. "Took you long enough."

"You know what they say, 'When you gotta go, you gotta go,'" She retorted.

"I guess," Shameis said as he sat up while rotating, so his feet were on the gray tiles floor before standing up. He then continued with, "We need to get going. It's super late, and I'd like to get home so that I can get some sleep."

"Sure," Sammie agreed with a pleasant smile, but I could see a couple of beads of sweat forming on her brow. The two then turned and walked toward the entrance. When they reached the hinged panels of glass, Shameis reached for one of the handles. As he did, Sammie stopped him and declared, "We need to go on a vacation soon."

"If that's what you want to do." Shameis granted as he turned back to look and probed, "Do you have somewhere in mind?"

"Not particularly, but there are a bunch of ideas over there," she responded, pointing to the cart of reading material. She then grabbed his hand and led him to the other end of the room, where they started thumbing through the neatly placed propaganda. After a few seconds and

18

several columns of jostled documents, Sammie asked, "how about we go on a camping trip?" While picking out a brochure for a campground near Hocking Hills National Park in Columbus, Ohio.

"If I wanted to sleep outside without a bed, with no running water or electricity, then I would just be homeless." He scoffed without inspecting the brochure Sammie picked out.

"What about a trip to Paris?" She continued while putting the campgrounds brochure away.

"That would be cool, but that would cost a lot of money, and we are trying to save up enough to buy a house. So instead, we could go rent a hotel room and go to one of the bigger amusement parks." Shameis counter-offered.

"But I want to do something sort of different. Something we can't do every day. How about a cruise?" She burst out as she pulled out another brochure and stuck it in his face. "That's not that expensive, and we could see a whole bunch of different places. You never know what will happen on the open seas!"

"You know how I feel about the ocean." He warned while lowering her arms.

"Oh, come on, Shamey, it'll be lots of fun." Sammie pleaded.

"I guess. I would do anything for you, Sammie," Shameis muttered as he took the brochure and stuck it into his right pants pocket before putting his left arm around her shoulders. The two then began to head toward the exit. As soon as Shameis touched her, my surroundings started to warp and distort as I finally felt myself being *pulled* to the next soul that required collecting. Finally, I could get back to my obligations, but I couldn't shake the bitter taste of not knowing why I was made to witness this. It all seemed so irrelevant. If my sole purpose is to collect the departed, then why would I be made to observe this? It just didn't make sense.

SHAMEIS ELI

20

Chapter Three

Upon becoming the ferryman of souls, something that I struggled to understand was the passage of time. You see, I do not possess the ability to process time the way a typical human would. The experience I deal with is similar to how a canine experiences time. I can feel time moving forward, and I can see days become nights as nights become days, but never am I able to take the time to understand my surroundings. I've collected souls in the presence of a clock or other time-keeping devices, through which I have noticed that I typically am present for one to two seconds at most. Being that I have existed since the beginning of recorded time, I have an everlasting feeling of time passing faster than it's supposed to. I assume this is my obligation to travel fast enough to collect each soul as they depart from this cruel world.

Some food for thought; just about one hundred forty-seven thousand, nine hundred and fifty-eight people move on from this world each day. These people are all located in different countries, time zones, and hemispheres of the earth. I've been engulfed in the darkness of a warm summer's night with nothing lighting my way besides the moon being diffused by the thick cloud cover of an oncoming storm, just to be *pulled* to the blinding white, snow-covered peaks of the Himalayan mountains. This is why I was so baffled when I was introduced to Shameis. My time seemed to pass parallel to that of the humans. I was able to partake in a human conversation, get a sense of location, and was even able to bask in the glow of the moon. It was bliss. I've hoped I would get a chance to experience a taste of humanity once again.

The feeling I experienced began to drive my actions and even pep into my dreary step. Deep within my bones, I knew I would get another taste of what the humans take for granted. I would continue to fantasize about that moment for months. I even began to keep track of the number of souls I collected to help keep a sense of time. Based on the previously shared statistic, I calculated a rough time estimate. Twenty-six million, six-hundred thirty-two thousand, four hundred and forty lost souls. My calculations counted about six months before I could get another taste of what freedom could be. At first, I didn't realize it, but the instance took place on a bright, warm, and considerably humid day.

The sun was high, and its rays were warming everything below to an absolutely perfect temperature. It would have been a glorious day to take off my tattered brown hooded black robes... if I had the skin to display. As the mid-day sun sat above, its light casted short shadows from everything it touched. I'd say that it was around eleven forty-five in the morning, if my knowledge of sundials is accurate. I do know the degree of the earth's axis has shifted a bit over the millennia, but my knowledge is typically on point.

While examining my newest surroundings, I found myself in the center of two parallel rows of vastly different types and colors of vehicles. From what I could see, there was a single open space sitting directly to my left. Looking beyond these initial columns, I found myself dead-center within a sea of vehicles of differing randomness. The blazing sun had caused the blacktop to become hot enough to cause blisters on

22

the feet of any human who dared to stand barefoot. Within seconds, an westward bound gust of wind blew past me, which carried a saltiness and the sound of seagulls. Oh, I love visiting the deep blues and crashing waves of the ocean.

After taking a moment to absorb my surroundings, a blue four-door sedan with a metallic sheen to the paint slowly rounded the intersection at the far end of the pavement before creeping toward me. The wind followed behind and blew past the vehicle, causing the salty breeze of the nearby ocean to fill my nasal cavity. I first assumed it was moving slowly due to my perception of time, but I was able to see the people inside were interacting with each other at a regular speed. This has made me realize that I would again experience the bliss I was craving.

Between the reflection of the sun's rays off the metallic paint and the shadow being casted by the vehicle's roof, I was unable to see their faces. I stepped out of the way, so I wouldn't have to waste energy letting the vehicle pass through me, and as I did, the approaching car slid into the space and sat idle before shutting off. A few seconds later, the driver's and passenger's doors opened as the occupying humans spilled out, which I instantly recognized to be Shameis and Sammie. In hindsight, I should have realized the occupants would be these two, but I wasn't expecting anything. One major difference from the last time I saw these two was they now donned shorts, graphic t-shirts, and sunglasses instead of their fancy dress attire.

Seeing the two of them moving regularly filled me with several different emotions. Initially, I was elated. As I said, I waited about six months for this exact moment. My delight then slowly melted into confusion, as I watched them walk to the rear end of the vehicle and release the latch holding the trunk closed. I know that when I am *pulled* to a location, it is to witness the moments before a human's passing. I theorized that I was *pulled* here to see an important event. It has happened often that I was drawn to witness the events before when I'm needed, like in the circumstances I described for Matthew Addams, but why would the conversations I observed at that rest area be meaningful?

As I stood pondering the new happenings in my life, I watched as Shameis pulled a pair of matching black suitcases from the open trunk. He then handed one of them to Sammie so they both could extend the hidden handles. Without saying a word to each other, Sammie set her suitcases onto their wheels and began walking down the path they had just driven. Seeing this, Shameis slammed the trunk of the vehicle shut before chasing after her. I knew I was here to be their witness, so I briskly walked to catch up and follow them.

"Did we grab everything?" Shameis inquired just before I reached them, to which she still did not respond, or even look at him. "Where do we have to go for this?"

"You can see the ship over there!" Sammie expresses aggressively while pointing primarily straight but veering off to the left of the direction we were walking. Following her point, I noticed a long line of palm trees standing in front of a single level building with a glass front. The whole building was similar to the rest area, except much more grand. However, between us and our destination was a busy street with many passing vehicles. On the other side of the building, I could make out the top layer and smokestacks of the white floating vessel these two intended to board. "So, we are going to walk over there and go through the building and all the security and everything. It's kind of like an airport but for a boat." She explained.

"Oh... cool..." Shameis responded with hesitation. The two fell silent as we walked past the empty vehicles, out of the lot, and up to the busy street before crossing at the earliest opening these two needed. We shortly reached the line of palm trees and noticed a clear paved path that

24

led past the foliage and up to one of the many visible entrances within the behemoth-sized glass wall. I should note that a drivable section of pavement connected the busy road up to many of the entrances. Still, I should be correct in assuming that Shameis and Sammie parked their vehicle in the lot as they had no one to deliver my unknowing companions to the building. Nevertheless, the walk from their car to the trees only lasted what seemed to be a few minutes, and then another one to enter the building on the other side of the trees.

Once inside the building, we were greeted by a blast of cold, refreshing air coming from a vast stretch of space in the room. It was a brilliant contrast to the scorching heat of the outside. The first thing about this room I noticed, besides the cool blast of air, was that the space contained several poles protruding from the marble-tiled ground. These poles were tethered together with nylon ribbon at the top of each metal shaft, forming several queues that led to a couple of desks on the other side of this entryway. Other than those obstacles, there was no object or a soul to block our path. The desks were fitted with various decals, each displaying a different company logo. There were a total of five desks with accompanying pieces of technology, but only the one in the direct middle had a young-looking woman standing at it, so Sammie led Shameis and me up to her.

The logo on this desk looked like a silhouette cruise ship with "the fractured son" underneath. That's a strange name for a boat, but humans are strange creatures. As we made our way through the queue, I continued to observe our surroundings and noticed that the room was oddly void of beings, compared to other terminals that I've had the displeasure of visiting. It was a bit eerie. Usually, places like this are bustling with people. The lack of voices allowed the squeaking of their shoes to echo.

Although feeling a bit empty, the room was decorated elegantly. The flooring was freshly waxed, so the off-white colored ceiling and extravagant crystal chandelier hanging from the center of the top reflected as if it were a newly polished mirror. The chandelier lights were illuminated, but the natural lighting of the exterior world is what lit up the room. The walls on both the left and right of the room had stone pillars with various shades of gray protruding from the off-white walls and reaching from the floor to the ceiling. I counted eight in total, four on each side of the room. It is essential to mention that an opening on either side of this specific desk gave way to the next portion of the building, but I wasn't paying enough attention to see what lay beyond. For the emptiness of the room, there was too much to take in. In my altered perception of time, I would have easily been able to absorb it all.

As we approached the desk, I received a better look at the receptionist. She appeared to be around twenty-five years old, had dark brown hair, and was wearing a black vest with a white, buttoned-up dress shirt underneath. Her shirt was tucked into a slick black skirt that reached down to just above her knees. Pinned to the left pectoral of the shirt was a white name tag that read 'Ellie'. I instantly was able to see the aura her soul was exerting. Her soul told me that she had a passion for acting. I would've been more interested in that tidbit of information, but this made me realize that I still haven't been able to see Sammie's aura. Interesting. I would have questioned it more, but just as I thought of it, Sammie yelled out to Ellie so her attention would be brought up from the computer. We weren't even halfway through this empty queue, what was wrong with Sammie today? Thankfully Ellie didn't respond until Shameis and Sammie were at her desk. Once there, Ellie simply responded with a sweet, "How may I help you?" I'm glad that Sammie's attitude didn't wipe that peaceful smile off Ellie's face.

"We have tickets to board 'The Fractured Son,'" Sammie informed Ellie forcefully.

26

"Oh, you showed up just in time. That ship is just about to depart. Can I have the name of the reservation?" Ellie continued.

"Shameis Eli," Sammie answered. As soon as his name grazed Ellie's ears, her smile dropped, her bubbly demeanor faded, and her eyes widened. I swear I could even see her lip start to quiver as her aura melted its teal shine of giddiness into a yellow fog of fear. I looked to my companions to see their reaction to this blatant display of realization from Ellie, but all I received was Shameis playing on his cellphone while Sammie squinted at Ellie.

"Hello?" Sammie questioned with growing irritation.

I understand that humans tend to grow impatient when faced with a lack of time. I frankly wish I could share the feeling. After Sammie tried to break Ellie's short paralysis, Ellie shook her head to refocus herself before quickly looking at her computer monitor. She then followed up with the stuttered question, "Could you spell the last name for me, please?"

That question instantly caused a skeptical glare to beam out of Sammie's eyes. She then answered the question with "Eli. E. L. I." In a very nasty tone.

"Come on, Sam. I'm sure she's had a rough day so far. She's trying her best." Shameis assumed while trying to break the tension, but everyone fell silent as Ellie clicked away onto the computer's keyboard.

Suddenly the silence broke as Ellie reoriented her focus back up to Shameis and Sammie while Ellie's machine emitted the sound of it pushing out two stubs of paper, to which she tore them away. She then turned to inform us, "Alright, here are your tickets. Security is right through either of these openings, and the entry ramp to the boat is just past that". It was easy to see that Ellie was still extremely nervous and a bit scared of knowing who these two were. However, she did this with a small smile.

Upon receiving the tickets from Ellie, Shameis and Sammie shuffled toward the left opening. Still, they were stopped once again when Ellie chirped, "Oh! You can leave your baggage here and we will have it taken up to your cabin for you." To this clarification, Shameis appeared to be reluctant to leave his property behind. Still, Sammie instructed Shameis to do so since they would be late. It took some persuading, but Shameis agreed to leave the two suitcases behind before proceeding on the path between the queue and desk.

The security area wasn't exactly just beyond the division. From Ellie's description, the security checkpoint was supposed to be "right through either opening." She failed to mention that the security checkpoint was down another corridor lined with shops containing flashing lights that were trying to peddel trinkets, souvenirs, and concessions. It sort of felt like the markets in Florence, Italy. Yet again, there was a void of people, which made this leg of their journey a breeze. We continued to walk down this corridor, following signs hanging from the ceiling that directed us to the security checkpoint. They seemed to be informed that the checkpoint wasn't much farther. It was just around the corner of this corridor. I would like to preface my observations here because I have never actually been through the check-in process of a commercial travel agency like this. Don't get me wrong, I have most definitely been in a building like this port or a standard airport, but it is usually farther beyond any checkpoint; since I'm only ever here to do one thing. With that being said, I found some matters to be a little off, even though I enjoyed the simplicity of these events. These matters were only twofold. My first question would be, why did the woman behind the desk look so scared to hear Shameis's name? Second, where are all the people?

Chapter Four

I can't express how excited I am to be boarding a watercraft under my own volition. I've given the statistic about how many people die daily, but I could break that statistic into more specific categories. For example, roughly two United States citizens require my services as the ferryman while boating every day. Of those two people, one person every other day had required my presence while on a commercial cruise line such as this. I mention this to put forth the realization that I have been onto one of these vessels much more than a handful of times, however, never once by regular boarding. I've always been *pulled* onto the boat and collected the soul before being cast away. This excitement instantly masked the confusion I felt in the foyer of this building as I began to see more signs of life.

Upon reaching the end of our path, we began to approach three sets of two rectangular mechanical frames, each constructed with flashing lights. These gateways were connected to other machines that seemed to consist of monitors and conveyor belts. The set up from left to right consisted of the conveyor and monitor, then two consecutive frames, followed by another conveyor. This setup was repeated two times to comprise the three sets I mentioned. A security officer manned each pair of frames, three in total, and the three of them funneled travelers through the six possible openings.

As for the conveyors, these were operated by two security guards each. These machines needed personnel so all the travelers trying to pass through this checkpoint could promptly put their belongings into plastic bins. As for the security members operating this system, one person would feed the material items through a metal box surrounding the conveyor while the second would observe the x-raying monitor. So, by my count, there were five security guards per set of machines, totaling fifteen. Not included in those fifteen was one last security personnel amongst the several travelers on our side of the checkpoint trying to direct the traffic. This officer repeatedly stated that electronics, bags, and everything metal needed to enter a plastic container before passing through the metal detector. I guess any form of checkpoint makes sense to provide a perceived level of safety to all these travelers, but it just seemed so trivial. It's not like we are boarding a plane.

Anything can happen on the open seas once the ship leaves port. None of this seems necessary, but I probably wouldn't understand since I have never been able to experience this portion of a human's traveling ritual. At least the mass of travelers all seemed to wear a form of relaxed or casual attire, similar to Shameis and Sammie, which in turn sped this process up a bit.

Upon observing al the machinery and the crowd of people, I finally noticed all security personnel wore matching uniforms consisting of black dress shoes, black slacks, a black belt with a large rectangular metal belt buckle, a light blue long-sleeve button-down dress shirt, and a tie. The only similarity between the two opposing groups was that they consisted of various races, genders, and walks of life. With that being said, the security was predominantly male.

Once the three of us reached the checkpoint, Shameis and Sammie entered the herd of cramped bodies as they filed one by one through these supposed metal detectors. I wanted to push past everyone to continue exploring the surrounding area, but I knew I was somehow tied to Shameis or Sammie, so I decided to wait by their sides. I felt like a puppy being put through obedience school, wanting to frolic about but needing to stay by my human's side.

The wait was excruciatingly long, even with all the directing and streamlining. I'm not sure if this was a regular human experience, but I would regret forcing myself to endure waiting like this. Human life is exceptionally short, so these souls should not squander their lives over waiting in lines. On the other side of this coin, I can sympathize with why humans think a checkpoint like this should be required for travelers. There have been so many moments where I had to collect a soul due to a horrible person smuggling contraband into a vessel and using it on another unsuspecting soul. It's truly a double-edged sword, but as I said earlier, nothing is stopping a rogue group of pirates from coming aboard with their weaponry. As for the idiocy of this wait, the number of humans wanting the exact same experience simultaneously will inevitably cause a backup. I don't even know why I am complaining. The universe has allowed me to live vicariously through Shameis and Sammie, and I have always wanted to experience what it is like to be human again. However, I should know that the glass is never wholly full of rainbows and sugar.

While contemplating the human existence, I didn't realize that we were slowly inching our way up through the line. Upon snapping back to reality, I noticed that Shameis's turn to step through the machine had come. He didn't have his carry-on items by this point in the process, so he must have removed them while I was zoned out. I watched as he proceeded up to his predetermined mechanical frame while Sammie began to place her belongings into a container. This was the point I decided I should relocate past the checkpoint. Plus, I was starting to get tired of the crowd.

31

I intended to walk through the section where the two frames connected while Shameis walked beside me. Everything was going smoothly until we were both halfway through when the machine suddenly began to flash a red light and blare a warning siren. I'm not going to lie; it did startle me. I've been *pulled* to extremely loud places to retrieve souls before, but it is infrequent for me to experience the dull roar of a crowd change to an ear-piercing loudness. Perhaps the sound seemed loud because I was actively phasing through the machine. As soon as it began to blare, I rushed through and spun around to examine what was happening.

I watched as the security guard overseeing these two frames began pulling Shameis backward while the one controlling the plastic trays came up from behind. The second of the two had equipped himself with a rectangular baton before making his way over. The Siren only pierced the room for a few more seconds after Shameis had exited before silencing itself. After it stopped, I could hear the security guards instructing Shameis to stand still while spreading his legs apart and holding his arms straight out to the sides. Once Shameis had assumed the recommended position, the guard with the baton began waving it around Shameis's body, starting around his feet before moving upward. This personnel kept swaying it around without receiving a reaction until the baton reached Shameis's right shoulder. Here, a green light on the wand lit up as it emitted a high-pitch whine, indicating metal was present.

"Sir, we require all metal to be put into the x-ray before entering the metal detector," the guard that was ushering people through the frames ordered Shameis. I was surprised to see how calm and collected Shameis was at this moment. A human usually becomes jittery when threatened. I can't say for sure if he completely emptied his person into the bin, but I know how demanding and self-righteous humans can be. Of course, Shameis tried explaining that he didn't have anything. His denial of the allegation and demeanor toward his accusers only irritated the security guards. "Sir, if you do not comply, we are going to need to take you to perform a strip-search," the guard threatened.

"I swear I do not have any metal products on me." Shameis protested. "I can show you right now if that'll help." Upon hearing Shameis's proposal, the two guards looked at each other without verbal exchange. After a moment, the two guards then turned back to Shameis. I couldn't see their faces, but I could see Shameis's. His face transformed from his stoic expression into a look of disbelief, which led me to believe the two guards had agreed with the suggestion.

So, Shameis slowly pulled the black graphic t-shirt off his torso to reveal himself to everyone. The siren may have caused a few people to stare out of curiosity, but this verbal shakedown caused even more bystanders to stop and watch what was unfolding. The commotion caused Sammie to blush as she hid her face in her hands to hide her embarrassment. Shameis, on the other hand, seemed to be confident in the way he looked and of how the situation was going. Upon revealing his torso, It was very obvious that Shameis was now a bit overweight, but had once actively exercised. However, his heavily scared skin was the reason why everyone had begun to stare, and as I gazed upon him, I could tell his scars weren't caused by burns or stitches. These were the scars of entry wounds that healed without proper medical assistance. Even with the scarring and the gained weight, I would deem this man attractive, but who is a walking skeleton to judge over appearances?

After seeing Shameis's bare torso, the guards allowed Shameis to put his shirt back on. They both apologized to Shameis, but the guard funneling people through the machine spoke more timidly than the other. He followed up his apology with, "Sir. I need to ask, is there by chance a piece of metal in your arm?"

"Yeah. I was hit by a grenade while serving. There is a piece of shrapnel in my shoulder blade. Or at least that's what I was told. I don't remember most of it," Shameis explained as he slid his shirt over his torso. The newly revealed information caused this specific guard to let out a defeated sigh as the pair of security guards returned to their positions. The one overseeing the frames then allowed Shameis to bypass the checkpoint so the sirens wouldn't be set off again. Once Shameis reached the side I was on, he instantly turned to the output of the conveyor belt and reclaimed his belongings. As he did so, a female security member monitoring the X-ray machine thanked Shameis for his service.

After Shameis acknowledged her, she inquired why he didn't lead with the facts about serving. "He didn't give me a chance. Also, I wanted him to feel as embarrassed as I would have felt." Shameis admitted. The woman chuckled in response to Shameis's ploy as she returned to watching the monitor. Within the time it took for Shameis to retrieve his possessions and quip with the security, Sammie had already made it through the checkpoint and began to collect her things. As soon as she had finished collecting her items, an announcement that was presented by an elderly woman's voice echoed through the corridors. The statement informed all the patrons that the watercraft my companions had acquired was about to set sail. This was the last call for boarding. This caused Shameis and Sammie to sprint through the crowd of travelers but still in the same direction as everyone else.

I wasn't planning on exerting my energy to keep up. There were still signs overhead that directed the passengers to their destination. I've never felt a need to rush while collecting souls, so why rush for an event as trivial as this? I was just going to walk there, but apparently, there were other plans. Within seconds of losing sight of Shameis and Sammie, I was *pulled* onto the deck of a large boat. This location had a large

34

boarding ramp stretching from a gap in the side railing to the ground near a large single-story building. Obviously, this was the vessel Shameis and Sammie were rushing toward, but a banner saying "Welcome Aboard the Fractured Son" hanging on the parallel wall confirmed it.

Instantly my confusion began to grow, inquiring why I would be *pulled* onto the ship instead of my companions. Why am I even still following these two? If the universe will pull me to a place, why would it not be to the next soul? I had many questions pressing against my skull, but I decided to use my time wisely and began to explore the ship. As I began to roam, I noticed masses of humans loitering over the deck and crowding potential walkways. They seemed to go on as far as my vision allowed me to perceive.

The populous I could see consisted of people reclining in white plastic chairs with their legs protruding into a clearly defined walkway while others were just standing around talking to each other. Then some people were walking in either direction, trying to maneuver the horde of bodies. As to the apparel of the lot, they were all wearing similar fabrics to Shameis and Sammie. T-shirts ranging in a rainbow of colors and shorts that ranged from athletic to cargo styles. Nine times out of ten, the elderly guests wore what they thought to be a tropical, short-sleeved, button-down dress shirt. I even saw several people dawning scandalous swim attire, not even trying to cover their exposure. There were so many genders and races of people! It felt like I was standing in the middle of a melting pot of experiences and cultures.

I tried to eavesdrop on some conversations as I walked through the crowd, but couldn't focus on anything. The one thing I did hear a little too much of was the word "act." Every time I tried to listen, I listened to that word in one way or another; acting, actor, to act. I even tried to read the people's auras to see why the word kept coming up, but that was also useless. There was too much going on. All the clouds of color merged and mingled to form a psychedelic mess. Finally, after all of this, I returned to use the one sense that I knew wouldn't fail me; my eyes. I saw groups of adults with their children walking while eating various flavors of ice cream in waffle cones. Some of the elderly occupied a section of the deck to play a game that required the participants to use metal sticks to push six-inch disks so they would glide across a ten-foot space on the floor. The players were trying to get their pucks to land within a segmented triangle that contained different numbers.

Speaking of the floors, its feel was soothing underneath my bare feet. It was a pleasant neutral temperature, not too hot like the scalding asphalt of the vehicle lot and not as cold as the soft, powdery snow of the expressway in winter. It was also quite reflective, as if it was freshly scrubbed spotless until they shined before travelers boarded.

Continuing to wander the deck, I dragged my boney hand on a railing along the side. It stood up to the bottom of my ribs. Although serving as a place to lean against, I knew its primary purpose was to prevent humans from falling overboard. In theory, this is a fantastic security measure, but I cannot count how many overboard souls I've been made to collect.

After twenty steps or so, I came upon a large entryway on my left that led deeper into the vessel's interior. This opening seemed to have a lot of foot traffic flowing in and out, so I decided to venture through to see what was on the other side. To my pleasure, the wood floor of the deck gave way to a soft, pillowy carpet.

What I had stepped into appeared to be something like a corridor, but the right wall was replaced with a waist-high glass barrier that served the same purpose as the railing that lined the deck. This balcony overlooked what I could only imagine being the main lobby of this floating hotel. Since these areas were essentially the same, the terrace and the lobby shared many features, such as the same pillowy carpet and the design of the walls and ceiling.

The carpet was a bright red color with golden swirls and floral patterns. Both the walls and the ceiling were the color of freshly churned butter. The walls had birch wood trim protrusions designed to make large elegant squares. Hanging directly in the center of the designated lobby area was a large crystal chandelier, which illuminated the entirety of both areas. I looked over the edge of the glass divider and noticed that a wall led up from the lobby floor to the edge of this landing, implying that the original shape of the lobby had a cut-out explicitly made to have this space.

There were only three other remarkable features of the area. The first was an additional opening directly across where I entered through. The light entering the space was extremely bright making me realize it was an additional entry from the other side of the vessel. Next, the third opening in this balcony was positioned directly in the middle of the opposing entrances on the left wall. It led to a grand staircase with thick golden railings. The overall theme matched the theme of the lobby, with a few other features that were not all too remarkable. This staircase presumably led down to the foyer below, causing the two spaces to truly be united. The final element of this room was an active fireplace lined in white marble and blocked off by a black gate. Clearly, the organization that owned the ship was trying to make this area look like an immaculate mansion, but there was no need to have a fire actively raging. After all, it was a warm summer day.

I decided to continue my adventure by going down the staircase to get a better look at the lobby, but as soon as I went to take my first step, I was *pulled* back to Shameis and Sammie. These two were currently on the boarding ramp to the vessel. Once I was able to see them again, I could see their entire faces were a bit more blushed than their standard pale complexion initially let on, and they were breathing a bit heavier than usual. These two indicators notified me that they had either been briskly walking, or running, to ensure they were aboard the vessel before the voyage commenced. After they finished climbing the ramp, the two of them paused for a bit so Shameis could ask Sammie a question that I wasn't close enough to hear. She nodded in agreement before the pair of them joined the flowing crowd, moving in the opposite direction I had initially chosen to travel. But, of course, I knew I had to follow. Why else would I need to be *pulled* back to them? So we began to walk, and within the same distance it took for me to find the lobby, we came across an inlet built into the wall. This inlet contained a set of vertical metal slabs set a couple of inches into the wall. I have seen this sight enough times to realize what we had discovered was an elevator shaft. Shameis hit a nearby button that pointed downward and then looked at Sammie. "What room are we in again?" He asked. I was glad to be able to hear his voice again, but realized my mind was beginning to throb from the roar of the crowd.

In response to Shameis's question, Sammie revealed an irritated scowl and interrogated with, "If you don't know which cabin is ours, why did you hit the down button?", which Shameis then responded with a shrug and a slight smirk before informing her that he was guessing. "One Hundred sixty-seven," She finally answered.

"That was a good guess then, huh." He gloated in response as the doors of the lift slid open. She was shaking her head in what seemed to be disappointment while the three of us loaded onto the empty elevator. I'm pretty sure it was better than a good guess. Based on the boat's design, the deck we entered was seven floors up from the very bottom, with only three more above us. He had a seventy percent chance of being correct, but I appreciate the effort he took to make a joke. Why Sammie was starting to be hostile? They were just starting their vacation. There was no reason for Sammie to behave like this. Following our entering of the lift, Shameis quickly spun to press a button at the very bottom of a whole slew of buttons, which then lit up with the number zero-one, and the door began to close.

After half a minute of lowering, the elevator stopped, and the wall opposite of the one we entered began to open. The way the interior was decorated, I didn't realize this lift had two opposing entrances, but it made sense with how the ship was designed. Once the elevator door finished opening, the three of us stepped out and found ourselves in the middle of a long corridor lined with doorways; each of which was spaced out by several meters. This hall had the same carpeting as the lobby area I was in earlier, and the walls and ceiling were painted the same creme color. Even the doors matched the type of wood that accented the lobby and possessed numbers that matched the golden railing in the grand staircase. A black sign that contained white numbers and arrows hung on the wall across from the elevator and indicated the rooms one hundred twenty-six through space one hundred seventy-six were to the left while all the others were to the right. I'm not sure how they chose how to number the suites, but I assumed that this and every floor were composed of two parallel corridors with conjoining halls and started the numbering in the front right of the ship and then snaked back around. They decided to follow the direction of the sign, which caused us to only have to pass ten sets of opposing doors to reach their cabin, confirming my hypothesis.

Immediately after reaching our destination, Sammie slid a card-like piece of plastic into a mechanism built into the door handle. The instrument then flashed a green light and produced the loud clunk of an unlocking deadbolt. I couldn't recall seeing her be given a piece of plastic like this. Perhaps I missed it when preoccupied with examining the lobby of the port. Anyway, she opened the door to reveal a quaint little cabin with a single king-sized bed, and a dresser with a flat-screen television mounted to the wall above the dresser. Again, the carpet was the same as what I've seen twice now, and the walls and ceiling were the same creme color. I noticed an additional doorway that became hidden by the cabin's open entry that must have led to the loo and shower. The bed was dressed with a white comforter and pillow cases while accented with a deep red bed scarf. Shameis quickly realized that their luggage wasn't present, but Sammie disregarded the observation and concluded that the baggage would show up sometime soon.

After observing the room and noting their luggage was absent, Shameis went over to sit on the bed, and Sammie decided to confront him about the ordeal that happened at the security checkpoint. She scolded him for treating them so poorly, citing that they were just doing their job. Shameis defended himself by suggesting that the guards not letting him speak wasn't his fault. His defense caused Sammie to roll her eyes and demand that they "Just go see what the activities on the ship were," to which Shameis hopped up off the bed and obliged her request. So, the three of us instantly left the room. After re-entering the hall, he retraced his path down the corridor but continued past the elevator we initially used before turning down a connecting passageway. In this smaller hallway, there was another lift with a sign posted in front of it. This sign indicated that the lift led to the ship's main deck. Shameis used a button outfitted to this lift to signal it to come down, and the doors instantly slid open as we began to board. Once inside, Sammie pressed a button that indicated the elevator would be taken to the deck the sign mentioned, which caused the sliding metal doors of the elevator to close. As soon as the elevator started to go up, a loud and deep horn blared from above us. This horn was very distinct, and I knew exactly what that meant. We were about to disembark.

40

Part One: Decending into Madness

Chapter Five

I think I am starting to enjoy myself. As I'm sure you're aware, I've been forced to work day in and day out. Death does not get a holiday, a vacation, or a day off. If it is considered, the only "break" I get is when I have to meet with my overseer. So, although I worry about the ramifications of not performing my actions for this long, I can at least say I am enjoying myself. Yes, some of the hurdles I have observed within the last few hours may have been tedious and wasteful, but they seem to be part of the modern human experience. Being aboard this vessel with Shameis and Sammie is probably one of this millennium's greatest moments. I don't think anything that could happen would top this. Receiving my freedom would beat this, but that is not a viable option. Who would collect lost souls if I was gone? The only aspect of this experience I wish I could change is to interact with Shameis or Sammie or anyone else I could see. Even though I cannot, the raw emotions they've portrayed have been more than enough to let me feel like part of their event. I am happy to be part of this though, since all I typically get to see is sorrow, anguish, or contempt from those on the receiving end of my eternal punishment. Rarely do I ever know the happiness that Shameis released during the altercation at the guard stand. Sammie's compassion at the rest area in Northern Ohio last Winter was an emotion I was hoping to see again, but all I've seen from her is the same contempt I've always seen.

A perfect example of this is what is happening right now. We were riding up an elevator to the top deck of a cruise ship, and Sammie was sulking with her arms crossed. It was silent, and she was radiating tension. Shameis ended up breaking the silence by asking about some of the attractions that were on the itinerary. To that question, she instantly turned to him and accused him of not wanting to be on this vacation. Shameis defended himself by explaining that he doesn't like the concept of a cruise ship and listed all the reasons I mentioned previously. He even sprinkled in some facts about international law and the no man's land that the sea is. Yet after covering all his objections to the event, he stated he was willing to have a good time for her.

I wish I could receive such words from a person who cared for me. Someone willing to put aside their fears to ensure my happiness. Sammie is a lucky girl. I could see that his chivalry broke through Sammie's cold exterior and brought forth a tiny smile before turning to look at Shameis. "Okay," she muttered sweetly. "Well, I know that as soon as the boat took off, there was going to be a lounge set up with a complimentary all-you-can-eat buffet and free cocktails. I recall seeing that a comedian was going to perform every day at some time. Unfortunately, I don't quite remember that time. The last thing I recall from the booking website was the company planned on airing an advance showing of a superhero movie." As soon as the mention of superheroes grazed Shameis's ears, his eyes widened as he became filled with pure excitement. He was really into superheroes. That seems to be a good piece of information to know.

"Which one?" Shameis inquired excitedly. "I know there were several that were going to be released soon. Is it about the Starseeker or Crossfade? Inkblot and Moonlight are supposed to come out soon!"

"I think it is called 'Crossing the Isle' or something like that." She answered as apathy flowed from her voice.

"Oh," he responded disappointedly. "That one is supposed to come out next week. I really don't care to see it, but I'll go if there is nothing else."

"Do you know everything about that one?" She asked while trying to mask her apathy.

"Well yeah, he's a member of the Council of Supers. He's just not one of my favorites. He was replaced by a new character a few years ago. The new guy is ten times as brutal as the original, but this movie is supposedly only about the first guy." Shameis answered. Sammie looked as if she was about to ask another question, but just before the words could flow out, the elevator gave a slight jostle as it finished ascending. With a faint chime, the doors slid open. I would have loved to hear more about these heroes and what makes them super. Were these characters anything like those invented through the ancient Greek and Roman mythologies? Of course, this conversation was thrown to the back burner as my companions and I mosied out of the lift.

Instantly, the ear-piercing screams of children mixed with the incomprehensible conversations of fully grown travelers filled the once peaceful space that the lift provided. With that, my vision was instantly impaired by the overhead sun while following them out. The lack of overhead protection from the descending solar rays beaming through the cloudless sky confirmed we were now on the main deck of the ship. As I looked around, everyone seemed to be huddled into cliques within the overall mass of bodies that talked amongst themselves. Most were standing around while others walked to and from a gigantic building-like structure that spanned the entire width of the ship; where this specific elevator was built into. Then some were sitting around in the same white plastic chairs I saw before and trying to soak up the sun's warmth. While all this commotion served as an unwelcome distraction, the one sound I kept returning to was the people screaming while swimming inside a large pool in the middle of the deck. Bloodcurdling screams could be heard from that area every five seconds. I swear I thought this would be the real reason I was here; to save a drowning victim. As we marched forward, I looked to gauge the reactions of both Sammie and Shameis. Overall, Sammie seemed underwhelmed, as if she was expecting something different. What was she expecting? How was she not overwhelmed by this madhouse?

Still, I don't know her life. Maybe her line of work is usually pretty loud? Not everybody's profession deals with serving one soul at a time in near silence. As for Shameis, his mouth was a gap. He was clearly in awe of the sights, but his attention was principally directed up toward the sky. He was staring at a wooden frame tower possessing a staircase wide enough for a single person to occupy any given space. This staircase climbed up the tower's frame toward the entrances of three colorful tubes large enough for people to slide down in. I observed as these plastic tubes twisted around each other and the tower before depositing both joyously screaming humans and gallons of water into the before-mentioned pool. I could tell that Shameis had every intention to climb the stairs to this behemoth, but he turned to Sammie to get her approval.

"You're not even wearing a swimsuit!" She instantly scoffed.

"We're on a boat! Do you think I would board without wearing a pair?" He informed her, which caused her to look down at his shorts.

"Those are khakis," She shot down.

"They're nylon. Waterproof. These things are supposed to look like khakis. That's the joke. They even have the netting and everything." Shameis pointed out. While saying that last sentence, he turned out his pocket and revealed that his current apparel did have a net-like material lining the inside. I found it hysterical that he was prepared for an occasion such as this, but Sammie wasn't as amused. I was expecting her to give some pushback to Shameis going off on his own, but instead just rolled her eyes and notified him that she was going to the bar to get a couple of drinks. To that, he smiled giddily, leaned in and kissed her on the cheek, then took off toward the base of the tower. Between these two, I chose to follow him. If I am going to be forced to endure this ship, I might as well do it with someone enjoying themselves. That, and I was hoping to get away from some of this noise.

I watched as he made his way through the crowd. It appeared as if he was all but slithering, not touching a single person. I was impressed. He moved almost as if moving through groups or cluttered areas were second nature, pure instinct. Instead of attempting his maneuvers, I decided to casually pass through like I always have. Another sad aspect of living this existence is that I will never have the ability to contact another living soul. I can only come in contact when needed to make a collection. I know, I know; Woe is me.

Nevertheless, I walked casually through the crowd of people and could catch up to Shameis at the base of the stairs. Standing underneath this wooden spire provided a warped sense of perspective. It looked as if it was simply a few stories tall from where we had just been, but now as I look up from the base, it seemed to stand as tall as the Eiffel Tower. After taking the view of the structure, I continued to follow Shameis up the stairs toward the summit. The queue of people began about halfway up these stairs, causing us to stop our ascent. I began to realize that there were quite a bit of people in line, and more started to file in behind us. Just like the queue for the metal detectors in the port, we inched forward every minute or so.

Waiting here with Shameis caused time to feel like it was beginning to slow. The roar of the crowd below had fallen to a slight whimper. Although I was enjoying myself, this was better than on the ground. The first outing for a being that hasn't experienced a crowd for an extended period of time in more than a millennium should not be instantly dragged upon a commercial sea vessel. As we stood in this line, I began to realize that this was also a first. I refer to receiving the choice of waiting around for the sake of waiting. In the security line, we moved slowly so Shameis and Sammie could be processed, but never have I been able to choose to wait. I have established that I haven't enjoyed life on earth for a long time, but I know that I could never stand around and do nothing. Even when I walked the world, I always had to remain busy.

Humans always think that I am sitting around waiting for the elderly or the sick to pass. No, I always arrive at my intended location before I am needed. Even if the soul passes due to a freak accident. I am made to take in as much of the surroundings as possible. This form of torture seems to be the universe's way of dangling a carrot in front of my face. Except ever since this instance of being by these human's sides, I was finally able to grasp my desires instead of staring at them. I realize that not a single human would want to wait in line, but the small things in life make it worth living. Theoretically, I could simply use my abilities to enter the void between realms so I could relocate myself up to the top while I wait for this human, but that wouldn't be the human experience. However, now that the thought of leaving Shameis's side has come to mind, something deep inside me is wanting me to stay close. What was this feeling? I don't think I have felt something like this before. This feeling was faint but

46

strong enough to notice. Was the roar of the crowd overloading my senses enough to miss this? I looked to Shameis as soon as I felt this feeling, and it appeared Shameis was even starting to look around while getting antsy.

I chose to ignore whatever that was as we escalated up the winding path. Pushing the feeling aside, I began to scan the sea of people from this new vantage point. I wanted to try and understand who they were and why they wanted to take this vacation. I thought that maybe I could use my aura-seeing ability to get an overall sense, but of course, I was instantly overwhelmed with the loudness of everything merging. I couldn't look long, but as soon as I looked away, one word stood out to me. The one word that I could hear over and over again. "Act." I had no idea what it could mean, but our surroundings didn't seem quite as perfect as I initially imagined, minus the screaming. I tried to push my worry aside with a few rationalizations. Perhaps there was some sort of convention that was taking place on this ship while others were vacationing? Maybe these people talked about celebrities since those conversations have increased in frequency as societies have advanced?

Although I knew it was a bad idea, I decided to try scanning over the sea of people one last time to see if I missed something. I've said it before and will probably repeat it; the human soul does not reveal itself until it is ready. But unfortunately, I cannot control what I can see with my ability. So, as I looked around, I did notice something my initial glance missed. Radiating from two different points within the massive structure that contained the bar, elevator, the captain's quarters, and presumably where the other attractions would be held were two auras that were as black and wretched as the stormy night sky. One was located towards the top of the building, and one was at the bottom. I've seen an aura like these several times before. Every time I come across one, they are emitted from the vilest of humanity. Murderers. Dictators. Terrorists. The scum of society.

I was tempted to pop over to examine the face of who was giving off such a terrible presence, but Shameis and I were about to reach the apex of our trek. This meant that I had to face an ultimatum. My curiosity wanted me to interact with these sources of evil, but that strange feeling deep within me was instructing me to stay by his side. There that feeling was again. Would it even let me leave? For as long as I can remember, my condition has made every choice for me so even if i couldn't actually leave, the notion that I could choose for myself filled me with joy. I would have left Shameis to wander if it wasn't for this feeling. Knowing I couldn't fight it, I turned back toward the direction we had been climbing and prayed that those wretched souls wouldn't eventually hurt Shameis or Sammie. Once again, all my searching had caused me to zone out, but upon snapping back, I realized that we had finally reached the summit.

At the top, the only people up here were Shameis and me, three people sitting at each pipe entrance, and a staff member monitoring the vacationers that entered the attraction. He allowed the fun-seekers to choose one of the three slides before giving them the signal to shoot down. This human was essentially staring into space as he mindlessly instructed guests to proceed. I noticed that the three humans preparing for their journeys were staring at the staff member, so I went to stand behind and look over his shoulder to see their expressions. They were all waiting with anticipation. Once I got behind, the staff member shouted, "Go ahead," which indicated that the three people could take off. After a few seconds, the controller instructed that three more people in line could take a seat.

Upon hearing this, Shameis stepped onto the water of his chosen tube and looked down the pipe. I could see the joy in his eyes. Just as he was about to sit in the water, the staff member called out to Shameis and informed him he couldn't go down in anything other than a swimsuit. In a beat-for-beat recap of the conversation with Sammie, Shameis recited his spiel about his shorts. He even turned out his pocket again. He was again smug about his attire, but as he turned from his pocket to the employee, the joy drained from Shameis's eyes, and they widened with fear. He tried to turn his torso so that he would be squared with the employee, but he tripped on the part of the plastic tube and fell to a sitting position with an echoing thud. The employee jumped up from the wooden stool to try and help Shameis back up, but before this person could reach out, Shameis had accidentally slipped into the tube and began his descent.

I was instantly confused by what had just happened. There was no reason Shameis should have been scared of this child. He was wearing the correct attire. I just continued to stand there baffled by what I had just witnessed until I was *pulled* to the outlet of the tubes, where I continued to stand in confusion. Within twenty seconds, I noticed a pulse of water gush out of the tube before Shameis was dumped into the heavily populated mass of chlorinated water. Once in the pool, he quickly swam to the edge and climbed up to where I was standing. He then stood beside me, hunched over and was coughing. Being that he had descended with all parts of his attire still being worn, he was soaked from head to toe with water dripping from his shorts and shirt. He continued to stand there, trying to catch his breath. "It's about time ya got down heya!" A woman shouted from behind me. I turned to get a glance as to who was calling, and as I should have guessed, a slightly intoxicated Sammie was marching toward us. She was the only person who would be expecting Shameis, but the way she was pronouncing her words threw me off. "I didn't expect ya ta take three hours!" Shameis didn't respond right away and instead stayed hunched over, trying to breathe. His actions did cause Sammie's anger to subside enough for her to show a bit of compassion and ask Shameis what was wrong.

"There... There was... I can't... I don't know.." He gasped.

"Shameis, come on. Tell me what happened." She instructed.

"There was... a skeleton!" He shouted as he looked up to her while slowly moving to an upright stance. "There was a standing, moving skeleton wearing a tattered robe!" Upon hearing that, my attention instantly jumped to him. If I had eyeballs, they would have jumped out of my sockets. However, I did lose control of my jaw as it hinged open. He saw me! He actually saw me! I have no idea how he was able to. It isn't possible. It shouldn't be possible. Now his instant fear made sense, but why? How? This settled any questionable concerns in my mind. The moment he said he could see me, I decided to stay by Shameis's side. I needed to discover why this particular human could do what no others could.

My astonishment was short-lived as it was interrupted by Sammie's drunken cackle as she questioned, "What are ya blabberin' about?" in a demeaning tone.

With the most severe expression I have seen on his face, he looked her dead in the eye and continued with, "I saw a five-foot-tall skeleton wearing a tattered black robe with a brown hood." Shameis exclaimed. As he described my exact wardrobe, I felt my jaw begin to quiver. Hearing someone acknowledge my existence filled me with an emotion that I couldn't even explain. It was the combination of overwhelming joy, relief, and excitement all wrapped up together. On top of that, I was filled with hope. A human saw me. A human actually saw me! I wish he wouldn't have seen me as a skeleton, but he saw me nonetheless. Once again, my joy was cut short as Sammie started to laugh even more aggressively. I found this quite rude, but she was not in control of her facilities. As if I could do anything, so I let it slide. Shameis must have as well since he changed the subject by asking, "Did you say I was up there for three hours?."

50

"Yeah!" She shouted as she grabbed Shameis and began to drag him toward the building. "The movie is about ta start! Ya said ya need ta see it!"

As we started to walk over, I tried to put all the pieces of this puzzle together, but it just wasn't making any sense. There was no way we were in that line for three hours. I know I lose track of time when I zone out, but three hours? That must have been thirty minutes maximum. Even if I didn't perceive time correctly, I knew three hours was incorrect. Everything just seems like it is getting out of hand so quickly. The people present. The lapse of time. Sammie's demeanor. The two sources of evil. The fact that I'm able to be here. I knew it was all connected, but I had no idea how. There is no way this is all just a coincidence. That is not how the universe works, so I knew there have to be other forces at play and needed answers. I need to understand this puzzle. I doubt it'll help, but perhaps being able to experience a film for the first time will calm me enough to wrap my head around this whole debacle. Either that, or it will get me to the point where the universe will finally release me from this trip so I can continue with my obligations. After all, the lives of any human are supposed to be out of my hands. Even if that human could see me.

SAMMIE

52

Chapter Six

There is an expression I heard that is used to cope with one's actions. It says that one cannot see red flags while looking through rose-tinted glasses. The meaning behind this typically refers to the attraction between two humans, where one displays signs of toxicity that the partner ignores due to their infatuation. Since I do not have a partner, I use this motto when I need to take a soul. Without my rose-tinted glasses, I would fall for every plea to return the lost to their mortal vessel. There have been instances where I nearly relented, but my role is unwavering. The infinite wisdom of the universe knows what is best. So I've always ignored the warning signs, bribes, pleas, and defiances while following the motions laid out for me. I bring up the notion of wearing rose-tinted glasses because I am trying my best to ignore all the coincidences that are springing up, but the evidence was overwhelming. Overwhelming to the point that I was starting to realize that I was here for a specific reason, as opposed to a fluke mistake the powers above have made. No, I was meant to be here. Initially, I was informed that my only purpose was to collect souls, but all these oddities are making me think there is more for me. If I am made to do everything these two humans do, then so be it.

In my eternity of walking the earth, I never thought I would be presented with the simple opportunity to view a picture show. Yet here I was, walking with Shameis and Sammie as we meandered through the crowds. Upon entering the entryway positioned to the left of the elevator, we found ourselves within a corridor that was wide enough for a group of eight people to stand shoulder to shoulder. I looked around the corridor and noticed the decor matched all the other interior spaces I had seen before, but the smell of fried food filled the air. We ended up passing a few entryways that led into locations that were made for people to enjoy. The first was on the left, and led to a lounge and a full-service bar on the other side. Through the doorway, I was able to see the buffet that served as the source of the mouthwatering aroma. I assumed this was where Sammie had ventured to while Shameis and I climbed the wooden tower. The next entry was also on the left and led to a different part of the same lounge. Here, a group of employees set up a stage for some sort of performance.

A third potential entry sat directly across the entrance to the stage, but was blocked by a set of closed doors. After passing these three, We finally came upon the room we were searching for, and many people were flowing into it with very few exiting. Through the crowd, I noticed a metal post and sign with a note printed on it. The message read, "ADVANCED SCREENING OF 'CROSSING The Ile' STARTING IN TEN MINUTES." Oh, I.L.E... not I.S.L.E... I didn't expect that word to be Turkish for 'with', instead of English for a small island. That was a strange choice for a title, but I'm sure I was going to learn why it was made.

As expected, we followed the flow of bodies into the room. Although I have not been able to observe a film, I have seen the inside of a theater more times than I can count. The ambiance matched what I've come to expect from a standard theater, only mixed with the design

54

elements of the ship. The entrance was at the top of an inclined floor filled with bolted-down reclinable seats. The mass of seats consisted of ten rows with approximately sixteen chairs per row. To allow easy access to each row, the landing we entered split to the left and right, which then led a series of steps on either side of the theater. As for the individual seats, the portion of the chair that the humans actually sat upon was built with spring-loaded hinges so the unused position was upright to allow others to easily pass by. I could also see that the cushions were lined with a leather exterior. This was brilliant. There is no easier way to reduce water damage in cushions than repelling moisture. Of course, all the seats were facing forward toward a projection screen that hung from the catwalks above a large stage.

Seeing the stage made me realize this was just a standard theater, not strictly one for movies. Perhaps there was going to be a live production here later? That would explain all the people using the word 'act'. As for the rest of the room's walls and ceiling, they one again had creme paint, birch wood, and red carpet with gold detailing. The only difference in aesthetics from the rest of the ship is the lighting. There were lights on both the left and right walls of the room that shot beams of light upward and downward. Above us was standard house lighting scattered across the ceiling. Most of the seats were occupied when we entered, but Shameis and Sammie descended the stairs and found an aisle with two conjoined and unoccupied seats. I decided to hang back by the entryway just in case the theater filled. There might be an additional unoccupied seat next to the couple I was unfortunately stalking, but someone could end up sitting there, and I hate the feeling of occupying the same place as a living body for too long. Upon taking his seat, Shameis began to look around the theater nervously, presumably to see if I was still around.

As I stood patiently, I decided to use my ability to view the auras portrayed by the populous of the enclosure. Although the room was packed, there were significantly fewer people in here than outside. I felt as if I might better understand the travelers since this room had less to take in. Unfortunately, I was instantly overwhelmed by the sea of rainbow auras that were spouting the word 'act.' I was, however, able to detect the void of one black aura radiating from amongst the crowd. I wish I could've, but I was unable to determine who the owner was. Still struggling to scan the crowd, I noticed the second black aura was also here and was pleased to see this one wasn't mixed into the crowd. Instead they were standing against the back left corner of the theater. Upon disabling my ability, I saw this second aura emanated from a short and stocky man who was balding but possessed a thick gray beard and a pair of circular bifocal glasses. If it wasn't for my ability to see the evil in his aura, I would've mistaken him as one of the other elderly voyagers. He was wearing a blue button-down shirt with a colorful floral design, khaki shorts, and sandals. He seemed to be fixated on a person in the crowd. I am hoping whoever that is will not be his next victim since I don't want to be collecting a soul right now.

I tried my best to keep my attention trained on this particular individual, but I was *pulled* away when the lights began to dim and a bright beam projected onto the screen. I wanted to keep my eyes on the man, but apparently, I was enthralled by the light show. After diverting my attention, I quickly turned back, but he had mysteriously vanished. The temptation to find and follow him did arise, but I felt that strange feeling instructing me to stay where I was. Oh well, at least I'll be able to enjoy a film without having to collect a soul. So, I simply leaned back against the wall and watched as snippets of upcoming films of various genres began to play. I know we are here to watch a movie about The Ile,

56

but as I watched these clips, I noticed they were predominantly action filled and of other heroes, which I was happy to learn about the other superhumans.

The first of the series of trailers was for a heroine named Starseeker. She appeared to be an all-powerful entity that possessed the ability of levitation and super strength. Following her trailer was a clip for the hero named Crossfade, who started off as a standard human but could transform into a living skeleton. I wouldn't wish being a skeleton on anyone, but at least this hero gained the ability to run at the speed of sound. The last clip about superhumans was for a duo of heroes named Inkblot & Moonlight. This clip told the story that a couple lay dying after a terrible car accident, and a pair of angels reached out to save them. The contact resulted in the team receiving extraordinary abilities. The male character went by the name of Inkblot, and he possessed the ability to control and produce shadows, even in a bright mid-day sun. Moonlight had powers that allowed her to create light from her body and even use the light as a projectile to inflict damage. Of these three clips, the last one felt the most far-fetched. I know for a fact that an angel can't reach through the Vale between realms. If they could, then there would be no use for me.

Once the trailer for the Superheroes ended, the house lights shut off completely as the sound of electric guitars, bass guitars, and drums filled the room. The instruments were airing a distinct melody as the visuals revealed the company's name that produced this film; 'Consnetrious Comics'. I was instantly engrossed by everything and felt like I could not take my eyes off the screen. The film did start rather slowly, but from what I understood, the premise was that the main character was a young private investigator named Issac Levi Enderson. The actor portraying this character appeared in his late thirties with a slightly muscular build that didn't seem to be overdone.

The cinematographer provided the audience with a scene where his physique was displayed via a tastefully placed shirtless scene near the film's beginning. I would have been into this scene as much as the other ladies if I was mortal. As the movie progressed, this investigator took several cases in which he helped people catch cheating spouses, corrupt cops, and other acts of impurity. I'm sure this was meant to help frame the character, but he eventually found himself sinking into a rut and beginning to loathe how he kept hurting people and ruining lives. After a couple years of living in this mind frame, a case came across his desk that would lead him to face off against two gangs that were warring with each other. He used the opportunity to pull himself out of his slump but was quickly discovered by one of the corrupt organizations. The leader tried to kill Isaac, to which Isaac had to fake his own death to get away.

This caused Issac to dive deeper into the case while realizing he needed a way to disguise himself. After all, dead men don't reappear. So the character designed a costume that looked like many other mercenaries you'd see in pop culture. He donned a black leather helmet, a pair of black goggles, and a black facemask with the outline of a skeletal grin. To go along with his headwear, his costume dawned a black leather trench coat with plenty of belts and straps with accents of spikes and other pieces of metal, black leather pants, a pair of black leather gloves, a pair of black steel-toed army boots, and the silver armored chest plate depicting a strange white skull-like design that was missing the lower jaw. Interestingly enough, this skull design sort of looked like the skin on Shameis's face that wasn't covered by his facial hair. It seemed that the only part of Isaac's ensemble that wasn't black or dark gray leather was the dull armor plating. I assumed that the clothing he chose for the identity must have had a kevlar weave within the leather since there was a scene in the film where he was being shot at, but the bullets didn't affect him.

58

After creating this new identity, Isaac loaded himself to the teeth with weaponry so he could fight the gangs the same way they were attacking him. Upon arriving late to a massacre and viewing the carnage, he decided to ditch the firearms. That was the moment Isaac vowed to never take a life. He knew he needed to be better than his adversaries. Realizing that he didn't have it in him to kill another human, Isaac took down this ring of villainy with his bare hands and his specialized suit, leaving unconscious bodies for the police to clean up. It appeared that he had received training in a couple of martial arts combat forms, but the film never explained how or when he went about getting this knowledge. He just had it. Anyways, his quest lasted several days as he took down many members of both gangs. Because of this venture, Isaac realized this was exactly what he wanted to do with his life.

The idea of becoming a superhero caused him to take his initials and create the name for this new identity of 'The Ile'; reflecting this identity was now part of him. He then took this experience and used it as the origin story of this above-average hero. After his run-in with these gangs, he trained in hand-to-hand combat and gained additional gadgets to assist him in his future crusades. The character didn't seem overly wealthy, but he worked with the money he made solving cases as a private investigator. This man developed an affinity for being The Ile and using his new identity to protect the city he lived in. The story then progressed a few years into the future, where Isaac received a case from a disgruntled mother that said her son had been kidnapped. The mother explained that the authorities weren't in the position of lending a helping hand. In response, Isaac told the mother that he too couldn't help but that if she were to give the information, he knew someone who could, referring to his alter ego. The case eventually led The Ile to a cemetery, where he found a disgruntled scientist experimenting on the boy in a secret laboratory underneath.

Within this laboratory, The Ile started to confront the scientist, who summoned several robots that were programmed to attack intruders. He held his own for a while but inevitably was overwhelmed by the swarm. They then pinned him down in a kneeling position and forced Isaac to listen as the mad scientist began to monolog while approaching the defeated hero. Once within arm's length, the scientist plunged a syringe into the neck of the hero and spoke the words, "It looks like The Ile is no more." For some reason, I was suddenly stricken with a sense of déjà vu. It was as if I'd seen this scene play out before, but I couldn't put my finger on where I saw it. Perhaps it was just one of the many other times I was collecting a soul within a torture room, morgue, prison, or another of the billion places I've been, but something about this specific scene tweaked a nerve. I continued to watch the screen as it faded to black before the end credits began to crawl up the screen. As the text slowly ascended, the theater lights illuminated the audience again, and they all began exiting the room. I just stood stunned for a bit. Why would a story end like that? I thought stories were supposed to have uplifting endings. The only explanation I could think of is that these storytellers were planning a sequel.

While baffled, I waited in the corner until Shameis and Sammie were close enough for me to start following. Thankfully they traveled the path they entered upon instead of exiting up the opposing stairs. It didn't feel like we were in there for too long, but it was enough time to completely dry Shameis's clothes. After they finally reached the theater exit, I began to follow as the two of them continued down the hall toward the main deck. Upon entering the salty open air, I noticed that the sky was dark and filled with glimmering stars and a vibrant full moon. Did that film really take several hours away from us? If the movie had started at five o'clock, it must have been at least four hours long. This

60

was odd, but there was something else that felt different. It was silent. I was relieved when I wasn't blasted in the face with the roar of screaming humans, but also a bit confused. Where was everyone? I continued to follow the duo toward a railing on the side of the deck and watched as they rested against it while looking out to the sea. They leaned and stared at the reflections of light that contrasted upon the dark ripples of water. I, too, leaned against the railing, but I looked up to the stars instead of to the water below. I've always found that looking at the stars is the easiest way to get a sense of my location.

I was expecting to find that we were somewhere tropical due to the weather. Somewhere like the Bahamas, the Gulf of Mexico, or somewhere along the Northern Tropic line. That's what I was expecting. But, to my surprise, the stars became another piece of this massive puzzle. Their orientation said that this vessel was currently positioned somewhere in the middle of Northern America. The only place I could think of that had water big enough to not see a coastline in the middle of North America would be Lake Michigan. Of all the things that have not seemed right on this trip, this takes the cake. How could we be here and have the scent of salt filling the air? Lake Michigan is purely freshwater! I was about to storm off and find an answer to this conundrum, but Sammie ended up breaking the silence.

"Did you enjoy the movie?" Her mellow voice questioned over the sloshing water.

"Yeah, it was alright. Better than I expected for a character without superpowers. I wish the movie wouldn't have ended in a cliffhanger, but I think they'll pick up the story in the Starseeker movie." He answered.

"Me too. I'm sure you'll get to see it soon," Sammie replied. "Do you know what time it is?"

"Uh, one sec," Shameis stalled as he scanned the environment for a clock or device that told the time. "Over there," he sounded off while pointing across the deck of the ship. "It says it is... Midnight? That can't be right. Wasn't it just five?"

After hearing that, Sammie quickly cut him off and stated, "Well, I'm pretty tired. Everything must be closed by now. We should head back to our cabin," before grabbing Shameis's hand, pulling him across the deck and back to the elevator. I still wanted to understand why things weren't making sense, but that feeling in me said I needed to continue to follow. In the lift, Shameis decided it was a good idea to spew out facts about the things he knew about the 'Superhero Universe' these upcoming movies belonged to, and how they were all going to be connected. He seemed to imply that 'The Ile' must have been a newer hero the company was trying to push since there isn't much information about him. Shameis seemed knowledgeable about the topic, but I was quite confused. How could this character be a new hero but already be replaced by a different character? He described these characters as real beings while Sammie just nervously smiled and nodded her head. It was as if she wanted him to believe she cared, but she clearly didn't and was uncomfortable by the situation. When the elevator finally stopped at the level with their room, we walked back through the halls until we approached their cabin door.

That was when my confusion finally became full-blown terror as I felt a cool breeze while following the couple into their pre-illuminated suite. I was the last to enter, so I watched as Shameis walked deeper into the room. Sammie, on the other hand, continued to stand patiently near the doorway. "That's funny. I don't remember leaving the lights on," he muttered before searching around the bed. "Our luggage still isn't here!" He then exclaimed frantically while continuing to search the room. That was when he noticed the porthole. "I didn't think that this could open," he spoke up one more time while sticking his right arm through in an attempt to close it. As soon as he turned away, Sammie rushed over and opened the top drawer on the dresser before pulling out a syringe. She then quietly walked up to Shameis and plunged the needle into his neck before emptying its contents into him. Out of instinct, I jumped forward and tried to grab onto her ankle, but ended up phasing through her. I knew I wouldn't be able to stop this, but I had a fleeting hope that perhaps my time away from my duties would at least allow me to interact with the two I've been made to watch. Alas, I was helpless as I watched Sammie pull Shameis out of the porthole, causing him to flop his still conscious yet paralyzed body onto the bed.

"Sam? Sam?" He struggled to get out.

"Oh come on, have ya not realized that's not my name yet?" She questioned in a mocking tone with a whiny, east coast city dialect. Her voice was identical to the one bleeding the restroom at the rest stop six months ago. Just as I feared, there were only two people back then. She had been presenting a false persona this entire time!

"What do you mean?" Shameis fretted as his words slowed.

She then sat on the bed and leaned over him to look him in the eyes. Her flaming red hair was obscuring her face, so I couldn't see the expression, but I could hear the mocking tone in her voice. She answered his question with, "So ya ain't put any of it togetha' yet? Well, I guess the Doc is gonna' have ta catch ya up." Within seconds, Shameis's consciousness began to fade and I could feel myself being *pulled* away. While trying my best to remain here, I quickly used my vision to see her aura, and sure enough, it was as black as a starless night sky. In hindsight, this should have been obvious based on how she was acting, but I guess my rose-colored glasses and desire to want the relationship they had allowed me to ignore the many red flags. I was devastated. Then, just

63

like that, I was *pulled* away without any additional information as to why this woman betrayed this man. This is the exact reason I try to ignore the affairs of humans. There is so much evil and deceit that it is hard to keep the truth correct. I still wasn't sure why I was there, but I now knew I was somehow tethered to Shameis since I was *pulled* away as his consciousness faded. This raised the wonder of why this man's consciousness has randomly started to ground me in a single place, but at least I now knew something bigger had to be at play. But that leaves the biggest question unanswered. What I really want to know is... why?

Chapter Seven

I know I've mentioned this before, but I haven't gone into detail about my situation. As an agent for the Higher Beings, I'm forced to travel for an eternity without rest. There have been many instances where I've wished to rest my aching feet, but time marches forward, and death waits for no man. For humans, the lack of rest will cause sleep deprivation, which can cause mood swings, poor balance, loss of memory, and even heart disease in some severe cases. In my position, the only symptom caused by my lack of rest is all my experiences blending into an ongoing fever dream. My solace to this never-ending nightmare is the hope to be released. That, or when I am *pulled* to meet with the Angel controlling me instead of my next soul.

Typically these meetings only happen when I am provided with special instruction for a soul. I am not privy to why these souls need special treatment; I only do as I'm told. These unique souls range from world leaders and political figureheads to souls that are pivotal to the course of human history. There have even been times I was instructed to fetch mass murderers. Now, many would expect that I can roam to whichever realm I want to, but the truth is that I am not allowed to leave the Earth except for a very few instances. One of which is these meetings, and the other is when I am ferrying a soul to their afterlife. Even then, I still cannot enter another realm besides the realm of the living. I am, however, able to travel into and lead souls across the Void between realms, an empty space where nothing exists. This is the space I get dragged through when traveling from one soul to another, and is why I can travel at the speed I can.

I've spent more time in this place than I care to acknowledge, but this time has given me the resources I need to understand and manipulate this zone. It acts as a corridor from one place on Earth to another; the doorway from Earth to whatever lies beyond. This Void is the only common ground for me to meet with the one angel I'm made to serve since neither of us can cross to the other side. I knew from the moment that I returned to this place that I would be returning to work. I guess my vacation is over. Now, being *pulled* here is usually a guessing game about what I'm supposed to do, so I began to wander. I intended to walk until anything happened, which generally doesn't take long. Only for a few yards at most, but this time was taking much longer. I was beginning to worry a bit., and my worry is very much warranted. I have learned the hard way that my energy is drained every second I'm in here.

I was beginning to think this was the universe's way of punishing me for slacking from my duties, like being punished with my greatest fear. Woefully for me, there isn't a handbook to being the ferryman of souls. Just the word of my overseer. Then again, I've realized long ago that being lost in the Void would be a welcoming outcome over the amount of pain I bring to the humans. I have toyed with the idea of forcing myself to stay here and end my existence. I hate the pain I cause to humans. The pain I caused has led me to desire an end, but my experience with Shameis brought me hope. If I was able to experience the joys of humanity, perhaps there is a way I can somehow be released from this

66

role. So, I dredged onward through the darkness. Eventually, a voice spoke out and made me stop in my tracks.

The voice wasn't as terrifying as the source wanted it to be. How could it frighten me? This voice is the same exact one that has spoken to me for multiple millenniums. Every time I'm brought to him, he tries to frighten me. He does this because of how fearful I used to be, but thousands of years have passed. This antic has become more irritating than anything else. Instead of reacting, I stood in place as I waited for him to appear. After a couple of minutes, a speck of light slowly presented itself. I watched as it floated at a height that was equivalent to the bottom of my ribs. It was bobbing in place for a couple moments until it froze as a column of light simultaneously ascended and descended out of it. It stretched until the anomaly stood seven feet tall before widening until it formed an ellipse. The light emitting from the newly formed ellipse appeared to ripple inward and outward from the middle, like how water would when a stone would be cast into a pond. Due to the waviness, the edges of this disk of light would not maintain a solid curve. Every soul I collect and lead through the Void is taken aback by this phenomenon, but I have long since become accustomed to this. As soon as it was finished stretching, a figure began to step through the portal. The action caused the light to flicker as it bobbed vigorously before destabilizing and fading away. I should note that for some reason, even though there is no source of light here, every entity that exists within the Void remains completely illuminated as if there is an overhead light source. I cannot explain why this happens. It just does. I wish I knew the answers as to why, but my captor is not keen on sharing his secrets.

As for the figure that just joined me, he was wearing robes similar to mine, except his was entirely brown instead of black with a brown hood. It was also untattered, while I have never been given another to change into. On top of all this, he decorated the exterior of his clothing with golden ornamental chains and shoulder armor. This entity's hood was obscuring most of his face so that his identity was shrouded, but again, I have been through this ruse more times than any soul can count. I wish I had the energy to be happy to see him, but I don't. Even if this realm wasn't drawing off of me, I still wouldn't care. This entity's presence has grown too tiresome. After a few moments of silent staring, he finally removed his hood to reveal the face I had grown to loathe. He had a smug grin and malicious intent in his crystal blue eyes. Upon shedding his hood, long golden hair flopped out and covered the left side of his face. In his left hand, I could see that he was wielding a scythe that appeared similar to the one I was entrusted with. Once this being was settled, he reached his right hand out as if to caress my face while questioning, "Are you not scared of me anymore? It has been a while since we've been together."

Before he was able to touch me, I slapped his hand away. The contact I made with him felt different from my contact with the human souls. It was as if something soft and malleable was covering me, so I looked to my hands. Sure enough, I found that my bony exterior was replaced with a soft, light olive-colored flesh. Oh, how I have missed my skin. I always forget that it returns when I leave the land of the living. After inspecting my hands, I returned my attention to the male figure standing in front of me. He seemed slightly irritated that I rejected his advance, but his smug look returned shortly after. "What's wrong, not excited to see me?" he continued to pester.

"When am I ever glad to see you, Azrael?" I responded as I continued to stare while hiding the fact that I was surprised by how high the pitch of my voice was. I know it has been a while since I heard my voice, but I always thought it was heavier than this.

"There was once a time when you adored my presence." He reminded me.

68

"I don't think that is the correct word." I corrected him. "The only time I have ever been happy to see you was when you revealed yourself for the first time. Even my reaction to you coming back after I was abandoned here with no inclination of what was happening wasn't adoration. You were the first face I saw in what felt like centuries. But you had to go and ruin my goodwill rather fast."

"It was only ten years," he gaslighted me, as if I hadn't already figured this fact out. Was that fact meant to make everything better? "Besides, that was the only punishment that seemed to fit your crime."

"Then why have you made me run your errands for all this time?" I grilled him.

Finally, his smug expression changed, but only to one of confusion. He then repeated himself. "This was the only punishment that seemed to fit your crime."

"You can see everything I see. You know how humanity has evolved. So many humans have done so much worse than what I did. Everything you have put me through is unjust," I pleaded. His response was to shout and remind me that I was the first, which shut me up since I did not want to incur the wrath of a deity once again. My silence caused Azrael's smugness to return with a vengeance while the tension thickened to the point it could be cut with a knife. After standing silently for nearly a minute, I broke the silence with the question, "What do you want from me?"

"Come on. Am I not allowed to want to see your face?" He cross-examined while shrugging his shoulders and bending his right arm so that his open palm was facing upward.

"No," I instantly shut him down. "You have never wanted to see me. You only show up when you want something. So if you don't mind, just tell me what you want. I have better things to accomplish and would like to return to."

"Like stalking a human?" He changed the subject after returning to his smug neutral position.

I was instantly taken aback by that question. I knew Azrael could see everything that I saw, but I wasn't there under my own volition. Not like I have a choice of where I am allowed to be at any given point. "You weren't making me follow him?" I wondered.

"And I thought you were starting to go rogue." Azrael playfully accused me, which created an impasse where both of us fell silent. This wasn't a long silence, as Azrael enjoyed hearing himself speak and broke the silence within a matter of seconds. "I guess it really doesn't matter. But yes, I need you to do something. I need you to bring him to me."

"Who?" I inquired.

My question slowly whipped Azrael's favorite expression off his face as he replaced it with another that I've seen more than a handful of times. He looked upon me as if I was an ignoramus, which I did deserve. I knew exactly who he was referring to, but I didn't want to believe it and hoped he would say another name. "The human you were following." He answered.

"You don't know his name?" I probed. Was it a good idea to poke at an angel's imperfections? Probably not, but there wasn't much he could do about it. I mean, I was already walking the Earth for all eternity as his go-for.

As expected, Azrael did get upset and began to bark at me while getting too close for comfort. He shouted, "It doesn't matter what his name is! Just bring him to me!"

Through this, I tried to keep my composure as best that I could. Moments like this are where I used to cower in fear before doing exactly as he ordered, but I just don't care anymore. For the longest time, I had hoped I would escape this role. I once had the thought that if I would push his buttons enough, he would just make me vanish. Unfortunately, I am still here, and it is only becoming easier to ignore. But now, not only is he requesting a soul that is still alive but one that has become one of the only lights in my bleak life. In a calm voice, I replied, "If you don't know his name, then clearly he isn't important. Why do you want him?"

Again, defiance caused Azrael's anger to build. I swear I could feel the heat from his anger radiating off his body. "I want him because of your attachment! Now bring him to me!" He screamed, causing his voice to echo through the Void. It is challenging to keep one's composure when getting yelled at, and frankly, I don't know how military personnel can stand it. I've witnessed humans murder each other over this form of abuse. I really wanted to keep my composure, but I could feel my anger rising and inevitably ended up raising my voice.

"No!" I challenged him. I expected him to continue his tirade, but instead, he fell silent. He just stared at me with intense hatred. "Bring him to me, or I will rip your body apart, molecule by molecule, and redistribute you throughout the human race so that I can imprison every single soul that you become part of." Now that was a terrifying thought, but I don't think it was possible. Again, if he could, he would have done so already. He has threatened me many times with acts that were so much worse than this, but I am still here.

"Go ahead," I muttered calmly.

"Excuse me?" He shouted again.

"You're not going to have him," I refused. "Rip me apart. I'm ready to die." For a moment, his anger became mixed with confusion. Clearly, this Angel has never been denied a demand. I then watched as he pondered my refusal just before he balled up his fists and tilted his head back to let out one of the loudest screams I have ever witnessed. When finished, he then returned his attention to me, brought his right arm up so that his fist was in my face, and snapped his fingers. Of course, I winced. If anyone was expecting something terrible to happen to them, they would do the same. I kept my eyes shut for a bit before opening them as I realized that nothing was happening. If his threat had followed through, it would have happened instantly. I then watched as he snapped again, pulled his hand back, and snapped a few more times while staring at his hand as if it was a broken toy. Finally, out of frustration, he snapped his fingers one last time and vanished in a flash of light, abandoning me in the Void.

Well, that could have gone better, but I expected as much. This Angel is so temperamental. Do all of these beings act like this? I once wished I could've had the opportunities to be more than just this one, but over all this time, this one angel has broken my faith. I'd be happy if I would never see one of these beings again. Nevertheless, I found myself alone again. I was a bit surprised that Azrael would go far enough to snap his fingers at me, but I knew nothing would come of it. It is just another reason to believe there is something bigger at play. So, because I was trapped here, what was I to do? I began to walk. The first time I was trapped here... before the fall. Still that was the only time I wasn't let out of the void shortly after Azrael leaves. By this point, I was starting to feel the wear of being in this zone, but I needed to push forward. Azrael would have to come to his senses eventually. After all, He wouldn't want to collect his own souls after another was doing it for thousands of years. I am essential to the entire operation.

Being trapped here ended up giving me some time to wonder about what was happening. Angel's are all-powerful beings that can control the universe with a literal snap of their fingers, but human souls have free will. We have the freedom of speech but not the freedom of consequences. So why was I still standing? Why was I still alive? What

72

does this have to do with Shameis? The moment Shameis's name came to mind, a gateway similar to the one Azreal entered through appeared in front of me. I assumed Azrael was about to step back through and act as if this whole meeting was just a joke, but nothing happened. This was meant for me. Was this portal finally meant to take me to my afterlife? No, that would be too hopeful, so I guess this is going to lead me to my next victim. There is no way Azrael is trying to be benevolent. He was probably toying with me so that I would actually follow his request. That would go right along with his modus operandi. Oh well. I wanted to know what was happening to this human, so I decided to walk through the vertical puddle of light. I guess it's time to get back to work.

CROSSFADE

Chapter Eight

The passage of time has always been a struggle to grasp, ever since I've become the ferryman of souls. The combination of my lack of rest and my ceaseless off-world travel makes time fly. As a matter of fact, from what I've been told by Azrael, the other realms experience the flow of time differently. It is impractical, but that's apparently how the domains were created. That would explain the idea that the world was created in seven days, as it was put forth from the Catholic religion. Perhaps it was seven days for The Almighty Presence, but billions of years on the face of the earth. Maybe. It's just a theory I use to rationalize my missing time. Cosmic mysteries like this are why I sometimes wish I was as omnipotent as Azrael. I hope I could be privy to the reasoning behind his requests or as to why I am still being punished for my mistake. Unfortunately, I only receive what Azrael is willing to tell me. I have pleaded with the tyrant, being that the knowledge of the universe would aid in my obligations. Nevertheless, I am bound to wander blindly and alone across the earth as I try my best to rescue lost souls. I was ecstatic to finally observe souls without having to rip them from their bodies, but now my break is over.

After returning to earth, I found myself inside a small room. It was no bigger than a ten foot square. Just as these portals usually behave, I entered from the corner so I could get the best view possible. The walls appeared to be constructed of bricks painted a dark gray color while the ceiling was made of white foam tiles, and the floor was composed of plain cement. The room's humidity was damp as the lingering smell of death filled the air. A beam of light poured into the dank room from behind me, so I turned to inspect it. The light source was the only window in the entire space, and it was built into a heavy metal door that mortals would use. As I turned to the rest of the room, starting at my left, a series of cabinets wrapped around nearly half of the room. There were two cabinet sets; one was suspended in the air above a countertop and a series of drawers and cupboards. They were all painted white, while the countertop itself appeared to be a cheap marble replica. Following the cabinets around the room, my vision came across another entrance. Diagonal from where I was standing were a set of two doors that hinged away from each other. Unlike the door behind me, these doors appeared to be loosely shut as if they could freely swing on their hinges and even had a gap between them that allowed a bright white light to bleed past them. These doors clearly led into another room, but it was impossible to see what was on the other side without investigating.

The wonder of this room's purpose and why it had such a heavy door to secure it did cross my mind, but a single piece of furniture quickly answered that question. In the middle of the room, directly between myself and the set of doors, sat a massive rectangular table on top of what seemed to be a cylindrical hydraulic system. At first, I assumed it was an artist's table since there was so much light coming from it, but more details began to stand out as I approached. For starters, I noticed several leather straps hung down from both of the longer sides and the shortest

76

side that was farthest from me. Then I noticed that the surface did not have light emitting from it but instead was reflecting it. I could see several divots and scraps in this structure's metal surface. This was an operating table, and those straps were meant to hold a conscious victim as any experimentation occurred. Upon realizing this, I instantly looked above the sight to find a sizable surgical lamp hanging from the ceiling. Whoever owned this room was using the light to illuminate this depressing place. The smell I have grown too familiar with made me feel uneasy, but the sight of this made me feel nauseous. That was when it dawned on me. People have died here, but I don't recall ever visiting this place. Yes, my memories do have a tendency to blend together, but at least I know where I've been. Clearly something was amiss. I was beginning to spiral, but a slight groan quickly caught my attention.

The final corner of the room seemed to be the only part cloaked in shadow. I guess the bright lights distracted me from this area, but now that it had my full attention, I was starting to feel my stomach knot. Built into the corner to the left of where I entered was a cage made of chain link fencing. It stretched from floor to ceiling and only offered a surface area of two feet by three feet. It was just big enough for a person to sit with their legs extended and back against the wall. I moved from the table toward the cage to inspect it, and as I did, another groan projected from the darkness. Once I was able to get a good look inside, I could see that Shameis had been propped up against the brick corner of the room.

His appearance matched that of a person who had passed from dehydration. His clothing was the same as what I last saw, but his skin had grayed, his body appeared to be skinnier, and he had bags under his eyes. It was as if he'd gone five days without water. I have no idea how he could be alive since humans can only last three, but here he was, groaning and starting to stir. This circumstance enraged me. Why do humans have to be so cruel to each other! I was about to go berserk, but I needed to keep my composure. I wish I could make that woman and the other person she was working with pay for what they've done to him, but I knew I could do nothing. I wish I was allowed to interfere with the affairs of the mortal world. Still it did seem like an odd coincidence, since it appeared as if he had just awoken. "Where am I?" he whimpered as he contorted his body so he could latch on to the fencing while looking around this dank dungeon. I continued to watch as struggling to get to his feet. If I had eyes in my sockets while on earth, my eyes would water at this sight. It was heartbreaking.

Within seconds of Shameis finally making it up to his feet, the set of double doors swung open, and a woman's voice poured out, "See Doc, I told ya I didn't kill him," in that whiny, east coast city dialect. That was when Sammie and the short, stocky, and mostly bald man came walking out. While Sammie was still in a casual attire, she now wore a bright red shirt, blue jeans, and laceless canvas shoes instead of the shorts and sandals I last saw her in. As for her partner, I instantly recognized him, but he appeared completely different from that fleeting glance. He still had a thick gray beard, but was now wearing a pair of circular bifocal glasses and a long white lab coat over top a white button-down dress shirt and red tie. To match his more professional appearance, he also wore a pair of black slacks, and shiny black dress shoes. Of course, these were the two. If only I knew sooner and could have done something about it. I could have taken his soul when I first saw his aura. If only I could interact with a still-living soul, none of this would be happening. Why must I be bound to these rules that Azrael has governed over me! I could make this world such a better place. Although Sammie came bursting through the doors, the man strolled methodically toward Shameis with his hands tucked behind his back while in a rigid upright position. From the way he carried himself, I could tell he deemed himself superior to anyone else.

78

"You're lucky he is still alive, Lilith. This man is critical to our endeavor. If he had expired due to your inability to administer a correct dosage, I would have shown you a fate worse than death." the man explained in a broad German accent as the two of them continued to approach Shameis. Once within an arm's length of Shameis's enclosure, the man in the lab coat began to speak directly to Shameis. "So, you are finally awake. I was worried, and you were absent for so long. Being in a catatonic state without access to the nutrients needed for survival usually results in a permanent coma or even death. You truly are as perfect as I was informed."

Shameis was still disoriented, as he completely ignored the man who had spoken and instead could not break his visual contact with Sammie. "Sammie?" Shameis whimpered while clinging to the links of the cage... "What... What's going on? Where are we?"

"Oh, Shamey. We're with the Doctor now. Everything will be alright." Sammie mocked while returning to the accent I originally had gotten used to.

"Doctor?" Shameis whimpered.

Apparently being ignored must trigger anger for the Doctor's superiority complex since he quickly turned to Sammie and shouted, "You irritating woman! Go back and wait until you are needed!" as he raised his left hand and pointed to the double doors. Instantly after receiving this command, Sammie scurried off while nearly tripping due to the instant momentum needed to enter a dead sprint. After watching her leave, he turned back to Shameis while fixing his tie. "Correct, I am the Doctor. My name is Victor. Victor Jakelyde. You are very sick, and I am going to help you reach your full potential." He proclaimed while trying his best to console Shameis.

"Jakel.. lyde... Like from the..." Shameis started to mutter before being cut off by the Doctor.

"I'm sure you are very confused. It must feel as if there are bits of information you are missing. But if you would've noticed the blatant red flags that Lilith was throwing out as she blundered her way to this moment, you might've understood your predicament. Then again, there was a low probability of you seeing them anyway. The naive personality I provided to you was meant to disguise that woman's mistakes." Victor continued.

"I don't... I don't understand," Shameis said while visibly becoming angrier. I concurred with Shameis. I also didn't understand what was going on. I wanted to ask a few questions of my own, but still, no one could see me. I hate being the ferryman of souls! "You have the wrong person." Shameis continued as he began to plead. "Please. Let me go. I promise I won't tell anyone about this."

To his plea, Victor began to monologue. "Oh, Shameis. Poor, naive Shameis. Of course, I know you are the pillock I seek. Your face will forever be seared into my memories. You see, in your past, you crossed me. You're the first to ever do so, and I did not appreciate that. There was not a chance I would let that transgression go unpunished. An amateur investigator wearing a ridiculous disguise managed to track down my laboratory. Thinking you could actually..."

"Hold on," Shameis interrupted. "I don't know who you think I am, but it sounds like you're describing...,"

"Don't interrupt me! Don't ever interrupt me!" Doctor Jakelyde shouted while interrupting in return, causing Shameis to recoil. This interaction caused Victor to lose his train of thought, as he couldn't continue his monologue. So instead, the Doctor picked up with, "To summarize my point, everything that you know has been fabricated to my design. Your life, your work, your parents, and even the love of your life. You don't even know who you truly are." After he said that, there was an extended silence that Victor shortly broke with the statement, "You may now speak," while Shameis Shook his head in disbelief.

"What are you talking about? You sound crazy! What you're describing is a comic book! Don't you think that if I was Isaac Levi Enderson, if I was The Ile, I would have some recollection or evidence of what I was?" Shameis questioned. As much as I would love to see all this be true, I agree with Shameis's denial. Merely implying that this character existed means that the other superbeings also existed. If the so-called superheroes existed, I would have encountered them at one point in my travels. It isn't possible.

"Oh, Shameis Eli," Victor muttered with pity as he turned away and started walking towards the double doors. "If only I allowed the capacity for you to see the truth, my gloating would be so much more lovely, but it is good that you can't. It means the incubation process was a success. It means that we are ready for the next step. And since it doesn't matter anymore, let me spell it out for you. Have you ever wondered why your name is spelled the way it is? Do you think your name was developed by the actors I have hired to portray your parents? No! The name you know yourself as is a derivative of the identity you once possessed. The moment you defied me, your life as The Ile was over. I wanted you to face this truth every single day. Even if you wouldn't have known. So long were the days of the spectacular hero known as The Ile. Thus beginning the days of Eli. Shame... is... Eli..." Victor continued to monologue as he slowly crossed the room, stopping just before the double doors. He then pushed one open and held it with his arm. "The three of you may enter." He proclaimed. As soon as he said that, he turned away from the door and began to pace back toward Shameis. Within seconds, the doors slowly opened as Sammie snaked through a gap that was barely wide enough for her scrawny body. Her bold demeanor had shattered by the way Victor spoke to her mere moments ago. I don't blame her. No person should be spoken to like that. The two of them continued to walk forward, but Sammie kept her distance.

As soon as Victor returned to the edge of the cage and Sammie was about halfway between the doors and Victor, the doors whirled open with a violent thud as the plastic barriers smacked the wall and the adjacent countertop. The noise was loud and quick enough that it caused Shameis, Sammie, and me to jump. Victor was clearly expecting this. Out through the gaping entrance stumbled... I don't even know what they were! What came through, just behind Sammie, were two... abominations! Crimes against nature! The best I could describe these monsters is as atrocities. They were walking upright as if they were humanoid, but were covered in thick dark gray hair from head to toe. They both stood taller than six feet, but had hunched backs and arms nearly dragging on the ground with plump, oversized forearms. When I say oversized, I mean that each forearm appeared as if each possessed a watermelon growing inside them. The clothes consisted of matching fabrics torn and tattered in different ways; presumably, from the mutations these poor humans underwent.

Their clothing consisted of black dress shoes that had burst at the seams to allow their enormous hairy feet to stick out, black slacks that had ripped at the knees and had holes forming in the thighs from the expansion of their muscles, the remains of a black belt with a large rectangular metal belt buckle, a light blue button-down dress shirt that used to have long sleeves before suffering an identical fate as the pants, and a tie that stretched from his collar to just above the pant line. After seeing their hulking bodies, I was quickly drawn to walrus-like tusks descended from their upper jaws as thick hair protruding all around their faces that formed bearded manes. I noticed that one of the two had feminine facial features and longer hair

82

growing from the top of her head tied into a ponytail, while the other seemed quite masculine with shorter hair. I think I was able to recognize the masculine one. His facial structures were similar to the security guard giving Shameis grief just before boarding the ship. Their eyes were cold and lifeless, as if they were walking corpses. I tried to see their auras, but there was nothing. It didn't feel as if they were hiding. No, instead, it felt as if they had no aura. Like their souls have been corrupted. What a terrible way to live... if they were still alive.

As the monsters entered the room, their pungent smell only added to the stench already present. The male was carrying a plastic rack holding many small cylindrical vials filled with various colored liquids. As it passed the counter, it moved to set the frame onto the countertop as the female beast stood just behind Sammie. After gently setting down the vials, the male creature joined the female. I turned my attention to Shameis to gauge his reaction, and all I could see was immense fear. The only time I have ever seen a human this terrified is when they stare directly into my eye sockets. Shameis fell back in fear as an audible thud sounded when his posterior hit the ground. His eyes were wide and unblinking. Sammie also appeared uneasy as the monstrosities loomed over her shoulder while Victor Jakelyde displayed nothing but confidence. No matter the expression they were communicating, all four of the threats were staring directly at their imprisoned prey as the room fell quiet. All that could be heard was the deep, heavy breathing the abominations needed to keep making to fill their distorted lungs with oxygen. This was too much. If these things can exist, maybe Victor's claim has some credence.

Suddenly, Victor broke the silence with a single command. "Get her on the table." I watched as Sammie's head perked up with a smile, just before her grin vanished entirely as her pale skin turned ghost white.

83

She realized what Victor had said. Without hesitation, the male beast placed each of his paws on Sammie's shoulders and effortlessly lifted her into the air. She let out a blood-curdling scream the moment she left the ground. Out of annoyance, the beast forcefully threw Sammie on top of the table, causing it to rattle violently. The sickening impact had the result that the monster was looking as Sammie's breath left her body. After watching her land flush on her back, I recoiled without removing my vision from the horror that was unfolding.

As her limp body laid on top of the metal surface, each beast lurched to the longer sides of the table and began to strap Sammie to it. They started by positioning themselves at the longer sides before forming loops out of the dangling straps and securing her wrists before securing one enormous restraint across her chest. They then roasted around the table so the male could strap in her ankles while the female beast pulled a neck brace out from the lower section of cabinets. Then, this thing placed it around Sammie's neck before strapping her head into place. This was the moment Sammie began to stir again as she rattled the restraints, but the daze she was in caused her actions to be weak. "Why?" She whimpered, but was unanswered. During this incursion, Victor did not relent his gaze from Shameis, while Shameis was paralyzed by his witnessing. I could hear his heart beating a mile a minute. Sammie's constant muttering ended up breaking the Doctor's concentration, to which he walked over and stood between Sammie and me, making it so I could no longer see her face.

"This is what you wanted," He declared before walking around her head to the other side of the table. To get out of the Doctor's way, The two beasts retreated and tucked themselves into the corner of the room. Both Shameis and I watched in stunned silence as this man walked to where the beast had set the vials, turning his back to the room. Once facing away,

84

the sound of a drawer opening followed by Victor rummaging it filled the tense silence. After a minute or so, he turned back around, and I saw he was holding a syringe and a vial of orange liquid. Seeing his possessions, Sammie snapped out of her daze as she started to frantically shake her restraints while trying to break free. "I change my mind! I don't want this! This isn't what I wanted!" She screamed in desperation.

"Of course it is. The deal was that if you brought Isaac to me when he was ready, I would try to make you as powerful as your sister. I'll try to make you a hero. Your genetic structure should be similar enough." He reminded Lilith with a deranged smile on his face while extracting some of the mysterious liquid with the syringe. He then plunged the needle into her arm and forced the liquid into her bloodstream.

"No!" She pleaded as she began to cry as she turned her attention to Shameis. "Shameis! Please! Help me! I'm so sorry! I didn't mean for this to happen! I lo... " She screamed in the accent she used with him before, but then her eyes widened as she looked up to the sky. This was odd. It was as if the liquid paralyzed her. Her mouth was agape, and she was staring blankly upward for a few seconds, but then she suddenly began to flail violently while entering cardiac arrest. It was as if every single muscle in her body began to pulse simultaneously. Her movements were causing the entire table to rattle. We must really be somewhere remote if this amount of noise can be made without drawing the attention of a random passer-by. Finally, after an unbelievably long minute of this excruciating torture, Sammie's body fell limp as her head rolled toward me. Her eyes were glassy and lifeless. "This is an unusual outcome. Her talents would have been gratefully appreciated, but I guess her genetic sequence was not as perfect as her sister's. Or perhaps they will have another plan for her." Victor muttered as he walked away from the table and back through the set of double doors. As soon as he left, the two behemoths unbound Sammie's limp body, lifted her up and followed suit. I was devastated. Yes, she was the driving force behind all this controversy, but I was still attached to her. Now, look at her. Dead. As if her life didn't matter.

I wanted to leave. I wanted to run away so I wouldn't have to witness this happen to Shameis. If this is what it means to be human... to lose the ones that you grow close to... to be betrayed by those that you are closest to just for them to beg for forgiveness when they are in the same position... then I no longer want to be part of their world. Honestly, I don't know why I was expecting anything else. Every single human life ends the same way. Alone. If I had it my way, I would take the soul of any person that takes another life. But, alas, that is not my role. I am merely an overseer and ferryman. So, as I fretted over the cruelty I witnessed, I turned to Shameis to see how he was coping, which wasn't well. He tucked himself into a ball while sitting practically motionless. I couldn't imagine what was going through his mind. So, I decided to phase through the cage wall and crouched down to rub his back. I knew that there was no way he was going to feel me, but maybe he could feel my presence and be soothed. It may be wishful thinking, but when I do this, I feel as if the border between the physical and meta-physical softens a bit. Very rarely has this happened, but sometimes the misery is replaced with complacency. Even if they can't see or feel me, sometimes understanding that there is no change or other outcome brings a sense of peace. So, I ended up barely grazing the back of his neck with the tip of my finger, but something unexpected happened. A small jolt of electricity jumped from his skin to my finger. I was freaked out, so I quickly pulled away and returned to a standing position. Forget the desire for complacency... What was that? How did that happen? I would've freaked out more than this little bit, but my attention was quickly subverted to a voice to me right.

86

"Scuse may," the voice scratched as I turned my attention to it while still holding my shocked finger. There I found Sammie sitting on the table with her feet dangling off the long edge closest to the cage. She looked a bit confused at first, but her eyes widened when she saw my gaunt face. Most humans are confused by their passing but understand their situation when they see me. "Wha.... What happened?" She asked. She didn't seem too scared, which I do understand. Those abominations the Doctor was controlling were more terrifying than a walking skeleton. I let out a sigh since her soul talking to me meant I needed to perform my duties, even though I didn't want to. I didn't want to take Sammie from this world. Alas, I knew what I had to do.

"You died," I replied while starting to slowly walk toward her. My voice was significantly deeper, just as I initially expected it to be.

"No, that ain't possible!" She exclaimed as she began to freak out. "How did I die?"

"Tragically," I responded as I phased through the cage and stopped within arm's length.

"No. They promised I'd be a superhero. They promised me immortality." She sputtered as she looked around the room.

"He lied, just like you did to Shameis," I stated unremorsefully.

"I didn't lie ta Shameis!" She barked as she turned her attention to me.

"Never?" I questioned, which caused her hostility to melt. I think she finally understood what was about to happen.

"Does... Does lyin' mean... Do ya know everythin' I've done?" She squeaked as her jaw began to quiver.

"I am not omnipotent, nor am I the judge of your soul. I am merely the ferryman to what lies beyond." I answered with a tone of repetition in my voice. I've had to use that line on countless amounts of souls.

"So I'm dead?" Sammie double-checked.

"Unfortunately," I confirmed.

"If I'm dead, then why am I still here? Does that mean I have unfinished business? Are they makin' me a ghost?" She continued to quiz optimistically, trying to find a way out of the inevitable.

"You're still here because I have not taken you to the other side." I continued to answer while reaching out to her so she could grab a hold.

"I don't wanna go to hell." she pleaded as she pulled out the most giant pair of puppy dog eyes she could muster.

"I am not in control of that," I reiterated. I'm glad that I didn't have that to weigh over me. Being the one who takes the souls across the void is enough weight for my weary shoulders. I try to stay impartial, even though my voice doesn't matter. Frankly, Sammie is the only one I wish I had a say in. She deserves eternal damnation. Yes, she may have been one of the only two I care about, but she betrayed the one who loves her. She does not deserve anything nice in the afterlife. I know this is harsh, but Sammie is the catalyst for all of this happening to Shameis. If everything Victor said was true, she abetted a maniacal mastermind into the kidnapping and brainwashing of another human as he was only trying to help others. Her soul is pure evil. She could have ruined countless lives with her tyranny, for all I know. "It is time to go, Sammie," I informed her as I pushed my open palm toward her.

"I guess it ain't gonna be good for me if the Grim Reaper doesn't know my name." She stated as she let out a nervous chuckle.

"If Sammie isn't your real name, then what is it?" I asked.

"Lilith, Lilith Cotter." She answered as she daintily placed her hand on top of my palm. As soon as we made contact, the human manifestation of her soul burst into a hulking inferno, causing me to pull back in horror. Never in my tenure in this position has that ever

88

happened. Whenever I take a soul from this world, I walk them through the void. This was new and it was terrifying. I could only assume that this meant her soul was whisked off to the place that she didn't want to go to. Would this happen to Shameis if he ends up being killed by Victor? I knew Shameis couldn't have seen what had just happened, but I still turned to him anyway. I need something to keep myself from absolutely losing my mind in the surrounding madness. To my surprise, Shameis was standing on his own two feet, and his skin was no longer grayed like it was before. He was gripping the fenced wall and was leaning forward with his head looking down toward the floor.

What the heck is going on? It is not humanly possible to recover like that. But as I thought about it, I concluded that this somehow had to be the result of me coming in contact with him. Perhaps some of my essences transferred to him and healed him in the process? Is this why I was warned never to come in contact with living human souls? Do I have the ability to heal the sick? No, I've touched the living billions of times, but this has never happened. None of this makes sense! Whenever I get some of the answers I am looking for, ten more are put into their place! As I struggled with my most recent existential crisis, I continued to watch Shameis. It looked like he was starting to prepare for what was to come next. Good, at least one of us was.

AZRAEL

Chapter Nine

One bad day. One bad day is all it takes to entirely uproot a human's life, and the outcome has always been anything but pleasant. I've seen loving husbands gruesomely murder their families, successful businessmen end their life over the loss of their empires, innocent mothers that were taken from this world due to tragic motor accidents, and grieving parents left behind as their child loses their bout with cancer. Of course, I will always be connected to nearly every human's "One bad day." Even now, when I am merely observing the ongoings of human life while the universe isn't demanding the execution of my obligations, death and despair still surrounds me. The incident with Lilith is the perfect example. Victor's procedure more than likely would have succeeded if I wasn't here. I don't know what Victor meant when he referred to her genetic perfection, but I knew that I would eventually have to take someone's soul. There isn't another being able to collect these souls.

Yet, I am still here. Before the end of this, I will have to claim at least one more soul, and it will be either Victor or Shameis. By the way things are going, it will definitely be the latter. So, I now ask, is today Shameis's "One bad day"? Or was it five days ago when Lilith plunged that needle into his neck? If Victor's previous enlightening can be believed, perhaps Shameis's worst day was when he was first taken and forced into this fake life. On the other hand, perhaps things are about to change, and today will be the best day for him. After all, that jolt of electricity is causing him to act differently, and it is affecting the atmosphere. There is a determined look in his eye. He seems more confident than a few minutes ago, even while falsely imprisoned.

I watched him with anticipation as confusion and excitement poured out of me. Shameis appeared poised, in control, and much healthier than he did moments ago. After collecting himself, he quickly looked up from the floor toward the set of double doors as ferocity burned in his eyes. "Hey!" He shouted. "Hey, Jak. How about you get out here and look me in the face! Come tell me what this is all about!" Within seconds, Victor busted through the set of double doors with his abominations in tow. His brow was ruffled and presented a scowl while staring intently at his prisoner through his thick circular glasses. Victor's reaction caused a smirk to grow on Shameis's face. "I'm glad your buttons are so easy to push," Shameis continued with a chuckle as Victor stormed over to the cage. "It's time to stop cowering like the rat you are and pay the piper."

Victor was speechless. He opened his mouth in an attempt to speak, but nothing came out. It took him a few seconds to compose himself, but all he could muster was the question "How?" as he examined Shameis. "What did you just say?" Victor then questioned rhetorically.

"You heard me, Jak." Shameis continued to mock.

"How dare you presume to speak to me in such an offensive fashion. No one has ever referred to me in such a foul manner since.." The Doctor started to say but froze mid-sentence as he realized the change in Shameis's demeanor.

92

"..Since a dashing, young vigilante found you in your laboratory underneath the Ivory Woods Cemetery. Yeah, yeah. I remember." Shameis picked up where Victor left off.

"No! This can't be right! The incubation process was a success. Your memories. Your past life. They were all erased. How? You're messing with me. Tell me what you remember, Shameis!" Victor worried as he began to sweat profusely while fixing the position of his glasses on his face.

"You know my name is not Shameis." Shameis replied, "I remember everything."

Upon hearing that, Victor was filled with rage again. "That is impossible!" He shouted. "The neural chip implanted into your mind cannot be corrupted! You can't have knowledge of anything other than what I have programmed! Even after my monologue, the fact that you are Issac should always be separated from your amygdala! No, this is not good. This might have compromised everything we have been working towards. Naturally, they will be angry about this. How did this happen?"

"No idea and don't care." Shameis quickly responded. "All I care about is getting out of this cage. Then I'm taking you in and returning to my life as The Ile."

"Do you remember anything from your time as Shameis Eli?" Victor pondered with the sound of defeat in his voice.

"Of course I do, and I will make you pay for what you did to me." Shameis threatened.

With that, Victor's eyes widened. I couldn't tell if this was the result of fear over Shameis's threat or a spark of hope from hearing that all his work hadn't been washed away. "Well, if you remember the past six years, then you would be aware that Isaac Enderson is no longer able to be in the public eye. Dead men do not rise from the grave, Shameis. The world has moved on without you, and another has taken up your mantle. So you might as well accept your role. Either you play nicely, or I will be forced to crack open your skull and repair the chip. But knowing The Ile wouldn't go down without a fight, I've already made the decision for you." Victor muttered as he turned to the lingering behemoths. "Get him on the table," he instructed.

With the command, the female beast stumbled past Victor and up to the cage. Once directly in front of Shameis... or Isaac... she aggressively pulled on the fenced wall. With the sound of snapping metal filling the room, the monster broke what must have been intended to be a door right from its hidden hinges. Apparently, Shameis was expecting this. He was ready. Shameis pounced and caught the female beast off guard as soon as the hole was formed. Shameis ended up striking her in the face with his balled-up right fist before following up with his left. This attack caused the abomination to stumble backward and topple over the table. Seeing the altercation, Victor scuttled behind the male abomination to cower, but upon seeing his partner being attacked, the enraged male beast charged Shameis with a loud growl and swung its large hairy right arm. It looked as if it was trying to slam Shameis backward into the brick wall behind him, but thankfully Shameis was quick on his feet. Shameis ended up dodging underneath the oncoming wrecking ball of flesh to zip around to the beast's backside. This was when Shameis began to furiously pummel the beast.

Utilizing a barrage of identical strikes to the kidneys and spleen, Shameis tried his best to take that thing out as quickly as possible. As expected, the beast was resilient and would not fall. However, the blows seemed to immobilize the creature as it grew increasingly unstable. I was amused by this display of Shameis's tenacity. I wish I could say that I've never seen someone move like this or has attempted to fight a beast

94

twice their size, but I have seen nearly everything. However, his sudden spur of knowledge and expertise does imply something that I have never experienced does exist; Superheroes. I'm not sure where this spirit came from or how it suddenly manifested itself, but I loved it. Shameis just kept whaling on this abomination until it finally dropped down to one knee. The fact that this ordinary, slightly overweight man was willing to fight for his life and was practically succeeding was starting to build hope within me. Once the beast had dropped to a single knee, it began to look as if it was about to pass out. "One blow to the side of the head will knock it out!" I shouted, and as if he could hear me, he wound up his right fist and pulled it back to deliver the final blow. After this, all that will be standing in Shameis's way will be the female monster. The female monster! I was too enthralled in Shameis's actions that I ended up losing track of the rest of the room. So I quickly turned my attention away from Shameis, and at that moment, the female monster sprung up behind Shameis. Without giving either of us a moment to react, it grabbed onto Shameis's right arm.

I was so focused on the way Shameis was performing that I didn't hear the beast get up off the ground and stumble over. Now she had a hold of him, and it was her turn for a surprise attack. Shameis looked over his right shoulder and tried to get a glimpse of her while trying to pull away, but he wasn't able to do so fast enough. This thing yanked Shameis away from her male companion so aggressively that Shameis flew across the room. I heard the sickening sounds of multiple bones cracking and flesh ripping during his take-off. His right arm seemed to remain attached, and no blood escaped his body, but it sounded as if he snapped like a twig. While airborne, he whipped around like a ragdoll while screaming from the pain and landed face-first onto the countertop. He tried to reposition his right arm to protect his landing, which caused more snapping and ripping sounds to air.

95

Along with the sounds of his body being torn apart, the faint sound of glass breaking could also be heard. I quickly rushed over to examine Shameis and noticed he had landed right on top of the rack of colorful test tubes. After all this, Victor began to scream at the two abominations everything got out of hand so quickly. I tried to listen, but It was hard to hear over Shameis's screaming. I watched in horror as Shameis rolled off the countertop, revealing that a majority of his right arm and face had become covered in these liquids. I've never been into chemistry, so I cannot explain why this happened, but some combination of the contact to his skin, the mixing of the chemicals, and the exposure to the air caused the liquids to start smoking as they began to melt Shameis's flesh. I swear, if I had a stomach, I would have hurled. The smell was repulsive. I would have preferred the scent of death to this. Almost instantly after seeing this horror, my surroundings once again started to fade into nothingness.

This didn't feel like the last time I was *pulled* into the void. It didn't even feel like I was moving from where I stood. It felt as if I was simply blinking for prolonged periods of time while the room faded out and would shortly fade back in. This was beyond strange. Starting with the fade-in after the horror show where he had become deformed, I was greeted with the sight of Shameis sitting on the table facing away from me. I wasn't able to observe much, but I could clearly see Victor Jakelyde wrapping his face in gauze. By this point, Shameis's right arm had been amputated at the shoulder joint as gauze wrapped around his bleeding wound and heavily scarred bare torso. That observation was the last before everything faded out for the second time.

When everything had returned, Shameis was strapped into a lying position on top of the table. Sometime when everything was cloaked in blackness, Victor attached a strange metal plating wrapped around Shameis's right pectoral and was now fitting him with a peculiar prosthetic arm. It was unlike any I'd ever seen! I know there have been many advances in technology, but this was futuristic. Typical prosthetics I've observed through history consisted of claws, hooks, and some with motorized joints to allow individual appendages to move. This one was nothing like those. The prosthetic attached to Shameis is pure metal with no visible joints. There did seem to be black rings where the joints should be, but there wasn't a bearing in sight. Perhaps the required mechanics were tucked inside the pale silver plating? Upon further inspection, it had black hexagonal shapes that covered the entire interior and exterior of the bicep as two streams of bright blue light rolled through a pair of mirroring crevasses on either side of the forearm. After attaching the prosthetic, Victor opened the external hexagon and started tinkering with the mechanics. Something else that struck me as odd was that sometime between the last sight and this one, Victor had changed Shameis's clothes. He was still shirtless, but now he was wearing a pair of blue jeans and black canvas shoes with white laces and white rubber soles instead of the cargo shorts and sandals. Also, the abominations were no longer in the room.

Before my surroundings could fade again, I quickly repositioned myself next to Shameis's head to see his face. The gauze wrapped around his head while leaving only his right eye exposed within a diamond-like opening. The skin around his eye looked unscathed, and as I gazed into his barely conscious eye, I felt sorry for him. This most definitely was a bad day. He woke up to the betrayal of his companion, learned the truth that the life he had been living was a lie, and now is a mangled amputee. Not even death is as cruel as what this mad scientist has done. At this moment, Shameis reminded me of myself. We are mortal beings that used to do what we thought was just, only to be turned into a presence that will strike fear in the souls of any mortal that gazes upon us. At least Shameis still had his humanity for whatever time he had left.

As I stood above him, Shameis's exposed eye began to slowly open as if it was a struggle to do so. When he finally managed to open it wide enough to see, he looked directly at me. His eye widened as it had at the top of that water slide. He looked directly into my eyes, into my soul, but not with fear. Instead, he was quietly begging for this pain to stop. I genuinely wish I could help, but all I could do was wait for this to be over. Once his soul leaves his body, then I could help. I watched as he started to softly rattle his restraints and looked as if he wanted to speak but couldn't find the strength for sound to escape his mask.

"Oh, Shameis. You've finally come through. I was beginning to fret that you wouldn't recover. The procedure caused you to lose a lot of blood and make quite a mess. I hope you don't mind, but I rummaged through your suitcase and found a change of clothing. Your shorts were heavily bloodstained." Victor rejoiced as he shut the panel he was working in. To this, Shameis limply looked over at Victor before trying to get a glimpse of the prosthetic. "Do not worry, Shameis. I have rectified the problem you have caused." Victor continued to boast. Shameis again tried to respond, but still, nothing came out. "What's the matter? Does a cat have a hold of your tongue? Nothing snarky to respond with? The blood loss was a great anesthetic, but you'll soon gain the strength to function properly. Well, that is a loaded statement. After all this, you'll be functioning the way they want you to function. Speaking of which, the microchip implanted into you is fully functional., so I have no explanation as to how you regained your memories. I'm assuming it was a lapse from the stress you are enduring. Science is trial and error after all. So, Shameis. Are you ready to reach your greatest potential? Are you ready to see why all of this is happening?" Victor monologued as he reached behind himself and grabbed a syringe filled with a pale green liquid from the countertop. It was clearly a different chemical mixture from Lilith's

98

injected chemical, but I feared it would have the same effect. I can only assume this has something to do with the different genetic constructs in each human, so each of these chemicals needs to be different.

This was when Victor moved around the table toward Shameis's left side. Seeing the inevitable about to happen, Shameis again rattled his restraints but was way too weak for anything to happen. Interestingly enough, the mechanical arm was not restrained. Victor must have realized that the bond was useless since Shameis did not yet know how to operate the machine. Regardless, there was no chance Shameis could escape. Shameis struggled for a bit, and I thought I saw the arm move, but he stopped after Victor began to laugh again maniacally. "Keep struggling! You don't have the strength to break free. But after this, you will." Victor gloated before plunging the syringe's needle into Shameis's left bicep. Like Lilith, the reaction was nearly instant as the muscles under Shameis's skin began to contort. I was sickened by the sight, but fascinated by how they seemed to shape themselves into a peak physical condition while depleting his cellulite. His eye widened again as he looked upon me in agony.

"Help... me..." Finally, Shameis was able to squeak out before falling limp while his muscles continued to distort themselves.

"I will be able to soon," I comforted him.

After a few more agonizing moments, the twitching finally ceased. Still, his eye didn't glaze over in the same fashion a typical corpse would. "Lightbringer?" Victor questioned Shameis's lifeless body before pausing to let silence fill the room. "No, This isn't possible! My calculations were sound! He was a one hundred percent perfect host! You even confirmed it!" He shouted as he quickly reached his right hand towards Shameis's neck to check his pulse. Within seconds, Victor regained his composure while presenting a puzzled expression. "The subject is still alive but in a catatonic state. Perhaps there is still time needed for the vessel to be claimed. If this is going to succeed, I am going to need to..." Victor began to explain just before the room faded into blackness again. Strangely enough, not everything faded this time. The walls, the floor, the countertops, the cabinets, the cage, and Victor Jakelyde all faded away. This only left myself, Shameis, and the table he was lying on.

I was still reeling from this experience. What force in the universe is causing me to witness all this tragedy? Why must I always be punished for something I tried to prevent? This has to be Azrael's way of showing me that my place is to do as he says. That is the only explanation I can think of. This is vile, but am I supposed to expect more from an angel? Still, if he is forcing me to bring this human to him, why would my connection to the surface of the earth randomly start to rely on Shameis's consciousness. There is obviously something I am missing, but I don't feel I'm in the position to know. I really didn't want to take this soul from this world. Everything he has done was for the good of society, and all he received in return was pain. It felt as if my heart was breaking, and I could feel the start of tears welling in my eyes. Humans are so cruel. Now, I guess I have to do the one thing I am destined to do; ferry this soul. I'm still bothered by many things Victor and Lilith mentioned in passing, but only one matter stood out the most. Was Victor expecting another being to inhabit Shameis's body? Because I know for a fact that once a human's time has come, no soul can return to it. That was first rule Azrael taught me. Yet I couldn't shake this feeling. Who is the Lightbringer, and Why was Victor expecting them to speak through Shameis?

Part Two: Encountering Those that Lie Beyond

Chapter Ten

Much like a book, the human lifespan is split into chapters. Many humans like to believe that their lives are divided by years for a straightforward recount, but I like to think the divisions are marked by life-changing events. Events like marriage, the purchase of a new home, the birth of an offspring, or beginning a new role of employment are all potential beginning points of new chapters. With that being said, death is the only common denominator that connects every story and pushes a soul into their epilogue.

Then again, I should know best that the death of the soul could be the starting point for a second story. At first, I thought that becoming the ferryman of souls would be the beginning of a great adventure. But as time dragged on, I started to fear that it was my epilogue. When I finally realized I was tied to Shameis, I began to think that I was meant to have a second act. Fear started to set in when his soul left his body, but now I am just confused.

Shameis's soul left his body. That means his story is over. Yet Victor proclaimed that Shameis's body was still functioning, but a body can't continue on without its soul. The rules of the universe are enforced. At least, I thought they were, but what do I know? When I finally understand what's happening, the plot is spun like a top. That's when I remember that I'm just a pawn in this cosmic game of chess. I'm under Azrael's control, and he has a tendency to force things into how he wants them to be.

Speaking of which, it's just like Azreal to force a helpless soul into the Void. Of course, he would overwrite my entire purpose when defied. I say I won't, and he makes me watch as he does it himself. I'm the guide; I am the Ferryman of Souls! I am supposed to know where I am at all times! Does he want me to feel useless? If he wanted me to feel hopeless, then he wouldn't have let me out to witness Shameis's death. Then again, the portal out of the Void only appeared when I remembered my tether to this man.

Why am I connected to Shameis? I have walked the earth for tens of thousands of years and have never been connected to another soul. I've never been anything more than a passing stranger. So why is everything changing now? I can accept that our lives have intertwined, but why did this all start on that highway? No, that is all just how it is. I shouldn't have an answer to any of that. However, I should have an answer to why this table is still here. One thing about a soul that I have learned is that they keep what is connected to them when they pass. Every aspect of a soul's identity is continued into the afterlife. I've heard stories that a soul is perfected when they reach the promised land, but I know for a fact that it is never before. I've ferried people with prosthetics, so I expected Shameis to keep the mechanical arm and the gauze on his face, but this table should not be here.

After spiraling within all these conundrums, Shameis finally began to sit up. I observed as he looked around while spinning until he was oriented toward me in a sitting position with his feet dangling over the void. He continued to look around for a second before hopping off without saying a word. Once his feet came in contact with the nothingness that constructed the ground, he spun around to look at the table as we both watched it vanish. So strange. How did the universe determine that piece of furniture was not part of Shameis? No, that's not what I need to focus on. I needed to focus on Shameis since he brought his full attention to me. Staring at him was when I noticed his iris. Through the sideways diamond-shaped hole in his gauze mask, I could plainly see that the color of his iris had changed from his natural hazel to a bright yellow. This was highly peculiar, and I knew this needed to be observed. As we stared at each other, I thought now would be a great chance to view his aura again. I was expecting to see his rainbow, but his aura had utterly vanished. It wasn't hiding like an unknown aura would try to do. It was as if his aura was present but invisible. While using my vision, I could feel fear radiating from him.

But, I can only feel these emotions when the aura is present in full force. After allowing me to stare at him for a bit, he broke the eerie silence with a single word. "You..." he muttered through the gauze. There was a definite quiver in his voice, indicating this man was terrified. Rightfully so. This is a significant change to what he is used to. But wait, the color associated with the emotion of fear is yellow. So, no. I may not be able to see his aura, but his iris is visually presenting his feelings. "I've... I've seen you before." He continued.

"It's a pleasure to officially meet you." I proclaimed sweetly through my high pitched of my voice that can only be heard while not on earth.

"You're the skeleton... From on top of that waterslide..." He questioned me while pointing at my clothing with his left hand.

"And in the back seat of your car last December. My apologies for the scares. You're the first human to ever see me." I confirmed.

"You've stalked others? How long have you been stalking me?" He instantly accused.

"I wouldn't call it stalking…" I began to explain before being cut off.

"How long!" He demanded with a bark. Instantly, I was taken aback. I understand that he was scared by what was happening, but there was no reason to bark at me. Thankfully, I recognized that his hostility was being brought on from his trauma, so I knew I needed to be patient with him.

"The universe put me at your side for a brief moment last December and again the moment you arrived at the terminal for the cruise ship. None of this was my decision, but I feel as if I was brought to you for a reason." I continued to explain. He grunted in response which I assumed meant my answer was satisfactory.

"So, where are we now?" He asked with much less hostility as he began to look around.

"This place is known as the Void. It is the Vale between Earth and a human's afterlife," I responded without looking away from him. Upon hearing my answer, he snapped his attention back to me and began to chuckle.

"No. Seriously. Where are we?" He asked again, clearly not accepting this answer.

"I am serious." I insisted.

"No, no, no. I'm not dead," Shameis stated while shrugging my answer off.

"I'm surprised to say this, but I think you're correct about that." I agreed. "From my understanding, something a human injected into you forced your soul out of your body. I didn't even know that was possible."

"Victor." He theorized as he looked down at his limp robotic arm. "Of course, this is his fault." There was a slight moment of silence before he brought his attention back up to me. "You said this place is between earth and the afterlife?"

104

"Correct." I continued.

"But I didn't die?" He repeated.

"Yes, that seems to be true." I concurred.

"Then put me back in my body." He then requested.

"I don't think I can. I've been at this for a really long time, and not once has this happened. I have tried to take a soul back to Earth before, but the Void wouldn't open a portal backward, only forward. We are going to need to talk to an angel about this, but I doubt he will allow you to go back since he wants you." I began to deflect before being cut off.

"Hold on. An angel?" Shameis inquired.

"Yes. Azrael, the archangel of death." I returned.

"Azrael? The Archangel of Death? Seriously? You're messing with me. None of this can be real!" He exclaimed as he turned and began to walk away. "This is all just a bad dream. Angels and demons don't exist. If they did, then that would mean all those religious nuts were correct." He ranted. Why is he walking away? We are in a void. There is nowhere he can go, yet that feeling in me is instructing me to follow. Unfortunately, the moment I took a step forward, I could feel the effect of the Void taking my energy. It hurt, but I needed to be by his side.

"In a sense, yes, but not a single religion understands the full truth," I shouted back to him. "They all understand a general idea but never see the full picture." Thankfully, this did get him to stop walking away and turn back around. He paused once he saw the twinge of pain in my face but shortly continued.

"If any of what you said is true and my soul really is out of my body and on my way to the afterlife, then that must make you the Grim Reaper." He projected in the way of processing everything.

"Yes, I am the ferryman of Souls," I affirmed confidently.

My answer caused him to pause his crisis and examine me. "You're joking, right?" he pondered as he eyed me up and down. Then, after a few seconds, he started to chuckle. "You do realize there is a stereotype for you. And after our first two encounters, I could've sworn they were true."

"Yeah, I know." I acknowledged. "Most humans want to believe that the only thing that can take them is the strongest of the strong."

"Very true. But many would go willingly if they saw the gorgeous face of a woman like yourself." He continued to joke without realizing how much that compliment meant to me. I hadn't heard that I was beautiful in such a long time. I mean, Azrael has called me pretty, but his cruelty often leads me not to believe anything he says. Frankly, I couldn't tell if this man was serious or not. After thousands of years of being manipulated, it is hard to accept any compliments.

"Thanks..." I spilled out awkwardly. "I bet you expected that I had pale, white skin as well." I ragged on him.

"You're right!" He admitted. "But I guess it makes sense that you'd have a darker complexion than I would expect. Lighter skin is a side effect of genetic mutation over a long period of time, and since you are the Grim Reaper, you've probably existed since modern humanity was conceived. You look like you could be from the middle east. Am I close with that assumption?"

"When I was a human, I was born in Israel. So you had the right geographical location." I answered with a smile.

"You used to be human?" He picked out of my answer.

"Yes, but that is a story that we don't have time for." I deflected.

"Right on." He retorted awkwardly before looking around the Void one last time. "I have a feeling that I'm going to need your help if I want to get back to my body." He then let out.

106

"It would be my pleasure." I obliged while a smile formed on my face. "I'm not sure how much help I will be, but I am willing to give you every bit of effort I can." He must have been relieved by this statement since his yellow iris started to morph back into the hazel I've come to enjoy. So, his iris does change with his mood. Why is our tether causing that? Is it caused by our tether? It could be from the serum that Victor forced into him. Whatever it was, I am thankful for it since seeing his expression from underneath his gauze mask will be nearly impossible.

"So... What do we do now?" He pondered as he stared at me.

"Well, typically, I need to hold onto the soul I am ferrying for a portal to open. So we could try that?" I suggested as I lifted my right palm upward and stretched it out.

"Or is that just your way of trying to hold my hand?" He joked while stepping toward me. I awkwardly laughed in response while trying to step forward, but being in this place for this long has caused too much of my energy to be drained. Instantly, I lost my footing and started to tumble. This, in turn, caused Shameis to leap forward and grab onto my left arm to stabilize me. He was using his left arm to support me instead of his right. This would seem insignificant, but I'm pretty sure he was right-handed. So, this meant he was either ambidextrous or couldn't use his prosthetic.

Nevertheless, I felt a slight shock on the back of my right hand during this accident. I must have grazed Shameis's sculpted abdomen, and the moment I felt the spark, the Void began to melt away to reveal a scenery I had never seen before; leaving me in awe. I took a step away from Shameis to have the freedom to look around, and as I did so, I instantly felt my energy return.

As I looked around, I noticed that we were standing at the base of an enormous tree. This beauty made trees on earth look like saplings and made me feel like an ant. From where I stood, I could barely see the

107

curvature of the trunk's diameter. Dark blue bark protected the plant that led up to a canopy of shimmering blue leaves that swayed in the breeze. Looking up, I noticed the sky was similar to the one on earth. The only difference was this atmosphere was filled with the phenomenon the humans refer to as the aurora borealis. These lights shimmered in various colors as they danced around each other. Then there was the faint smell of freshly baked apple pie that filled the air. I could even hear the sound of birds chirping. Turning from the sky to the ground, the land was covered in vibrant green grass that tickled my feet. Everything here was relatively peaceful. As I followed the grass toward the horizon, I could see that the ground cut off to form what must be a floating island. Of course, it could just be a ledge, but I theorized that this was an since similar chunks of land were floating in the distance. It seemed as if the island we were on was the only one to have a tree. If this place had anything more than just the giant tree, I would consider this paradise. I looked to Shameis and noticed he, too, was looking around in amazement. "What... What is this place?" Shameis wondered in a mumble.

"This was once the garden of Eden!" A familiar male voice blurted out from behind me. I turned around and witnessed Azreal strolling out from behind a series of massive roots near where we were. "Now, this is Purgatory. Limbo. Elysium. Bardo. Yomi. The Summerland. The great waiting room. But I like to call it... "Azrael rambled before freezing in his place once he laid his sight on me. "What are you doing here!" He then shouted.

"You weren't the one that let me out of the void to be with Shameis?" I questioned in response as he stormed up to me.

"I was planning on leaving you there to rot for a bit. Which angel helped you?" Azrael demanded to know.

"I don't know. All of the other angels don't seem to care." I informed Azrael, but he didn't seem to believe me.

108

Hearing this, Azrael huffed as he changed his focus from me to Shameis while walking past me. "So, you're Shameis Eli. Right? Why are you Shirtless?" He inquired.

"This is how I looked when my soul left my body," Shameis answered.

"You died shirtless? That's embarrassing." Azrael mocked.

"Well, it clearly wasn't my choice. Besides, I'm under the impression that I never actually died." Shameis clarified.

"Oh... OH!" Azrael uttered as he seemed to realize something important. He then looked back at me before quickly returning his attention to Shameis. "You know what, since I have you here, how about I make you the ferryman of souls. I need to decommission that fossil back there. Come with me." He continued as he spun Shameis and tried to lead him away.

"Hey!" I shouted at Azrael, which caused Shameis to look back at me. Shameis then pulled away from the angel and began to walk back toward me.

"Naw, I'm looking for a way to get back to my body. I don't want to be the Grim Reaper. But, she seems to have it covered." Shameis casually mentioned as he pointed over his shoulder.

"Excuse me?" Azrael barked, causing Shameis to turn around and look at the angel as Azrael's irises began to glow a pale yellow light. This was his attempt to display his power while forcing Shameis to submit. Azreal then began to pace toward us. "You do realize who I am, right? I'm Azrael! The Angel of Death!"

"Yep, She told me everything. You're clearly her boss, but she doesn't trust you. There has to be a reason for that." Shameis answered before attempting to turn his back again. Naturally, Azrael did not like this. Shameis's defiance caused his creep to change into a full-blown sprint as he unraveled the golden ornaments that wrapped around his cloak. Once loose, Azrael revealed that his robes were actually a pair of dark-colored wings wrapped around a suit of golden armor, equipped with a sword on his hip and his scythe on his back. This was the first time I actually was able to see an angel's wings. I always thought his wings were hiding underneath his robes, and he was too vain to display them. Still, I am no stranger to Azrael's intimidation tactics, so I held fast. Surprisingly, Shameis also didn't seem startled by Azrael's intimidation either.

"What, in the name of the divine presence, did you said to him, Cain?" He screamed in our faces.

"Cain? Seems kind of masculine." Shameis joked while quickly diffusing the tension Azreal was trying to create.

"Well. It's Welsh for fine, lovely, and intricate. So..." I played along.

"You're Welsh? I thought you said you were Israeli?" He cross-examined while turning his full attention from Azrael to me.

"Enough of this!" Azrael cut us off, bringing our attention back to him. Then, realizing that intimidation was not going to get his way, he pulled in his wings and reformed his robes while the glow in his eyes dissipated to the murky brown that I loathe. After doing this, he grinned as he began to speak. "She must not have shared too much if you are just now learning her real name."

"Says the Angel that refers to me by the name made up by a mad scientist." Shameis interrupted. I couldn't tell if this was him trying to get a rise out of Azrael or if he was being genuine. I guess I could refer to him as Isaac, but I know him as Shameis. Maybe I should call him Issac, but why does that feel wrong? I think I'm still going to refer to him as Shameis until he corrects me or I get a chance to ask what he prefers. It seemed that Shameis's interruption did derail Azrael's train of thought, which caused him to ball up his fist and scowl.

110

"How about I inform you of the ally you are choosing to befriend." Azreal threatened while disregarding Shameis's interruption.

Shameis looked back at me skeptically, and I could tell that he had already put two and two together. I was ashamed of what would come next, but If I wanted his trust, I knew Shameis needed to know everything about me. "You're right, Azrael." I agreed. "You should tell him. Shameis is going to find out eventually. This might as well come from an angel that is intentionally trying to hinder the goal I promised to accomplish."

"You want him to know? Fine!" Azrael shouted. "In your realm, there is a well-dispersed book that is full of a million metaphors on why humans should not be malicious. For example, an early parable depicts two siblings that fight over The Divine Presence's affection, and in this parable, one sibling ends up slaying the other." Azrael described.

"Yeah, the story of Cain and Abel. I've heard of it and know it well. Everyone does. It is the ultimate story of betrayal." Shameis acknowledged before turning his attention back to me. "I understood who she was and why you made her into the grim reaper the moment you said her name." Of course, he was able to put it all together that fast. I tried my best to gauge his emotions, but everything was neutral. Even his iris was still hazel. Shameis spent the majority of his life on earth fighting evil. He is a righteous man, and I am a murderer. If he really used to be a superhero, I am what he fought against. I know I don't deserve his trust, but hopefully, I can somehow persuade him not to sacrifice his soul.

"I know that this sounds bad, but I will explain everything," I interjected as I began to beg. "I will not keep any secrets from you. Call me crazy, but this feeling deep inside me tells me that we need to stay together. I have repented for my sin tenfold. Please trust me, and I will explain everything."

"So now that you know the ugly truth, will you please come with me? Your soul can't return to your body anyway." Azrael let out while extending his right hand toward Shameis. Upon hearing Azrael speak out, Shameis returned his attention to the angel.

"My soul can't return, or you won't let it ?" Shameis cross-examined Azrael's comment.

"Does it matter? Being my ferryman will allow you to walk the earth again. You'll be able to go wherever you want whenever you want. So become my Ferryman of Souls, now. Or rot with this murderer!" Azrael demanded.

"He's avoiding the truth. He would never willingly let your soul return to earth." I quickly interpreted, causing Azreal to scowl hideously and Shameis to look at me.

"Well, if you put it that way, I think I'd rather rot here." Shameis decided. "No, Cain, you're not crazy. That feeling you mentioned, well, I feel it too. So if we both have the same feeling, then we are going to have to stick together." Shameis's proclamation enraged Azrael, but this time, his tantrum went much farther than it ever has. While shouting, his rage caused the ground to shake, causing leaves and bark began to fall from the massive tree. After a few seconds, the shaking stopped just before Azrael raised his fist. His middle finger and thumb formed a rather suggestive gesture, but the tips were together and signified that he was about to snap them.

"This is not over!" He shouted before the clicking of his fingers could be heard. Azreal then vanished in a flash of blinding light.

"That was aggressive," Shameis muttered as he turned to me. "So, now what?"

I, too, turned to him and was about to inform him that I didn't have a plan, but a male voice with a British accent quickly intercepted the question. "Touch the tree," it instructed. We quickly spun around to see

112

who the voice belonged to, and we were greeted by a devilishly handsome, pale-skinned man who was sporting a black goatee, slicked back jet black hair, and dressed in a four-piece black tuxedo. His eyes were a piercing blue, and the teeth revealed from his smirk was pearl white. He was standing upright, with his heels together, left arm tucked behind his back, and his right arm stretched out with his palm upward as if he was simultaneously pointing and gesturing for us to inspect the tree. "Don't mind Azrael. He has always been a bit spoiled and wrathful if he doesn't get his way."

"Great, the Devil is here." Shameis joked, which only caused the man's smirk to grow into a full-blown grin.

"Guilty as charged, but I prefer to go by Lucifer." He poshly agreed as he retracted his outstretched hand and stuck it behind his back.

"Wait... You're seriously the Devil? Of course, you would show up to help. We can't trust an angel, but we can trust the Devil. That makes perfect sense! I'm not losing my mind at all! Maybe I should have gone with Azrael!" Shameis started to rant and pace. While shouting, he began to throw out wild hand gestures, including the use of his robotic arm as if he always had control of it. How does he all of a sudden have control over that thing? It's as if he doesn't even notice that he can use it.

"Yes, I may be the Devil. But If you are up to date with your scripture, you would know that I also was once an angel." Lucifer reminded us in an attempt to calm Shameis down. "I know you humans are wary of anything related to me, which is understandable since you tend to fear what is unknown. But when I was cast out from heaven, I was cursed with the inability to lie. Therefore, I may only speak the truth. I assure you, I can be trusted."

"He's right," I insisted. "While Azrael had me trapped in the Void, Lucifer was the only being to visit me. He didn't have the power to help me, but he at least came to keep me sane. He's the only angel that I can trust."

"I'm not going to pretend that I know what is going on, but that weird feeling I mentioned before wants me to trust you with every fiber of my being. I can't explain why, but I trust you more than I have ever trusted another. With that being said, my trust in you does not extend to Lucifer. But if you trust him, then I guess I will," Shameis stated as he cooled down before turning his attention to Lucifer. "I need to know, what is your endgame? Why do you want to help us?"

"Simply to atone. I will never ascend back to the spot I once shined, but at least I can grovel for forgiveness. I just want to be useful again," Lucifer begged as he bowed his head and brought his hands out in front of him into a prayer-like position. "All you two have to do is touch Yggdrasil at the same time, and you'll be off," Lucifer then instructed as he gestured to the tree again. That instantly caught Shameis's attention as he turned toward the massive blue tree.

"Yggdrasil? As in the world tree from the Norse Mythology?" Shameis questioned. "I thought that the angels were specifically in the Catholic religion?"

"It's all the same." Lucifer blurted out before looking and walking toward the tree. "Haven't you noticed that all religions have the same origins and recurring themes? How else would you explain the angelic Demi-gods of ancient Greece?"

"So touching the tree will get me back to my body?" Shameis changed the subject as he moved closer to the tree.

"It's the beginning of getting you back. But I'll warn you now, it is not what you know as Hell. There will be a few trials that you'll need to overcome to prove that you're worthy of returning to earth." Lucifer answered as he turned back and gestured to both of us before gesturing to Yggdrasil. "Touch. The. Tree." Lucifer repeated his instructions one last time in a demanding fashion. Shameis had already reached Yggdrasil by

114

this point, and I had almost caught up., but when I got to the base of the tree, he was raising his left hand.

Shameis slowly looked at me as he heard me rush up, and I looked at him. Once making eye contact, I raised my right hand. I could tell Shameis was hesitant, but I nodded to him to let him know I would be by his side. I hope this shared feeling between us is true because I know I would be terrified in his position. With a reciprocating nod of agreement, we simultaneously turned to Yggdrasil and placed our palms against the course dark blue bark. Instantly, a blinding blue light overwhelmed my vision as I felt myself being *pulled* into the tree. I'm glad Lucifer showed up when he did, becuase I would never guess to touch the tree. With that being said, I couldn't stop thinking of how peculiar his timing was. He must've felt that we needed some help like he used to do for me. I am very thankful for that angel's foresight and knowledge. I wish I had his foresight. Shoot! I should have asked him if the name "Lightbringer" meant anything to him.

VICTOR JAKELYDE

Part Two: Encountering Those that Lie Beyond

Chapter Eleven

This is vastly new territory for me. Everything beyond the void was always on a need-to-know basis, and I was never allowed to know. Is this what every soul is faced with once they leave my guide? It would make sense that I'd be the one to prepare a soul for what is to come next, but I guess it makes Azrael look better when I am incompetent at what I do. At least it is starting to look like I'll finally get some sort of understanding of what lies beyond for when I inevitably return to my obligation. Still, the question of why this was happening is burning in the back of my mind. I understand that he was once a remarkable human, one that would do anything to ensure justice was served, but why him? Why now? The emergence of our tether is unexplainable, but I guess I shouldn't complain.

Because of him, I could escape the oppression that Azrael applied to me and now can experience what lies beyond. I will be forever grateful for that alone, but I'm not looking forward to what will come after getting him out of here. This may be wishful thinking, but perhaps I'll be able to stay by his side! But, no. The Earth needs the ferryman of souls. How else would the souls be able to cross over? Still, I know that there is something special about this man. Not including the connection we share, he has already met two powerful beings on his plunge into the afterlife. There is clearly some information hidden from us due to this connection between Shameis and me. Hopefully, these trials that Lucifer mentioned will shed some light on the subject.

Speaking of which, our contact with Yggdrasil resulted in the pair of us being spat out somewhere strange. There was no hesitation between touching the tree and finding ourselves airborne a few meters above the ground. After a few seconds of falling, I easily landed on my feet but heard Shameis's body thump onto the ground beside me. I tried to look at him, but everything seemed so dark. I initially thought there was a black haze in the air, but I quickly realized my vision was obscured by my thick black hair. I completely forgot I had hair! I took a moment to quickly run my fingers through my hair before tucking it back into my hood before taking a look at our new surroundings. We were standing in a dank, moist field enclosed by a tall circular stone wall. It was about twenty meters tall and covered in branches of ivy. I could see a solid top to the wall but was filled with dread when the thought of climbing it came to mind. Perhaps a trick to prevent trial-goers from attempting to escape? I then panned across the field and noticed upward protruding stones scattered all about.

They all varied in height, shape, and size. Some were dull, and others were polished, but all were a similar shade of swampy green. In fact, everything besides the gray border wall was a shade of green. The grass, the storm clouds in the sky and the flashes of lightning that periodically bolted across it, and everything else was a different shade of green. I quickly looked to where Shameis's body smacked the ground and saw he was lying in a prone position, which caused me to start chuckling. "You'll get used to portaling if you stick with me." I joked. I guess not everything was green since his skin was still the color of fair beige and that his pants were still blue.

118

"I would have been ready if I knew it was going to happen," He chirped back as he started to get up before freezing in place. Seeing that, I stopped chuckling when and noticed that he had fallen right in front of a freshly polished and very reflective stone. Oh... This was the first time he his new mask... I watched as he brought his left hand up tot his face and stroked the gauze covering his left cheek while supporting his weight with his mechanical arm. I really didn't want to interrupt his moment, but the itch for an answer was starting to burn.

"Hey..." I hesitated. "When did you start being able to use that arm?"

"I'm not sure." He answered without breaking his attention from the reflection. "Perhaps it has something to do with Victor... Just like everything else that has happened to me."

"That can't be. You didn't use it when supporting me in the void." I pointed out, which caused him to look down at the prosthetic before looking back to the stone.

"Why does this say Lilith Cotter?" He questioned while changing the subject after a brief silence. His inquisition caused me to stoop down with curiosity while Shameis swapped which arm was supporting his weight so he could bring the blue lights in is metal forearm up to the stone. Sure enough, in a light gray text, the stone read, 'Here lies Lilith Cotter. A devout assistant who was always willing to do what was requested. May she rest in pieces.' After reading this, I quickly darted my attention around the field. I didn't notice this before but could when lightning lit up the area. Every stone had writing on it, and that was when I realized that we were not in a field. We were in a cemetery. With that realization, I turned to Shameis and saw he had already returned to a standing position. He didn't seem worried or scared, but his iris was currently a bright green, which didn't make sense. I couldn't feel any intense emotions flowing from him.

"I knew Victor would have killed her." Shameis remarked. "So this is her grave?"

"No, this can't be her grave. Graves are only found on Earth for the vessels." I asserted before focusing on the other part of his statement. "Did you know Sammie's real name was Lilith?"

"Oh yeah, well, once I snapped too." Shameis let out. "We go way back. She was a low-level thief that would get gigs working for crime bosses, gang leaders, and other syndicates. This superiority complex was always with her since her sister became the Starseeker. So working for Victor was the biggest thing she's ever done."

"Huh. I guess that makes sense." I let out.

"Yeah..." Shameis responded awkwardly before dropping the subject. "So this is Hell? I was expecting more fire and brimstone and less green and dreary."

"This is not Hell. Nor is this Heaven." A soft voice echoed through the musky air. "This is another realm entirely. One of seven designed to test the worthiness of a soul. None have surpassed the gauntlet, but two souls have not attempted the trials simultaneously. Please approach." I couldn't quite tell which direction the voice was projecting from, so we looked around until we were facing behind us. That was where I noticed that the tombstones formed a clear path leading toward a structure different from everything else. We followed the trail as the voice instructed, and as we came closer, the design became clearer. Just before the edge of the circular wall stood a large, muted pink throne covered in white ornamental sculptures depicting roses and doves. The throne itself sat atop a set of white marble stairs, and atop the throne sat a scrawny man that draped himself over his pedestal. As I observed him, I noticed he was pale-skinned with curly brownish/blonde hair and light pink robes detailed with gold jewels that darkened to a beet-red as they descended toward his feet.

120

As we walked down the aisle, I decided to use my aura vision to try and get some information about this guy. I was, however, met with another blinding light. The same result as seeing Azreal's aura. As we approached, he unenthusiastically let out, "I will inform you right now that there is no point in lying to me, as I will know."

"Okay?" Shameis questioned.

"You may begin." The man on the throne instructed as he flicked his right hand at us. This caused Shameis and I to look at each other simultaneously. He was expecting me to know what was going on, but I just shrugged. Shameis and I then looked back to the unimpressed man. "Well, go ahead." he insisted as his irritation grew.

"But we don't know what we are supposed to be doing," I informed the man.

"Of course you do. You wouldn't be here if you didn't." He let out as he sat up to get a better look at us.

"We were not informed. Lucifer..." I began to explain before being cut off.

"Lucifer sent you here? Right. He would be behind this. Whenever he is involved, he leaves me to explain." This man pouted as he slumped back into his chair before letting out a dramatic sigh. He then looked back down at us and asked, "Did he tell you who I am?" To his dismay, Shameis and I disagreed. "Did he at least tell you what your reward is if you're able to succeed?"

"Yes. If we get through this, Shameis's soul will be able to return to Earth and return to his body." I answered as I gestured to my new counterpart.

"Well, at least you know what you're fighting for." The man responded sarcastically. "I am Chamuel, the archangel of peaceful relations, and I am the juror of this realm. You have agreed to what we

Archangels refer to as 'The Inferno.' You will try and best all seven archangels while overcoming the seven deadliest sins. Or you'll perish in the process. Being that you are coming from Heaven or Hell means that your souls will forever be trapped in this realm or any that you fail in. Is that understood?" He explained.

"I do have a question," I followed up. "What if our souls have never been to Heaven or Hell? Would we go to one of those places first?" This question caused Chamuel to lean forward again with intrigue in his eye.

"What do you mean? If you did not come from either of those realms, how did you come to be here?" He questioned suspiciously.

"Lucifer had us touch the trunk of Yggdrasil, and it spat us out here," Shameis answered. This enlightenment caused Chamuel's brow to ruffle as he tilted his head in confusion as silence fell over the three of us. Clearly, Shameis and I were facing a predicament that was so unheard of that it even stumped an Archangel.

After a few seconds, Chamuel spoke again, but instead of addressing the concern, he picked up the conversation right where he left off. "This is the realm of Envy. The only way to pass is for each of you to answer the same question truthfully and without a hint of desiring what is not within your grasp. Is this understood?" He explained, to which Shameis and I nodded our heads in agreement. "Good. So, the one question that I feel is eating at your soul's, and what you need to answer is: 'Who are you now?'" What? That seems like a pretty basic question. Have souls actually failed this challenge? Wait, what did he mean by 'now'?

"May I ask a follow-up question?" I pondered, to which Chamuel threw himself back into his throne and let out another sigh.

"The light of truth radiating from a human's innermost self must be void of Envy to travel the road of righteousness. Envy is to internal as greed is to external." He let out without letting me ask my question. I'm

122

not sure what kind of metaphor he meant by that phrase, but it didn't answer the question, and I could tell that he wasn't going to let me ask. This is yet another reason why I dislike the angels. They request an astronomical amount from their underlings but refuse to clarify how to achieve the request.

Upon receiving Chamuel's 'explanation,' I turned to Shameis and saw him staring at me. He was as confused as I was, and was waiting for me to lead by example. Alright, I can do this. I need to be strong. Like a good companion, I needed to do this. When I was ready, I turned back to Chamuel and declared, "I am Cain, daughter of Eve, and I served as the ferryman of souls. I now serve as his guide and companion as we navigate these other realms''. My statement again caused Chamuel to lean forward, and he was again filled with intrigue.

"Did you just say your name was Cain? Are you THE Cain?" He followed up.

"Yeah... but I am not proud of my past and do not like to bring it up or even be called that name." I insisted, to which Chamuel grunted noncommittally before turning his attention to Shameis.
"And you?" Chamuel then questioned.

Once the spotlight was put on Shameis, he froze before what he wanted to say finally came out. "For a moment, I was starting to believe that I could reclaim my old life. I wanted to go back to the way things were and be Isaac Enderson again. I wanted to be The Ile! But Victor told me that my mantle is now held by another and that Isaac Enderson is dead. The reflection I saw on the gravemarker with Lilith's name confirmed it. So, I am Shameis Eli, and I am a soul that is lost and trying to make his way home." So he did choose to be called Shameis. Good. I know he had the choice, but somehow I knew that name would be the one that stuck.

After hearing this, Chamuel grunted again before slowly leaning back. "You know, I feel like you're telling the truth, but you're not telling me the WHOLE truth." He proclaimed. "There is a connection between you. I can feel it. There is a power in the air that is radiating from you two. You should have told me about this energy, and for that, I deny your approval." As soon as he finished his request, he raised his left hand and snapped his fingers. This caused a significant bolt of lightning to arc down from the sky and strike the ground between where Shameis and I stood and the throne's base. Less than a second after its touchdown, the ground began to shake violently. I looked around in horror as hordes of pale light green skeletons started rising from the graves and started to head toward us. The sound of rattling bones instantly filled the air. As they approached, I knew precisely what Chamuel meant when he said we would be trapped here.

"What do we do?" Shameis panicked as he turned his back to me.

"We have to talk about our connection!" I shouted in an equal amount of terror.

"The weird feeling?" He wondered. "I don't even know what is causing it!"

"I don't either, but it is there and is the reason we were brought together across time!" I continued to shout as our impending doom enclosed us. "Okay! Think! What caused all of the important turning points to lead us to this point?"

"Outside intervention! Victor killed me, and then the angel led us here!" He answered quickly.

"Can't be that! This is about us! Our truth!" I denied.

"Is it just fate and the universe?" He cross-examined.

"They are factors but not the catalyst!" I encouraged him since I heard the groans of the envious walking dead growing nearer.

"Us touching?" He then put forth.

"How would that cause this?" I then probed.

"Well, you grazed my neck when I was in that cage. That was when I got all my memories back. Then when you touched my stomach in the void, the blackness faded, and we found ourselves in the garden." He theorized.

"I guess! We don't have much time so let's go with it!" I agreed as I stretched my left arm out toward Shameis. Without a second thought, and just as the endless count of skeletons were about to reach an arm's length of distance, Shameis latched onto my hand with his left and squeezed tightly. The moment he grabbed on, bright flashes of imagery filled my mind. I couldn't understand what it all meant, but these images tried to tell me something. First, I saw the silhouette of an Angel made of pure light with massive, immaculate wings. Then there were a few flashes of two other silhouetted beings fighting with the first. The final moment I saw was the two additional silhouettes ripping the first one in half. The flashes only lasted for a few seconds before Shameis ended up letting go of me.

Shameis then shouted "ENOUGH!" in a deep, booming voice that did not sound like him. With that command, all the rattling of the bones ceased instantly as the embodiments of Envy stood motionless. After a moment of silence, Shameis and I turned back to look at Chamuel, who was now standing tensely with his full attention on us. There was fear in his eyes. I had no idea what was going on, but it was enough to scare an archangel. Was that even possible? Granted, I have only experienced Azrael and Lucifer, but I still was under the impression that angels could not be scared. At this point, I had goosebumps. "You know who we are," he then muttered in his regular voice. I was speechless and Chamuel couldn't take his eyes off of us. Without saying another word or breaking his eye contact, Chamuel quickly raised his left hand and snapped his fingers again as a portal opened underneath us. Shameis and I fell through it without a moment to react and were launched into the subsequent trial. What just happened?

Everything was going so fast that it didn't give me time to process. Shameis must know more than I do since he is the one that caused Chamuel to react peculiarly. Would he know who the angel I saw in my visions? It couldn't be the Lightbringer, since the angel was ripped in half. Also, Victor Jakelyde was expecting to talk to this Lightbringer through Shameis, so it is possible that Lightbringer could be some super powered villain on Earth that can control bodies with empty minds. Perhaps the Lightbringer is just someone Shameis going to have to stop after getting back to earth.

Part Two: Encountering Those that Lie Beyond

Chapter Twelve

After what just transpired, I'm starting to understand how unprepared I am for all of this. The doorman to the afterlife should have some inclination as to what lies beyond. Yet, I'm at a loss. How would not sharing what we don't know cause us to fail a trial about telling the truth? I thought that I at least had a handle on these sins, but I clearly need to re-evaluate myself. I used to be human and have experienced the temptation of all sorts of sins. I felt pride, greed, lust, wrath, and worst of all, envy. I'm sure that envy is the sin I am guilty of, but it is news to hear that it's an internal sin. I know I didn't feel greed since I did not covet my brother's possessions. All I wanted was the love he was receiving. Perhaps my condemning sin would be wrath since that was the sin that fueled my urge to shove him? I didn't hate my brother. I loved him, but I wanted the love he received.

Nevertheless, I know that I no longer possess envy in my soul. Yes, I do find myself wanting, but I have come to realize that what I once had will never return, and it sounded as if Shameis was under the same impression for his life. Still, after learning that the archangels will be helming these trials, I now know that there will be an ulterior motive to these tests. This is the angels' opportunity to demonstrate their superiority. But that begs the question, why did this power inside Shameis and I decide to reveal itself now? I would have liked to discuss this with Shameis, but now was not a good time.

After falling through the portal Chamuel opened underneath us, we again found ourselves being dumped unceremoniously into a new realm. Unlike the last, I couldn't tell how far above the ground we were. We were falling through a thick cloud of purple fog, but only for a second or two before we hit the ground. This time, I was the unsuspecting one. I tried to land on my feet but lost my balance and fell backward onto my posterior. After sitting on the ground for a bit, I tried to stand up, but it felt like something was pulling me down. It was like this place's gravity was heavier than anywhere else we had been. My attempt to get to my feet only caused me to rock back and forth a bit, so I decided to roll onto my stomach and push myself up with my hands. Thankfully I was able to get up with the help of all four of my limbs, and once I was on my feet, I noticed that the fog had dissipated enough to see Shameis. He was already firmly on his feet and looking around. "You were able to get up fast," I joked as I brushed myself off.

"I didn't fall over. Like I said, once I am expecting it, I rarely get knocked off my feet." He muttered in a grumpy tone.

"Oh, then I guess I have a few things to learn from you." I continued to joke, but far less confidently. After hearing his tone of voice and noticing that he was paying me no attention, I decided to look around our new surroundings, but there wasn't much to see. The dissipation of the fog we fell through formed a bubble of clean air. This bubble was still surrounded by the dense fog, so it felt like we were standing on an island within a sea of nothingness. Although I couldn't see the sky, the ground below us was a pleasant change. Instead of the moist green grass that bedded the cemetery,

128

this realm was lined with dry, warm, and soft light purple grass. It felt as if I was standing on a bed of feathers. No wonder I wanted to lay down. There was also several types of flowers varying in shades of purples, pinks, and grays scattered throughout the grass. These flowers filled the air with the scent of lavender and vanilla. Between the gravity and all the atmospheric elements to this place, I felt as if I should lay back down and take a nap. It was jut another fraction of paradise.

"So, these are the Mists of Torpidus?" Shameis muttered while looking around the air pocket before turning his attention to me, which showed me that his iris had again changed color. Instead of the bright green that overcame it in the last realm, his iris was now a light shade of purple. Okay, so green is for envy, and if the name he had mentioned means what I am thinking, then purple must represent lethargicness. "What? Why are you looking at me like that?" He questioned while catching me staring.

"Why did that name pop into your mind? That is oddly specific." I cross-examined as I ambled over to him.

"I... I have no idea," He responded as he began to look around in confusion.

"Interesting," I muttered before stopping once I reached an arm's length of distance. "We probably need to start moving," I then suggested.

"We're not going anywhere until I get a few answers." He proclaimed before looking back at me.

"I don't think now is a good time." I insisted before instantly getting confused as to why I rejected his request? Why wouldn't I share what I know to ease his transition and make our path easier to traverse?

"No, I need answers!" Shameis demanded as his light purple iris slowly gained a reddish hue. It was as if he was getting angry at my refusal to share. That was freaky, but the phenomenon gave me some good insight. His iris displays the emotion associated with each realm but adds color depending on his genuine emotion. So, unfortunately, it will be a while until I see his natural hazel iris again.

"No, we need to get moving!" I insisted, which only caused him to go silent. Between the thick fog and the heavy gravity of this place, I could tell there was a force wanting us to stay motionless. In a way, it was causing this friction between us and was trying to prevent us from making any progress. Initially, upon hearing the name of this place, I thought this would solely be a physical challenge, but perhaps it was also mental. This force also made me understand that even though I am the ferryman of souls and have a lot of experience with the spiritual, I am not immune to the power these realms have. One of us has to bend to proceed, but Shameis may not realize that this place is messing with us. I'm assuming that my experience with the spiritual is the cause of my self-realizations, so I know it is on me to break this cycle. "Okay, okay. I will answer whatever you are wondering." I relinquished.

"I'm wondering about what the hell just happened!" He started aggressively.

"I'm as in the dark as you are. All I got was a few flashes of some kind of fight, but that's it. You're the one who told Chamuel that he knew who we are." I answered.

"That was only because a voice in my head told me to say it." He informed me. "As soon as we touched each other, it felt as if someone was screaming. The screaming stopped as soon as I *pulled* away." How strange. He heard a voice, and I saw imagery, but only while we were touching? This connection between us was starting to act more and more bizarre. "Since we don't have an answer for that, how about you explain why you killed your brother. Tell me how you became the Grim Reaper." He then suggested as the red in his iris began to fade.

130

"I would rather not talk about such a dreary topic," I muttered in an attempt to avoid the question. This time, it wasn't the realm forcing me to avoid this. I genuinely dislike bringing up my past. For so long, I've felt as insignificant as a leaf blowing in the wind. I've learned that people don't care to hear my sorrows. Humanity has grown so selfish over the years.

"You promised you would, and I find it difficult to trust liars and murderers." Shameis pried. Did he genuinely want to know more about me? I should have realized he was willing to listen and believe me. I might as well share my story since we need to stick together to get through this, and there is no sense in having unneeded turmoil.

"Fine," I folded as I crossed my arms in an attempt to support myself through the inevitable emotions I was going to feel. "Being that you do know the basics of who I am, I'm going to assume you know a bit about your scripture." I presumed.

"I'm not religious but I know the stories." He subverted.

"Even after seeing all of this?" I questioned.

"I've always felt that SOMETHING else existed; I just wasn't sure what did. But now I know that EVERYTHING exists in one form or another. However, all religions essentially being the same thing is still baffling and hard to believe. Do you know how many people were killed over differing belief systems?" Shameis reminded me.

"Trust me. I know. This is a lot to take in," I concurred.

"So start from the beginning and explain everything. I don't need all the details, just the gist of what happened to you," Shameis requested.

"Okay. Well. Although the human's scripture has a few similarities to what actually happened to me, it's obviously not the entire truth," I started. "Before I go in-depth, I need to inform you that I am not, nor have I ever been a man. Also, I need to insist to you that I did not kill my brother, but I was the cause of his death."

"So, involuntary manslaughter instead of first-degree murder."
Shameis pointed out. "Look. Accidents happen, and I can understand
that more than anyone else. I am not here to judge or shame you for what
happened at the beginning of time. All I want is to know who the person I
am entrusting my soul with." Shameis then let out as he firmly placed his
right hand on my shoulder. Hearing that someone finally was willing to
listen to me instead of starting to judge me almost made me tear up, but I
needed to stay composed for this next bit.

"Right." I stuttered hesitantly. "Well, just like the story goes,
Able and I would travel to the top of a nearby mountain every day to
pray and offer sacrifice to The Almighty Presence. In return, Abel's
harvests became increasingly bountiful. Unfortunately, the only thing
I received in return was my livestock becoming increasingly sickly.
So, one day, we were coming down from the mountain, and I decided
to voice my grievance, and we entered a debate that quickly became
heated. Inevitably, I ended up shoving him. I didn't think it was that
hard, but he ended up tripping, falling backward, and hitting his head
on a large stone."

I tried my best to stay composed for Shameis, but I could feel
myself start to break down as I recounted the incident. "I didn't mean to
hurt him, but as soon as he hit his head on the stone, I was *pulled* into the
void and was face-to-face with Azrael's evil grin. I wasn't even given a
chance to help my brother." As I recounted my brother's tragedy, I could
feel tears roll down my face as my nose began to stuff up. I've always tried
to keep this memory repressed, but I knew he would need to know. It
shouldn't matter this much since it is widespread amongst human culture.
It is just that what they know is nothing more than a massive rumor that
is dramatized for their enjoyment. This memory is why I feel so alone.
There was only one person in my life I was supposed to care for, and I

am the reason they were taken from the earth. I deserved to be punished, but what I received was far more than that. I was physiologically tortured with nothing but my thoughts before being forced to watch as everything I knew turned to dust around me.

After feeling the chill of my liquefied sorrow roll down my cheeks, I suddenly felt a cold press on my face. I stared at Shameis as he wiped away the tears that had fallen from my eye. Although still purple, his iris now had a hint of deep blue. Was he really saddened by the pain I felt? All this caused me to weep even harder, which caused a few awkward moments where all I could hear was my blubbering. I wanted to keep my attention on him but decided to look toward the ground. I really shouldn't be so emotional. I know better than anyone else that loss is just a part of the human experience. I could have stayed composed if it wasn't for Shameis's compassion and willingness to listen to me. After letting me wallow for a bit, Shameis then caressed my left cheek with his metal hand and lifted my head so we could look into each other's eyes. Again, he wasn't saddened on my behalf. The blue is actually the indigo hue of compassion.

"I'm sorry I was being aggressive." Shameis apologized. "Thank you for trusting me with your story. We all have our issues, and no one is perfect. It sounds like all you had was a slight accident before Azrael went off the rails. He will pay for what he did to you, just as Victor will pay for what he did to me." He assured me while trying to comfort me. No other human has ever attempted to console my worries. I couldn't have asked to be stuck with a better human. "I have a hard time trusting others. So many have tried to manipulate me, and they have all ended up in a jail cell. But you, Cain, even after hearing your story, I am still willing to trust you with every bit of me."

"I'm not like any of the humans on earth," I whimpered as I wiped my remaining tears in an attempt to collect my composure.

"I know! You're THE Grim Reaper!" He proclaimed enthusiastically." Even if we didn't have this connection, I would still be inclined to trust you for that fact alone. I just needed to know why you became, well... you." I was flattered by his enthusiasm and the excitement growing in his voice. As he said this, I began to feel warm on the inside. Was this happiness? True happiness? It had to be since I was happier than I had ever been.

"So I told you about me. How about you tell me a bit about your life before Victor took your memories." I requested so I could have some time to compose myself.

"You saw the movie, right?" He then inquired.

"You know that I've been with you for a while," I responded.

"Then you already know everything about me. I was a P.I. that became a vigilante before losing my first face-to-face with that psychopath." He confirmed.

"But that movie said that there were other superheroes on earth." I recounted with uncertainty.

"Yep." He agreed.

"I've never encountered a soul that is more than average. I haven't even gotten a hint of the existence of superheroes before I met you." I cross-examined. "How long have they existed?"

"I don't know why you haven't, but I can promise you they exist." He guaranteed. "There are only seven powered heroes, but they did pop up once every few years, starting fifteen or so years ago. I think I was twenty when the first one showed up. Anyway, I was the only powerless hero that was allowed onto their team." Shameis explained as he began to amble past me. "But those powered villains popped up like clockwork. We were able to capture them and keep them contained, so maybe that's why you haven't seen one of them. I do feel sorry for them. A majority

134

of them acted as if they were just people that had completely lost their minds. I would have taken pity on them if they didn't have those powers. Now that I think about it, they also seemed to start popping up about the same time as the first hero did." He explained before turning back to me as he changed the subject. "So, you suggested that we start walking. Why was that?"

"Oh! Because of the name you called this place. The root word is torpid, which essentially means Sloth. So this is the realm of Sloth." I answered as I moved toward him.

"So you think wandering into the fog will solve this problem?" He pieced together while following me as I passed by his left side. My movement caused him to turn around, and with us now facing the same direction, I was now on his right.

"I'm not certain of it, but it hopefully won't hurt," I answered as I led us toward the edge of the bubble.

"Well, Grim. I think we should head out as well." He suggested. The name he called me caught me by surprise. My real name is just as easy to say, so why give me a nickname?

"Grim?" I wondered as I looked away from the wall of fog toward my companion.

"Yeah! Grim!" He exclaimed as he too looked from the fog to me before beginning to justify himself. "I figured that you would dislike being called your real name since it carries all that pain and suffering. Also, I thought that since we are essentially starting new lives, we might as well have new names. So that's why I'm sticking with Shameis and going to call you Grim."

"Right. I like that." I agreed. "Let's get going." Then, thinking that we should try our best to not get separated, I decided it would be a good idea to reach and grab onto his metal hand.

"What's going on here?" Shameis inquired with a weird inflection in his voice as he looked down at our hands. It was almost as if he was trying to mess with me while being genuinely surprised.

"We were about to go into the fog, and we really shouldn't get separated..." I muttered in a fluster.

"And you thought that holding my hand would make it so we wouldn't get separated? Good thinking. You know, if you wanted to hold my hand, you could've asked." He toyed with me.

"Well, I already am, so let's get going," I muttered with embarrassment as I tried to step into the fog. I say tried because the moment my foot left the bubble, our environment repositioned itself and put us back into the middle. Seeing this, I quickly let go of Shameis's hand and looked around. Everything was the exact same except the smell of lavender and vanilla had increased. Although the scent was pleasant, this was definitely a bad sign. I wanted to walk toward the edge of the dome to try and exit again, but I could not move from this position. My feet seemed to be stuck in place! I turned to look at Shameis, and he, too, seemed to be struggling with moving his feet.

"What the hell is going on!" Shameis shouted as we struggled to break free, which seemingly caused us to sink into the warm, soft ground. It was almost as if the grass had turned into quicksand. "Okay, panicking will only make us sink. Got it. Grim, don't worry. We will figure a way out." Shameis realized while trying to comfort me, but I should have been trying to comfort him since he was the one with the tremble in his voice.

"We really should have started walking earlier," I mumbled as I tried to look around for something to grab onto. There was nothing, just the grass, flowers, and fog. That was when a loud yawn sounded from behind us, causing Shameis and I to try and turn around to see who made the noise, but that only made us sink until we were shin-deep.

"Are you not even going to try and look at me?" A light, female voice pondered through another yawn.

"We would if we weren't sinking into the ground!" Shameis barked back.

"Ugh. Why do I have to do everything?" The voice complained. Right after that, the ground around Shameis and I began to shift. It didn't let us out but instead rotated us individually toward the voice. This made it so that I was on Shameis's left side instead of his right. Now that we were facing her, I could see that the voice originated from a light-skinned woman with long and messy dark brown hair. She was wearing an oversized light purple t-shirt and matching purple shorts. It looked as if she had just woken up from a nap. Besides her clothing, this woman's appearance was similar to an average woman on earth. She could have easily passed as human if it wasn't for the pair of immaculate pearl white wings that stretched out from her back. "Do you two realize what is going on, or am I going to need to explain it to you." She jeered at us while yawning before turning her direction to Shameis. "Too lazy to put a shirt on?"

"You're one to talk, bedhead." Shameis retorted, which caused her to laugh.

"We are new to this. We obviously have until we are completely submerged to overcome whatever the realm of Sloth wants us to prove, but that is all I know." I followed up.

"You don't even know who I am?." She then asked while still giggling.

"Nope." Shameis quickly responded.

"Well, I'm Ariel." She informed us.

"Ariel... Like the little mermaid?" Shameis then joked.

"Same spelling, but I'm an archangel. A fitting analogy since I am the Archangel of nature and animals." Ariel retorted as she let out yet another yawn. "What else do you need to know?"

"What we need to do to pass this trial!" I shouted as I realized that the ground was now up to my stomach.

"Right. No need to shout." She let out. "So, your idea of moving and doing the opposite of whatever lazy urges you felt was good and all, but you need to discover your hidden potential to overcome sloth." She exclaimed.

"And how are we supposed to do that? The ground is already up to our waists!" Shameis questioned, but I quickly responded as to not upset the Archangel.

"She doesn't know. It is on us to figure it out." I answered as I looked at Shameis.

"Or in us," Shameis muttered.

"In us?" I questioned.

"Yeah! That connection we have. The thing that made Chamuel put us into this realm. I think now is the time we try to figure out what that is!" Shameis answered.

"That's a good idea, but we already touched while we were here. Remember, I grabbed your hand." I pointed out.

"You grabbed onto the metal one. Maybe this only works if we make direct contact. Skin to skin." He suggested.

"You're probably right!" I concurred as I stretched out my right hand. "Don't let go this time," I then instructed. He nodded in agreement and reached out with his left hand. As soon as he grabbed onto me, the feeling I felt in the last realm washed over me. It felt as if a surge of energy was coursing through my body. However, it wasn't accompanied by flashes of imagery this time. I felt so strong, but then the power suddenly

138

felt like it began to change direction. Instead of flowing into me, it was going into Shameis. It wasn't just the energy, but it now felt like I was being pulled into him myself. As if I had blinked, my vision went black before quickly returning returned. That was when I found myself floating in the middle of the air. I looked to my limbs to see what was happening, but I couldn't see them; it was as if I was invisible. Talk about your out-of-body experience. Although this was odder than even becoming the ferryman of souls, I strangely felt relaxed and at peace. With that being said, I don't like not having my body. While looking down, I could see that Shameis's body was still present and stuck in the ground, but within seconds, he uprooted himself as if he was stepping out of water onto a beach. It was nearly effortless. Seeing all this unfold in front of her caused an expression of wonder and disbelief to be plastered onto her face. But I now know why Chamuel expressed terror. I was mortified to see all this, and she should have been too.

"What... How did you... What happened to the other one?" Ariel blabbered while limply pointing toward Shameis.

"Both of these souls are under my protection!" Shameis proclaimed in the booming voice I heard in the last realm. That voice was not Shameis's, but it implied that both Shameis and I were safe, so I could only assume that Shameis's soul was in a state similar to mine. But, it is still concerning to think about where this voice came from. Perhaps the Lightbringer may be an alter ego Shameis has? No, That can't be. There is different, since I'm part of whatever is happening right now. I was then snapped out of my hypothesizing by seeing a single, beautiful wing sprout from Shameis's left shoulder blade. What the hell is going on? Seriously? I don't know what is going on between Shameis and me, but our connection has somehow turned us into an Angel. An angel with only one white wing that transitioned into black feather points.

"It... It is true," Ariel whimpered just before she started to beat her wings in an attempt to flee.

"No!" The voice coming from Shameis's mouth ordered, which instantly caused her to stop. "The Challenge Is complete. You see what you requested. Now allow passage to what lies beyond."

"Of course." Ariel continued to whimper. "The other two had the right idea. The portal to the next realm is in the mists."

"And you intended to cheat them into failing this trial, just as Chamuel did?" The voice then interrogated.

"We archangels are supposed to challenge the souls." Ariel let out. "It would be pandemonium if any unworthy soul was allowed to return to earth."

"And yet you punish the worthy?" The male voice continued to press.

"I'm just doing what I am told. Please spare me. Let me go." Ariel groveled. Whatever this connection is, it not only is strong enough to turn Shameis and me into an angel, but it is strong enough to command an Archangel. This was a game-changer.

"Fine." the voice granted, to which Ariel instantly used her wings to propel herself up into the haze above us. Once we were alone, Shameis's body turned around and looked up at me before looking a bit to my left. His iris now was a pale glowing light instead of the purple this realm made it. If the wing and the voice weren't enough of a giveaway, that light confirmed that our touch has caused an angel to take over our bodies and souls. "Stay close," he muttered before following Ariel's lead and propelling himself upward, to which I instantly I felt myself being yanked from my floating position toward the angel. Within seconds, I found myself floating over his left shoulder while the angel hovered in the dense purple fog.

140

Once whatever I had reached whoever was possessing Shameis, it then began to fly straight through the fog as I remained on its shoulder. This was all just a little too much and more than I was able to understand, but I sure was not going to be the one to look a gift horse in the mouth. I wish I was able to understand how fast we were traveling. It felt like we were soaring at a high velocity, but the only aspect that gave any insight was the wisps of mist that rolled by. I couldn't even feel the wind on my face. Yes, at first, I thought that whatever was happening felt good, but I was starting to dislike it. Even with all this power coursing through me, I felt less in control than I ever have. If this is what I felt, I wonder what Shameis was feeling. I dislike being in the backseat, but at least I can notice things that the driver is missing. Like, as we are zooming, it nearly sounded as if a female's voice was trying to call out through the fog. I couldn't tell exactly what she was saying, but I did hear Shameis's name a few times. I guess whoever that was, it doesn't matter since a circular portal opened directly in front of us and didn't give the angel a second to react. Ready or not, I guess we are en route to the subsequent trial.

STARSEEKER

Chapter Thirteen

Although I've been Azrael's puppet for a majority of my existence, I've always been in control of my own actions. I never would have chosen to inflict the pain I have brought to those grieving humans, but my efforts were still my own. Regardless, I think I would prefer an eternity of being forgotten in the void over an eternity of being trapped in the backseat of an all-powerful entity. Right now, all I felt like was a camera that was viewing the action of an avatar in a videogame while everything I could see was just a cutscene. I couldn't even move or look in a different direction than what is straight ahead.

How can so much power cause me to feel so powerless? At least I could feel this immense feeling starting to dissipate with every passing second. I didn't recognize it when I first became a disembodied consciousness, but now I can feel it with certainty. It's kind of like a reverse of what the void does to me. There was a ticking timer on this angel's control, and I was ready for it to be over. Still, I did wonder why our combined power was starting to fade. If this being was powerful enough to command an archangel, then why couldn't he hold his control over us? I tried to inquire as to why this was, but he either couldn't hear me or was willfully ignoring me. Whatever the cae was, the dissipation of this could not occur fast enough. I can't wait to regain control of my body! Well, I guess I could wait until we were safely on the ground.

Upon exiting the portal from the Mists of Torpidus, we went from gliding through deep-purple clouds to soaring through a lemon-yellow sky. The air was mostly clear, with minimal wisps of light goldenrod-colored clouds scattered as far as the eye could see. Below us were plains of golden wheat fields that stretched on for miles without a single path or road to cause division. The realm's sun sat to the left of the direction this angel was taking us and was casting dramatic shadows across the fields of wheat. The surroundings and the knowledge that I would soon be separated from this being did leave me at peace, but feeling like a captive to this one-winged angel left a sour taste in my mouth. I do wish I could get a whiff of the fresh air we were zooming through, but I'll just have to experience this realm's scent once I have my nose again. Now, what do I do? I know that when I was neglecting my duties as the ferryman of souls, I was at least busy studying Shameis. But now, I have nothing other than to sitting back and enjoy the ride. I wish I could, but it is kind of hard to enjoy when I can't feel the wind in my hair. What I really needed to do was get out of my own head and understand what was happening. I should be wondering is 'Why does this angel only have one wing and how are they flying able to fly? Why are they projecting themself through Shameis's scarred body instead of...'

"Fret not. This portion will be all over soon." The angel's voice boomed as if he was screaming right next to me. That was when I noticed a small light in the distance. That had to be where our subsequent trial was going to take place. Would crossing these fields actually be part of the trial in this realm? It was as if these Archangels really were trying to cheat any challenging souls out of an honest attempt, so I guess it was

144

for the best to have our angel in control. As we approached the glimmer, the shine grew more prominent, and a low hum started to fill the silent sky. The glow morphed into a metallic bowl-like shape with a massive opening at the top while the buzz bellowed into a hellacious roar within a matter of seconds. Were we really traveling that fast?

Once we were directly above, I recognized that this random structure in the middle of a wheat field within a realm unknown to mankind was a modern-day sport's stadium. It was complete with spectator seating surrounding a rectangular field made of a soft orange turf. I could see that the building was lined with tiny moving specks that occupied each seat of the spectator's section. We were too far away to see any distinct details about them, but I was able to see limbs flailing wildly as they cheered. I then looked to the field to try and get an idea of why they were cheering, but the track-enclosed turf was vacant. They were cheering just to cheer. Once the angel decided to descend, the crowd's roar grew into a near deafening scream! I think I'd prefer the roar of the cruise ship to this. I really wish I had my hands to protect my ears from this noise, and in that exact moment, I felt the connection flowing from me to Shameis's body snap. Instantly, I felt my body rematerialize around me as Shameis and I plummeted to the ground below for the third time.

This may have been the wrong time to get my body back, but not the worst. If Shameis was in a similar state to me while the angel was in control, then I'm assuming his energy was sucked back into his body. So we were ten feet above the ground, the grass below was in plain sight, and we were both braced for the impact this time. I theorized that Shameis and I were going to land at about the same time, but some wonky physics messed up my idea. I didn't realize that my body rematerializing would cause my descent to slow, so Shameis reached the ground well before I could. The extra few seconds allowed him to quickly reposition himself underneath me and catch me in a cradle position. Why did he go out of his way to do this? I didn't have much time to think as to why, since I was instantly overcome with the joy of not coming in skin contact with him and fueling or overtaker again. So, once in his arms, I looked up at his face and noticed his iris had transitioned to orange. That makes sense. Everything else in this place was orange, so his iris should be too. But that begs the question, if green is for envy and purple is for sloth, then what is orange representing? I wonder this for a bit as I gazed up at him for a few moments, but he then quietly asked if I'd like to be put down. I could barely hear his question of the roar of the crowd, but after realizing what was happening, I began to squirm as he gently put me onto my feet. "You know I am old enough to take care of myself." I playfully let out as I brushed out robes so it would lay properly.

"So I've heard," He played along as he continued to gaze at me. "Do you have any idea what happened this time?"

"I thought you would know since he talks to you," I responded as I started to look around the stadium. Now that I had my body, I was able to get a scent from this place, and it wasn't enjoyable. It was a combination of cooking meat, salty body odor, and rubber. I wasn't expecting much else for a sports stadium, but it was still not great. Besides the smell, there wasn't much to see. All around us were the fans in the crowd cheering ferociously and the metal constructing this arena. However, two large digital monitors that displayed a red lightning symbol with a blue background did stick out. Each monitor was hung above the crowd parallel to the longer sides of this rectangular field. While in a stadium, one would expect to see various sizes, shapes, and ethnicities of beings commingling, but all of these fans seemed the same. I couldn't get that good of a look, but it seemed like they all had gray skin.

146

"He didn't talk to me this time." Shameis clarified while drawing my attention back to him. "It was like I was just floating over my own left shoulder without being able to contol own actions." He recounted.

"The same thing happened to me, but I'm pretty sure that was an angel. I don't know how or why this is happening. I can only assume that my spiritual energy is trying to merge with your physical conduit, but that wouldn't explain how the new entity that comes from us. I've never touched a soul that still has a living body, so this is new ground" I theorized.

"Does that mean we are angels?" Shameis wondered.

"Unlikely, but something inside us conjured one," I answered. Before I could finish my thought, The crowd instantly and unexpectedly was whipped into an uproar. The chanting was so loud that Shameis and I both tried to cover our ears, but even while trying to protect myself, I could still hear them perfectly. In unison, they chanted the name 'Michael' over and over. I frantically began looking around for whatever caused the uproar and found that a dark-skinned man had appeared on the field and was walking toward us. He was wearing a sleeveless shirt, extremely short shorts, sleeves that covered his forearms and shins, and a pair of running shoes. Everything he wore was snow-white with red lightning bolt designs. Just like Ariel, this man had a set of massive light gray wings that exploded from his back. As the crowd's chant would suggest, this being is one of the most well-known archangels; Micheal, the warrior Archangel. Shameis and I watched as he approached us while trying to talk to us from a distance, but it was impossible to hear him. Our lack of response caused Michael to stop in his tracks and stare with a puzzled look defore turning toward the stadium.

"Enough!" He boomed as an eerie silence washed over the stadium. I swear you could hear a pin drop in this silence. "So you two are the infamous Seraph that Chamuel and Ariel are blabbering about." Michael proclaimed as he continued his approach. "You don't look so tough to me!"

"Isn't a serif part of a font?" Shameis questioned under his breath, which caused me to let out a sigh.

"What you're thinking of is, but what he is referring to is spelled differently." I clarified. "A Seraph is a type of angel. Scripture explains that there was once a hierarchy to these kinds of beings. They are sometimes known as Cherubim, but a Seraph only took orders directly from The Presence. After the Seraphim, the hierarchy unfolds with the fates, powers, and dominions in the second tier. Finally, Archangels lead the angels in the third tier." I quietly answered Shameis before speaking to Michael. "The Seraphim don't exist anymore. Azrael explained the tale of their demise long ago."

"And why do you think that is?" Michael inquired rhetorically before letting out a chuckle. "After seeing the fear in Chamuel and Ariel's eyes, I can understand why Azrael wanted you to believe that. That archangel feared that if you found out you were only half of something greater, then you would search for your other half. His only task, other than collecting the departed, was to keep you two separated, but look how well that worked."

"Hold on a second... Are you saying that Shameis and I are two halves of an all powerful Seraph?" I cross-examined Michael's statement aggressively. "And Azrael was torturing me so I wouldn't find out?"

"And if he was supposed to keep us separated, then why did he make it her job to collect all the dead people's souls?" Shameis added.

"That was the intention, but we archangels are all guilty of pushing our duties onto others." He confirmed as he finally reached us. "And now it falls on me to rip you apart. So, bring the big guy out. I want to beat him instead of two weak souls."

148

"We are not doing that again!" Shameis quickly retorted.

"You don't have a choice, mate!" Michael rejected. "You already know that we archangels rig the challenges, so puny human souls like you have no chance of competing. Why do you think my crowd is so massive? You think these souls want to be here to cheer for me? No, they are all humans that tried to challenge me." He then shared as he raised both of his arms to show off all the spectators, which they roared in response before falling silent as he lowered his arms.

"No, I agree with Shameis." I let out as I sided with my ally. "Yes, it is a shock to hear that we are two halves of a powerful Seraph, but I am my own person, my own soul. There is no point in fighting for our lives if we are going to have to sacrifice them in the process."

"Then you're going to make this easier than I thought!" Micheal exclaimed before raising his right hand and snapping his fingers. In a flash of light, the three of us were then teleported from the middle of this empty field to the far right end. Along with our position change, a tall circular gate with an opening facing the field now surrounded us as a warm concrete circle sat beneath our feet as a foot of turf separated the two. There was also a rack holding three metal balls on the turf opposite the fence's opening. The last change was that the two monitors were now displaying a close-up live feed of us so the once again roaring crowd could see what was happening. "This trial is going to consist of three games. You lose one, and your souls are going to be trapped here forever." Michael quickly explained as he moved toward the rack of balls.

"I'm surprised you don't lean toward the ancient tradition of feeding the losers to a lion." Shameis retorted.

"I used to when this place was similar to the coliseum, back when I was referred to as Hercules, but I wanted to get with the times. Plus, I enjoy the masses cheering my name." Michael quipped back as he picked up the middle sphere and hoisted it just above his right shoulder. Once in possession of this item, he turned about-face before heading back to us. "You may want to get off the circle." he then suggested, and we complied.

"Right, everything is connected. But even I know Hercules was a Greek demi-god, and the coliseum was roman." Shameis pointed out. "Then you should do more research. I'm fairly certain I was named Hercules in both mythologies." Michael responded as he reached the middle of the concrete circle. Once in position, Micheal pulled the sphere from his right shoulder and used its momentum to spin around two full times. Then, he released the chunk of metal on his third rotation and allowed it to soar across the field until it landed near where we used to be standing. "You guys know what shotput is, so I shouldn't have to explain the rules. All you need to do is beat my distance, and we can start game two." He then let out.

"Your throw was halfway across the field!" I protested.

"Yep. Rules are rules. And you're up." He then ordered as he pointed toward the rack. I did grumble with resentment but followed his instruction. Unfortunately for Shameis and me, I am not competent at performing physical labor. The only reason Azrael even gave me a scythe was because I was complaining about how challenging the task of collecting souls is. Nevertheless, I walked around the concrete platform and up to the rack. Once there, I placed my hand onto one of the metal balls and tried to lift it up, but it didn't budge. Okay, I know I may not be the strongest, but I am not weak. Instantly after trying to lift it with one hand, I then grabbed it with two and tried again, but it still didn't move an inch. As panic began to set in, I turned to Shameis and shouted, "I can't pick it up!"

"Well that's because they are Deitanium." Michael blurted out. "It's a metal that only celestial bodies can pick up. No human soul has a chance at lifting that metal, and neither a special cloak nor training to collect souls will give you the ability to lift it."

150

"What about a robot arm?" Shameis then inquired as he began to walk around the circle toward me.

"Umm..." Michael stuttered. "That arm is part of your soul. You might as well forfeit now."

"Yeah, we heard that lie before." Shameis let out as he finally reached the rack. Once here, he reached past me, placed his right metal hand onto the sphere I tried to pick up, and lifted it with little effort. He even started to toss it up and down like a baseball. Once this orb was in his possession, he walked to the middle of the circle while staring directly into Michael's eyes. Shameis then chucked his ball without saying a word or warming up. The moment the ball left his hand, I moved my vision to one of the mega monitors and noticed that a camera was trying to keep up with Shameis's pitch. I watched in awe as this hunk of metal flew through the air, then let out a cheer as the camera displayed our orb had landed three-quarters of the field away. The rest of the stadium fell silent while realizing their champion had lost the first challenge. With a furious grunt, Micheal raised his hand and snapped his fingers to cause another flash of light, and within seconds, I found that the three of us were back near the middle of the field. More specifically, we are just on the inside of the outermost edge. Then, mirroring our position on the other side of the field was a series of five targets that depicted rings that decreased in size, leading to a center in the middle.

"Oh! Archery!" I exclaimed.

"I won't be able to do this one," Shameis admitted, which caused me to look at him." I have terrible aim. That's why I was a hand-to-hand brawler as a hero." Shameis let out.

"I thought you stopped using guns because you didn't want to kill people?" I cross-examined his statement.

"You can use guns to protect yourself and your community without killing others, but my lousy aim didn't aid my cause." He explained.

"Oh... Well, don't worry. This reaper used her skill of archery to protect her flock, and I've had a long time to perfect my aim since then." I assured him before turning my attention to Michael. He was already aiming at the targets with a bow in his left hand, string pulled back to his chin with his right, and a quiver of arrows on his back. He was waiting for our attention to be on him before beginning, and once watching, he released his shot before drawing another. He did this repeatedly in quick succession until Michael had launched five arrows. Then, as soon as he finished, the crowd was whipped into an uproar. The cheers caused me to look up at the monitor above the targets where I saw that each of his arrows had sunk into the target with a perfect bulls-eye.

"So all I have to do is shoot better than you?" I then questioned without looking away from the monitor. This question caused Michael to start laughing uncontrollably.

"There is no way you can outshoot that!" Micheal gloated. "Not even a Seraph could do better, but why don't you let him try?"
"Naw, I'm a pretty good shot," I admitted as I turned to Michael. "Do you have a bow I can use?"

"Sorry. Fresh out." He gloated as he trotted away. Hearing that, I spun around to wink at Shameis before turning back toward Michael.

"That's fine. Shameis isn't the only one of this duo that has a trick up his non-existent sleeve." I muttered. Michael abruptly whirled around, and if looks could kill, I'd be six feet under. Being that they couldn't, I *pulled* my scythe from within my robes with my left hand and rotated my body so I could point the tip of the handle downrange. This made it so the blade was curved back toward me. Once I was in this position, I brought my hand up as if I would pretend to use my scythe as a bow.
152

"So you do have a scythe!" Shameis let out in excitement. It just dawned on me that this was the first-moment Shameis saw it.

"Yeah, I try to keep it hidden and only use it when I need to," I affirmed.

"But why use it now? You need a bow, not a blade." Shameis cross-examined my thinking. Instead of responding, I looked over at Shameis and winked again before looking downrange. That was when I observed as the monitor above the targets switched from admiring Michael's perfect bulls-eye to me pointing my scythe like a doofus. This is my time to shine! Since the line my blade and staff made was aligned at a perfect ninety-degree angle with the ground, I took a slow and deep breath to calm my nerves before holding my breath. Once ready, I pulled my right hand to my chin. This gesture caused a thin string of light to manifest, starting at the tip of the blade and looping around my right index and middle fingers before connecting to the end of the staff. I held this position for a bit as I aimed my sight at the first target. Once I was sure of my shot, I released the illuminated string. This, in turn, caused the string of light to snap forward and transform itself into an arrow made of pure light before flying down the range. Upon reaching the target, my arrow pierced the end of Michael's first arrow, which caused it to splinter and explode. Just as Michael did, I repeated this action four more times with the exact same results. Again, the crowd fell deathly silent.

"Nice shooting, Robin Hood!" Shameis shouted as he ran up to me. "But how does your five perfect bulls-eyes out do Micheal's bulls-eyes?"

"Because he had an entire target to hit. I gave myself the tip of his arrow." I answered quickly, but before Shameis could respond, Michael rushed up to us while screaming.

"No fair!" Michael shouted as he grabbed onto my left shoulder and forcefully spun me around. "That was cheating! That doesn't count!" Seeing how aggressive Michael was acting, Shameis pushed his way in between us and started back.

"Says the one that wasn't going to provide the tools we need to participate!" Shameis accused the angel. It looked as if Michael was about to respond, but he quickly shut his mouth and raised his hand before snapping his fingers. Unlike the last two times, this snap didn't cause a flash of light to occur. Instead, the monitor switched from displaying my arrows to two sets of the number one hundred separated by a think line. Michael's name was listed above the one hundred on the left side and had a red background, while the one hundred on the right only was listed as 'Other' with a blue background. Since my attention was drawn to the monitor, I looked back at where the targets were and saw they had vanished.

"Alright. You want a game that any soul is prepared for?" Michael incited while getting my attention. I watched as he took a few steps past Shameis and me before stepping onto the racetrack and positioning himself to the right of a white strip crossing the black pavement. "Our last event is a race. One hundred laps around the track. The first one to finish wins." He explained before taking off in a blur, moving faster than I could keep up. Due to a combination color of his skin and the clothes he was wearing, a streak of brownish-gray quickly enclosed the track for approximately three seconds before Michael reappeared in the exact same position he was standing. "So which one of you three think they can match my speed? The shirtless wonder, the nightmare-fuel, or the Seraph?" That question made Shameis, and I look at each other.

"He moves as fast as Crossfade!" Shameis fretted.

"There is no way either of us can keep up with him," I muttered in response.

154

"I don't want to…" Shameis whimpered, to which I hung my head.

"Me neither, but there is no other option?" I agreed as I held out my left hand. Shameis hesitated for a bit before letting out a sigh and latching onto me with his left. I instantly felt my energy flow into Shameis, and within seconds, Shameis's body sprouted that single left wing to signify the Seraph was present. Strangely enough, this instance of transference was different from the last. I felt more in control and was able to move freely. Did the Seraph actually heed our concerns and try to make this situation more enjoyable? This had to be the case since this time, I noticed a crystal blue orb surrounded by a light blue smoke floating just beyond Shameis's possessed body. That had to be Shameis's consciousness. As the Seraph walked onto the track, I decided to inspect the orb, and it too chose to approach me. This orb and I could not communicate, but I could feel that it was definitely Shameis. Does that mean I am also a floating orb? After a second or so, I turned to look at the Seraph in Shameis's body and saw that both he and Michael had entered a sprinter's stance.

"Oh, this is going to be good. I'm going to show my brothers and sisters that there is no reason to be scared of you. It's time for us archangels to know we are stronger than the Seraphim ever were!" Michael proclaimed to the Seraph.

"Even at half my strength, I have the power to best you in a foot race." The Seraph responded before turning his attention to Shameis and my consciousness. "Wait there." He ordered before returning his attention straight ahead.

There was a second of tense silence before Michael decided to shout, "Let the race commence!" Instantly, a flash of light appeared on the track in front of our Seraph and Michael. Once it dissipated, a familiar red-headed woman wearing a tattered red t-shirt, ripped jeans, and a pair of black canvas shoes stood where the flash originated.

"Lilith?" I wondered with concern as I tried to rush over to her, but the Seraph's command wouldn't allow me to move. Without saying a word, she slowly raised a flag she was holding in her left hand before raising a second in her right. She held them up for a second before throwing them back down to her side to indicate the racers could begin. Immediately, Michael and Shameis whizzed by her. I guess this was an excellent choice to summon the Seraph since it could move as fast as Michael. This speed caused Shameis's body to appear as a two-colored streak with pale white on top due to his wing and exposed upper body with a blue underneath due to his jeans. Their streaks were relatively translucent, so I could see the start of the seating on the other side, but it seemed as if Lilith had vanished the moment the two beings whizzed by her.

I didn't even try to keep up with the streaks since it was nearly impossible. Instead, I wrenched my vision upward to see the only tool I knew would be reliable. If I wasn't mistaken, the monitor's display stated that the Seraph's tally was decreasing at a faster rate than Michael's. Our Seraph was faster! Within minutes, the Seraph's count reached zero while Michael still had ten laps left, and once it reached zero, The Seraph stopped just beyond the starting line while waiting for Michael to finish. He appeared to be standing impatient with his flesh and robotic arms crossed. They didn't even break a sweat! Michael finished only a quarter of a minute after the Seraph, but he reappeared in a hunched-over position while struggling to catch his breath and dripping with sweat. Seeing that Michael had lost for the third time, the crowd began to boo and rant that we had cheated again.

"You will allow us to leave," The Seraph ordered Michael while staring at the struggling archangel.

156

"One... more... game...?" Micheal huffed in between his deep breaths. To this question, The Seraph uncrossed his arms before walking over to Michael, grabbed Michael by the back of his tanktop, and hoisted him into a standing position.

"You will allow us to leave." The Seraph commanded more firmly while staring directly into Michael's eyes. Michael did not respond verbally, but instead, he nodded and snapped his fingers while his hand was down at his side. Much like what happened in the realm with Chamuel, the noise caused a portal to open, but thankfully it was not underneath either of us. This time it was floating above the track near where Lilith had manifested. Seeing the portal open, the Seraph let Michael loose and marched toward it. "Come along, you two." He ordered both of our consciousnesses, and before I could respond or even move, I felt myself being pulled behind him. I was still not a fan of being controlled, but at least I could move on my own actions when I was not being commanded. There was now no difference between being in this state versus being in the Ferryman of souls.

Nevertheless, I still wanted this to be over quickly. It had to be. That race dispersed so much energy that I nearly felt the way I did when my body rematerialized while falling into the stadium. Why is this Seraph not holding onto control of his manifestation longer? There has to be something wrong if I can feel his grasp slipping. Still, it seems pretty easy to allow the Seraph to regain control. All Shameis and I need to do is make skin contact while holding onto eachother. Knowing this, I wonder how the archangels will rig this next trial.

SHAME IS ELI (THE FACELESS HERO)

Chapter Fourteen

I can't believe it is another beautiful day! Waking up to the sound of birds chirping and the bray of sheep always lifts my spirits. The only thing that could make each day better would be my brother enjoying it with me. Still, I do have to admit that each day had become better since Able refused to wake up. I think he would've been happy with what I've been able to accomplish. Once I was in control of both of our farms, I expanded our little homestead into one of the largest agricultural businesses in the known land. We could barely provide for ourselves while he was alive, but now I provide my wares to several kingdoms and nations. I even receive generous payments in return for what I offer. Our lack of funds was the cause of why my herd was growing sick while his crops could survive. He reasoned that he wanted our operation to serve The Presence above. Still, now that I started making a profit, I've been able to provide work for the workless, homes for the homeless, and opportunities for those seeking them. As a side effect of my expansion, our small village has expanded into one of the largest cities in our home nation. Travelers from many lands even travel to our immaculate bazaar to buy, sell, and trade wares. Although I would like my brother to experience this with me, I'm starting to believe that this might be a blessing. However, all this success has come with the side effect of terrible, recurring nightmares.

It's always the same, reoccuring dream. Abel and I are traveling
down the mountain, we get into an argument, I push Abel, and he trips and
hits his head on a rock. The moment he gets injured is always the moment I
wake up from a cold sweat in my luxurious swan feather bed. My husband,
Raphael, has consoled me about my night terrors, but he'll never truly
understand my experience or why my memories haunt me. So much blood
poured out of that wound, and I was young enough to have no idea how to
help. I couldn't even recall an instance where one human caused this type
of injury to another. So what would any good sibling do in that situation?
I tried my best to clot his wound and struggled as I dragged my brother's
limp body back to our home. I felt so guilty over hurting him, but was
surprised that no other member of our village saw what had occured. Once
in our cottage, I tried my best to heal his wounds, but to no avail. He just
wouldn't wake up. Finally, I realized that his eternal slumber was my doing,
so I took it upon myself to take over his duties while handling my own.
I even performed his sacrifices on his behalf in hopes that The Presence
above wouldn't notice. There were many opportunities to come clean over
my transgressions, but I simply told them that I was not his keeper when
the villagers asked about my brother. I know it was probably incorrect to
say, but I didn't know what else to do.

I should have told someone so they could have helped. There was
no way a young woman would've been able to tend to all those chores and
devote the care her brother would have needed. So I let his care decline
as I tried to keep up appearances. Perhaps I was just in denial and refused
to believe that my brother had lost his life while on that mountain. Still,
the influx of support and coin was so great that I closeted my fear before
expanding my land, hiring more help, and eventually establishing a better
economy so my village would no longer be oppressed by the ruling kings.
Without realizing it, my brother's death signified an age of peace for my
160

town in which I was labeled as a lord and a savior. The praise and the wealth I received had been more than I knew what to do with, yet I could feel the need for more starting to grow within me. Over the years, I tried my best to fill the void left by my brother's absence, but nothing could replace him. I have wealth and power. I'm wedded to a wonderful man who is known the world over as a healer of the mind and soul, while his flawless olive skin, piercing blue eyes, and dark brown hair all contribute to his angelicness. I even hired a woman named Lilith Cotter as a personal servant. It's not often that you see Fiery red hair on top of a woman's head, so I knew that I had to have her, but she still wasn't enough. There was something in this world that I knew I needed more than anything else.

That's why this day was going to be sweeter than any other. Today was the day I would going to find what I was missing. So, unlike every other morning where I lay in my bed as I let the sun's golden rays warm my silk bedding, I quickly hopped out and glided across my acacia wood floor to my almug wood wardrobe. Strangely enough, my husband was not present, but I paid that detail with little attention since he is often traveling in exotic lands. Besides, I was preoccupied with dressing for the day. I had an urge to apply one of my more delicate garments, but nothing seemed to fit my mood. Bright orange with blue flowers? Pink with red wisps of clouds? Yellow with golden sun rays? No, none of these felt right. None until I pushed past all my brightly colored robes and came across my first one. It was pushed into the back of my closet as if it was trying to hide. Probably because it was a severely tattered. Usually, I wouldn't be caught dead in this thing, but today it was calling for me. Something about the black and brown felt right. So I pulled it out and slipped it on, and within seconds of doing so, my chamber door swung open as Lilith barged in; nearly scaring me half to death. "How many times do I need to tell you to knock before entering?" I shrieked.

"I'm sorry, but do ya not recall what ya instructed last night? Ya asked me ta wake ya up early this mornin'." She reminded me in a polite tone. "I'm surprised you're already up." Her statement caused me to pause and think for a bit. I don't recall giving such an instruction.

"Why did I request that again?" I questioned.

"Ya wanted ta go ta the Market today." She answered. I guess that makes sense. The bazaar has everything a person is looking for. I just find it strange that I don't recall informing her of wanting to go. "Do ya plan on goin' out lookin' like that?" She then inquired.

"Yes, I will be," I responded.

"But ya have so many betta' ones." She protested.

"I know, but this is the one I've chosen to wear today," I responded aggressively, causing an eerie silence to fall over the room while we stared at each other. "Do you intend to come with me?"

"Of course. I'm your loyal servant." She assured me. "I'm supposed ta stay by your side whenever you're up and about."

"Then I guess we should head out," I suggested as I headed toward her. She nodded in agreement while waiting for me to lead. So, I walked past her and into the rectangular main room of my house. With the amount of money I made from my business, I could've afforded my castle, but I wanted to live modestly so my neighbors wouldn't become jealous and covet my goods. My home was a single-story structure with walls and a ceiling made of polished sandstone, acacia wood floors, and almug wood furniture. Of the furniture in this room, a long rectangular table sat in the center with three matching throne-like chairs on each of the longer sides and one on each end. Several structural and decorative boards of acacia ran up the walls to match the floors. Just because I want others to think I live modestly doesn't mean I will live poorly. Once I heard the loud clunk of my chamber door closing, Lilith moved past me

162

toward a large door on the right slide of this room before pulling it open. Unfortunately, this caused the bright light from the desert outside to bleed in. Without hesitation, I followed Lilith across the room and out the door, and once outside, I was greeted with the sound of the not-so-distant city's bustling. The golden sand was pleasantly warm beneath my bare feet. Thankfully the yellowish-green sun had not climbed to a point in the sky to cause the sand to be scorching. With Lilith by my side, the two of us set off to our civilization's bazaar. I found it odd that Lilith wasn't trying to have a conversation with me since she is typically a chatty girl, but I was grateful for the silence since a feeling deep within me was telling me not to talk to her. The trek only lasted fifteen minutes as we crossed the barren desert, but once we arrived, everything seemed as if it was just another average day for the patrons. People were talking loudly while bargaining over various odds and ends.

I was recognized the moment I stepped onto that street as the vendors started to call my name in an attempt for me to purchase their wares. I paid these people no attention as I grazed my sight over their stands to find what I didn't know I was missing. Not seeing what I needed, we strolled deep into the market, but nothing was catching my eye. We just kept walking and looking until we crossed about three-fourths of this market, but stopped when I heard a different form of ruckus begin to arise. People were shouting while others screamed as mothers coddled their children and ran in the opposite direction I was walking. I could even hear the sound of wood and ceramics breaking up ahead. It sounded as if a brawl had begun in my bazaar, so I rushed toward the noise. My intent was to end the disruption. However, I found that it had been completed moments before I reached it. Many residents of my city were thrown about the bazaar, with bodies draped over stalls and lying in the street, but ten prominent men were able to subdue the assailant. They were able to hold the pale-skinned man in a kneeling position, but it was unclear why it took ten of them. It didn't even seem as if this man was trying to put up a fight.

As I gazed upon this unusually pale-skinned man, I noted how peculiar his clothing was. He possessed blue fabrics that wrapped around each of his legs and stretched up to his waist while bandages engulfed his entire head beside his right eye. This scandalous lack of clothing left his scarred torso exposed to everyone around, but that's how my attention was brought onto something new to me. This man's arm! It was like he was wearing white-ish porcelain as armor over his right arm. There was no way he was wearing ceramics; it had to be a type of metal. Whatever it was, I knew it was what I came here for. "Come, Lilith." I beckoned as I trotted up to the group of men. The instant this man laid his one exposed eye on me, he quickly shredded their grasp while rushing up to me. I was caught off guard by the way he was trying to talk to me as if he knew me, but I couldn't understand a word he said. All I could do was stare into his bizarrely colored, greenish-yellow iris. The ten men holding him down then rushed over and tried to pull him away but struggled to do so.

"Master, do ya know this guy?" Lilith then interrupted his blabbering.

"No. I don't think so." I answered uncertainly. I am confident that I have never seen this man, but something deep inside me told me otherwise.

"Oh, well. this guy seems ta know ya by name." Lilith then informed me. "Ya are pretty famous, but it's weird that he also knows me."

"That is odd. Wait... You understand this man?" I then cross-examined her.

"Well, yeah. He came from the same land that I did." Lilith continued to enlighten me. "I have no idea what's goin' on with this guy, so

164

we should leave." She then grabbed onto my shoulders and tried to turn me away, but I needed his armor, so I turned back toward the incident.

"Hello, my friends," I greeted the subduers. "What seems to be the problem here?"

"This guy was harassing the vendors. We don't know what he is saying, but I heard your name quite a bit." One of them answered.

"I need this man to come with me. I shall pay for all damages he has caused." I informed the men, to which they begrudgingly pushed him toward me with vulgar expressions on their faces. Once away from them, the men walked away from us as I turned to Lilith. "Tell this man that he is to follow us. I have some business I would like to discuss," I instructed. She grumbled but then did as I suggested. As soon as she finished speaking in her native tongue, I turned around and walked in the direction Lilith and I originally came from. This was a conversation I wanted to have at home. Through my confidence, I didn't even look back to see if he was actually following, but after a few minutes, I could hear Lilith and this man speaking in their native language. I couldn't tell while in the bazaar, but once we reached the barren desert between the city and my home, I could tell that they were bickering. I did feel a bit left out, but I allowed them to chat with the hope Lilith would share what they were talking about while trying to seem friendly. Every so often, I looked back at this man, but every time I looked at him, I could see the look of confusion in his eyes. It seemed as if the more he saw, the more he became confused. "Lilith? Is everything alright back there?"

"Yeah. He's just goin' on and on about nonsense. There's no need ta worry about it." She answered.

"Okay..." I responded hesitantly. So, I led the three of us across the desert and up to my house. Without taking a second to think, I let us in and instantly headed to the right end of my table before plopping myself in the seat. Once settled, I gestured to the chair to my left and instructed Lilith to offer the seat to our guest. She, of course, did as required, to which my guest headed my suggestion. This left Lilith standing awkwardly at the door. "You may sit to my right." I then offered it to her. "I will need you for this conversation." She then nodded her head to me before walking around the table. This put her directly across from our masked guest. Once they were all seated, I turned directly to the stranger and spoke toward him. "I'm sure you're wondering why I brought you into my home," I uttered before a long pause occurred. The delay caused me to look at Lilith before speaking to her. "You're going to need to translate what I say," I informed her grumpily.

"Oh! Right." Lilith responded before sparking up a small conversation in their native language. "He seems ta be more preoccupied with why we're actin' like we have no idea of who he is or why you can't understand him." She interpreted.

"Tell him that I meet a lot of people, and it is hard to remember some individuals. Especially the ones now in masks." I explained.

"His response was only him askin' what he needs ta do ta get this over with." She continued to interpret with confusion growing in her voice.

"Right to business! Good!" I responded excitedly. "All he needs to do is give me the armor, and he can be on his way. I'm willing to pay handsomely."

"He said that the metal is not armor, but his arm." Lilith enlightened me. An arm made of pure metal? I could conquer kingdoms in the name of the almighty Presence with an object like that. "He doesn't want your money." Lilith then informed me.

"Well, tell him that I am willing to give him whatever he wants. I am going to get it from him, or he will not be leaving this house." I then instructed. This was the point where my adversaries usually would become disgruntled by my advances, but my requests seemed to do nothing but relax him. It was as if he was washed with unwavering clarity, and his confusion melted from his eye. How peculiar.

"I'm startin' to get a little lost," Lilith informed me as she touched me on my arm. "He said somethin' about the sin of greed affectin' ya and that an angel has taken over your mind?"

"I haven't believed in anything religious since my brother was taken from this world. I am not a greedy person! On the contrary, I'm one of the most generous people I know!" I assured her before growing offended by his accusation. Of course, she translated what I said. I admit that I am a bit zealous with my ventures, but I'm not greedy. If I was greedy, I would have left my brother to die on that mountain. "Listen here! I am not greedy." I shouted as I pointed at this man while standing up from my seat. "I do not want your tool for personal use. I need it to better serve my people!" As Lilith translated, this man grew increasingly relaxed. I couldn't quite tell, but I felt as if an expression of smugness grew underneath the fabrics on his face. This caused me to be more engaged and confused, so I ended up stopping my scolding. The moment I stopped, the man spoke up so Lilith could translate.

"He apologizes for insultin' ya and is willin' to offer you his arm for nothin' in return. But he does want to add the stipulation that ya have ta shake his hand without changin' your mind." She returned as he extended his normal left hand toward me. After hearing and seeing this, I slowly slumped back into my chair while stunned by this man's generosity. Was he really willing to give me what I desired for nothing in return? I've never met a person that was willing to surrender their valuables, but I did not want to pass on this opportunity, so I nodded my head and reached out with my left hand to shake his. But, just before I could reach him, Lilith grabbed onto my right arm to pull me away. "I don't think ya should touch him. He's a street urchin and probably tryin' ta harm ya."

"Unhand me!" I shouted to her as I aggressively pulled away. "I'm a handshake away from filling the emptiness inside of me and will not be stopped!" I quickly reached this man but ended up barely grazing his flesh. The touch caused a spark of energy to shoot up my arm and into my brain, filling my mind was instantly filled with memories that I'd never had. It was as if I was looking through someone else's eyes. There were many sights of this person collecting ghosts of the deceased and guiding them through a vast emptiness. It seemed like this person had traveled far to see horrors I would never want to experience. I was shown flying metal birds filled with humans crashing into the ground before being engulfed in flames, tall reflective towers tumbling as their inhabitants try to jump to safety only to meet the cold hard ground below, a massive ship striking a piece of ice before splitting in half and sinking to the bottom of the ocean as the people inside drowned, and even a pile of burning books within a nation where their government was committing mass genocide. I don't know why I saw these sights, but I wanted them to end. Whose memories were they? Were they mine? They had to be. Why were my memories so dark and dreary? I wanted to cry, but then I was shown some happy memories. Recollections about the man and how he and I were working toward a goal. We were jumping from world to world, intending to get him back to his own. Back to mine. This world isn't real. It's all just been an illusion of the sin of greed. What was this man's name? Shameis Eli. Suddenly, I snapped back to the table we were sitting at by Lilith's shrill voice. "What did you do!" She shrieked at Shameis.

168

"I didn't do anything," he smugly responded. I could understand him!

"Shameis? Wha... What's going on?" I questioned.

"And just like that, it's all coming back to you." He quoted with a chuckle.

"Yeah... My memory is still a little fuzzy... but it's getting there." I responded.

"That's how it was for me." He comforted me. "I'm just happy to get your memories back."

"Well, at least I don't gotta pretend ta be your servant anymore," Lilith interjected, to which Shameis and I looked at her in confusion. "Did ya say his name is Shameis?"

"Why are you even here?" Shameis then questioned while ignoring her realization that this man was the guy she screwed over while on earth.

"Tha angel wanted me ta watch over ya and try ta make sure ya didn't touch." She admitted.

"Why are you working for the Angels?" Shameis continued to interrogate.

"Well, a skeleton sent me ta hell. But I was promised by this one guy that if I did whateva the angels wanted, I would neva go back." She explained.

"If you would've stayed locked up in Gyles-Helmsley, you wouldn't have been caught up in this mess, and she wouldn't have ferried your soul!" Shameis then shouted at her.

"So ya are tha Ile! I like tha new look. Tha Doc musta messed ya up good." Lilith let out before pausing for a bit. "She? Ya know tha Grim Reapa?" Lilith picked up before looking at me as her eyes widened. "You? You're tha Grim Reapa? Is that why he wanted me ta be with ya?"

169

"That's not important right now." I deflected. "I need to know which angel helped you out of Hell." but in that exact moment, everything around us began to shake violently. During this, unlit torches that hung on the wall were ripped from their mounts, the sound of cooking-ware rattling could be heard coming from the kitchen, door latches came loose as they all slowly swung open, and even the stone that made up the walls started to disintegrate. It felt as if a sudden earthquake with a magnitude of five point five was rolling through. Of course, the three of us snapped to our feet, but the shaking was so bad that we had to use the table and our chairs to support ourselves.

"Not this one," Lilith muttered, implying that this shaking was being caused by a specific angel. As the seconds passed, the shaking grew increasingly violent, which meant the angel was approaching. This caused the structural supports of the building to begin collapsing around us while we were essentially frozen in place by the instability of the ground. It felt as if the house was about to entirely collapse on top of us, but then the shaking suddenly stopped as an eerie silence fell over the room. We all darted our gaze across the room to look at the damage, but then the slow creak of the front door opening demanded our attention. We watched in suspense as the massive silhouette of a cloaked man ducked underneath the doorframe to enter the room. Once inside and no longer disguised by the harsh exterior sun, I could see this man possessed flawless light olive skin, similar to the color of my own, and was wearing a soft blue tunic with a blood-red sash wrapping around his torso and right arm. This man's eyes matched the color of his robing, and his dark-brown hair hung down onto his shoulder.

"I am Raphael, and I am here to retrieve your souls." The man stated while breaking the silence.

"Yeah, this trial is over," Shameis responded while trying to defend us. "But we are not going with you. We won your rigged game."

170

"On the contrary." Raphael denied. "A deal has been struck in favor of greed."

"But there was a stipulation!" I corrected him. "For the deal to be completed, I had to shake Shameis's hand and still want his arm."

"She's right! Lilith even translated for us. So she can attest to the outcome!" Shameis backed me up.

"I don't know. This guy seems ta have a reason to need ya ta lose whateva is goin' on. And If I help him, I don't have ta go back ta Hell." Lilith pointed out, which suggested that she would cause us to fail.

"Well, if you help us get out of this, we won't only keep you out of Hell, but we will try to get your soul back to earth." I offered desperately.

"Grim!" Shameis barked disappointedly.

"What? We need her help." I questioned defensively.

"Enough!" Michael boomed, causing the entire building to shake once again. "You clearly do not understand the gravity of this situation. This trial is over, and you have failed."

"Sorry, boss, but these guys are right. Their deal never was agreed upon. They didn't even get ta shake hands." Lilith verified to support our claim.

"The acquisition matters not. A deal was struck while greed possessed the soul." Raphael decreed again.

"I only suggested that because I knew that would jumpstart her memory." Shameis pointed out, which is fair. That was precisely how he regained his own.

"A realm's effects cannot be overwritten," Raphael pointed out.

"They definitely can. We found out that there is a Seraph inside of us, so strange things happen when we touch." I clarified, which caused Raphael to pause and become speechless.

"And we know that you Archangels rig these trials, so the Seraph gives us a fighting chance," Shameis added in.

"The four Seraphim vanished from existence before time existed. How dare you claim to possess powerful beings inside your souls that aid your bidding?" Raphael cross-examined while slowly starting to approach us.

"We do not claim to know this information for certain." I clarified. Realizing that Raphael was possibly approaching to take our souls, I started to blabber on about the supporting facts. "All I know is that Chamuel was frightened by this energy, the being forced Arial to obey its commands, and it was able to overpower Micheal. Micheal was the one that kept calling us a Seraph. We even grow a wing!" I stated desperately as I turned my attention to Shameis and reached out.

"NO!" Raphael shouted, causing me to stop just before I could reach Shameis. After stopping in my place, I turned to Raphael and saw that he had stopped approaching and instead looked as if he was beginning to cower. "I can feel the energy increase with every inch you two come closer. I believed the surge to be the realm indicating that this trial had concluded, but I am now inclined to believe your testament. This means that his prophecy is coming to fruition."

"What prophecy?" Shameis inquired, but Raphael did not respond. He instead stared at the three of us blankly.

Chapter Fifteen

The moment I was forced into the role of being the Ferryman of souls was the moment I abandoned my faith in pursuit of knowledge. While living, my faith meant the world to me, but I soon realized that I couldn't devote myself to beings that didn't respect the existence of humans. Although I was engulfed by the mystics of my former faith, the separation grew with every terrible moment Azrael applied to me. I always hoped the other angels would treat me better, but the last four trials have proven that all angels are the same. Every single one of them would prefer to punish or screw over a soul. At least the one inside Shameis and I is willing to protect us, but I wonder if it is only because we serve as its vessel.

Well, seeing all this with Shameis at my side has done wonders for my curiosity, knowledge, and faith. It just didn't have the effect many human zealots would prefer. I can say for sure that there is more after a human's life and that there is more life in the Universe other than what humans can see, but the religious system is essentially upside down. From my experience, those deemed righteous are self-serving, and the one considered the ruler of evil was willing to provide helpful guidance. But now I know that there is more to this story than what was initially given to us. When we embarked on this quest, I thought the goal was to get Shameis back to his body, which would be the end of it. The whole Seraph thing explains why I was drawn to Shameis in the first place, but it is unfortunate to hear that the emergence of this being means there is so much more going on that we don't know about. Not like the archangels would be willing to share that information anyway. Nevertheless, Shameis and I, and now Lilith, found ourselves in yet another realm based on a deadly sin. We have endured Envy, Sloth, Pride, and Greed, which means we only have Lust, Gluttony, and Wrath left.

After leaping through the portal, I found the three of us standing at the edge of a circle that transitioned from a non-existent light source into the surrounding darkness. It was as if the Mists of Torpidus and the Void between worlds had merged. As the ground faded in from the blackness around, I could see and feel the soft deep-blue grass leading to a simple wooden picnic table that served as the focal point of this realm. This place also had similar flowers to the Mists, but these flowers were various colors of greens and greys while letting off the aroma of fried chicken, waffles, and maple syrup. Instantly after getting a hint of that smell, my mouth started to salivate, and I knew the sin we would now be faced with was gluttony. There was an eerie silence to this realm, but it was quickly broken by Shameis's voice. "How about we don't stand around too long this time?" He joked, to which I chuckled in response.

"What? What's so funny?" Lilith questioned obliviously.

"Nothing. This place looks similar to the second trial we were in." I explained. "That place was based in the sin of sloth, and the ground started to swallow us."

"The place with the purple fog?" Lilith quested for clarification. "I rememba that place, but I didn't see no open air."

"So that was you that was calling out through the fog?" Shameis then interrogated.

174

"You heard her too?" I cross-examined his question.

"Yeah, that was me. But that was when I had no idea what was goin' on." Lilith clarified.

"Why did they put you there?" Shameis continued to grill her.

"That's top secret." Lilith countered. "It's a need-ta-know basis, and ya don't need ta know."

"Well, if we are bringing you back to Earth with us, then we need to know!" Shameis barked.

"Oh yeah? Whatcha gonna do monsta man? She already said ya would get me back." Lilith pointed out while trying to act big.

"You do realize I'm going to lock you back into Gyles-Helmsley the moment we get back to earth, right?" Shameis informed her while stepping closer. "But I have half a mind to leave you here."

"You're moral code wouldn't let ya leave me." She retorted while getting in his gauze-covered face. "The Ile always tries his best ta help people in need."

"And you know I'm not The Ile!" Shameis shouted. "You don't know how Victor messed with my mind. Between him and all this, I'm a new man. As you said, I'm monstrous. Maybe I'll take you back to earth just so I can kill you myself!" This not only caused Lilith to recoil in fear, but it also scared me a bit. I always thought this man to be righteous, so would he have the strength to retake her life? "Now, if you want to avoid being on my bad side, I suggest you tell us everything you know." See, that statement confirmed the thought that he was using the threat as an intimidation tactic. I understand that these two have a deep history with each other, so I'm assuming this was part of his hatred for her, which I can understand why he does. The betrayal she performed while he didn't have his memories would be enough to push anyone over the edge.

"She's not going to tell you anything." A childish voice then echoed around us. Instantly, we all turned to look at the lone picnic table and saw a young boy staring at us and waving daintily. He appeared malnourished with grayish-pale skin, brown eyes, and darker brown hair curled into a small afro. I swear that this child was no older than twelve years old, but wore a calming and gentle smile below his voluminous hair-do and murky eyes. As opposed to any of the Archangels we encountered thus far, this one was the first to actually feel inviting. As for his apparel, he was wearing a pristine white tunic robe accented with golden chains that wrapped from his right shoulder and around his torso to his left hip. Because this kid was too short for the table's attached bench, I watched as he swayed his legs forward and back. I also noticed that a stereotypical angelic halo floated above his head while puny feathered wings fluttered on his back. "But, I'll tell you lots of stuff." He continued after giving me a bit to observe his presence.

"And which archangel are you?" Shameis then questioned the child.

"To align with my brothers and sisters, I am currently known as Gabriel, the messenger, but I much preferred when I was known as Thoth."

"The Egyptian god of knowledge?" I questioned.

"And the moon, sacred texts, mathematics, the sciences, and recorder of deities." The child agreed as he touched the tip of his nose. "I always enjoy feasting on new information."

"Okay... So, what impossible task is the Archangel of messages planning on demanding of us?" Shameis then inquired after pausing for a bit to process this child's claim.

"What of the Seraph are you wanting to see?" I followed up.

"Please do not bring him here." Gabriel pleaded as he perked up in his seat. "After witnessing what my brothers and sister have done to you, I have come to the conclusion that forcing your souls to fail my trial would

176

be impossible. Especially with the Seraph. No. My trial will be simple and to the point. Nearly impossible to fail. Come and take a seat, and we can start." He chirped as he gestured to the bench across the table from him. This caused Lilith, Shameis, and I to look at each other out of suspicion. Shameis and I knew we couldn't trust the Angel but didn't actually have a choice over what our next course of action would be, while Lilith looked at us as if she was wondering what was going on. This was also when I noticed that Shameis's iris changed color to match the deep blue of the grass. Weirdly enough, I felt as if I wanted to stare into them for hours, but I needed to stay focused for once. So, Shameis and I began to approach, which caused Lilith to follow suit, but Gabriel ended up stopping us as soon as he saw this. "Umm...Lilith, it is good to see you made it out of my brother's realm of greed, but you're not supposed to be here." He uttered before stretching out and slowly arcing his hand from left to right.

"No... wai..." Lilith screamed before vanishing into thin air, leaving Shameis and me to stare at where she stood in stunned silence.

"I'm sorry, but this trial is meant for the two of you and the two of you alone," Gabriel explained while breaking the silence.

"Well, that solves that problem." Shameis joked before proceeding toward the picnic table. I was further stunned by the uncaringness of Shameis's action, but again, there was no love gained by her presence. I guess there is no point in fretting over Lilith's disappearance since we've seen her in every realm we've been to, so we will probably see her again.

"Are you not concerned at all about how he could just wave his hand to make a soul disappear?" I muttered to Shameis as I followed behind him.

"I didn't want to bring her along in the first place." He answered without looking back at me. "But if you're worrying if the angels could do that to us, I counter by wondering if they could, why haven't they done it yet? They've had plenty of opportunities, yet we are still beating them. Things are not adding up, and I intend to find out why." He does make a good point. Another reason why this guy is a perfect match for me. He's able to be more direct while I overthink the situations.

"That's an astute observation," Gabriel interjected himself just before we were able to take a seat. "I'm more than willing to answer whatever you ask... if you ask."

"Why can't you tell us now?" Shameis then inquired.

"Because that is my trial!" Gabriel exclaimed. "I don't have to answer anything until you sit down. And when you do, we all have to answer each question asked to us with the utmost truth. So you feed me, and I will feed you."

"What's the catch?" Shameis followed up.

"The only catch is that we each get three questions, and all we can do is ask our three questions and provide an answer." The child informed us. "Now, please, have a seat." He then gestured to the bench across from himself for a second time. This caused Shameis and me to look at each other hesitantly, but again, we didn't have another option. So, I watched as Shameis climbed over the bench and slid his legs under the tabletop, and once he was seated, I did the exact same thing. The moment we were seated and comfortable, we looked at Gabriel, to which he gestured to us with an open palm without saying a word. This was his way of informing us he wanted us to start. Seeing this, I turned to Shameis to tell him he should speak first, but I couldn't get a sentence to leave my mouth. Gabriel wasn't lying when he said all we would do was ask our questions. So I get three and only three. I wanted to make these count, so I needed to ponder over the best questions to ask.

"What role does Lilith have to play in this game?" Shameis blurted out after realizing that I needed a moment to think.

"She was originally registered to have an impact on your life as a former lover, so she was going to be used as a pawn to throw you off your game and trick you into losing a trial. However, after seeing the hatred you two share, her role will be altered. Don't worry, you will see her again." Gabriel answered. It looked as if Shameis wanted to debate this topic, but the trial prevented it. I watched as he quickly gave up and pinched the bridge of his nose through his gauze mask. If only the angels cared to research a soul's history, they would know that was a bad idea. At least I know that their relationship was under false pretenses. So, when Gabriel finished providing his answer, he pointed to me and indicated my turn to ask a question. Any question that my heart desired.

"What is the history of the four Seraphim?" I inquired after thinking long and hard.

"Now that is a good question," Gabriel let out through a cracking voice as he bounced in his seat with joy. "As I'm sure you are aware, the Seraphim were essentially prototype angels. The Presence created them before anything else by duplicating his power and giving each of them one-fourth. Once constructed, he named the four of them himself. Jalliel the Timekeeper, Zatael the Worldforger, Despiel the Lifegiver, and Samael the Lightbringer. Once created, The Presence instructed the Seraphim to construct everything we know and don't know today. As their name explains, Zatael first created the seven realms that contain and limit sin, Hell, Heaven, and the Earth. He then connected them all with the world tree to allow travel between the realms while putting limitations on how to travel between the realms can be done and who can cross the doors. So you can thank him for the portals you keep walking through. After Zatael was finished, Despiel created the life that was to exist in these realms. This includes the Archangels, demons, fates, humans, and even the animals. Once Despiel created life, Jalliel then

179

created the time for these beings to keep track of the events they would experience. Finally, Samael created the Sun in each realm and the stars in the night sky to light the way for these beings. When they were finished, The Presence was pleased with everything they had accomplished and decided to rest while viewing over what he deemed to be his. Zatael was happy that the work was sufficient, but the other three were enraged after feeling slighted. That was when the Timekeeper, the Lifegiver, and the Lightbringer decided they needed to overthrow The Presence and take back what they created. While preparing their crusade, the three realized that they alone would not have the power to challenge The Presence. They needed The Worldforger. Of course, the Worldforger would deny their proposal, so the Lightbringer instructed the Lifegiver and the Timekeeper to rip the Worldforger apart, curse each half of the soul so he could never permanently become whole, then send each half in opposite directions across the Universe. This violent act caused The Presence to curse the Timekeeper and the Lifegiver to wither until they were weaker than humans. The Presence then entered a deep sleep due to heartbreak. Once in this slumber, The Lightbringer proposed that if the Timekeeper and Lifegiver would allow him to consume their power, he should be able to challenge The Presence. Being as gullible as they were, they agreed, and the Lightbringer proceeded to consume the Lifegiver and Timekeeper. Once uniting their power, The Lightbringer enlisted the help of us Archangels to face off against The Presence with the hope that all of our power would be enough to seize control. Unfortunately, we severely underestimated the might of The Presence. The Presence quickly awoke from his sleep, to which he cast the Lightbringer to rot in Hell while forcing us to oversee these trials in an effort to show us that a soul is more than what they seem. But as you know, we quickly realized these trials can

180

easily be manipulated. As for The Presence, after losing all four of his first creations, The Presence decided to vanish from the Universe, so we could do what we pleased."

Well, that is a lot to take in, but was some well-needed information. The story also gave enough context clues to answer other questions I had. One of the first images I was shown when I felt the Seraph's presence for the first time was two silhouettes ripping a third in half. That thought had to be depicting The Lifegiver, the Worldforger, and the Timekeeper. Gabriel's story also implies that the Worldforger's soul could eventually reconnect for a temporary amount of time. Using all these clues, I can conclude that Zatael, the Worldforger, is the Seraph that is part of our souls. Still, that tale raises even more questions. I was about to let another out, but Gabriel lifted his tiny hand to stop me before pointing to himself. "What do you two think Raphael was talking about when he referred to a prophecy?" Gabriel then inquired. Upon hearing this question, my head started to throb as thoughts that I didn't even know I possessed began to fill my mind.

"The Worldforger has been revealed and stands as both the key and adversary to the Lightbringer's end goal." A deep voice bellowed from my mouth before transferring to Shameis. "The Worldforger and the Lightbringer will need to engage in a final battle for the realms, and the result will cause The Presence to take notice." Hearing the voice of Zatael bleed from our separate mouths filled Gabriel with joy while I was left with confusion. I thought Shameis and I had to be touching to cause the Angel within us to manifest. Then again, I'm confident that Zatael's spirit is the reason Shameis and I were brought together. Out of joy, Gabriel started to clap his hands. How can he be happy with the response of a Seraph if he didn't want the Seraph to be present? Well, when he finished clapping, he quickly indicated it was our turn again.

"Can you please explain as to why a human was expecting to speak to the Lightbringer through Shameis's body?" I requested.

"Oh, that's a simple one." Gabriel boasted. "Besides the Lightbringer's goal of usurping The Presence, he is also trying to conquer all of the realms. He enlisted our aid, so he probably reached across the Vale to speak to the humans. The rules that apply to us Archangels don't apply to the Seraphim in the same way, which I'm sure you're aware of by now. It is a good thing you have a Seraph of your own. If the Lightbringer would've been able to get into your body, you wouldn't be able to get back." Great, so not only do we have to worry about a mad scientist on earth, but we're going to have to worry about a supreme angel trying to take over the world. Gabriel is right about having a Seraph of our own. Although Shameis and I don't care much for being controlled, we will need its strength to face the Lightbringer. That is, if a damaged Seraph would match a Seraph with the might of three. At least we would have the Superheroes on earth to aid our cause. Well, since I just asked my second question, It was Shameis's turn to ask another, and he did so just as soon as Gabriel finished answering.

"Why were Grim and I chosen to be the hosts of the Worldforger's soul?" He quickly inquired.

"Because you're special," Gabriel joked in response. "Not every human is born with the genetic makeup to host a celestial being as powerful as a Seraph. In fact, only one comes into existence every several Millenium. Cain, you were the first in existence. We knew you could host the Lightbringer, but for some reason, he couldn't get into your body. At first, we assumed it had something to do with the rules that Zatael established when creating the realms. Between these two reasons, The Lightbringer commanded Azrael to scoop you up. Little did we know that a part of Zatael had already latched onto your soul."

182

Gabriel explained before taking a long pause and a deep, drawn-out breath. "The Lightbringer soon realized that he not only needed a human vessel to exist on earth but also a human soul. Many humans have the genetic potential to host beings like us, but rarely are any born perfect. Shameis was the second ever to be born perfect enough to host a Seraph, but his wild nature was thought to be the reason why the Lightbringer couldn't latch on. That's why the Scientist was instructed to remove that portion of you and was hoping to speak to the Lightbringer. None of us realized that Zatael was part of either of you until he emerged in front of Chamuel." So, essentially, Shameis and I are in this position due to pure coincidence. After realizing that, another realization about something Gabriel mentioned clouded my mind. He noted that humans have the genetic potential to host Angels, so if the Lightbringer was able to command Victor to alter Shameis into being a different person, then Victor's experimentations had the potential of preparing a human for any other angel to come to earth. Was that why Zatael finally decided to pull us together? Since Shameis was so close to the Doctor, Zatael must have watched the progress. Shameis and I were itching to get more information, but neither of us could let it out since it was Gabriel's turn. "Do you think that you can achieve your end goal when you get back to earth?"

"Yes, I will definitely be able to stop Victor from experimenting on another innocent life." Shameis quickly belted out.

"And with Zatael's help, we will try our best to keep the Lightbringer at bay," I added on. Okay, this time, it was my own thoughts and voice, but speaking it still felt forced. Since the responses were our own, they left Gabriel less than impressed. In response, he slumped in his seat, placed his elbows on the wooden picnic table, and propped his head up before limply pointing at Shameis.

183

"Since you are working for the Lightbringer, why are you helping us by sharing all this information?" Shameis inquired as if he was trying to sympathize with the tiny Angel, which caused Gabriel to perk up a bit.

"I don't want to be under his thumb. We made a deal to serve him a long time ago. But ever since he consumed the Lifegiver and Timekeeper, his mind has been in retrograde. My brothers and sisters still follow him without conviction, but I can see his stability is dwindling." Gabriel answered before pointing to me.

"Could you tell us why there are super-powered humans on earth?" I asked with genuine interest.

"I wish I could, but that is the only thing that the Lightbringer has blinded my knowledge to." Gabriel let out. Well, that was a bit disappointing, but I guess the phenomenon is so recent and outrageous that even Thoth wouldn't know. Even now, I felt a bit cheated that he couldn't answer my final question, but I would prefer this kind of cheating over what the four other Archangels did. Nevertheless, that was the last of Shameis and my three questions, which meant it was time for Gabriel's last. "I understand your hesitation toward us Archangels since one has been torturing you for hundreds of thousands of years, but if I was willing to get away from Lightbringer, would you allow me to join your crusade?" Gabriel requested. He had one last question, and that was what he asked? He could have asked anything he wanted to, but he asked if we would take him in? I was shocked and confused by this. I don't think I would ever see the day when an angel would ask a human for help. Of course, I instantly turned to Shameis to gauge his reaction, but he looked as confused as I was. Then, while looking into his deep-blue iris, I knew how we needed to respond. So, I turned back to Gabriel and spoke from the heart.

"If our path is going to lead to us facing off against the Lightbringer, then we'll need all the help we can get," I muttered.

"But when the time comes, you will need to prove that you are willing to stand with us instead of playing both sides." Shameis then pointed out, reminding me that Gabriel is still under the Lightbringer's command. Hopefully, Zatael would command this Angel if it came down to it.

"You have a deal!" Gabriel let out as he hopped out off of his bench and turned away from us. Instantly, he snapped his fingers and caused a portal to open just beyond the right end of this table. "You should get going. I've kept you here long enough."

"Have fun telling your brothers, sisters, and the Lightbringer about everything that happened here!" Shameis joked mockingly as he and I struggled to exit the picnic table.

"The only thing I have to report is that you two know of the prophecy, but everything after that is our little secret." The child uttered as he turned back to wink at us. "Oh! Don't think your last two trials will be as easy as this. I took it easy on you since I want you to succeed, but my brother and sister may not have the same thoughts." This wasn't exactly new news since we haven't faced off with Azrael's trial yet, but I was at least hoping the other would be easy. So, once we were free from the table, Shameis and I began to make our way to the portal, but he quickly rushed over to my left side and nearly tripped over the table in the process. I was confused by what he was trying to do, but was surprised when he grabbed onto my left hand with his metal one.

"What's going on here?" I let out in a half-joking, half-excited response.

"Just trying to make sure we don't get separated again." He answered as he looked at me. As I looked back at him, I could see that the deep blue of gluttony now had a tint of pink to it.

"Or are you trying to hold my hand?" I joked as I felt myself begin to blush.

"I'll let you decide that," he then mumbled. I'm not exactly sure as to what spurred his decision to hold onto me, but I definitely liked it. Even if he was grabbing onto me just so we didn't get separated again, I still felt a strange feeling growing inside me. A feeling that I haven't felt in a very long time, and judging by to tint in his iris, he was probably feeling the same way. Ever since I first laid eyes on him, I knew he was special. More remarkable than holding half of an almighty being inside of him. I knew he would be special to me.

"Will you please get out of my realm! You're starting to gross me out!" Gabriel then shouted, causing us to look at him before back at each other. Gabriel is right. This is not the time or place to be worrying about feelings. Perhaps in the realm of Lust since that is one of the two that we have not visited yet. So, hand in hand, Shameis and I proceeded the rest of the way around the rectangular picnic table and into the portal with our minds stuffed with new knowledge. I think this was the first time I was ever thankful for an archangel's guidance, being that he was able to answer more than three questions that I had. We now know about the Angel within us, who the Lightbringer is, why the Archangels are helping him, and what the Lightbringer's goal was. We even got another source of motivation as to why we need to not fail these last two trials. Yet, it would have been great to figure out how the superheroes on earth fit into this equation and what the Archangels get out of it. I'm sure those questions will be answered eventually, but it would've been nice to know now.

Chapter Sixteen

This adventure, thus far, has been the most incredible experience of my life. So many humans would expect that being the ferryman of souls would be vastly rewarding, and in many ways, it was, but my experience with the role has been nothing more than depressing. Seeing the wonders of the world is a fantastic experience, but it gets old when you don't have a traveling partner. The solitude can be maddening; leaving one to ramble on inside their mind while aimlessly traveling. Having Shameis by my side has done wonders for my self-health, being that he was the key to unlocking the shackles placed upon me. Together, we have seen segments of five realms that lay just beyond earth's borders while meeting and facing off against mighty angels. I can't believe I would never have known about these places if Zatael hadn't pulled Shameis and me together.

Nevertheless, this adventure is wondrous, but I don't think those were the best part. The best part is having Shameis by my side. I really needed a friend and someone to talk to other than myself, but as we progress, it feels as if our friendship is blossoming into something more. Yes, a few boundaries would keep us from having a normal relationship. Obstacles like his gauze mask, his metal arm, my lack of a physical construct on the surface of the earth, and the Seraph that begins to manifest when we make skin contact, but I think we have a chance of making it work. At least my robes are enough to insulate our skin so we can hug each other, or I can hold his metal hand like I am now. Yeah... This could work. I genuinely want to be by his side for as long as he would let me, and I know it's not just because of the realm we are walking toward.

With every step we took toward the portal, I could feel an insatiable passion growing within me. Not just to be with Shameis, but my head flooded with thoughts about everything I enjoy. Because of this growing passion while still in the realm of gluttony, I wasn't surprised that this next realm was the sin of lust. However, I was surprised to see the next archangel waiting for us just beyond the portal. Once crossing the threshold, we were greeted by a curvy, well-endowed woman with light mocha skin. Her black curly hair formed a soft, bouncy afro that faded into a neutral brown at the ends. As for her attire, she was wearing a tight black dress with long sleeves and a low "v" tailored into it; embellishing her chest. As I gazed upon her, I noticed a large section of fabric missing near her left foot tapered up and ended on her left hip. Thankfully her garments covered everything necessary, but it clearly left the temptation for her future victims to desire more. Although she was standing plainly in front of us, I could not see any wing associating her with being an Archangel. Through this, I assumed that, much like Azrael, the dress she wore was her wings that wrapped around her body.

This thought also led me to fear what she would display if she decided to show off those appendages since she showed off a lot of skin with no apparent straps. Besides her dress, this woman also wore a golden necklace with a large heart-shaped pendant, sizable golden hoop earrings, and golden bracelets. When she saw us enter, she began to hop slightly up and down while lightly clapping her hands, causing everything about her to

188

bounce. "Oh yay! New playmates!" She shrieked. I don't know why, but this caused another feeling to rise within me. This woman is voluptuous, beautiful, and perky, while even though I know I'm attractive, I'm still a walking skeleton. I can leave a lot to be desired while she is in the game of fulfilling them. Was I jealous? After seeing what she was doing, I turned to Shameis to gauge his reaction. Although his iris was a bright pink due to the realm of lust, his expression gave off more of a creeped-out and worried vibe.

"I don't think we are interested in what you're selling..." Shameis sputtered, causing her to stop her display while relieving some of my jealousy.

"Oh, come on. You'll never have another chance to be with an Archangel." She offered seductively as she slowly began to approach with a lustful gaze.

"Except we already have a Seraph inside us." Shameis declined with a double entendre. I nearly choked on my laughter when I processed his claim and watched as the archangel froze in place and began to laugh uncontrollably.

"Fair enough." She squeezed out between gasps before backing off and turning her attention to me with an attempt to compose herself. "So you're the first human to ever service us Archangels? You're cute. If only I knew about you before this trial, maybe I would have pulled you away from Azrael and kept you for myself."

"No, I think I would have preferred Azrael's command over what you have in mind." I rejected.

"That's what they all say before getting a moment with me," she suggested lustfully. "But I suppose that you also are not affected by my aroma."

"Thankfully, I am not. However, I do believe that Zatael has proclaimed that we are under his protection." I rebutted.

"Then I guess we are going to have to do this the hard way," The Archangel shrugged as she turned away from us and showed off the realm we were in. "This room is part of what is known as the Chambers of the Wanting, Specifically, the waiting room." This finally broke my attention from the scandalous woman, to which I examine our new surroundings. I saw that we were standing in a square room no longer than ten feet in any direction. The walls were covered in a tacky dark pink wallpaper with white pinstripes and various light pink hearts. I could also see that the floor was covered in a soft red velvet carpet, the ceiling was covered in mirrors, and several heart-shaped pieces of furniture were scattered throughout this space. The centerpiece of this room was a massive heart-shaped sofa that could double as a small bed. It was as if this place was trying to look like a stereotypical sleazy motel. If they were to take away all the elements that add to this place's 'ick factor' and replace them with standard features, this place wouldn't be that bad. Basically, keep the carpet and replace everything else. I like the way it feels on my bare feet.

Anyways, besides all those parts of this room, I noticed an oak door in the middle of each of the three walls I could see. I did look behind us to where the portal used to be and was greeted by a wall with matching wallpaper but no door. "And these doors lead to the Chambers where you will face what you desire most. This trial will consist of three parts, one part behind each door. Kind of like Michael's trial, but far more intense. Each of you will go into these doors and face what you covet most. If you can get out without succumbing to your desires, you win. My trial is just that simple, just not that easy. Oh! And do remember, souls can lust over many things, not just love." She laid out before turning back to us. "Any questions?"

"Yeah," Shameis let out. "I can tell that you are clearly meant to be Aphrodite for the Ancient Greeks, or maybe Venus to the Romans, but what is your name now?"

190

"Jophiel, The Archangel of beauty." She answered smugly as she poofed up her hair with her hands. When she finished peacocking, she then strutted over, slid between us, and forced us to let go of each other. Once we were separated, Jophiel interlocked her fingers with mine in the same fashion Shameis and I were. Then, after grabbing onto me, she led me toward the door on the right wall. "You're up first, sweetie," she whispered, to which I immediately began to freak out.

"Wait! Why isn't Shameis coming with me?" I fretted as I turned back while trying to reach out for him. I could see he was worried and was trying to follow, but it was as if he was stuck in place.

"Because he needs to see what you desire most. No good relationship is based on jealousy." She answered as she pulled me up to the oak door.

"But we were holding hands to make sure we wouldn't get separated," I informed her, but she obviously didn't care. Instead, she reached to the doorknob with her left hand and opened it to reveal an empty pitch-black space. "No!" I did not want to be left alone in nothingness while not knowing what I needed to do. Not again! I tried my best to prevent her from putting me in there, and I was doing a pretty decent job at defying her strength. "I don't want to go in there."

"Don't worry!" She grunted while trying to push me beyond the doorway. "Your boyfriend will be in my safe, tender, and loving hands." She assured me, which did not comfort me in the slightest. Wait... Did she just call him my boyfriend? Apparently, this was enough of a distraction to allow Jophiel to give me one last shove that sent me stumbling into the darkness. Once I found my sense of stability, I turned and watched as the archangel closed the door. Straight away, I ran in the direction that the light from the waiting room once originated, but stopped when I realized I had passed where it had been. I was trapped in here while that succubus could do whatever she wanted to my partner. Upon learning that, I felt the start of a nervous breakdown build up within me as I freaked out over how quickly everything was transpiring. I felt myself begin to hyperventilate, shiver, and sweat, but almost as quickly as it started, I felt a rush of calmness wash over me.

"No, everything will be okay." I thought to myself as I began to justify the situation. "I've been playing their game all by myself for a very long time, and he has just recently come into play. I've experienced darkness like this before, and I've come out the other side. Yes, he is a crucial part of why I still exist, but he is not the most important thing to think about right now. I need to focus on what I need to do to get past this and trust that he will do the same. We must not succumb to the lust of this realm, and I hope the Worldforger will be able to help us stay on our path. All I need to do is push forward." I muttered to myself as I began to take my first step deeper into the darkness.

Suddenly, the darkness lightened as a scene around me became visible. Within seconds, I found myself standing in what seemed to be a small, concrete bunker that was no bigger than the room I was just in. This new place was trashed! There was a hodgepodge of mangled computer towers sitting on top of a damaged table and underneath a wall of damaged monitors. It was as if someone swung a baseball bat at it all, leaving components scattered across the room. Much like the computers, there were stacks of shredded documents and torn books littered throughout the room. I could see bloody rags and clothes tossed into the corner mixed in with used gauze and other bandages, two overflowing trash cans, and scraps of crumpled-up paper littering the floor. It even looked like whoever did this adhered documents to the wall opposite the computer monitors. At least that's what I initially thought.

192

As I carefully maneuvered through the mess, I examined the wall of papers and found that these were not pasted with randomness. Instead, it was rather meticulous. The paperwork consisted of pictures and newspaper clippings haphazardly connected by red strings of yarn flowing in a clockwise circle around the organized chaos. I've seen one of these before! If I recall correctly, I'm pretty sure it's called a "conspiracy theory" board, and whoever made this was trying to prove something about a malicious person! So, I followed the strings while starting in the top right of the story and found several titles of news articles. In order, they read: "United States Government Hires Premier German Scientist," "German Doctor to Create World's First Super-Soldier.", "German Scientist Kills Thousands in Failed Super-Soldier Experiment.", "German Scientist Resigns, Now on the Run After Children Bodies Found." and ended with "Child abducted Near Chicago Cemetery." These newspaper clippings had a second piece of string that led to a large photograph of Victor Jakelyde directly in the center of the board. I knew this man was vile when I saw his aura, but I never had the whole story. I don't even need to read these articles to understand how terrible this man is! This is sickening! I guess it's true what humans say; The scariest monsters are often found in human skin. Yet, this can't be right. If thousands of people had died this way, I would have remembered such an event. Mass casualties are hard to forget. This had to be the realm feeding into my desire to take this man away from his self-proclaimed profession.

So, trying to distance myself from that hatred, I examined the room again. This time I noticed a piece of furniture that seemed relatively unscathed from the carnage engulfing the rest of the room. On the wall across from where I entered, and adjacent to the wall of newspaper clippings stood a tall and black one-door cabinet. Some scratches revealed it was wooden with a black finish. It also had a cracked mirror connected to the front of the door that reflected me and the rest of the room. I know how mirrors work, but I was startled by the reflection. This was the first instance in a really long time where I was able to see what I honestly looked like, and if this was correct and not the realm feeding into my desires, I could see I was still young. There was no single wrinkle or pimple on my flawless light olive skin, nor could I see any gray strands in my long flowing black hair. There wasn't even discoloration in my hazel eyes. It was as if I didn't age a day after being plucked out of my life. How old would that make me? Twenty-five? I didn't realize that I would still look this good after all this time! "No wonder Shameis is interested in me." I joked to myself. As I continued to gaze at my reflection, I caught a glimpse of a humanlike outline standing on the other side of the glass.

Apprehensively, I took a step back while realizing that this was a two-way mirror. I couldn't exactly see to whom the silhouette belonged, but I assumed it had to be from someone watching my progress. So, I reached for the cabinet's handle on the right side of the box and attempted to open the door, but it was locked. The thought of breaking the glass did cross my mind, but I noticed a small switch hidden on the right of the cabinet near the handle. Immediately, I realized its purpose and flipped it to the opposite position, which in turn caused a lightbulb to illuminate and reveal a mannequin wearing a familiar set of clothing. I could clearly see that this thing was displaying the costume I had come to recognize as The Ile. With that realization, I spun around to look at the room and pieced together that this was Shameis's former base of operations. By the state of disarray, I had to assume that this was Victor's goon's handiwork from searching the base for any vital information after capturing Shameis the first time.

194

While looking back at the room, I noticed that there still was no sign of this trial's ending. I agree that Shameis becoming The Ile again is not really a desire, but getting rid of Victor is. I rejected the board and have no attachment to the suit, so what else do I need to do? Besides the cluttered mess, the only part of this room that I didn't correctly inspect was the desk. So, after taking everything else in, I crossed the trash-covered floor. As I saw before, it was primarily piles of damaged books, torn papers, and a heap of computer parts. Except, I could now see a detail I missed previously and wouldn't have seen from across the room. There was a note with the nickname Shameis gave me next to a glass syringe with a mysterious liquid mixed in with the mess. Being the curious person I am, I opened the note and read it.

"Grim, I've found a way that allows us to be able to be together. Take this, and you'll be human again." Without hesitation, I dropped the note and picked up the needle to examine it thoroughly. The liquid was shimmering a gold color while excreting a similar light to what I saw in Azrael's and Shameis's iris when the angel and Seraph were exerting their Angelic power. Is it possible to restore a soul? No, this can't be right. This has to be a trick. I just saw that I was human. What I need is a vessel to host my soul. Some liquid couldn't help, right? Am I human? Maybe my reflection was the trick? I needed to double-check, so I walked to the middle of the room to look at myself again.

"No!" I shrieked the moment I saw the reflection of the skeletal curse I possessed while on earth. "But... I just saw my skin... I thought I was human... but wait... how is there a reflection? I thought I left the light on."

"Take the serum." A soft voice instantly echoed in my head.

"No... I shouldn't... What if Shameis needs my power? What if we need Zatael?" I hesitantly defied.

"Take the serum!" It ordered once again, this time much louder.

"Well, I do want to have a normal relationship with someone. And I know Shameis likes me in the same way I like him. So maybe our love would be worth the sacrifice?" I justified the request as I rolled up my left sleeve and held the tip of the needle to a vein I could see in my forearm. "Will it make me human again?"

"Take the serum!" The voice ordered once again with an ever-increasing volume.

"But me taking this and becoming human won't fix Shameis's gauzed face or metal arm." I countered.

"TAKE THE SERUM!" The voice now boomed.

"But, things are good the way they are." I hesitated.

"TAKE THE SERUM!" The voice boomed once again as my skeletal reflection stretched out of the mirror and across the room. As it approached, it whipped at me in an attempt to grab my right wrist so it could forcibly plunge the needle into my arm.

"No!" I shouted as I backed away. I also pulled my right hand and needle away before moving it down to my side. "This isn't right! This isn't real! I... I need to get back! I'm not a monster! You can't be me!"

"TAKE THE SERUM!" It boomed again, but this time loud enough to cause me to try and cover my ears.

"NEVER! Shameis NEEDS ME!" I shrieked. "If you want this so bad, then you take it!" I barked as I threw the syringe at the outstretched skeleton. I watched as it phased through the manifestation before coming in contact with the previously cracked mirror. The impact then caused both the mirror and the glass syringe to shatter. Eerily enough, the manifestation of my skeletal form suddenly was covered in spider-like cracks as its demeanor transformed from aggression to sorrow. Finally, it again reached out toward me, and as it did, it began to morph its shape

196

into a woman wearing a red t-shirt and blue jeans with red hair and pale skin. "Lilith?" I wondered as I took a step toward her. The look in her eyes was one of pure terror.

"Please! Help me! I'm so sorry! I didn't mean for this ta happen!" She admitted before shattering like the mirror, except as she shattered, the pieces vanished instead of scattering across the paper-covered floor. This just left me and the mannequin wearing The Ile's super suit to stare at each other. It still blows my mind that Shameis used to wear this thing while running around the streets of his city to fight crime. As I continued to stare at it in shock over what had transpired, I noticed something peculiar. Reflecting off the goggles on the mask was a shimmer of bright light.

Immediately after seeing this, I turned to the opposite wall and found a heavy metal door acting as the entrance and exit to this room. All the creases around it were glowing a bright pale light, symbolizing that I was able to go back! I guess my wanting to be human again was my greatest desire, and in hindsight, I know is obvious. So, without a second thought, I rushed over the disastrous floor and grabbed onto the door's handle and pulled it open. I was instantly greeted with Shameis standing in front of the door with the love-themed room and Jophiel sitting on the heart-shaped futon as his background. Strangely enough, the futon had rotated to face the wall that I was re-entering through. Without a word, he pulled me out of the room I was in and into himself so he could give me a firm hug. It felt like it lasted quite a while, and it was wonderful to feel again.

"Is this a sign that something bad happened while I was gone?" I joked timidly while fearing the answer.

"I wish!" Jophiel answered. "But your Killjoy wouldn't let me do anything. He was too busy worrying about you."

"Then what is this for?" I questioned Shameis, to which he let go of me and backed up a bit so he could get a better look at me.

"We saw everything that went on. I know what's going on between us is a problem, but we will figure something out. We will make it work." Shameis said bluntly.

"So you do have feelings for me? It's not just the pink in your iris from the realm of lust?" I then cross-examined optimistically.

"Of course!" He admitted. "No other person has given me the dedication that you do, and superheroing does not provide a lot of extra time for a love life. Lilith was the most commitment I've given to a relationship in my adult life, and that wasn't even my doing. But I'm willing to take a chance on a literal soulmate." I knew it! I knew it wasn't just this realm. I mean, maybe it is causing these emotions to be shared more effortlessly, but at least I know that they exist.

"I'm glad the feeling is mutual," I muttered as I blushed.

"Wait... What do you mean my iris is pink?" Shameis then exclaimed as he lifted his metal hand up toward his eye.

"Oh! I completely forgot I didn't tell you. Your iris has been changing color with every realm we enter. It's as if it is showing your emotion, like a mood ring, while filtering out the emotions given to you by the realms. Maybe even for the both of us since I haven't really been affected either."

"Alright, love birds!" Jophiel again interrupted in an attempt to push us along. "If you two are just about done, it's Mr. tall, muscular, and mysterious." I then watched as she peeled herself off of the couch, walked over to us, and grabbed onto Shameis's left hand to pull him away. I tried to follow them, but it felt as if I was stuck in place.

"While I'm in there, she's going to try and proposition you. Don't fall for it!" He warned as he was being led away toward the door directly across the room from where I was put.

"Don't worry, she's not my type!" I assured him.

198

"And what is your type?" She then inquired as the two of them reached the door.

"Men," I answered simply. Instantly, she looked at me with a look of intrigue that I didn't care for. Once there, She opened the door, Shameis walked in, and Jophiel closed it behind him. Once it was just us two in this room, she snapped her fingers which caused the couch to rotate clockwise until it was facing the door Shameis had entered.

"Why don't you come join me?" She muttered seductively, which put an uneasy feeling in my stomach. I then watched as she slowly sat on the far left end of the couch. Trying not to be rude, I did walk around so I could take a seat and did so at the far right end, leaving a lot of room between us. The moment I sat down, she repositioned herself to stare at me, worsening my uneasy feeling. Shameis really needs to hurry up in there, so I don't have to be alone with her. Will I get to see what he has to face? I only assume I will since Shameis mentioned watching what I encountered. Why is she staring at me? I know it's because she wants me to succumb to desire, but I do not desire this. And knowing that she is an Archangel doesn't help the matter. I mean, She is only the second archangel I have ever been alone with, if I don't include whatever Lucifer is, and she is the second to want something from me. Shameis, please hurry up.

GRIM

Chapter
Seventeen

I don't know why I'm all of a sudden feeling like this about Shameis, and I can't tell if I'm enjoying it. I've been alone for thousands of lifetimes. I am an independent and self-sufficient woman! So why does it feel like my insides are twisting, not that Shameis and I are apart? Is it because of the realm of lust, trying to have me fall for the desire of a relationship with him? Maybe this is Zatael's desire at work? He finally had a taste of freedom and now is trying to keep us together.

On the other hand, this could be because both issues are working in tandem. The realm of lust could be perpetuating my wanting to be near Shameis while Zatael is trying to pull us together. I've always thought the universe to be strange, but I'm starting to realize it is far more complicated than I could've ever imagined with every realm we visit. Nevertheless, my desire and circumstances leave me here, sitting on a heart-shaped couch anxiously waiting for Shameis to return. And Jophiel continuing to make the situation unnecessarily strained didn't help my emotions and overactive thought process. I know I'm overthinking the situation. My desires are my own, and I know that an Archangel cannot force me into service. That is something that can only be consensual. Still, it doesn't help that an attractive and overtly sexual woman will not stop staring at me with her lustful gaze. Perhaps it comes with the territory of being that archangel over this realm? I really shouldn't be the judge over the books I haven't read. Still, she could stop staring at me for a few seconds.

"So, how does being on this side of the wall work?" I forced out as I turned toward Jophiel while trying not to make eye contact.

"Oh, you'll see in a bit." She responded softly as she sat with back was leaning against the armrest and feet on the seat; leaving her knees near her line of vision.

"How long would that be?" I then inquired while turning back to the door.

"I'm not a fan of awkward situations. Are you?" She redirected as she began to lean forward as if she was trying to approach.

"Awkward situations don't bother me as much as they used to," I answered as I slightly turned my attention in her direction. Out of my peripheral, I could see that she was now on her hands and knees as she slowly approached in a crawl. This act instantly enveloped my attention as I turned to stare her in the eyes. "I am not interested."

"It's because I'm a woman, right. But, you know, I can turn myself into a man if you'd like me to." She followed as she looked me up and down.

"No!" I barked. "I'm not interested in anything you're trying to offer. All I'd like is to focus on this trial, so Shameis and I can get out of here."

"But he'll be in there for a little while. He won't even know anything will happen out here." She muttered in an attempt to persuade me.

"I said no!" I barked again. "Besides, you're an Archangel!"

"What does my status have to do with anything?" She scolded me as she moved back into her original position.

"Shameis and I know that you're working for the Lightbringer, and the Lightbringer is the Mastermind as to why Victor put us into this mess," I answered bluntly. "All you Archangels have done is mess with us. You've rigged these challenges with that intention of forcing us to lose. Clearly the Lightbringer thinks he can take Shameis's body if we aren't in the way."

"Well... I know that Gabriel wasn't too awful on you guys. And maybe I do not want to be either?" Jophiel rebuttled while rotating herself, so she was in the same position I was. "All I was looking for was a little fun, but neither of you is letting me! There aren't many visitors that I could go multiple rounds with. After all, I am the Archangel ruling over the realm of lust. But judging me based on my angelicness would be like judging you because you're just a ferryman."

"What do you mean by just a ferryman?" I picked out as I turned to scowl at her. I'm not just a ferryman, I am THE ferryman. It is just like an archangel to belittle a soul that isn't at their level. As I observed her, I watched as my question caused her to look at me blankly for a few seconds before finally responding.

"I was referring that you, as a Ferryman of souls, are unique because you are half of a Seraph inside you." she stammered before falling silent as we both turned to the wall ahead of us. "You know that you can't be with him, right?" She then mumbled after a few more seconds had passed. This question struck deep.

"Wh... What do you mean?" I struggled to get out. "Our souls are connected." This caused Jophiel to turn her head back toward me. Thankfully, the lust in her eyes had dissipated.

"Exactly. By a third soul. One of the most powerful souls in existence. As long as Zatael exists within you, you'll never be able to embrace each other." She answered, causing a feeling of defeat to roll through my body. I thought this was the case, but I didn't want it to be true. Of course, the all-powerful being inside us wouldn't allow us to be together. He'd never let us touch without conjuring himself, and he'd never let himself play the third wheel in a mortal's game. But then, Jophiel muttered something that, unbenounced to her, would render her point mute. "If you two want to be together, you should release the Worldforger and let the Lightbringer take the body."

"But the Worldforger is the only reason we are connected and why Azrael hasn't blown me into cosmic dust." I debated.

"The Lightbringer would keep you together." She tried to assure me, but I doubted her claim.

"The goal of all of this was to get Shameis back to earth, so he can stop Victor from hurting more innocent lives. And Victor somehow works for the Lightbringer. So if we gave up this easily, then we would doom the earth." I pointed out while refusing her offer.

"How are you two able to say the same thing when not being together?" She then let out with a chuckle. "Fine, if you want to keep going, then I guess it's time for the show to start." After stating this, she then leaned back and pointed to the wall. Following her finger, I looked to the wall and watched as it began to vanish and presented Shameis standing in a cement room. I was fascinated to see that where Shameis was elements that combined Victor's operating room with a morgue. The holding cage and both sets of upper and lower white cabinets were all present on the left side of the room. At the same time, multiple operating tables and a wall of square morgue drawers were present on the right. Then directly across from where Shameis was standing sat a familiar bald man with his back toward all of us. He was sitting at a desk and typing away on his computer. As I watched in rage, Shameis slowly crept toward the figure. I may not've been able to see his face,

204

but I could feel the anger radiating from his soul. This was precisely what I was expecting to see as Shameis's greatest desire. The one issue is that I never took a minute to think as to what we would do once we finally found Jakelyde. Presumably, we would have him thrown in jail. After all, Shameis is a hero. Well, he was... Six years is a long time to be out of commission from a profession. At least the injections that separated Shameis's soul from his body instantly prepared us for an encounter like this.

Just then, the sound of metal rattling began to fill the silent room. As I tried to figure out the source of the sound, I noticed Shameis's robotic hand began shaking from what I thought to be the anticipation. This finally caused Victor to look up from his computer monitor, but he still didn't turn around. "It's about time you've come back to me." He muttered causing Shameis to stop in his tracks and the rattling to ceased. After a few moments of silence, Victor returned to what he was working on while continuing to speak. "Lilith, come over here so I can assign you your next task," to which Shameis took that as an invitation to charge the man. Within the blink of an eye, Shameis reached the seated doctor, thrust his robotic hand against the back of Jakelyde's neck, and forced Victor's head to smash into the keyboard. Seeing this caused me to sit straight out of shock. How violent of a hero was Shameis if this was the first action he would make toward his adversary? Not greeting or interacting. Straight to the attack. Then again, I would probably do the same thing in his shoes.

After this initial display of force, Shameis pulled Victor back into an upright position before letting go of the doctor. After the surprise attack, Victor slowly peeled himself out of his cushioned chair and turned to face his assailant while holding his forehead. "Who are you..." Victor questioned in a daze before realizing who was standing before him. Instead of responding or giving Victor another second to continue his thought, Shameis grabbed Victor by the front of his neck and lifted him into the air. I was so surprised by Shameis's ruthlessness that I instinctually rose to my feet. I'm not sure if it was the shock or increased horror, but this was the only thing I was able to do. I've never seen Shameis act like this before! Was this the action of a vengeful hero? Or was this an action of pure hatred? What happened to the man that was cracking jokes with me in the face of Archangels? Although I know Victor deserved so much more than this, I don't like how Shameis is acting. I really hope that this was just the intense emotions the realm of lust was fueling him with.

"Who am I?" Shameis questioned with a growl in his voice. "Here's a hint. You killed me! TWICE!"

"Isaac?" Victor struggled to get out of his clenched vocal cords. "How? The Lightbringer was meant to take your body." With that, Shameis grunted and threw Victor toward the left side of the room. The force and trajectory caused Victor to fly into the middle of the upper cabinets before falling to the floor. Upon impact, the wood blew out, and everything inside spilled out on top of the grounded Doctor. Seeing this, Shameis started to approach as Victor used the lower set of cabinets as support while trying to stand up.

Out of shock, I rushed toward Shameis to talk some sense into him but was stopped by the invisible wall. Yes, Victor deserves to pay for everything he has done, but Shameis can't kill him. After all, if you murder a murderer, the number of murderers hasn't changed. Also, this wasn't really him! So, in horror, I watched as Shameis reached the manifestation of Victor just as he was up to one knee. Shameis then stood over Victor and watched as the old man struggled to get up. After running out of patients, Shameis grabbed onto the back of Victor's neck with his

206

ight hand and forced him up. Once on his feet, Shameis then placed his left hand onto the front of Victor's neck while letting go with his right, and in one swift motion, Shameis pushed Victor onto the counter of the lower section of cabinets so that Victor was pinned with the back of his head against the concrete wall. That was when Shameis pulled back his right arm and formed a fist.

I knew exactly what was going to happen next. This realm wanted Shameis to feed into his greatest desire and Shameis could give in so easily. I swear it looke like Shameis was about to pop Victor's head like a balloon. We were one swith motion away from genuinely losing. Was this how Shameis felt when watching this realm nearly tricking my into taking that fake serum? For me, I lost all sense of reality the moment I found my test, so I'm sure he has no idea if what he is facing is real or fake. Now, if I was allowed to be with him, I think could talk him down. Thankfully, it looked as if Shameis was facing the same mental conundrum I did since it appeared that he was frozen in place and contemplating his decision.

Just then, Victor's voice broke the tension. "I understand. Do it."

"How could you possibly understand?" Shameis shouted after leaning toward his his adversary.

"I've gotten away with so much over the years. I tortured you, ripped your life away, and then ended up killing you. I've always been one step ahead of you, but now you've caught me, my old friend. Now my chickens have come to roost. You have come to exact your revenge, and I deserve it." Victor whimpered. I really wish I could gauge Shameis's reaction, but I still couldn't see his eye. All I could see were dramatic shadows being cast across Shameis gauze covered face due to this poorly lit room. "What are you waiting for? Go ahead! Kill me!" Victor barked.

"No! No, no, no. That was just Lilith trying to coax Shameis to give in to his desire as she did to me!" I shouted even though he wouldn't be able to hear me. Shameis was right. I really should not have trusted her. I'm glad that the Angels have taken her back!

"Well, of course, it is. Did you think that a mortal soul would succumb to lust if it was solely on themselves? There is always an external force pushing them to do what they do. No soul is born inherently good or evil, but with the slightest nudge, we will see who they will become." Jophiel spilled out before Lilith, portraying Victor, spoke up after a few seconds of her and Shameis's prolonged silence.

"I knew ya didn't have what it takes ta be done. This is why Tha Lightbringer needs ta take your body. I'm not even sure how ya made it as a vigilante for as long as ya did. You're a coward. You're weak. No wonder tha Doc was able ta beat ya so easily. Ya couldn't even save a child." She mocked as she tried to wiggle out of Shameis's grasp, but then, Shameis let out a massive cry before forcefully thrusting his metal hand forward faster than I could react. Within a millisecond, The sound of metal crashing through stone could be heard as a cloud of dust filled the room.

"No! Shameis! What have you done!" I shouted as I pounded on the invisible wall separating us. "No..." I felt my heart sink in my chest. This was his trial, everything I've done was for him, and he just threw it all away. I guess even Zatael wasn't strong enough to guide the desire of a human soul. Why did he have to fall under the pressure? I guess have no room to talk. The only reason I didn't fail is because my fear of being a monster outweighed my desire of becoming human again. Even though this realm made me feel like I could eventually be human again. "I guess you won, Jophiel," I admitted as I slowly walked away from the wall and slumped back into my seat.

208

"As nice as it is to hear you admitting defeat as, I do believe that this is not over," Jophiel uttered, which caused me to perk up and continue to watch. Through the debris-filled air, I could hear the exasperated breathing of Shameis. I could listen to the frustration and anger leave his body with every breath. Finally, as the cloud began to dissipate, I could see that Shameis was now facing us with his robotic hand embedded in the concrete, to the right of Lilith's head. Now, when I say Lilith's head, I don't mean Lilith appearing as Victor, but I actually mean Lilith. Just like how my skeletal reflection turned into her. "You really should have more faith in your partner." Jophiel then let out.

"Pathetic." Lilith patronized Shameis, cutting off his sorrow. "You're pathetic. Ya had one job. All ya had ta do was kill me, and ya couldn't even do that right."

"You're not worth my time, Lilith," Shameis muttered as he forcefully pulled his arm out of the wall before beginning to walk toward the exit of the room.

"Ya really think ya can beat the Doc by bein' soft?" She continued to mock.

Upon hearing that, Shameis froze in place and started to address her. "Just because my tactics are brutal does not mean I am willing to take a life." He mumbled softly as he hung his head.

"But some people deserve ta burn in hell." Lilith disputed as she rolled off the countertop.

"Are you speaking from experience?" He responded while picking up his head. Then, finally, I was able to see his iris, and just as I felt, it was the blazing red of rage. "I was not a murderer while on the earth, and I am not one now. Just because I will be reborn as a monstrous shell of myself does not mean I am willing to kill."

"Wouldn't ya sleep betta' if ya took anotha murdera of the streets?" She cross-examined while trying to poke holes in his moral code.

"How could I?" He retorted as he spun around to face Lilith. "The hydra that is villainy will always grow two more heads when one is removed. So if I decided to kill one, I would need to kill them all. But there is nothing more that people fear than to be locked away." He explained before turning back toward the door he entered through. "Now, if you don't mind. I'm leaving." he uttered as he walked over to the door he entered though, and turned the doorknob. The moment he did this, the transparent wall and door quickly reappeared. Seeing that he was coming back, I promptly hopped onto my feet and rushed over to the door he was re-entering through. After seeing that display, I was hesitant to embrace him while still elated that he did not succumb to his temptations.

"Is that how I looked when you returned?" He joked rhetorically as soon as he laid his eyesight while the door closed behind him. His iris was still beet red, so I could tell that his emotions were still running high.

"Are you okay?" I muttered.

"Yeah. That was no joke. I'm sure it seemed easy to walk away, but I had a voice in my head telling me to end him. I wanted to put my fist through Victor's skull." He confirmed.

"That's exactly what happened to me, except the voice really wanted me to inject myself," I assured him.

"Too bad I didn't. We could've finally gotten rid of Lilith." He joked in response.

"I'm starting to understand why you don't trust her." I let out as I approached my partner while grabbing onto his metal hand and gazing longingly into his eye. "We will stop him. I promise." I then mumbled. This finally caused the red in his eye to subside as it returned to the pink this realm was feeding through him.

210

"I'm holding you to that." he chirped pulled me into a tight hug.

"Alright! One last chamber to clear!" Jophie quickly projected as the sound over her voluptuous body hopping off the couch and onto her feet could be heard. The noise, in turn, cause Shameis and I to seperate as I turned to see what she was doing. "I was really hoping one of you two would give in to your desires before we got to this point, but I guess we will see how this is going to." She let out exacerbatedly as she walked towar the final door

"Which one of us is going to have to do this again?" I inquired as Shameis and I began to followed her.

"Well, there are three of you, right?" Jophiel questioned in response while peering over her shoulder.

"Thankfully, no. We do not want to be affiliated with Lilith." Shameis answered. "That's why I left her behind in there."

"Not her. I refer to the Worldforger." Jophiel redirected as she turned to look at us after reaching the door.

"You really are going to test the desires of a Seraph?" I responded. She has to be joking, right? I understand testing Zatael's strength, but his desires? Can a Seraph even have desires?

"You see, I also think this is a bad idea. Letting the Worldforger loose will probably not be good for us, but I, unfortunately, have orders to follow." She spilled out before opening the entryway for us. "Both of you have to go in."

"And how are we supposed to summon The Worldforger without losing ourselves," Shameis questioned hesitantly.

"No idea, but good luck." Jophiel answered as she gestured to the blackness on the other side of the open entryway.

"Well, I guess we should have expected that we would have to let him out again," Shameis mumbled as he proceeded forward.

"At least we are expecting this time." I followed up as I shadowed him past Jophiel and into the darkness. Like for my section of this realm, Jophiel closed the door behind us and left us in total darkness. Thankfully, I was able to look up to the right of where I was standing and saw Shameis was illuminated the same way he was while in the Void. I was happy that I didn't have to face this by myself. So, While standing here waiting for this final hurdle to begin, my mind began to race. I knew that we would have to sacrifice our spirits to bring forth Zatael, but I was starting to worry. Since we learned he is the reason all of this exists, could he finally take control? I mean, since the Lightbringer, the Lifegiver, and the Timekeeper cursed Zatael, I really shouldn't fear his overtaking. That is, if Gabriel's information could be trusted. But what would happen if we summon the Seraph and he instantly gives in to his own desire? Would that mean Shameis and I would immediately fail? Well, I guess the outcome of this sixth trial rests on Zatael's shoulders. So now all Shameis and I have to do is hold onto each other's hands and hope for the best.

Chapter Eighteen

It is always odd to think about one's desires. I've often thought about what I wanted most while dredging onward as the Ferryman of souls, but I never thought I would face them and then reject them. I've dreamed of being human again for an eternity, but I turned it down. So what does that mean for what I want out of this experience? I agreed to his endeavor with the thought that I would help a lost soul, but so much more has come out of it. Perhaps I simple desire the touch of another on my own flesh without the need of taking them across the void or to have a fear of being taken over by an almighty Angel? My desires have clearly shifted. I feel like my new priorities are to help bring peace to the world as Shameis's grim counterpart. We could be like Inkblot and Moonlight, defeating evil as a super duo. That is... If I can lend him my strengths after we return to the Earth.

There is still the mystery of what will happen to me once we return. I assume my soul will be able to walk the Earth in a similar spectral state I did before, but that's where my train of knowledge ends. Will I remain at Shameis's side, or will the forces at play cause me to return to my role as the Ferryman? Would I be allowed to help Shameis thwart the Lightbringer after dealing with Victor? I have to stay by

Shameis's side, right? There is no way Zatael would allow himself
to be separated after pulling us together. All these thoughts were just
hypothetical. We still have this last part of this realm and one more to go.
So now, it was Zatael's turn to overcome his desires, if he had any, and all
Shameis and I had to do was hold hands. That's why I chose to stand at
his left side after entering this darkness. So, I looked up to him and saw he
was already staring down at me.

"Are you ready?" He inquired while peering into my soul with his
bright pink iris.

"As ready as I'll ever be," I responded as I looked away from his
face and down toward his hand as I wrapped my arm around his and
interlocked our fingers. Instantly, the jolt of electricity associated with
Zatael's coming started to pulse down my spine and into our hands, and
I closed my eyes to endure the pain. At first, this felt like what happened
last time, but it quickly felt as if my hand was starting to warm up. I don't
know why this feeling must change every time we summon Zatael, but
I decided to roll with the pain and clench my grasp even harder. As the
seconds marched on, I could feel the heat start to burn. I tried to ignore
it, but the pain, along with the fact that Shameis and I had not been
possessed yet, broke my concentration. So, I looked down and saw a
blinding ball of light had engulfed our hands up to our wrists. This sight
caused me to freak out, and I tried to pull away from Shameis, but his
grasp was also quite firm.

"Grim, What are you doing? We need to summon Zatael?" He
questioned while focusing on the distance.

"Look!" I mustered out, which did cause him to look down toward
our hands. Upon seeing the orb, Shameis let go of me so we could both pull
away, and as soon as we escaped the light, it exploded into thousands of
particles. With that, I watched as the specks fo light particles scattered all
214

around the darkness before freezing in place. I was overwhelmed with so many emotions that I didn't even know what to feel. There was the fear of whatever just happened and being struck by the light, the relief that there was no longer a burning sensation on my hand, the worry for Shameis's safety, and the overall confusion about what just happened. So, as I wondered about this, I looked around to the aftermath. That was when all my other emotions melted away and left only pure amazement as I stared at the tiny specks of light. The sight was beautiful. It resembled the star-filled night sky prior to the existences of metropolitan cities. Through my awe, I turned back to Shameis and saw that he, too, was looking around at the specks of light that contrasted against the black void.

"What... Just happened?" Shameis stammered as he looked around.

"Something truly remarkable," a deep voice boomed in response. Just then, a single speck of light began to streak across its black background until it positioned itself off in the distance until it reached a resting point fifty yards away. I was about to start approaching, but refrained as more of the specks started to follow suit and began to merge with the first. We watched as they coagulated into an ever-increasing mass and brightness, which eventually caused Shameis and I to turn away. With the merging and traveling of all these specks, a whooshing sound similar to flame in the wind also became audible and increased in volume as a strong wind started to blow. It was so mighty that the gusts pulled the hood off my head and began to blow my hair around. "Be not afraid." The voice then boomed.

"We're not afraid," Shameis shouted in response. I didn't think that the noise coming from the light was that loud, but I could barely hear him over it.

"Then why cower?" It boomed again.

"The light is too bright." I, too, shouted in response.

215

"My apologies... Does this help?" The voice then questioned, this time in a much softer tone as the wind died and the sound muted. Upon hearing this, I cautiously peered toward the light source and was astonished when I saw that every bit of what surrounded us had inverted its color. The darkness was replaced with a sterilizing white speckled with black flakes, and the blinding source of light was replaced with a humanoid silhouette from the waist up that had to be the height of at least ten men. I was so enthralled with what was in front of me that I could feel my eyes starting to strain from the lack of blinking. It was hard to tell, but it seemed like the silhouette was consuming light around it, similar to how a black hole would. "The expression on your face and silence on your tongues tell me you are as shocked by this situation as I am." The voice spoke once again.

"Zatael?" I somehow was able to get out through my shock.

"Correct." The silhouette confirmed as it shifted its position.

"How... What? Wait... If you were able to manifest yourself like this, then why have you needed to take over our bodies?" Shameis sputtered.

"Shameis! You can't question a Seraph!" I quickly scolded him.

"Why not?" Shameis asked. "We defied all the archangels and are plotting to fight a different Seraph. So why can't I question this one? I think we deserve some answers for everything we are going through!"

"Enough!" Zatael boomed, causing us to fall silent. "Although the situation is bizarre, we are one and need to work as one. But, yes, you two deserve clarification over our purpose. Because this section of your trial is meant for me, I am meant to face it. However, I am the Forger of Worlds. If my authority is scrutinized, then the challenge will be manipulated to my will."

"So you're in control of this realm now?" Shameis followed up.

"Precisely, but only due to the design of this realm. But as you know, my presence has an expiration. We must act fast." Zatael acknowledged.

"What do we have to do?" I inquired.

"Nothing," The silhouette answered.

"What is that supposed to mean?" Shameis requested.

"This realm is designed to test one's desire, correct? There is no desire in my soul, as I simply serve as a means to an end. My purpose is inevitable." Zatael informed us.

"If we're not going to be tested, then why don't you let us out so we can move onto the last realm." Shameis pointed out while taking a few steps toward the where door once stood.

"I could, but I would then be forced to retake your vessel. This is also the only chance we will communicate directly within the foreseeable future" Zatael enlightened us, which caused Shameis to walk back to my side.

"Fair point." Shameis agreed. "So, do you have something in mind that will pass the time?"

"I thought I would take this time to address any concern in our partnership." Zatael's suggested as his silhouette gestured to us.

"I like that idea," I muttered as I looked to Shameis, to which he nodded in response.

"Me too," Shameis agreed.

"Since the three of us are in agreement, I would like to start by sharing some misinformation that was provided to you by the messenger Archangel." Zatael Started out. "From what I could decipher, the being was genuine in the answers, but one piece of information lacked clarity about why you two were chosen to be my vessels."

"Are you going to tell us that we aren't that special?" Shameis joked.

"On the contrary. You two are among the most important of all humanity." The Seraph disputed. "Few lineages have the genetic makeup to host celestial beings. Cain, daughter of Adam and Eve. It was correct that you were the first to be born with the ability to host my soul. You were also the purest host. As humanity aged, the likeliness of a candidate as perfect as you would surface. I watched as The Lightbringer tried to claim a host time and time again with no success. And over the millennium, there was never another soul pure enough to play host to the might of a Seraphim. That is until the miraculous conception of the soul known as Shameis Eli, formerly known as Issac Enderson and descendant of Enoch. Thankfully, I was split into two by the being we seek to thwart and was able to claim you both."

"Okay..." I stammered out while trying to process Zatael's claim.

"Who is Enoch?" Shameis then questioned ignorantly.

"A man who was once allowed to live for three-hundred and sixty-five years." Zatael released. "Now, I would like to address the matter of your souls avoiding touch."

"We are sorry about that." I interrupted. "I know that you probably wish to not be trapped within us, but..."

"Do not apologize." Zatael cut me off as he raised his massive left hand toward us before bringing it back to himself. "To fear is human. My time has ended long ago, and the time of the Seraphim is drawing to a close. I only bring up this point to inform you that I have and will only manifest when needed."

"What do you mean? Every time we made skin contact, you were brought out." I pointed out.

"Correct, but that is because you made direct contact twice, and I was the result, so you correlated the events. But neither of you have your bodies here. Both of your constructs are purely your souls. Your clothes, weaponry, and mechanics are all extensions of you. No matter how you've touched, your souls have come in contact. I have not had a chance

218

o inform you, so I am now. From this point forward, as a token of good faith, you have my word that I will not manifest unless needed." Zatael elaborated.

"So all this time, we could've not worried about touching each other?" Shameis cross-examined, to which I apprehensively grabbed onto his left hand. This time, the only feeling I felt was his skin on mine. No pains, burnings, or sparks of electricity in my spine. Just flesh on flesh.

"I'm just happy to know that now," I uttered while staring at Shameis, as he turned to me. I was stunned to see that his irir was not the pink. I mean, there was still a hint of pink, but the base color was definitely hazel. Why was that? Was the effects of this realm been diverted by Zatael's trial? If that is the case, am I seeing Shameis's infatuation with me?

"You're right," Shameis agreed gingerly while staring into my eyes and squeezing my hand tightly. "But that just leaves one more problem." He then verbalized as he turned back to Zatael's silhouette. "I'm sure The Lightbringer is going to throw his Archangels at us in an attempt to evade us, and since it seems that you can't hold your control for more than a few minutes at a time, how do you expect us to challenge the Archangels or the Lightbringer."

"You'll be able to help us on the Earth, right? Gabriel said that the Vale between the realms is not as strict on the Seraphim as the Angels." I added on.

"Unfortunately, I will not be able to manifest my presence on the surface of the earth." Zatael denied. "My condition renders me too weak, and the Vale is too strong. Only the Lightbringer, backed by the might of the former Lifegiver and Timekeeper, has the ability to squeeze through. That is until the Vale is broken."

"Does that mean the Archangels will be able to interfere with us? I continued to ask.

"Is that how The Lightbringer plans to try and take over the Earth?" Shameis Followed up.

"This only acts as an inevitable bridge to the point you refer to." Zatael began to clarify. "Without a permanent conduit or my essence to match the might of The Presence, the Lightbringer stands no chance of fulfilling his desire. However, Cain, once the Vale has broken, all beings will be free to travel to any realm if a means is acquired."

"How do we keep the Vale intact?" I continued.

"That requested information is unknown. My foresight does not show how the Vale falls. All that is known is that the fall is inevitable." the Seraph answered.

"Okay. Let me get this straight... Once we get back to Earth, we will stop Victor from experimenting on people, so he doesn't somehow create a host for the Lightbringer. However, the Lightbringer will be able to get to Earth and try to steal my body while breaking the Vale and allowing who knows what into the Earth." Shameis rambled on, intending to clarify the objective.

"Precisely." Zatael agreed.

"And how do you expect two mortals to take on a seraph and seven Archangels?" Shameis grilled.

"Once the Vale falls, we will be able to summon him again." I reminded him.

"Although that is true, after this moment, you will only encounter me only twice more." Zatael then informed us. "And that leads me to my last declaration before this gathering will adjourn. With this nearly impossible task being placed on your shoulders, I wish to bestow gifts of immense feats upon you."

"What is that supposed to mean?" I then wondered out loud.

"Similar to how several humans have developed abilities, I wish to bestow upon you the strengths that will be needed." Zatael elaborated.

"He's going to turn us into Superheroes?" I let out giddily.

"He's going to make us into POWERED superheroes," Shameis pointed out, reminding me of the fact that he was once a powerless superhero. Like I needed reminding. I was just more focused on the fact that I would help humanity instead of taking their souls.

"Are you two ready for my gifts?" Zatael quickly followed up, to which I rapidly nodded my head. "Good. Shameis. Unto you, I have provided a gift that you may have already noticed; the strength of a Seraph. Although it will appear as above-average strength while on the face of the earth, your physical strength will not be matched by any other while in the nine realms. I lent you my strength when I knew you'd face Micheal in the physical trials, but I would now like to permanently provide this to you. I also offer the knowledge of any mechanical tools you will contact. This will be needed when you return to Earth."

"So that's why I randomly had the knowledge to use this thing?" Shameis pieced together as he let go of my hand to touch his right shoulder.

"No. As I've stated, every bit about you is your soul." Zatael reiterated. "This construct you refer to is a manifestation of your soul. It is part of you. But this ability I am granting you will allow you to circumvent the learning process such a piece of machinery would require. This will be required to unlock it's greatest potential."

"Then I am thankful for this," Shameis uttered as he brought his hand back down to his side.

"Since I am part of you, I know your thoughts and understand that you do wish to remain as human as possible, so I leave you with just these two gifts and your humanity intact." Zatael proclaimed before pausing, which caused me to slump a bit. "Grim, unto you, I proclaim that you will be released from the obligations as Ferryman, but you shall retain all the abilities you have honed in your role. With this, you will have control over access to Yggdrisal's limbs. Furthermore, once on Earth, I will be granting you the additional capability to heal his mortal wounds upon contact. The pair of you shall remain tethered through me. Even with this ability, do be aware you are not immortal. Your vessel can still parish from specific mortal wound, which would inevitably plunge the world into eternal damnation. Is that understood?"

"Yes, sir!" I proclaimed as I bowed my head to the silhouette, elated that I am officially free from my imprisonment. I then looked back up to the silhouette since there was one bit of his statement that puzzled me. "Could you please elaborate on what you mean by controlling Yggdrisal's limbs?"

"You will now be able to open rifts into and from the river Styx. These rifts will lead you to other points within the realm you reside in, as long as you can imagine the location you wish to travel to." He explained.

"The river Styx? Is that the same as the Void between realms?" I followed up.

"Yes." He affirmed.

"Does the healing thing mean she will be able to heal my face?" Shameis quickly interjected.

"No. That wound has long since healed. You're scars will be your burden to bare." He denied.

"But it..." I started to argue, only to be cut off by Zatael raising his massive hand.

"Our time has come to an end. It was a pleasure to meet both of you mortals. Please serve me well." Zatael let out before the whirring noise of wind instantly filled the white nothingness.

222

"Wait!" I shouted as I tried to keep my balance trough all these intense gusts, but it was no use. So, I blocked my face with my left forearm as I reached out and grabbed onto Shameis's left hand with my right. The wind did make it hard to see, but I watched as the black hole that was Zatael's silhouette gradually shifted back into the blinding light we once saw. I guess it was Zatael's power that was causing the change to realm, since as soon as his silhouette morphed into an amorphus blob, the white background with black specks to invert once again. As I continued to watcht he phenomenon, the rest of the particles around us found their way into the orb of light before slowly splitting into two streams of light that flowed toward Shameis and I.

"One last thing!" Zatael boomed over the roar of the winds. "Please remember these last two facts! The Lightbringer's growing madness is his undoing, and no matter a soul's place in the realms, a soul is a soul!" After those words were uttered, the streams of light finally reached Shameis and me, respectively. That was when an enormous flash of light forced me to close my eyes as a burst of energy caused me to let go of Shameis and knocked me off my feet. Strangely enough, the moment I landed on what consisted of the ground below me, both the wind and the noise ceased. So, I opened my eyes and found that Shameis and I were surrounded by nothing again. However, I did notice that Shameis stayed on his feet.

"Are you okay?" He worried as he slowly walked up and stood in front of me.

"Just peachy," I muttered as I rubbed my hand on my sore bottom. "I wish that I could've been given super strength as well." I then joked.

"Well, how about a hand?" He countered as he reached down to me with his left hand.

"Are you sure you want to test this now? The moment he left?" I questioned hesitantly.

"He's part of us. We can't live in fear of him." He answered.

"Right..." I agreed. I was still hesitant about what would happen, but he was right. So, I reached up and grabbed onto him. I was expecting to feel the sensation that has always accompanied Zatael's presence, but instead, all I felt was Shameis' flesh against mine before being hoisted from the ground. Within seconds, I found myself on my own two feet and wrapped loosely in his arms. As he stared passionately into my eyes, all I could feel was pure happiness. This was going to work. Everything about our unconventional relationship will work. I was so happy to know that Jophel was incorrect with her claim. Zatael was entirely on our side. So, what was I to do when in the arms of a man that was willing to accept me for all my transgressions and experiences? Without a second thought, I wrapped my arms around his torso and squeezed him tightly, just before I rested the side of my head on his chest. "I needed this." before letting a somber silence overtake us. I wish I could've left well enough alone, but after a few seconds, I spoke up again and asked "So, what do we do now?"

"Probably go through that door," Shameis uttered, causing me to pull my head up from his chest to look behind me. Sure enough, the oak door we entered though had reappeared and was outlined in a pale glow.

"Great! We get to go to the last realm!" I let out as I left Shameis's arms to take a few steps towards the panel of wood before stopping.

"Exactly. And we know exactly which sin we'll have to overcome... And the Archangel who will try to stop us...." Shameis added as he walked up to my right side and grabbed onto my hand. I still couldn't get over the fact that we are actually allowed to hold onto each other! This is going to need some getting used to. Anyway, while hand-in-hand, Shameis and I walked up to the door. Once we reached it, he let go of me before grabbing onto the door handle with his right hand, opening the door, and gesturing for me to walk through. In turn, I smiled and nodded before doing just as he implied.

I was expecting to see Jophiel waiting for the two of us, possibly with the intent of getting us to succumb to our lust one last time before we left her behind. So I'm sure you can understand the shock I felt when we returned to a barren room. The furniture was removed, the walls were stripped of the heart-covered wallpaper, the two other doors had vanished, and even the velvet carpet that covered the floor was ripped away. All that remained were grayed wooden walls and ceilings with holes in the planks and a cracked concrete floor.

As soon as I heard Shameis close the door we just used, I spun around and watched as it too vanished, leaving nothing but the decaying wood behind. As I watched it disappear, I had the worry that we were now trapped in here, but once I completely lost sight of it, a gust of wind blew my hood off my head and my hair into my face. I, again, spun and saw that the portal to the final realm of sin had opened and was trying to pull us in. "Are you going to put your hood up before we head in?" Shameis questioned over the sound of the whirling winds. I simply shook my head from side to side before reaching my right hand out to him, to which he grabbed onto without a second thought. As soon as I felt his grasp, I looked at him with a smile before nodding my head and leading us across the cold concrete floor and through the portal. This is it, the last of the seven realms of sin. Unfortunately, we will have to go through the Archangel I despise most to achieve our goal.

226

ZATAEL

Chapter Nineteen

An aspect of anticipation always causes a soul to act out of sorts. Through my experiences, I've witnessed several occurrences of terminal lucidity brought upon by the uncertainty of my once inevitable coming. Somehow, the hormones spurred upon by the anticipation in one's soul have always momentarily caused them to bounce back while laying on their deathbed. I could never explain this phenomenon while I walked the earth as the ferryman of souls. These humans knew they were dying, and some were embracing it, yet, to my bewilderment, I watched as many souls somehow made a full recovery before fading away. I've always presumed it was a sick joke the universe played on loving families, but I think I am starting to realize why this would happen.

As both Shameis and I walked hand-in-hand through the portal from the realm of lust into the final realm of sin, I could feel that I was filled with the happiness and anxiousness that comprises the anticipation that I have observed through their auras. After all this time, I was finally able to latch onto another soul, one that is, literally, my other half. One that is willing to stand beside me, even after understanding the evil that I unleashed onto the mortal world. A soul who understands that although I was the first murderer on the earth, my actions were only an accident put forth by fate. My happiness did not want me to let go of Shameis, yet my anxiety told me that thought would be fruitless. With six of the seven Archangels dealt with, the one Archangel that we were going to face last was the architect of my confinement. After learning about what lay beyond my grasp, I should have realized that Azrael is the Archangel that oversaw the sin of Wrath.

My worry now is that even though I've stood up to Azrael before, this upcoming situation is vastly different from the last. Even though I was unaware of Zatael's protection of me, I was at the point of thinking I had nothing left to lose. However, this whole ordeal has changed everything for me, and now, Azrael will try to stop us from completing this task at all costs. Azrael is extremely spiteful and equally vindictive. In my opinion, he is the closest an angel can get to being a demon. I've witnessed him banish tyrants, humanitarians, dictators, and benevolent rulers all to Hell out of spite. I guess you don't become what is known as the Archangel of Death by being caring.

I am not excited to face him. I can't even begin to prepare for what lies before us. I mean, there is no way to know what the trial would be until we experience it, but after learning that I was being kept alive for the sole purpose of being a potential host for the Lightbringer, is there a need to keep me now? If I was taken out of the equation, and subsequently the second half of Zatael, it would probably be easier to persuade Shameis into being the vessel.

As we walked out of the portal into the final realm, one thing I was expecting would've been Azrael to be standing at the other end of the gate, similar to Jophiel. I was expecting him to be waiting for us while we readied for an onslaught. But instead, we exited the portal to a flat, rocky surface that led to a tall rock wall leading up to a plateau. I wasn't entirely sure since we were all but directly underneath the landmark, but it didn't seem to come to a point.

228

As for the rocks that comprised the ground were a reddish, gray material, almost like granite. The sky was a light shade of red and filled with pink, cotton candy-like clouds, while a bright orange sun pierced through them. The sunlight was warming the ground we were standing on, and I could feel my feet starting to burn, but there was no pain. It was as if this heat was trying to penetrate our souls and fill us with a fire of rage. The moment the breeze pelted my face, I began to sweat. What a fantastic realm to be stuck wearing a black, long sleeve, and full-bodied robe. At least my robe was tattered enough for a cross breeze to flow across my skin and it was an excellent decision not to wear my hood. I slowly turned to Shameis and saw that his skin also had a sheen of sweat that glistened in the overhead sun.

"Geez, it's hot!" I grumbled.

"Then take the robe off," Shameis suggested.

"I can't." I continued grumbling.

"Why not? Are they connected to you, or are you not wearing anything underneath them?" He joked as he looked toward me. Once again, the color of his iris changed to match the emotion this realm wanted us to feel. As he stared at me with his blazing red eye, I felt myself begin to blush as I turned my attention from him down toward my feet. "Oh... It's the latter." He answered for himself. "We don't have enough time to unpack all of that right now. We need to get moving."

"Right..." I agreed As I quickly shuffled forward toward the massive rock formation in front of us, but froze after a few steps when a low pitch growl echoed from in front of us. This caused me to stare at the location of the noise, but I couldn't find an origin for it.

"Did you hear that?" Shameis whispered as quickly yet softly walked past me. So I wasn't just imagining things... Good... So, I followed him forward but still couldn't see anything. That was until we

229

were about halfway between the vertical rock face and where the portal once stood. Once we approached this position, I noticed something ahead of us was shifting about amongst the rocks and shadows of the cliffside. I couldn't see what it was exactly, but I could tell it was stalking us while trying to stay hidden.

"What is that?" I inquired as I tried to focus on whatever this creature was.

"Do you see something?" Shameis wondered as he stopped and turned back to look at me.

"Yeah, something is moving over there," I answered. I guess I must've responded too loudly as the creature let out a blood-curdling scream before scaling the rocks.

"We need to catch it!" Shameis shouted as he began to run toward the cliffside.

"There is no way we will be able to! It's moving too fast!" I shouted back at him as I tried to keep up, which caused him to stop dead in his tracks and turn back to me.

"We could if I threw you!" He suggested.

"That is a terrible idea." I shot down instantly. "What we should do is try to cut it off."

"And how do you suppose we do that?" He inquired.

"Zatael said that I can open portals to the Void between realms if we know where we need to go, so we could be up at the top of that cliff in seconds!"

"Right! I forgot about that." He admitted with a chuckle.

"Because you were more focused on the healing I'll be able to do while on earth." I pointed out as I started to walk past him while *pulled* my scythe out. "Now, let's see how this is going to work," I muttered. I didn't know how this was going to work since I've never in control of how I went

230

rom one place to another, but there is a steryotype of me that does depict now such things could happen. So, once I was a fair distance away from nim, I grabbed the staff of my scythe with both hands before slashing at the air. Just as I hoped, a string of light appeared and quickly widened into a similar-looking portal to the ones we've been traveling through. Honestly, I was slightly surprised to see it opened on my first try, but I'm assuming it nad to be because Zatael's grace. So, seeing that it worked, I turned back to Shameis and held out my right hand to him. "Let's go." I let out, to which ne briskly walked up and took my hand to lead him through.

Once in the darkness of the Void, I instantly could feel my energy start to drain. How did not expect this to happen, expecially after learning that is place is one in the male as the mythical river Styx. However, I did notice something wasn't the same as what I'm used to. As the ferryman of souls, when I was *pulled* to the Void, I would have to walk as my energy was drained until the second side of the tunnel was opened. This time, I could see the other end instantly. Strangely enough, it felt like the energy being taken from me was more aggressive than the previous times I was here. Almost immediately, it felt like I was wearing cement shoes. Was this a side effect of using Zatael's power? Whatever it was, I need to lead Shameis across the darkness. At least I knew we weren't going to be here for long. It was maybe twenty steps, but I was thankful that we made it through.

Just as expected, we exited the Void and found ourselves at the edge of the cliff. Instantly after exiting, I looked around to try and find whatever we were chasing, but all I could see was more of the protruding red rocks scattered across the flat surface. As I scanned our surroundings, I noticed a few weapons like swords, shields, maces, and bows were scattered amongst the rocks with plenty of signs that there has been a massive amount of conflict here. It was like we were at the edge of a battlefield. I know that this is the realm of wrath, but were we expected to fight? Were we going to have to fight Azrael? There is no chance we would stand a chance if we had to go up against the Archangel of Death.

"I guess that was easier than trying to fly up here," Shameis admitted as he looked around with me.

"Yeah, but that thing isn't up here." I pointed out as I walked toward the edge and looked over. I was expecting to find what we were looking for, but I didn't expect it to be this close. As soon as I looked over, I saw a pair of glowing red eyes staring back at me. The moment we made eye contact, it let out an ear-piercing screech that caused me to instantly jump back in shock. As soon as I did, I watched as whatever it was launched itself up into the air and over us before landing on the other side. Finally, we were able to get a good look at this... Demon? Is this what they look like?

It was a bipedal humanoid with red, scaly skin and long arms stretched below its knees. It stared at us with a twisted smile full of razor-sharp yellow teeth. It looked like this creature had goat-like legs and hooves with dark gray rocks replacing its fur from the waist down. To match the rock-like features, it had blades that stretched at least six inches off each finger and two long pointed horns placed symmetrically on its forehead. I also noticed as its veins glowed bright orange as if it had lava instead of blood. Overall it looked rather skinny, but I was intimidated by its stare.

"Is that... a demon," Shameis stammered as he slowly backed away from it.

"I... I don't know... It has to be..." I answered timidly as I, too, backed away from it. After seeing us back off, the creature started to stalk us like prey and began to approach. "Stay back!" I shouted at it as I pointed the blade of my scythe at it, to no avail. It just slowly kept creeping forward as Shameis and I backed off to the point that I nearly stepped off the ledge.

"I don't think it is going to stop." Shameis worried as he looked back to see that we had nowhere else to go.

"Then I'm going to make it stop!" I shouted as I decided to be brave and approach the beast. Bad idea. Seeing me step forward caused it to lunge at me with its sharp claws stretched out. I really didn't want to hurt it, but I instinctually swung my scythe and sliced it diagonally across the chest. This action caused whatever this monstrous creature was to fall limply just before it could reach us, and I just stared at it to ensure it wouldn't get back up. I could feel myself start to breathe heavily as anger began to fill up my body.

"That was probably not the best idea," Shameis proclaimed as he came up behind me while placing his right hand onto my shoulder and left onto the staff of my scythe.

"What do you mean by that?" I snapped at him while pulling away.

"If this is the realm of wrath, it is probably best to not act out of malice." He pointed out as he held up both of his palms with the intent of showing he was not a threat.

"It was going to attack us!" I countered.

"Yes, and I am thankful that you protected us. But all I am trying to say is that we still don't know what we need to do." He stated while trying to de-escalate the situation.

"Aren't you the one that nearly bashed Lilith's head in while she was pretending to be Victor?" I questioned while verbally attacking him.

"I regret acting out of malice while in the realm of lust, but now is not the time to have raised tempers." He reiterated through now gritted teeth.

"Whatever." I sharply responded while turning away from him. "Can we at least get away from the ledge? I don't want to fall off."

"Of course." He then muttered before directing me deeper into the surface of the plateau. However, after getting a few yards away from where we left the defeated demon, we heard a spine-shivering cackle come from behind us. Immediately after the laugh crossed our ears, we instantly turned around to see two identical creatures climbing over the edge as the one I had struck down began to return to its feet. I watched as the demon's wound poured out its bright orange blood before rapidly sealing off.

Yes, I was terrified to see those demented smiles, but the rage this realm was pumping into me was overwhelming. The frenzy drove me to charge at the three demons with the intent to attack. I did hear Shameis shout my name, but it was too late. I saw red. After seeing me approaching, the three demons sprung at me. With one shift of my momentum, I skillfully slashed the first demon we encountered across the abdomen and the second across the top of its chest without being touched. They both dropped to the ground instantly, but that was when the numbers caught up to me. As I swung at the third demon, it was able to catch me on my left bicep with its razor-sharp claws. Not only did I feel it leave four cuts on my arm, but I watched as it sliced through my already tattered robe to do it. So, I swung my scythe again and caught the demon in the neck as a response. With one fatal swoop, I decapitated it.

"Grim!" Shameis barked as he grabbed onto my right bicep and forcefully spun me around to face him.

"What?" I snapped back. "They are demons! Monsters! They regenerate! They'll come back!"

"Do you not recall what Zatael said?" He interrogated me. "A soul is a soul! We learned from Micheal that those who lose in these realms become trapped here! Those things were probably once human! And you're hurting them!" As soon as he pointed that out, it felt like the fire within me was instantly snuffed out. Why was I wanting to hurt the souls I so desperately want to protect?

234

"Shameis... I'm sorry..." I muttered as I lowered my weapon. I was expecting to be scolded, and was supprised when Shameis quickly pulled me in and hugged me tightly.

"It's okay," He whispered in my ear as tears began to roll down my cheeks. "It's this realm. I can feel the anger within me swelling up, but I can focus on other things. We just need to figure out what we need to do to get out of here. But I bet those things are too far gone to be..." Shameis went on to make me feel better before being interrupted by yet another set of maniacal cackling. Then, of course, the laugh caused me to turn back around, and I saw the two wounded demons had already returned to their feet as an army of identical beasts were climbing over the edge of the cliff. As I continued to watch in shock and horror, the decapitated body of the last demon I struck limply rose to his feet before bending over to grasp its lifeless head by the horn. It then placed its head back on its neck, which caused it to spring back to life and let out a horrific scream. That scream signaled the rest of the surrounding army to charge at us. "We have to go!" Shameis shrieked as he lifted me into a cradled position before sprinting away from them.

"What do we do?" I inquired as I watched the demons chase us while holding onto Shameis for dear life. "They're right on our tail."

"Can you shoot those light arrows like this?" He returned as he focused on the ground ahead.

"Of course! But I don't want to hurt them." I answered.

"Well, don't aim to kill. Aim to stun." He implored. Now that, I can do. So, as Shameis was running us away, I pointed my scythe behind him with the blade pointed toward me and did as I had before. I pulled on the imaginary line between the tip of my blade and the end of the staff. Once the string of light appeared, I let go of it so it could transform into a bolt of light and go screaming into one of the demons in the front row of the oncoming horde. I watched as the bolt struck the single demon in the knee, which caused it to topple over. In turn, my bolt caused even more behind it to trip and cause a massive pile-up. It was pretty comical to watch, but now was not the time to be sidetracked. I needed to buy us some time, so I continued to shoot off bolts of light into the crowd. And I continued to do so until Shameis stopped running and put me down. "Why are we stopping?" I questioned as I turned to him and watched while he quickly bent over and picked up a rusted sword lying nearby.

"They're surrounding us. We are going to have to fight." He muttered as he gripped the hilt with both hands.

"But we can't. Those things were once human souls." I reiterated his own words.

"Yes, but I'm not letting them kill me." He remarked as he focused on the enclosing horde. I, too, looked around the ever-decreasing unoccupied space as all the piercing red eyes kept coming closer.

"What if we aren't supposed to fight them?" I quickly put forth.

"I am not letting them kill me!" Shameis reiterated.

"Think about it! This is the realm of wrath, and we are standing in the middle of a massive battlefield. Azrael wants us to fight them, and we are in this situation because I provoked them. We chased that first one up here. The first demon sprung at us because I attacked it. After that, more monsters showed up because I kept attacking them, and we are at this point because I was shooting them." I pointed out while still looking at the wall of demons before stowing my scythe back in my robes. "I surrender." I then shouted, which caused Shameis to let out a defeated sigh.

"I really hope you know what you're doing," he muttered as the sound of the sword clanging against the rocky ground could be heard. I was still focused on the incoming demons, so I wasn't looking at Shameis,

236

but I imagined he was also raising his hands as he admitted defeat. At least I knew we were both disarmed. "They're not stopping!" Shameis then pointed out.

"They will once they're close enough to see we won't attack; they'll stop," I responded confidently as the clopping of their hooves increased in volume as they approached.

"Grim!" Shameis shouted with a slight tremble in his voice.

"I got us into this mess! I will get us out!" I declared as I turned to him and then back to the approaching army. "We will not succumb to our Wrath!" I then shouted at the demons. After I screamed that, I noticed that they started to slow down and watched as the demons went from a full sprint to a slight gallop, then to a trot and walk before just stopping to stand around us. All I could do was look around the twenty-foot circle at all of the identical smiles and burning red eyes. Every single one of these demons was precisely the same. All except one. A single demon came strolling out of the wall of monsters. I guess I didn't realize that the demon I decapitated was the first demon we came across, but I realized that fact after noticing the glowing slash across its chest and ring around its neck. "Shameis..." I quickly whispered, to which he whooshed around to see what I was seeing.

As this demon ambled creepily over to us, it pointed to its chest and then to its neck with the talon on its right index finger. "I guess the trial was about staying as nonviolent as possible." Shameis pointed out.

"No, it's not that. Yes, these things want us to be violent, but only so they have a reason to lash out at us." I denied Shameis's claim before speaking directly to the approaching demon. "We will not attack you!" I shouted at it again. This caused it to pause, tilt its horned head, and cackle before preceding closer. While I felt myself trembling, I knew I needed to stay as calm as possible. With this thing's animal instincts, any slight movement could provoke it into attacking, but once it was within arm's length, it raised its right hand as if to intimidate me and show that it was willing to strike me down. "Go ahead. I will not strike back, I deserve what you're about to do. I 'm sorry." I let out as I slowly held my arms out wide and closed my eyes.

Once I did this, I heard the sound of flesh being torn and bones being broken, which instantly caused my eyes to spring open. I was surprised that I didn't feel pain, so I looked around my body to see what happened, but there was nothing. After realizing nothing had happened to me, I looked up to the demon and saw it had vanished. In fact, every single one of them were gone. "See Shameis! I told you refusing to fight in the face of certain death was the key to succeeding!" I boasted as I turned to my partner. That was when I received the frightful sight of him impaled from his back and thought his stomach by the blade of a golden greatsword. He stood there looking down at the blade with both of his hands loosely wrapped around it.

As blood poured out of him, I watched as the tip slid out his torso before he dropped to his knees. Through my panicked sight, I forced myself to look at the assailant and found the heinous, golden-haired angel that I loathed so very much. I wanted to scream, but I couldn't get the air to escape my lungs. I was speechless. I was stunned. I was furious, but I was frozen in place by what I witnessed. This isn't right... It's unfair! How could we be expected to compete when an Archangel snuffs out the one soul that did everything correctly. As I stood motionless, Azrael broke the silence with a single phrase through that smile I wanted to cut off. "I hope your vow of passivation applies to the Angel of Death."

Part Two: Encountering Those that Lie Beyond

Chapter Twenty

This wasn't supposed to happen and shouldn't even be possible. The one excuse Azrael always used as to why I wasn't allowed to vacate my role as the Ferryman of Souls was because Angels were not allowed to interfere with the destiny of humans. He always preached that the universe has a function for every being, and mine was to guide the souls to the afterlife since he could not reach the humans, nor could he hurt their souls. In hindsight, it's obvious that everything he preached was a load of hogwash, but I didn't have another choice but to believe the Archangel. But what is that old proverb? Seeing is believing? Well, rose-tinted glasses be damned, I'm now seeing red.

Why did Azrael have to do this? Was this to punish me after seeing how close Shameis and I have grown? Was it because the Lightbringer ordered him to get us out of the way so He could have Shameis's body? If it were the latter, this still wouldn't solve the issue of needing a soul to bond with. Perhaps it was a ploy to convince me to be the soul he binds to? That would solve the problem of his missing portion of power The Lightbringer needs inorder to face The Presence. The wicked grin on Azrael's face gave me the sinking feeling that this had something to do with all three reasons. If that is the case, they haven't been watching us close enough. Since being with Shameis, I've grown more substantial than ever before.

But at this moment, all I wanted to do was to *pull* out my scythe and destroy Azrael for hurting my partner. I've seen too many people die from wounds like this, and I know that is Azrael's intent. But I couldn't do that. There is no way I could stand up to an archangel alone. So, all I did was stand in a numbing rage as I watched as the cool, deep red liquid that flowed throughout Shameis's veins begun to spill onto the reddish-gray ground beneath his knees. Through my blinding rage, I could see that Shameis was barely clinging to life, which instinctually caused me to run over to Shameis and kneel into the forming pool of blood so that I could wrap my arms around him. I could feel myself start to sob uncontrollably as I squeezed him tightly and focused on Shameis's struggling breath. That was when I remembered that Zatael gave me the power to heal his wounds. So I quickly let go and placed my hands over Shameis's laceration as tried to remember what Zateal just informed us. I'm able to heal Shameis's body while on Earth, but am I able to heal his soul? Hopefully, I pressed onto him with the desire of helping him, but the only result was my robed and hands becoming covered in the cool liquid while the pour slowed to a trickle. Even after seeing that nothing was happening, I still applied pressure to the wound to stop the bleeding while most of my robes became soaked. I didn't even know how Shameis's soul was bleeding, but that didn't matter. I just needed to stop!

"Now, look at what you made me do." Azrael mocked as I saw him begin to slowly walk around us out of the corner of my eye. "This wouldn't have happened if you had just listened to me. I could have saved you all this trouble. He wouldn't be dying here if he had accepted my proposal. But I guess it isn't that big of an issue since The Lightbringer will be able to take this human's body." That statement caused me to look up from Shameis as I tried to stare daggers through my tear-filled eyes.

"Even with the body, the Lightbringer still needs a soul," I informed him through gritted teeth.

"And that's where you come in. So get up and come with me." Azrael then ordered.

"Never! I will never help you!" I barked at Azrael before turning back to Shameis.

"Do you really want to go back to being one of the Ferrymen?" He then questioned. I know that he was trying to get a rise out of me, but this question instantly seared into my brain.

"What, do you mean 'one of'?" I growled as I looked back at Azrael.

"Have you really not put that together?" He answered as he crouched down to look me dead in the eyes. "Of course, there are more than just you that serve me as a ferryman of souls. One hundred and twenty humans die every minute. Do you think you are fast enough to collect all those souls? Ha! You are the slowest ferryman out of the thousands I oversee. You're not special. Why do you think the Lightbringer has that human doctor working on modifying the genetics of his own species? We don't need you to get to Earth. As soon as the Vale is lifted, we will be able to crossover." He boasted before rising back up to his feet. "Now be a good little girl and come with me. If you want to be special, then you will agree to the Lightbringer's request."

"No! I will not leave him!" I shrieked as I quickly wrapped my arms around Shameis and squeezed him tightly.

"This is enough of your insolence! Rise to your feet right now!" He ordered.

"If you want to kill Shameis, you're going to have to strike me down as well!" I defied.

"You dare order an Archangel!" Azrael boomed.

"I have dared once before, and I will dare again!" I shouted back.

"Then I will finish what I started!" Azrael boomed again just before the swoosh of his sword cutting through the air could be heard. Once I heard the sound of our impending demise, I quickly closed my eyes and buried my face into Shameis's chest. I didn't want to die, but I was willing to if it meant that I would be with Shameis forever. And knowing Azrael, I was expecting him to follow through. Yet, quickly after cowering, I felt Shameis's body jerk away from me milliseconds before the sound of clanging metal echoed over the silent caprock. That was when that familiar jolt of energy finally shot up my spine. Yes! Finally, the mysterious member of our trio has come to help us in this dire situation. Frankly, my rage and worry over Shameis's wellbeing almost made me forget that Zatael could spring forth at any second, so I was surprised that it took him this long.

"What... What's going on?" I heard Azrael worry as I looked up to see him struggling to pull his sword out of the grasp of Shameis's right arm.

"These souls are under my protection!" Zatael's voice boomed from Shameis's mouth.

"No... I thought... How could you catch my blade? That arm isn't even real metal!" Azrael questioned in distress. That was when Shameis lifted his head, and I saw that his red iris was glowing once again.

"You can not use Deitanium to strike down the creator of Deitanium!" Zatael boomed as my vision was momentarily engulfed in white light before I found myself floating well above where Shameis's body and Azrael remained. Once in the sky, I glanced at my right and saw that pale-blue glowing orb I noticed in the realm of pride. I was so happy to see that Zatael had come in time to save Shameis! Honestly, for the first time since Zatael began inhabiting our souls, I was elated to see him. I didn't think I would ever be grateful to see an angel. So, turning back to the ground, I watched as the single wing sprouted from Zatael's back as he made his way to his feet.

242

"No. No! This is not your fight! Bring them back!" Azrael screeched while trying to yank his sword out of Zatael's hand.

"You should know by now that the two seek to get rid of are part of me, and I am part of them. Their fight is my fight." Zatael declared as he finally let go of the blade, which caused Azrael to stumble backward. That was when all of Shameis's spilled blood began to return to his body. It was as if the liquid was flowing backward. To try and get a better look at this phenomenon, I circled Zatael and was amazed that the wound on his torso was healing instantaneously. Even the blood that was spat out onto his gauze face-wrappings slowly vanished. Due to the healing process, a wicked scar was left in the wound's place, but I did not mind it since Shameis's torso was already covered in them. "If you know what is best, you will allow us to pass," Zatael suggested.

"You dare command an archangel?" Azrael questioned as he charged at Zatael while swinging his sword, to which Zatael quickly deflected it with Shameis's metal arm. Zatael then swung his left hand as my scythe manifested out of thin air. I watched as Azrael quickly dodged backward while nearly avoiding the blade. Even though it was a counterattack, it seemed that Zatael's intention as not to attack since proceeded to holding out his left hand and point the blade and tip of the staff toward Azrael.

"I dare," Zatael confirmed.

After recovering from Zatael's perry, Azrael aggressively ran his fingers through his long golden lox in an attempt to calm down. "Okay, let's just take it easy. How about I make you a deal? If you agree to back down, I will grant those two splinters a permanent seat as general of the Lightbringer's army. It's a pretty good deal. We'd make sure nothing bad will happen to them, and they'll get to be together!" Azrael offered. Zatael did not respond, continuing to stare directly into Azrael's eyes.

"Like hell, I'll never work for him again! Don't back down! Get us out of here!" I cheered, even though I was pretty sure no one could hear me.

"They have declined your offer." Zatael denied after a long pause, catching me by surprise. He can hear me? .

"Well, I tried... Get Him!" Azrael then shouted as his anger instantly returned. With this command, the horde of vanished demons started to claw their way out of the rocky ground. Within seconds, dust across the rock cap was kicked up, leaving a ring around the Angels. Within seconds, thousands of sets of those burning red eyes piercing through the dust while maniacal laughing grew louder than the sound of shifting rocks. If I had been in his shoes, I would've been scared out of my mind, but as expected, Zatael was calm and confident. He simply scanned the oncoming army before quickly spinning in a circle while pumping his wing. This caused a gust of wind to blow, wholly clearing the plateau of the dust and demons. It was fun to watch all those demons be launched over the edge of the cliff. The gust even knocked Azrael off his feet, although he recovered quickly. Once on his feet, Azrael let out a scream as he unwrapped his dark-brown wings and revealed his golden armor before charging Zatael.

Now, from all my time of being the... a... ferryman of souls, I know that the one thing a warrior should never do is shout while trying to attack. This action has many terrible outcomes on many battlefields all across time. It can leave you breathless and causes the defender to focus on the attacker. Has he not learned anything from all the sould I brought to him? Nevertheless, I watched as Zatael stood motionless while Azrael approached. Once withing striking distance, Azrael swung his sword, to which Zatael swung my scythe to clash the blades.

"You're... You're weak." Azrael grunted as he struggled to hold his position.

244

"You're the one that is breaking a sweat," Zatael responded.

"I'm the Angel of Death! I'm stronger than any of my Brothers or Sisters!" Azrael shouted.

"And I am the Worldforger!" Zatael shouted back as he pulled his scythe away. The withdrawal caused Azrael to plunge his sword downward and bury the blade in the ground. "You may be a powerful Archangel, but your might does not stand up to that of a Seraph!" Zatael then shouted while throwing a punch with Shameis's right arm, landing on the middle of Azrael's chest. The blow was so powerful that a fist-shaped indentation was left in the arm as Azrael was blown several feet backward, landing on his back and leaving the sword embedded in the rock.

"You... You can't do this to me... I'm the most powerful Archangel!" Azrael shouted while attempting to get off his back.

"You are not the most powerful Archangel. Power does not reside in strength alone. Power is received from generosity, benevolence, diligence, modesty, and understanding." Zatael corrected Azrael as he switched the hand holding my scythe from his left to his right before effortlessly pulling Azrael's sword from the ground. Once in possession of both blades, Zatael began to pace toward Azrael, while the archangel attempting to get to his feet. However, Azrael decided to get into a kneeling position instead once seeing Zatael was in control of both blades.

"Oh, please, tremendous and powerful Worldforger! Please cease this unnecessary violence." Azrael began to beg just as Zatael entered striking distance. "The Lightbringer has given me one last option to offer you."

"We are listening." Zatael boomed after pausing for a brief second.

"The Lightbringer offered that if you were to sacrifice yourself, we would allow your two hosts to live out their remaining days together on Earth. They'll be able to live as a normal couple and have a normal relationship." Azrael offered. Frankly, that offer did sound nice and would be a dream come true. I'd love to be able to have a regular, steady relationship with Shameis. To be able to wake up together. To eat and drink together. To be a proper human again. I think I would prefer that than to being a Super Soul that heals Shameis's body; even though that would be great in itself.

"No." Zatael then rejected, snapping me out of my brief daydream.

"What do you mean 'no'?" Azrael questioned as he dropped his begging demeanor.

"Although I do wish for these two to one day live peacefully, the moment The Lightbringer gets my soul, the Earth, the realms, and everything we know as it is will cease to exist. With the Lightbringer's declining mental capacity due to the corruption of the Lifegiver and Timekeeper, The Lightbringer will inevitably destroy everything while aiming for his impossible goal." Zatael explained.

"Then good luck getting the portal out of here to open up without me!" Azrael let out as he quickly spun on his knees while preparing his wings to blast him out of here. Before I had a moment to react to this, Zatael quickly jolted forward into a blur before the sounds of metal clanging against rock and Azrael screaming in agony washed over the battlefield. Within the blink of an eye, Azrael went from kneeling to laying on his stomach with Zatael stepping on his back with his left foot. He also was holding the sword in his right hand instead of my scythe. I initially thought that the scream was from Zatael possibly kicking Azrael over, but then I noticed that the blade of my scythe was pierced through his wing and buried into the ground. Now that was shocking. As much as I loved to hear Azrael's shrieks of pain after all the years of torment, I was stunned to see that it was possible to hurt an angel. And that I've had an instrument to do this all along.

"Your lack of empathy should have disqualified you as an Archangel long ago!" Zatael boomed as he touched the tip of Azrael's blade to the

246

ground between Azrael's head and right wing. After seeing the blade, Azrael began to freak out and tried to pull away, which only caused the scythe to cut his wing more. The movement, in turn, caused a shining liquid to spill out of Azrael's wound. Angelic blood? They can bleed!

"No! Please! I beg of you! Have mercy!" Azrael pleaded desperately.

"Do you deserve mercy?" Zatael cross-examined.

"Yes! Of course!" Azrael lied.

"I'd beg to differ," I muttered off-handedly.

"That's what I thought," Zatael responded before pulling Azrael's sword away, which caused Azrael to let out a sigh of relief. "Azrael. You are an archangel. You're designed to serve benevolently, but instead, you act selfishly under a being that will be the destruction of us all. Therefore, you do not deserve the gifts you were given." And with that, Zatael drove the blade down through the Angel's wing, severing it and causing Azrael to let out a bloodcurdling scream. His shrieks were so loud and echoey that they bordered on the line of eerie and terrifying. For the first time, I think I actually pitied him.

I continued to watch as Zatael dropped Azreal's sword while stepping off of Azrael and pulling my scythe from the angel's severed wing. While Zatael did this, Azrael continued to scream as he rolled about in shimmering pale blood before struggling to get to his feet. There was so much Angel blood. The glow of it made his golden armor seem dull in comparison as it spilled all over him. Oh, this was gruesome, but its effect was similar to many of the vehicular accidents I witnessed on Earth. I just couldn't look away. I just continued to watch as Zatael caused my scythe to vanish once in his hands as Azrael floundered like a fish. Then Zatael began to stroll over to Azreal, causing the Archangel to try and scuttle away. Thankfully, Zatael could walk faster than Azrael could crawl.

"That is enough of that," Zatael muttered as he reached down to Azrael. His eyes grew wide as Zatael placed his left hand over the Angel's mouth to muffle the screaming while scooping his right hand under Azrael's head. When Zatael firmly held Azrael, the Seraph hoisted the Angel to his feet. From this angle, I could see the fear in Azrael's eyes while frightened tears glistened in the orange sun as they rolled down his cheeks. "I have watched you torment my host for too long. Heinous acts you performed on her have no punishment to match, but ridding the universe of a cancer like you will have to suffice." Upon hearing that, Azrael began to tremble, which caused his armor to clatter as he stared into Zatael's one revealed eye.

"You are one hundred percent correct. Please do the cosmos a favor and rid it of this stain." A familiar British-accented voice followed Zatael's proclamation. The voice instantly drew my attention, and I found it was coming from that devilishly handsome, pale-skinned man I know as Lucifer. I was astonished that he was accompanied with a terrified Lilith, where they stood just a couple of yards away from Zatael. "However..." He continued, "If you do this favor to the universe, you will voluntarily admit defeat. Which means the two souls you are trying to help will be trapped in this realm forever."

"This act is not out of wrath." Zatael declared without looking away from Azrael.

Yes, but acting out of revenge for another can be misconstrued as Wrathful." Lucifer pointed out. "You've already marked this one as one of the fallen, like you or I. So Azrael will never return to the kingdom above. Is that not punishment enough?"

"If the one he serves fulfills his plans, this one will be able to return even if marked as a fallen." Zatael countered. "It is best to take a pawn off the board when the chance arises. It is best to cripple the opposition."

"Unless this is a moment where pieces are meant to be exchanged," Lucifer suggested. That was what caught Zatael's attention and made him look from Azrael.

"What do you mean by this?" Zatael inquired.

"Well. As you are aware, the role of us Fates is to drive what it meant to be. With that being said, please know that what I say next is only in service of my role." Lucifer put forth. So that's the classification of Angel that Lucifer is. I would have assumed that he would've been more substantial from the stories, but that explains why he has never lied to me. Still, it begs the question as to why he was cast out of heaven in the first place.

"Out with it, Fate." Zatael boomed as he slowly squeezed Azrael's head, causing the Archangel to squeal.

"Issac and Cain are meant to return to the Earth, and Azrael is meant to return to the Lightbringer's side. I know that the Will of a Seraph outweighs the Will of the Fates, but I have reached out to the Lightbringer and have struck a compromise. If you return the souls of the Archangel, the Lightbringer will allow the return of this one." Lucifer laid out.

"My two host are not fond of that soul." Zatael then stated.

"I am amply aware of that, but if they are the heroes they claim to be, then they surely would prefer to save a soul whenever possible." Lucifer coaxed in his suave tone of voice. That is a fair point. Although I have seen a lot of horrendous acts from humanity, with Lilith committing more than her fair share, she still deserves to be saved. But, would we be allowed to bring her with us? Shameis and I were forced to face every trial independently, while she only showed up to torment us. That doesn't seem right.

"How would she be able to pass through the Vale? She has not completed the trials that my hosts had to go through." Zatael then questioned as if he heard my ramblings.

249

"Oh, great Worldforger. Although you crafted the very ground you stand on, the rules that have been put forth have changed drastically while you've been away." Lucifer informed us. "All a soul needs to do to cross the Vale is simply to visit each of these seven realms. No set task needs to be completed. That is why the archangels were placed as the doorkeepers; to prevent souls from proceeding. But, while they fought to stave off the threat you three posed, they failed to realize that they made another able to return. With this one's unique circumstance, she now fits a particular role that needs to be filled on the Earth. All that is meant to be can not proceed without this one." With that, Zatael let out a sigh.

"I will let this archangel return to his master in exchange for safe passage for my hosts' souls, but the decision for whether her soul goes with them is not mine to make." Zatael agreed as he let go of Azrael's head, causing the Archangel to fall onto the ground before crawling away. Once Azrael was far enough, I felt Zatael's hold over Shameis and I instantly lossen as my vision blackened. Then, as it came back, I found myself standing on the ground beside Shameis. As I looked at him, I saw that a bright red portal was floating silently just on the other side of him.

"Ah, good. Isaac and Cain. I'm glad the Worldforger allowed you to return safely." Lucifer stated to us.

"You know those aren't our names anymore," Shameis responded bluntly.

"Yes. What is a name beside a means to get one's attention? Shameis and Grim. What say you in the matter of taking this one with you?

"We don't have a choice. But, as you've said, Lilith still has a role to play in all of this. I just hope she remembers that even after all the bad she has done to us, we were still willing to help her." Shameis responded as he stared directly at Lilith. During this, I noticed Azrael finished crawling to Lucifer's feet and was now resting.

250

"I couldn't have said it better myself!" Lucifer agreed as he lifted his hand from her shoulder, signaling Lilith to run toward us and the portal. This, in turn, signaled Shameis and me to turn toward the exit as well. "Oh, and do allow her to cross before you."

"Why?" I questioned as I turned back to Lucifer.

"Although she qualifies to return with you, that portal is meant for you. If you cross before her, then it will close behind you." Lucifer explained. I guess that make sense. I've come to understand that doors like these have a security measure, so unauthorized souls do not stumble upon them. So it stands to reason that this portal would follow the same principle. So, as Shameis and I watched Lilith's soul run through the portal, I grabbed onto his left hand and interlocked our fingers. My action caused him to look down at my grasp before looking back up at me. With our sight locked, I noticed that the redness on his iris had subsided, and all that was left was the hazel I love. There was a subtle hint of pink mixed in there, but I didn't mind.

"So we don't get separated." He joked to me through a whisper before turning back to the portal. That was when I took my first step forward and began to lead him towards it.

We didn't have far to walk, as it was just a couple feet away, but we were once again stopped as Azrael spoke out to us in a quivering voice. "This isn't over!" He shouted, causing Shameis and me to turn back, to which we saw Lucifer helping Azrael to his feet.

"Of course it is. They're going somewhere you're not allowed to be." Lucifer responded to Azrael before turning back to us. "Don't worry about him. I hope to see you again."

"Thank you for everything, Lucifer," I responded before turning back to Shameis and nodding to him. The moment he replied with a nod of his own, I proceeded forward and stepped into the portal. I was glad to be heading back to Earth. And now, we will face Victor together and stop his reign of terror. Finally, we will be able to take down the Lightbringer's means of finding a perfect host! And with Shameis and I being the first souls to return from the other side, I was feeling invincible! This was fantastic! And we wouldn't have been able to do this without Zatael. Sure, our trio had a rocky start, but in the end, he stayed true to his word and served the pair of us without taking control. I'm just hoping that our journey on Earth won't be as mentally draining.

Part Three: Desiring a Resolution

Chapter Twenty-One

I can't believe that all just happened. How am I supposed to accept that we were allowed to walk away from the seven realms of sin? Am I supposed to believe that we are allowed to roam freely on the face of the Earth? If it wasn't for the strength that Zatael provided, I'm sure the Archangels would've ensured that the dead stay dead. I know that fables are all but a fever dream concocted by the mortals in charge of the entertainment industry, but let's take a moment to think about this. Where would a soul returning to Earth even go? I know our situation is unique since Shameis's body was somehow still alive when his soul was separated from it, and I'm tethered to his soul through Zatael, but if a regular soul would somehow slip through the seven realms and back to Earth, where would it go?

If their mortal vessel perished, it would begin to decay. There is no way a soul could return to that. After going through that mess, I'm reasonably sure that Zatael had something to do with the consistent state of Shameis's body. I mean, I still haven't determined why this phenomenon happened, but that is my hypothesis until it is confirmed. That would explain why the Lightbringer couldn't take it after Shameis's soul left. On the other side of this coin, I am still shaken to have learned that I am not the only ferryman of souls. I've never met or seen any other one of them, but it would explain why I didn't remember ferrying a single soul from Victor's multitudes of murder. I wasn't being kept around because I had a job to do. They kept me because Zatael was protecting me from obliteration. If it wasn't for him, I wouldn't be here today. I wouldn't have been able to help Shameis return. How many souls have I unknowingly delivered to Azrael that are now under his tyranny?

Well, at least I will no longer have to serve that monster. And with Shameis and Zatael, there are other fears I need to worry about. Mainly the worry that we may not be able to find Victor. With resources like his, I'm sure there are an infinite amount of places he could hide. I would never have the thought to look for him in a secret laboratory under a cemetery. So, I guess it is good that I am partnered with an investigator.

Another fear lingering over me is the fate of Lilith's soul. I have no idea what she returned to. Her body could be a corpse for all I know. Then there is a fear of how long we've been away. Because time passes by differently in the other realms than on Earth, I have no idea how long we were gone. It could've been months or even years. My last fear is that even though Shameis and I were holding hands when leaving the spiritual realms, Shameis was now nowhere in sight.

Since the process of returning to the Earth was severely abnormal compared to every other instance I've experienced, I found myself standing in a room I'd never seen before. At least being in a random place I hadn't been is actually pretty standard. It's more of just showing up here. I could only assume that this was because of the power of the realms. When I open the portals, I'm manipulating the magic, so it drains me, and I have to experience walking through the tunnel. However, when a realm does it naturally, the transport is instant. That's all I can assume. I could also assume that Shameis was nearby, but I had no idea where.

So, as I looked around my new surroundings, I found myself standing alone within a rectangular room. The walls consisted of bricks that were painted dark gray while the ceiling consisted of gridlike foam tiles and the floor was concrete that had been painted a light gray. Along with that, a musky, dank smell made this place seem so familiar. I even noticed a set of matching white painted countertops and cabinets lined the wall, but what gave this room away was the set of 'push-to-open' double doors in the corner. This room is the space connected to Victor's Operating room!

As I continued to scan the room, I found a set of nicely folded jeans topped with a pair of black canvas shoes with white souls sitting to their right on the middle of the countertop. I instantly recognized that these belonged to Shameis, so I immediately feared the worst and further investigated. There was a small workstation computer sitting upon a desk pushed up against the shortest wall furthest from the doors. This was where I found Shameis's metal arm wired to the terminal, which led me to believe Victor had decided to perform some software updates. The computer monitor was still on and displaying a slideshow of generic geographic locations, which meant that either this machine was set to never enter rest mode or that Victor had just been here. to the left of this workstation, there was an antique wooden coat rack holding a white lab coat. Being that I have only ever seent his man in a lab coat or a tropical vacation shirt, the presence of the computer lent credence to the notion that Victor, in fact, had just left.

For the rest of the room, I then noticed that the long wall across from the countertops was filled with doors I recognized as morgue drawers. This had to be where Shameis was! So, with that thought I decided to approach them and that was when one of the panels began to rattle. I won't lie, the rattling did catch me off guard, but it was nothing to be terrified about. So, I looked up and down the wall until I found the square that was the culprit of the noise. "Shameis?" I questioned as I slowly approached it before reaching out toward the handle. I was hoping that Zatael would have provided me with the ability to interact with physical objects, but as I reached out, the door swung open, and my arm phased right through the metal.

Yep, just as expected... I wish that I could've grabbed onto it or that it would've hit me, but just as it was before, it went right through me. Frankly, I would've preferred the pain of the slab of metal slamming into me over knowing that I was going to be invisible to the world again. I guess I'm just going to be Shameis's silent partner, healing his wounds whenever he is hurt since he too most likely won't be able to see me. I guess I am just destined to ride in the passenger's seat of another person's story which means I was back to being a walking skeleton.

Anyways, as I continued to gaze upon the opening, I watched as a pair of bare feet poked out, followed by a couple of naked thighs. Knowing what was going to follow, I quickly turned away out of a sense of self-preservation. I really shouldn't be peeping at Shameis's naked body if he doesn't even know I'm looking. I mean, I really shouldn't be spying on anyone, but I especially didn't want to be peeping on Shameis.

On the other hand, I've seen hundreds of thousands of unclothed mortals' bodies. I've had to collect so many naked souls, so why am I all of a sudden concerned with seeing this one? So, I just stood there and listened as Shameis struggled to climb out before I heard the consecutive plops of his bare feet smacking the concrete floor. "Hey, Grim! We made it!" Shameis's voice called to me, which quelled the fear of being alone. If no one else could see me, at least the most important person in my life will be amble to. Well, that did quell the fear of being entirely alone.

"Hey, Shameis," I responded nervously without turning back to him. "We sure did."

256

"Is everything okay? Why are you facing away from me?" He asked.

"Umm...." I responded.

"Oh! You think I'm naked! Well, I am, but there was a sheet in there with me." He clarified. Hearing that, I hesitantly turned back to face him and saw that he did manage to wrap a sheet around himself in a similar fashion as an Ancient Greek toga. As I looked at him, I did expect to see the metal plating that covered his right pectoral, but I was a bit surprised to see that his head was still covered in the gauze wrappings. I guess this should have been expected since there was no way for Victor to heal his wounds. Still, as I continued to stare at him, I noticed that his one exposed iris was still his natural hazel color. I guess everything he saw in the other realms caused him to no longer fear the skeleton following him. "You know, even if I was completely naked, it would be okay for you to look. We have feelings for each other, so it is only natural. And besides, since I'm the only one of us that has a body and you're going to be by my side, there are probably going to be times where you're going to see a lot of me." He joked, trying to break the apparent tension.

"Haha... right..." I chuckled nervously. "Um, your clothes are over there." I then informed him as I pointed to the countertops on my left.

"Great! Thanks!" Shameis responded while shuffling past me. I Still felt a bit uncomfortable by the situation, so I decided not to allow my gaze to follow Shameis until he redressed himself. "Oh, man! He didn't leave me a shirt!" He then let out as the thumps of his shoes being dropped to the ground echoed through the room.

"There is a lab coat next to the computer," I informed him.

"You really think I will fit in Jakelyde's jacket? I'm nearly a foot taller than him." He responded as he zipped up his pants, which meant it was now safe to look at. So as I turned around, I watched as Shameis struggled to put on his socks and shoes.

"Why dont you use the chair?" I inquired, accusing him to stop and look up at me before walking over to the computer station, pulling out the task chair, and sitting so he could finish.

"Man, this would be a lot easier if I still had two arms." Shameis muttered while letting out a sigh of defeat.

"Then why don't you connect your arm? Hook it up, and we can get Victor!" I inquired since he must've seen it. It was right behind him.

"It's wired to the computer. I don't know if unplugging it would damage its hardware." He responded as he turned toward the computer monitor and awkwardly reaching over the prosthetic so he could jiggle the mouse. The slideshow stopped playing as soon as it moved and revealed that it was still unlocked and on the main desktop. Seeing this, I looked closer and saw a single open program that had previously been minimized. I will admit that I don't have a lot of experience with computers other than from what I've seen human souls use before I collected them, but I can say for sure that I did not recognize that icon. It seemed that Shameis didn't realize it either since he instantly clicked on it. As soon as he did so, the screen that popped up had a loading bar that was completely full. Overtop the bar, a pop-up message was displayed stating an update was complete and the prostetic was ready to disconnect. Seeing that, Shameis yanked the cabled connecting the prosthetic to the computer before closing the hexagonal panel on the outer bicep that was open. Once disconnected, the pop-up and loading bar vanished and left a pictograph.

"Now, what do you have to do?" I then pondered.

"Umm... Based on this... It says that all I need to do is hold the joints together, and they will connect." Shameis explained me as he lifted hs prostetic and turning to see the connection. Sure enough, So, the two joints reached out and grabbed onto eachother as the sounds of bolts and screws could be heard fastening them together.

258

"It's just that simple?" I wondered.

"It's just that simple." He answered as the lights in the forearm lit up again. Once they were consistently glowing, Shameis started to move the arm about to ensure that it functioned properly.

"Great! So, now that you have the arm, are you going to use that computer to find out where Victor is?" I pushed.

"Slow your roll, Grim. I'll get to it, but before I close this program, I want to find out what was added in that update." He stated as he grabbed the mouse with his right hand instead of his left and clicked on a tab to the top of the pictograph labeled 'features.' This tab brought up a list with more pictograms started with things we were already aware of. Replicated human movement, superstrength, and the ability to light any dark area were all included, but after those three, there were three more abilities on the list. So, I leaned in to read the descriptions and saw that the fourth item on the list stated that there were voice controls. This did not provide a list of these commands or how to program them, so that was a bit useless. The fifth was that the arm could extend itself from every joint up to three times the arm's natural length there wasn't an explanation as to how it would activate this ability, so I guess it it good thing Zatael gave Shameis the knowledge of technology. The sixth and final feature of this prosthetic is to remotely hack into any other piece of machinery. The pictogram shown the palm of the arm touching a computer, but there was still no explanation. Why does Victor have to be such a narcissist? Could he not include details into his own computer program "Well, that's neat." Shameis expressed as he broke my irritation while looking to the palm of his arm before placing it at the top of the monitor.

"Wait, wouldn't you need to put it onto the tower, where the computer hardware is?" I questioned.

"Do you see a tower?" Shameis retorted.

"No..." I muttered.

"That's because Victor prefers his technology to be as simple as possible. This piece of machinery is two-in-one." He explained as the monitor began to cycle through and flash hundreds of files and folders a second. After thirty seconds of scrolling, single file folder containing three files causing him to pull awat and have a better look.

"What did you search for?" I pondered.

"Anything involving his name or office locations. And these are the only files that came up." Shameis answered without taking his eyes off the screen. I was becoming a bit confused about why he was so transfixed on the three files, so I leaned in to see what was going on. Each of the three icons that appeared was identical to each other; with a rectangular shape with the top right corner folded inward and a light blue circle in the center of the rectangle. Inside the ring sat a triangle pointing toward the right and underneath sat the phrase 'MP4'. From my limited knowledge of these machines, I am aware that this type of file is supposed to be a video, meaning that once one of these is selected, something will begin to play. I was still confused about why he was staring so intently at the icons, until I noticed a small labels uder each rectangle that each depicted a different name. I recognized two of them! One label spelled out 'Isaac Enderson' and the other spelled 'Lilith Cotter.' There would be something wrong with me if I couldn't recognize these names by now, but I was unable to recognize the third. Also, I was a bit confused about why these three files came up when searching for Victor's name, but then I noticed that the files were listed in a folder called "Jakelyde and Lightbringer."

"Who is Dennis Wayne?" I wondered.

"Dennis was the child I failed to save," Shameis muttered as he fixated on the file.

"Oh," I responded sorrowly. It is a bit tragic for Shameis to be reminded of his greatest failure, costing him six years of his life and his role as the protector of his city. However, seeing this file did fill me with a bit of optimism. "So... wait. If Victor made a video file about this boy and grouped it with a file for both you and Lilith, does that mean the boy is still alive?" I put forth. This notion caused Shameis's attention to be unglued from the screen and returned to me. His eye was watering, and his iris had changed from his hazel to a solid shade of deep blue. I understand that this moment was sad for him, but I was surprised to see that his iris was still changing color depending on his mood. I was starting to think that ability was just something that happened in the realms. "It was just a thought. I mean, I know Lilith died, but she came back to life. So, perhaps Dennis is still alive. I wasn't summoned to collect that soul from Victor, but I guess one of the other ferrymen could have."

"So the only way to know is to open the link," Shameis confirmed as he quickly looked back at the monitor. But then he hesitated.

"I understand why you dont want to. I spent so long being tormented by my greatest failure; the loss of my brother. But all we can do is move on and hope we can somehow make the situation right." I consoled Shameis as I rested my left hand on his metal-plated right shoulder. Seconds after I did that, he gently nodded his head before slowly dragging the cursor to the icon labeled 'Dennis Wayne' and double-tapping the mouse's right button. This action caused an image of Victor's menacing head to appear on the screen while the 'play video' logo floated over the doctor's face. The background Victor used was the dark gray brick wall covered with the square hatches that Shameis had climbed out of, indicating that this video was filmed in this exact location. Within seconds of the video's viewer window opening, Shameis slowly dragged the cursor to the 'play video' logo before clicking it. This instantly caused the cursor vanished and the image of Victor began to speak. I could only assume that this was meant to act as a video diary to serve as personal use.

"Dennis Wayne: entry 108. Date: August twenty-fourth." The image of Victor started, causing Shameis to grip the mouse, pause the video, and take note of the date at the bottom right corner of the screen. As I too looked to it, I noticed that the computer registered today's date as what Victor stated. I initially thought this was great since this confirmed my theory that he was just here and should be close. Besides the date, I wondered what happened to the other one-hundred and seven entries, but perhaps Victor relocated each entry when he records a new one. That, or he deletes them when the subject of the video passes on. Whatever the reason, I was about to share my delight with Shameis since we were close to Victor's tail, but Shameis started to speak with the slight sound of panic in his voice.

"No, no. That can't be right." Shameis worried.

"What can't be right? Is it not good that Victor was here earlier today?" I cross-examined.

"No, grim. That's not the important part." He remarked.

"What's more important than that?" I continued to question.

"Today is August Twenty-Fourth." He pointed out again.

"Yeah? What's important about that date?" I pondered.

"The last date I remember was July twelfth, and that's before I was unconscious for five days. So we were in those seven realms for over a month!" Shameis freaked out.

"Well, yeah. Time passes significantly different for the other realms. One day for a celestial being like The Presence or an archangel

262

could be millions of years here on Earth." I explained. Apparently, he was not expecting my response, as he stopped panicking, turned toward me, and stared at me with a blank expression, revealing that the blue in his eye had begun to fade. "There are a lot of aspects that I still struggle to understand, but I have grown accustomed to losing days at a time while ferrying souls."

"So, we were there for what felt like a day, but it was actually more than a month?" Shameis questioned. "Victor was allowed to run around and do whatever he wanted for a month?"

"Unfortunately," I responded, to which Shameis let out another sigh before turning back to the monitor and hitting the spacebar, which resumed the video. Without hesitation, Victor's image picked up where it left off.

"The subject's aggression has begun to increase as of late. I am starting to suspect that it is starting to understand that its life is not typical for a living being. I did not want to keep this subject for nearly as long as I have, but I have yet to unlock the secrets as to why it was the only human to survive the experiments to create a potential host for the Lightbringer. I have matched the subject's race, age, gender, blood type, and disposition, but I have not had any other successes. Compared to all blood samples from Issac Enderson, this child meets nearly every requirement the Lightbringer has laid out. I have every intention to wait until Isaac's body wakes or passes until I continue with that experiment. Still, without receiving any updates from the Lightbringer, I feel the urge to adjust to this child's genetics. Unfortunately, I fear that the strength exerted by the subject Dennis Wayne will eventually cause the experiment to lead toward a more drastic solution. This completes the summary of this weekly Log." Victor's image rambled until it stopped playing by itself as the encircled play symbol reappeared on the screen.

"Could that child really be a host for the Lightbringer?" I fretted as I looked to Shameis. Without hesitation and without a response, Shameis quickly stood up from the desk.

"We need to get going. We are wasting time here!" He demanded as he stepped away from the computer.

"Are you not going to watch the other clips?" I wondered, which caused him to turn back toward me as he stared intently with a blazing red iris.

"There's no need. I know more about my situation than he does." He pointed out.

"But what about Lilith?" I continued.

"What about her? She doesn't matter. Victor probably threw her body away like all the other failed experiments." He answered.

"Shameis! Where is this coming from?" I barked.

"Not saving that boy is my greatest failure!" He barked back. "Hearing that he is still alive and being tortured... Victor deserves to pay for what he's done! Only to add insult to injury, now I know that the reason the boy will continuously be experimented on is that I won't hand over my body and soul! We need to find Victor, and this place will not give us the information we need!"

"Shameis, I understand that this realization is troublesome, but don't you think we should be going at this with a level head?" I suggested, to which he continued to stare at me for a bit longer before dropping his head and letting out a third, more exaggerated, sigh. "We will get him. We will make sure Victor doesn't hurt another soul. I promise." The moment I made that promise, he lifted his head back to me. His iris still had a hint of red to it, but it was not as vibrant as it once was. Without saying a word, he nodded in agreeance before walking up to the coat rack and pulling off Victor's lab coat.

"I really wish he would've left me a shirt." He then muttered through a defeated sigh as he stared at the jacket. "I'm really tired of not having one."

"Hopefully, we will be able to find you one after we beat Victor." I comforted him as I walked up to his left side.

"If I still have any belongings..." Shameis let out as he struggled to put on the too small jacket. At least the sleeves came down to his wrists. So, he turned to me once it was on, and I was stunned. Between his white gauze face wrappings and the long white coat, he kind of looked like an inverted version of me. "Alright, Grim. Let's go," he then smoldered as he blew past me toward the set of double doors. I really wish I could've done something to make him feel better about everything he just learned. I know what would make him feel better, but I fear what will happen when Shameis finally comes face-to-face with the man that caused all of this to happen. So, as I followed him out of this room, I had a hope that I really didn't want to see, even though I knew it would be good for him. Shameis needs to let out some of that anger.

AZRAEL IN ARMOR

266

Part Three: Desiring a Resolution

Chapter Twenty-Two

I'm starting to realize that knowledge is more than just a tool for making ones existence more straightforward. As of late, it feels more like a double-edged sword that could potentially injure the user. The one thing I've always loved about knowledge is that there is no leeway for interpretation. Truth is truth, and I often used this to my advantage when trying to convince souls to come with me when I served as a ferryman of souls. If the soul allowed, I would show them their corpse and explain why they have passed on. Initially, I wouldn't let them see their loved ones since the emotions would complicate the process. Still, my quest for knowledge and my increasing disconnection from my feelings allowed them to see their still-living family.

I guess this drive for knowledge kept me by Shameis's side initially, instead of reporting what was happening to Azrael. After everything we've learnd and seen, my quest for knowledge ultimately connected me with someone whom I couldn't stand to lose. I will forever be grateful. And not only did I find my partner, but learning everything about the other realms has re-engage my desire to live. I even have the drive to help people in dire situations. Finally, I have a chance to be a hero! All we will have to do is stop the Lightbringer's nefarious scheme of taking over the world. Then, we will be free to help anyone in need. The only thing that lies in our way is Victor. Not only because he is hurting humans in the name of the Lightbringer, but also for Shameis's sanity. And all we have to do to reach that goal is find him.

That brings us to where we are now. After following Shameis through the set of doors, we found ourselves in the same room I speculated to be here, and it remained virtually untouched. I could feel the trauma Shameis endured and the sadness I witnessed as the stench of death permeated the air. The metal table still had the overhead light shining on it, illuminating the dried blood from Shameis's disfigurement. As I continued to look around, I noticed a section of the waist-high countertop had all but disintegrated. If those slipped chemicals can do that to wood, then we should feel luck that all it did was scar Shameis's face. With the countertop, even the cage that Shameis was held in was left in disarray.

As I looked around the room in shock over how Victor could leave it like this, I nearly ran into Shameis. The moment he entered the room, he froze while fixating on the table. "Shameis?" I questioned as I reached out to him. I wanted to gauge his reaction, but before I reached him, he snapped into a violent rage. He rushed to the closest edge of the table. Without hesitation, he placed a hand underneath the tabletop and ripped the slab from its hydraulic system and swung it toward the holding cell with little effort. Upon contact, the sound of breaking and twisting metal filled the small room. With the noise, the wirelike fencing of the cage mangled as the table passed through. Zatael was not messing around when giving Shameis the gift of strength.

After making short work of the inanimate object that helped ruin his life, he quickly turned his attention to the countertop that had taken his face and right arm. Within the blink of an eye, he balled his metallic hand into a fist and forced it through the countertop. Then, with a quick

268

pull, he ripped the section of the lower cabinet between the double doors and disintegrated section from the wall. I was stunned to see how strong Zatael had made Shameis, but it was also obvious that these cabinets were poorly constructed since the container and the top instantly separated once free from the wall. This left Shameis holding the section of countertop, to which he blindly through it off to his left side; directly at me. It did startle me to see the chunk of wood hurdling at me, but knowing that I can't interact with the physical realm as one should, I stood in place and let it pass through me. I know Shameis wouldn't intend to cause me harm, so I could forgive this transgression. Still, the sound of the wood smacking the wall before bursting into pieces was a sound I didn't expect to hear. It was comparable to the sound of lightning striking a tree.

I felt like I should intervene, but I also knew that this rage had been building up for a long time. Experience has taught me that sometimes the best thing to do is stand by and watch as a soul gets it out of its system. So, all I could do was watch as Shameis continued by grabbing the remains of the cabinet that fell tot he floor and chucking it behind himself. As this container flew across the room, various documents, medical supplies, unused syringes, and vials of different colored liquids spilled out and scattered across the newly vacant tile floor. I watched as the glass vials shattered, causing more of the liquids that took his arm and face spilled out. They began to mix as the did before while being absorbed by the loose documents, but there was no reaction. I guess they outlasted their expiration. As all that occurred, the box itself collided with the heavy metal door that separated us from whatever was outside this room.

Upon decimating this section, Shameis turned his attention to the cabinets directly in front of his face. Once again, he balled his metal hand into a fist before swinging it across his body and through the side of it instead of punching right through the cabinet. The force he exerted,

269

in turn, caused the first door and the bottom to blow apart from the walls as more medical supplies and nondescript documents fluttered through the air. That was also when I noticed something unique that was sent airborne. I couldn't see it well, but it glistened a bronzish-gold color as it reflected the light. Also seeing the reflection, Shameis turned and reached his right arm toward the glimmering object without warning. As his mechanical arm rapidly stretched out, Shameis ended up catching it in his fingertip while it was mid air.

So, As soon as Shameis grabbed the object, the faint chime of clanging metal filled the tense atmosphere. Then, after ensuring the flying piece of metal was in his grasp, he slowly retracted his arm. Now that it wasn't flailing through the air, I could see this thing had a small chain that formed a loop hanging from it. I sure didn't know what this thing was, but Shameis definitely recognized it, causing his entire demeanor changed. It was still quite hard to tell his exact emotion through his masked face, but I could tell that his anger changed to depression as he slowly backed up to the freshly cleared wall, placed his back against it, and slid down until he was in a sitting position. Since he appeared to finish raging, I took this as an opportunity to approach.

"Shameis?" I questioned again as I walked toward him. My utterance of his name was only met with silence mixed with the subtle sound of him sobbing. I don't know what I should do to fix this. I understand why he was so angry when he first saw this place, but I don't know what could've caused this change. So, I simply walked up to him and squatted so I could look him int he eye. While doing this, I observed him as he kept his head bowed and vision fixated on this piece of metal while continuing to sob. "Shameis... Is everything alright?" I asked while trying to show some sympathy. I knew that

270

something was wrong, but I just wanted him to look at me so we could get through this together. Thankfully, he did look up to me after the second question. His iris was a deep blue, while the white of his eye was now bloodshot. Even his exposed skin around his eye was blushing and puffed up as a stream of tears rolled down his face.

"I can't handle this..." He forced out through tremble before looking back down to what he was holding.

"You were just letting out some anger. I would have done the same thing if I was in your shoes." I confided in him. "I know the pressures on us are high, but we are the only people that can handle this. You and I are the only souls with a Seraph, and only we can stop the Lightbringer. Maybe we can get help from the other heroes when the time comes, but this is all up to us."

"No..." He denied.

"Shameis... We didn't go through hell   just to give up on the mission now." I tried to persuade him.

"I know..." He muttered in response.

"Then you're going to have to handle it, and I'm going to handle it with you," I assured him as I wrapped my right hand around the outside of his left. This act of kindness brought his attention back up to me before letting out a sigh.

"It's not the supernatural stuff... It's the superhero stuff..." Shameis let out as he showed me the piece of metal he caught. Now that I could see it better, I saw that it was a medallion connected to a chain so someone could wear it around their neck. Its shape resembled a crescent moon that nearly formed a complete circle with a simplified lightning bolt swishing across the gap.

"What is it?" I asked, as I genuinely did not know what it was supposed to represent.

"It's the key to the team of heroes I was once a part of; The Council of Supers. The shapes are supposed to represent the 'C' and the 'S.' Having one of these not only recognizes us as one of the most respected heroes in the United States, but it also gave us access to any locations we used as a means of operation." He spilled out.

"So now you have proof that you were The Ile! That's great! You're one step closer to regaining your old life." I reassured him with glee.

"That's the part I can't handle. I will never be able to return to that life, Grim. Look at me. The only reason the people of Chicago respected me was because I was just like them. Now I look like one of the villains that we locked away. I can never go back to being a hero." he disputed.

"Didn't you say that one of the heroes on your team was a walking skeleton that shot out lightning?" I questioned, trying to find his reasoning.

"Crossfade uses his Identity to strike fear in the hearts of villains. The Ile was supposed to be a spark of hope in the dead of night." He sulked.

"I thought we both agreed that the old us are gone? You're Shameis Eli, and I am Grim. No more Isaac and Cain." I reminded him.

"Right... but how am I expected to face a different person wearing my clothes and running around in my identity?" He countered.

"Well...from the sounds of it, there are different types of heroes. Yeah, you may never be able to take up the mantle of The Ile ever again, but Shameis Eli has yet to give his debut. You are the hero resurrected. You're the hero that not only conquered death but got her to fall head over heels for you. No longer will you have to wear black to hide in the shadows. You could, and should, let your adversaries know that you are coming for them. After all, what gives off more hope than a come-back story; a redemption arc." I blabbered on, trying to raise Shameis's spirits.

272

"Azrael really didn't let you anywhere near the Superheroes..." He pointed out as he hung his head. "I wish it would be that easy, but I'm a science experiment. Victor has been letting soulless monsters loose all across this country. Enough to the point that they have been labeled as one of the greatest fears a civilian can face. I would be hunted by the other heroes just for looking like this. They would never give me a chance. I would never be accepted..."

"Then don't be accepted!" I shouted at him as I stood back up to my feet. "They may be superpowered, but you have a literal Seraph inside your soul! They may think they are high and mighty, but you have the grace of an all-powerful angel! So, they'll either need to get with the program or get out of the way. We don't need them!" As soon as I shouted that last sentence, Shameis quickly looked back up and showed me that his iris was still mostly blue, but it was slowly being overtaken by a light shade of pink while the bloodshot started to dissipate.

"Head over heels?" He then questioned softly.

"I wouldn't have come all the way back to Earth if I didn't have feelings," I joked as I watched him slide the medallion over his head before leaning forward and picking himself off the ground.

"I'm pretty sure you didn't have a choice," He joked back with a grunt as he finished standing up. "But of course, I would never willingly leave you behind." He then let out as he leaned in to wrap his arms around me. So, I cringed a bit since I knew that he was about to pass through me. This is about to be one of the worst moments I would face while on this Earth; almost worse than what caused me to become a ferryman in the first place. But, at least I would be able to talk to him, and he would see me. So, I prepared myself for what I thought was inevitable, but something unexpected happened. As he wrapped his arms around me, I felt his grasp grow tighter as he pulled me into himself.

"What the hell is happening?" I questioned as I began to freak out.

"It's a hug," Shameis muttered as he began to pull away. "I was trying to show you some gratitude since you're the greatest thing to happen to me... but I can stop if you'd like."

"No! No." I rejected before quickly wrapping my arms around him and pulling him back toward me. "You just caught me off guard. There have been a few instances where I couldn't touch anything while we've been back. I didn't think I could touch you!"

"Well, It's probably because of Zatael." Shameis pointed out.

"That makes sense. Zatael was the reason I was able to touch you before when you got your memory back." I agreed as we stood in this interlocked position for another minute or so. After that time passed, quietly I muttered, "We should probably get moving," even though I didn't want to. With that, I felt him nod before trying to back away again.

"Woah." He muttered after looking at me upon pulling away.

"What?" I giggled. "Did you not enjoy hugging a skeleton?"

"Well. It didn't feel like I was hugging a skeleton, and apparently I wasn't," Shameis remarked.

"What are you on about?" I pondered skeptically.

"I'm not gonna lie, you did look like a skeleton just a few seconds ago... but now... Does your skin usually vanish and reappear?" He cross-examined. His question caused me to look down at my hands, but all I could see were boney phalanges. There were no tendons, blood vessels, muscles, or skin; just bone.

"I have no idea what you're talking about," I confessed.

"When I first saw you in the back of what I thought was my car, you were a skeleton. That's how you looked on top of the water slide. Then when we went to the Void and seven realms, you looked like you do now, with cute olive skin and silky black hair. But you were

274

just a Skeleton before this while saying all those nice things to me. So, can you control that?" He spilled out as his iris began to turn back to normal. Everything made sense up to now. My curse makes me appear as a skeleton while on Earth. I am still a skeleton and that is just how it is. I guess my look of confusion gave my surprise away since he followed up his own question with another. "Wait, you really don't know what is happening?"

"No, I have no idea what you're talking about. I can clearly see that I'm still a skeleton." I responded as I held up my hand.

"I swear, I see you as yourself." He assured me as he reached out to my hand and grabbed the tip of my right index finger with his left index finger and his thumb... except he didn't.

"What... What the..." I stammered as I watched his slight grip hover around my bone, but I could feel his touch. With that, I froze as I continued to stare. "Can you really see me like me?" I begged. I swear that I could start to cry if I had tear ducts.

"Of course I can. You're beautiful. There is no need to cry." He tried to comfort me. Great. Just great. Now he will be able to see my emotions. "Okay, so this is just another thing that we have to figure out. We need to find a way to communicate with Zatael. We'll find a church if we have to." He uttered as he moved from holding my individual finger to holding my entire hand. "But as you said, we need to get going." Although I was still stunned from knowing that he could see me correctly, I nodded in agreement. I just couldn't believe that my curse wasn't as cut and dry as I thought. There is a way to break it; I just have no idea how to.

Nevertheless, I followed him as he guided me across the cluttered room toward the solid metal door, and once there, he slid the section of cabinet out of the way before trying to push the door open, but to no avail. He tried to push a little harder, but it still did not budge. That was when Shameis decided to ram the door with his right shoulder. Between the sound of the door's locking mechanism breaking and the jolt of him throwing himself forward, I finally snapped out of the existential crisis I was having.

Once the door was open, Shameis shielded his eyes from a blinding white light bleeding from the other side. I guess that is one benefit of having a curse that makes me an otherworldly specter; my eyes don't have to adjust from dark spaces to light. So, since Shameis was temporarily blinded, I now began to lead him into what was beyond this door. I was half expecting to lead us out into fresh air and open skies, but instead, I found that we were entering a sterile white hallway. The tile floor, the smooth walls, and the flat ceiling were all bleached white. As I looked don the long corridor, I noticed lights that were periodically scattered throughout the ceiling as evenly spaced out birch wood doors lined the walls.

As I led Shameis through, we passed several of these doors. I honestly didn't know where I was heading, but I knew that we wasted enough time in that terrible room. However, as we passed the doors , I noticed that they all had a rectangular brass plaque near the center of the barrier at eye level. These indicators each had the name of a different doctor engraved on them, indicating the space behind may be an office or workspace. After reading a few of the names, I decided to try and blow past the rest since the hall veered off the left, but was suddenly jerked backward. This cause me to turn to Shameis, were I found him staring at a door on the right side of the hall. "Were you going to just blow by this one?" He asked, causing me to relook at the nameplate. Of course, it had Dr. Jakelyde written on it.

"Sorry, Shameis. I didn't expect him to have more than one room." I admitted.

276

"Well, if he was just on that computer, it is possible he is in here." Shameis let out as he walked me up to the door.

"You really think he is in there?" I returned.

"Not a chance. If he was here, he would've heard my rampage and ran for the hills." He answered as he reached for the door handle with his right hand. Within seconds, he turned the latch, and the door popped open.

"Did he leave the door unlocked?" I inquired.

"No... I broke it." Shameis retorted as he led me inside. Once crossing the barrier, I was greeted with a room that was darker than the blinding hallway, but not as dark as the operating room. The electrical light must've was turned off, but a window on the opposite wall of the door poured natural light in. Oh! I was so excited to see the surface of the Earth again. So, I let go of Shameis's and rushed to the window to take a look outside. It was midday, and the sky was a marvelous shade of blue overtop the building we were in. From this point, I noticed that we were nearly ten-stories above an almost filled parking lot, indicating we were in some sort of massive building. Perhaps an essential laboratory of some sort? As I looked around, I saw that the enormous parking lot was surrounded by a decently sized strip of vibrant green grass that was, in turn, surrounded by a line of luscious trees.

This would be a great day to have a picnic if it wasn't for our circumstances and a dark, ominous stormfront looming over the city skyline in the distance. Thankfully we were nowhere near it, so I could enjoy the warmth of the sun. I wish I could open the window so I could feel the breeze. Well, since I can control when I go into the Void between realms, I could pop over to that patch of grass for a bit while Shameis continues to do whatever he needs. What was he doing? With that thought, I turned away from the window and found him rummaging through a desk near the entrance. I guess the light from the window wasn't enough for him to see what he was doing since Shameis had illuminated a desk lamp.

277

As he snooped for Victor's location in the desk's several drawers, I scanned the rest of the room. Overall, it looked to be a standard rectangular office. I noticed that the shorter wall between the window and doorway had a small leather sofa pushed up against is as the opposite short wall was completely covered by a massive bookshelf. Seeing that it was filled with hundreds of books and several small house plants, I decided to walk across the rough gray carpet and past a glass-topped coffee table that sat in the middle of the room to get a better look at them all. As I approached it, I studied the titles on the spines and noted that most of these books were related to biblical texts, while others seemed like titles for pieces of fiction. I guess Victor dove headfirst into the paranormal after learning about the Lightbringer.

"There is nothing here!" Shameis grunted as he slammed a drawer of the desk closed, which startled me and caused me to spin toward him.

"Is everything okay?" I worried.

"Everything is fine," he muttered as he leaned forward while using his palms to rest on the desk before looking at me. "Is there any chance you found anything?"

"Nothing besides a lot of books. It looks like learning about the Lightbringer rocked his world." I concluded as I pointed over my shoulder to the bookshelf. "Why do you think he needed so many books?"

"There are a few reasons." Shameis let out as he made his way over toward me and the bookshelf. "One, he's a mad scientist, so he would do anything in his power to prove or disprove what he didn't understand. Two, he's really into collecting books. I'm not one to judge what a psychopath does in his free time, other than the activities that ruin other people's lives." After listing those two options, he raised his left hand up to one of the shelves and rested his hand on it before pausing

278

bit to examine the piece of furniture. "Or three, the option I'm leaning toward, Victor is using this to hide something behind it."

Now that is why Shameis was an investigator. I would never have thought of that. I know humans have a tendency to make secret hide-aways, but that idea didn't even cross my mind. "What do you think is behind there?" I questioned excitedly, to which he quickly moved his left hand from the shelf toward my face and held up his index finger as he shushed me.

"Did you hear that?" He whispered.

"No," I responded quietly. I hadn't heard anything. I was too preoccupied with how Shameis deduced this fact that I must've shut off my surroundings. But, on the other hand, I definitely should've heard something since I've used my curse to listen to the beat of a human's heart time and time again. So, I listened intently as I leaned closer to the bookshelf, and sure enough, I heard a faint groan, the rattle of chains, and the beats of two different hearts coming from the other side of this false wall. "There are two people bound up in there..." I informed Shameis as I turned to him while backing away.

Without responding, Shameis cautiously reached up to one of the many shelves with his metal hand and grabbed onto it. Once firmly held, he tried to gently pull the unit toward us. I was expecting it to come sliding toward us or start toppling over, but the force Shameis generated caused the wall of books to hinge at the center-most vertical supports. The movement revealed that the shelf was built in two sections connected by metal hinges and placed onto a track for easy opening. As I gazed upon the wonderment of human innovation, Shameis gently folded the sections and revealed another room.

As he moved the wall, I tried my best to see what was there, but the only light that reached this space was from the single window and the small desk lamp. I tried to move around Shameis to try and get a better look, but it was no use. I was just going to have to wait until Shameis finished opening the wall. Except as he did so, I was slapped with the overwhelming sensation of a terrible odor. What was that? It was not only the smell of death but excrement and decaying flesh. How could Victor willingly leave people chained up in a place like that? This is awful. So, I held my bony hand up to my nose and tried to block the smell, but it was no use.

That was when Shameis nearly finished opening the wall, and enough light shined in to reveal what was on the other side. It was not a who, nor were there two people. This was definitely a what, and it for sure had two different heartbeats. It was terrifying. It was hideous, but I couldn't take my eyes away. As I stared at this thing, the room fell silent as Shameis joined me to stare at this creature. After a few moments of prolonged staring a silence, it picked up its drooping head and began to stare directly at Shameis with peircing, reflective red irises. Then, in a deep, dark growl, this thing spoke a single word in the tone of a question. No, one word was not terrifying, but the realization that came with this word was. I mean, how else could this be? This one comment sounded as if he was trying to call out for help or for the person that had been 'caring' for it. "Doc...tor...?"

Part Three: Desiring a Resolution

Chapter Twenty-Three

Every so often, something new pops up and catches me off-guard. There was a moment right before meeting Shameis where I thought I'd seen it all. I've witnesses miraculous developments in producing energy, evolutions for how humans communicate and travel, and fantastical civilizations dwindle to mere ruins. I've existed long to witness enough man-made horrors develop and become mundane; just be replaced by even greater horrors. I feared for humanity, but evidently lost that care as I continued to watch modern day mortals sit behind their screen while their lives passed them by. I've always been impressed with the ingenuity of this species. Yet, I feel so much sorrow for those that choose to squander the graces they are given.

That was why I was ecstatic to be introduced to the heroes that Shameis mentioned. As fascinated as I was to finally see what lay beyond the Void, I've been surrounded with the metaphysical for so long that I was just ready to see something new on Earth. To witness a human woman soar through the sky or to see a man transform into a skeleton as he ran at the speed of sound would be more than I'd ever expect. I'm still not entirely sure how power humans is possible, but I'm sure it has something to do with the... thing... that knelt before us.

All things considered, I am yet to see a true superhuman other than Shameis and his superstrength. I believe Shameis's words when he says they exist, but I am yet to see these beauties. All I've seen are these three horrors connected to Victor. I don't need to be an investigator to realize that this means Victor is responsible for the monsters Shameis has fought; all innocent lives that Victor corrupted in the name of the Lightbringer. I know evil has many shapes and strengths, but the two abominations I saw before have nothing on the one we were face to face with now. All this talk about monsters begs the question, where do I fall on this spectrum? I've spent so much time causing pain and misery that I've thought myself to be the worst of them. That is why I want to become a hero so badly. But the realization that there is an unknown number of other ferrymen and that these monsters are not one-off occurrences have caused me to realize that there is so much worse in this world than me. At least I can start to atone for my transgressions since I had been freed from my shackles, unlike this poor soul. But based on his terrifying appearance, I can only assume he has no intention of performing heroic deeds.

Sure, seeing a walking skeleton is enough to send a soul running for the hills, but I'm not even able to manifest myself. Only the souls that have left the physical plane, and Shameis, can see me. Based on the appearance of this thing, it could easily maim, destroy, or kill anyone or anything. I don't even know where to start the description of this monstrosity. Maybe its head? This thing had long, stringy, and greasy black hair that covered most of its face and spherical skull. The monster's eyes were yellow with red irises that reflected the minimal amount of light reaching them as teal scale acted as its skin and razor-sharp teeth filled its unlipped mouth. I guess its lack of a nose kept the monster from being affected by the stench surrounding it.

Moving toward its torso, the teal scales continued past its thick neck and onto its chest, but transitioned into grayish flesh as it reached its abdomen. I could only assume that this monstrosity was male since its shirtless physique revealed two sets of sculpted pectorals stacked on top of each other. That's right, this thing had a total of four arms, with the lower two being scrawnier than the top two and matched the gradient of the torso. As for its other two arms, they were wildly different from its torso. Its major right arm was covered in bright yellow fur and had a hand that I can only describe as a cross between a paw and a human hand, but with three fingers. As for its major left arm, it appeared to have a bright red exoskeleton that led down to a pincer of a fiddler crab. All four of its wrists and neck were encased in metal shackles that were in turn chained to the floor, with the chains only being long enough to keep it in a kneeling position.

"Doc... tor?" The monstrosity repeated through a gruesome smile while fixating on Shameis's head. Although it was in a kneeling position, its eye level was nearly in line with Shameis's chest.

"No, I am not a doctor." Shameis denied with a trembling voice.

"Not... Doc... tor... Jakel...yde?" It grumbled as it tried to lean forward but was stopped by its restraints.

"I'm sorry. I'm so sorry. I will make him pay for what he has done to you. We will." Shameis assured the beast before looking at me. His iris was a bright yellow with a hint of red, symbolizing the fear he felt while angry that this was allowed to happen.

"Make... pay? We?" The monster quizzed while still staring at Shameis.

"Yes. Grim and I will make sure Victor is locked away for a long time because of what he did to you." Shameis promised.

"Who... Grim?" The beast continued to integrate.

"My friend. The pretty lady standing beside me." Shameis answered as he gestured to me. The monster slowly looked in my direction before turning his attention to Shameis.

"No one... there." It replied.

"Of course, it can't see me." I quickly followed up to Shameis without looking away from this abomination. "This only cements the fact that only you can see me since we are connected."

"Right..." Shameis agreed. "Then that means he never died... Right?"

"That's what I was leaning toward." I concurred. "Wait, do you know who this is?"

"Of course. Is it not obvious?" Shameis questioned in response. This time, The creature growled at Shameis to get his full attention.

"Who... Talking to?" The beast interjected.

"My friend." Shameis reiterated before bluntly asking his next question. "You are Dennis Wayne, correct?" This question caused the beast to lean back as it hung its head.

"There is no way that is the child Victor took!" I shrieked but was quickly interrupted by Shameis holding up his right index finger.

"Dennis?" Shameis then questioned the beast.

"Dennis?" It then parroted in its deep growl. "Not hear... that name... in long time..." It then confessed.

"So that is your name? Dennis Wayne?" Shameis requested for clarification which caused the monster to lift its head and reveal its wicked smile as its eyes reflected in the sunlight.

"Yes..." It confirmed in a long, drawn-out growl before falling silent.

"No... No. No. No. No! This cannot be that child! This is not what children look like!" I raved as I returned to my rant.

"It has to be. He can't be lying. Dennis's appearance matched the clues that were in that video."

"But you said this was a child!" I grilled Shameis.

"Correct. Dennis was only six or seven when Victor got his hand on him." Shameis confirmed.

"Then that would make him... What? Fourteen? Maybe Fifteen? This is not what fifteen-year-olds look like!" I pointed out.

"And we know that he is a nearly perfect host for Lightbringer. We don't know what the infections in a human's DNA can do to them when a Seraph tries to take them. We are the only two!" Shameis reminded me without looking away from the beast's stare.

"We need to free him!" I then blurted out as I began to walk toward it.

"No!" Shameis shouted before grabbing onto me and pulling me back. "There is a reason Victor keeps him locked up and hidden. He is not the first... big guy... that I have dealt with. So we need to let other people handle him. There are people for this type of situation." Shameis laid out. I guess that is true, and Shameis would know more about these matters than I. I just wish there was a way to help this child, but the damage has already been done. There is no way to roll back the time. So, I simply nodded before Shameis and I turned to walk away.

"Wait!" Dennis shrieked as it forcefully rattled its chains, causing both Shameis and I to turn back to him. "What... Your name?"

"My name is Shameis Eli," Shameis answered.

"Shameis... Eli... Don't... Know that name... How... You know me?" Dennis questioned. This caused Shameis to freeze in place as he hesitated to answer.

"Well... I tried to save you before Victor did this to you." Shameis responded.

"Save... Me?" Dennis inquired ignorantly.

"Yeah, but I was known by a different name back then." Shameis continued. "I was Isaac Enderson. The Ile."

"The... Ile..." Dennis muttered.

"Yes. I used to be a hero." Shameis confided in him. "But Victor did this to me. He turned me into a monster too."

"The... Ile..." Dennis repeated a bit louder.

"Yes..." Shameis also repeated, now getting a bit antsy.

"THE... ILE...!" Dennis now screamed as he yanked on the chains in an attempt to get up. They did seem to hold their rigidity at first, but as he continued to pull, the metal links started to bend until several connected to each of his massive arms shattered and fell to the uncarpeted floor beneath the 'child'. With these arms free, he quickly reached to the chain connected to his neck using his crab claw and cut a few links before following suit to the chains on his smaller arms, and once entirely free, he quickly started to rise up. Immediately after bringing his right leg forward, I was able to see that the mutations I noted before were not all that had changed. I couldn't tell where the change began since this beast wore a pair of jeans that had been ripped into shorts, but his legs appeared as a hybrid of tiger limbs and human legs. They were covered in black-striped orange fur, leading to furry white paws with black claws protruding from its toes. Although the fur covered the entirety of his lower half, it seemed that the mutation took place below his muscular thighs.

Once to his feet, Dennis stood tall and showed off his actual height. It towered over Shameis and me as its lanky arms dangled at its sides. It began to walk toward us, we started to back away, and we observed as it had to crouch as it exited the hide-away. This 'child' had to be standing nearly ten feet tall! As we backed away, Shameis almost tripped over the glass table that sat in the middle of the room, but when this beast reached it, it stepped right onto and through the glass with complete disregard. The beast kept driving us backward until there was

286

no more room to travel when Shameis finally entered a 'ready' stance. Seeing this, I decided to get out of the way and ran to the darkening window. "You don't need to do this, Dennis," Shameis fretted.

Unfortunately, this attempt was in vain as it only caused Dennis to strike a pose and let out a frightening screech before charging at Shameis. Shameis may have anticipated an attack, but he must not have expected Dennis's overwhelming might. Within seconds, Dennis rammed his furry yellow shoulder into Shameis's torso, launching him back into the wall over the leather sofa. Then, after Shameis smacked into the wall, he fell on the couch in a sitting position. That was when I noticed the drywall that absorbed Shameis's impact had severely weakened with a massive impact mark.

"Not... Name... Anymore!" Dennis shouted before letting out a terrifyingly loud howl.

"Okay. I understand not wanting to be yourself anymore." Shameis listened as he slowly rose to his feet while raising his palms in a non-offensive position.

"Shameis! What are you doing? You need to fight back!" I warned Shameis, but he just looked at me and shook his head in disagreement before looking back to Dennis.

"That's why I am not The Ile anymore. So, tell me what I should call you." Shameis continued.

"CHIMERA!" Dennis let out with a long, drawn-out growl before raising its giant yellow fist and throwing a haymaker. Upon contact, Shameis was again blasted toward the wall behind him, but this time he went straight through the drywall and wood beams. Following Shameis into the next room, Chimera blew through the wall destroying the couch in the process and nearly taking down the entire wall. I wasn't too worried as I knew Shameis could hold his own

287

against this brute, but I wondered why Shameis wasn't fighting back. It had to be because this horror was the child he failed to save. This was the only reasonable answer.

So, as I followed behind the Chimera, I peered into the next room and the exact same display as Victor's office. It had identical furniture in the same position, the carpet was uniform, and even the desks were twin. I guess I didn't hear it from all the wall debris that was falling to the ground, but Shameis ended up flying far enough to crash through this new room's glass coffee table, meaning that they too were now identical. The only reason I could think of as to these rooms being identical was for the sole reason of stashing away Dennis. And if that is the case, that would explain why Shameis couldn't find any information about Victor here.

So, as I peered past the now demolished wall around Dennis's hulking body, I watched as Shameis slowly sat up on his bed of glass while his hands were still raised in a non-confrontational position. I guess putting on the lab coat was some good foresight since it protected him from the shards of glass. "Dennis, please. I am not trying to hurt you." Shameis proclaimed as he tried to get up.

"CHI...MER...A..." Dennis shrieked in response as he pounced on Shameis, wrapped his massive fiddler crab claw around Shameis's neck, and hoisted him to his feet and into the air. While this was happening, I quickly crossed into the new room and positioned myself near Shameis.

"Why are you... doing this?" Shameis struggled to get out. "I just... wanted... to help..."

"You... no help... Is... Ile fault... I... like this..." Chimera growled as he pulled Shameis's head closer to its own. Shameis did try to free himself from Chimera's grasp, but it seemed that Shameis's gifted strength was no match for the animalistic ruthlessness.

288

"It wasn't me." Shameis gasped. "It was Victor. Dr. Jakelyde. He did this to you. Victor wanted to kill you. To give you to the Lightbringer."

"Doctor... Fault..." Chimera repeated.

"Yes! Doctor's fault. Let me go. We can find him together." Shameis begged.

"Ile think... Doctor... Lock up Chimera... Torture Chimera?" Chimera questioned as he tightened his grip around Shameis's neck. "Doctor... lock up Chimera... to protect Doctor. Doctor... tell Chimera... Chimera is monster... because Lightbringer... Doctor save Chimera... Lightbringer make Chimera... Ile no save Dennis..."

"I tried to save you." Shameis wheezed. "Victor kidnapped me too. Victor turned me into a monster for the Lightbringer too. I look like this because the Doctor hurt me. The Doctor hurt you. The Doctor turned Dennis into Chimera."

"Doctor... Fault..." Chimera parroted again. "Ile... Fault too..."

"No, you're not listening! Ile help... Doctor Hurt..." Shameis pleaded.

"Doctor say... Ile bad. Ile say... Doctor bad... Both hurt Chimera. Chimera kill both." He professed as he extracted a razor-sharp black claw from each tip of the yellow paw-like fingers on his right hand and slashed Shameis diagonally across his abdomen. Instantly, a deep red liquid began to pour out of Shameis as his body went limp. Seeing this, Dennis let go of Shameis's neck and let him fall back onto the bed of glass.

"No!" I shouted as I followed Shameis's body to the floor and knelt beside him as I quickly placed my hands onto the wound to try and prevent as much blood from leaving his body as I could. Due to how he had fallen, his bleach white coat was bunched up underneath his shoulder

289

blades, so Shameis's blood began to pool and mix with the shards of glass below his bare back. Thankfully this attack didn't kill Shameis on impact, but I was still frightened that this would quickly escalate. "Not again," I repeated to myself over and over as I pressed onto him. How could I expect to be a hero like Shameis? How could I wish to save another soul if I can't even save my other half? Unfortunately, unlike last time Shameis sustained a fatal wound, we won't have Zatael's help. We are on our own, and I have no idea what to do. Wait! Yes, I do! I have the power that Zateal gave to me! I could heal him! "Don't worry, Shameis! I'll save you!" Let's just hope this wound isn't too drastic to recover from.

Part Three: Desiring a Resolution

Chapter
Twenty-Four

I'm starting to question my decision on wanting to become a hero. I just don't understand why anyone would choose this. I know it takes a lot of determination and bravery to stand at the model you want your society to live up to, but is it worth putting yourself in harm's way just to do what you think is right? Shameis is lucky that I am here because if he would've sustained a wound like this without me, there would've been no way he could've recovered. This just makes me wonder how he acted while serving as The Ile. Was he this reckless, or did seeing what lay beyond and learning of the entity in our souls open his mind enough to become like this? I mean, I know Zatael's power is what drove Shameis into becoming a hero, but he would have acted like this before, right? If monsters like Chimera existed before, then there was no way a regular human was this open. That has to be why Ile's costume was so black and armored, so he could hide and protect himself.

It's almost as if Shameis is now the exact opposite of what he used to be; besides the desire to do good. He's wearing a bright white mask, a white and now tattered lab coat, and blue jeans with no armor other than his metallic arm. From the few interactions I've seen, he's willing to talk and try to get through to his opponent while quipping instead of his "I'm here to get things done" attitude I saw in that movie about The Ile. It's so strange, and don't get me wrong, I do like that he is willing to try and get to the bottom of the mystery as opposed to punching first and asking later, but still, I find it odd that all this changed as soon as he got his memories back. I may not understand what it takes to be a hero yet, but I am willing to stand by Shameis's side as he shows me what it means.

With that being said, I have no idea how to heal him. I know I can. I just have no idea what to do to activate the power Zatael gave to me. I'm not a healer and never been. Throughout my entire existence, all I've done is take life. My brother, the souls on this planet, heck, I could barely keep a flock of sheep healthy. All I've known is death. I guess I should've realized that my time in my body was a foreshadowing of the rest of my existence. But now is not the time to reminisce about the past. I need to push forward and embrace my new life! No more self-pity. No more death! I may be the Grim Reaper, but I will not allow this life to slip through my fingers! So, as I pressed onto the wound and as Shameis's cool blood flowed through my fingers and pooled under my robed knees, all I could think of was what happened in the realm of Wrath. Shameis's blood flowing backward into the orifice just before Shameis waking up and taking control of the situation. At this moment, I was hoping for Zatael to manifest and possess both of us so he could handle everything like he did last time, but this was on us.

Then, as I gazed down at Shameis's wound, I observed a miraculous sight. My hand started to glow that pale light that I've associated with Zatael's power. Seeing this, I pressed down onto Shameis's wound a little bit harder. That was when the light transferred from my hands to Shameis's injury and, in turn, his blood began to flow backward once again. "What... Happening?" Chimera inquired from overtop of me. Yeah, this was a bit miraculous, and I'm sure it would be even more so for a child with little grasp on anything it can't see. Although I wanted to see

Chimera's expression, I needed to focus on Shameis. As I kept alternating my attention from Shameis's glowing wound to his expressionless face, I started to worry that this might be too late since it was taking what seemed to be a really long time. That was until Shameis's closed eye sprung open to reveal that his iris was once again glowing the same color as my hands and his wound, but only lasted for a few seconds before fading into his natural hazel iris. I was so elated to seet hat he was okay. So, I used this knowledge to ease my nerves and look back down to the wound. Except it and all the spilled blood had vanished! There werent even scars from this attack! However, the massive scar Shameis sustained from Zatael's sword had manifested instead. I was worried about the implications this might mean, but I didn't have much time to think about it as Shameis quickly sat up and looked directly into my eyes.

"I knew you could do it." He muttered.

"At least one of us did..." I muttered back.

"Hey, you had no idea about how to use that power." Shameis comforted me as he reached out and put his right hand on my shoulder. "Zatael is glad you were able to figure it out."

"You spoke to Zatael?" I cross-examined excitedly.

"Slightly. While out, I was *pulled* into my subconscious for a split second, where Zatael explained a few things to me. So I know what we need to do. He also where we will find the information we need." Shameis explained. "He also said I wasn't going to see him again..."

"Right... Zatael did say we would see him only two more times after the realm of lust. And I guess the realm of Wrath was the first of the two." I recalled. As soon as I said that, Chimera let out a ferocious growl.

"Who... Talking to? Why... Not die?" Chimera shrieked, to which Shameis quickly rocked onto his feet as the glass crunched beneath him and as his unstained lab coat unraveled.

"I was not talking to you." Shameis declared as he turned toward the Chimera while bushing excess shards of glass off himself. Seeing him do this while talking to the Chimera made me realize that I, too, needed to get up off the ground. So I did and quickly rushed back to the gaping hole in the wall.

"No one else... Here!" It continued to shriek as it lunged at Shameis with its crab claw, but Shameis easily dodged underneath and spun around.

"Just because you can't see them doesn't mean no one else is here." Shameis professed as Chimera spun and tried to swipe at Shameis with both its razor-sharp talons and jagged pincer while Shameis dodged. "This isn't your fault Dennis. I now know that your mutation isn't because of me or Victor. This is because of the Lightbringer. The madness affecting him from the Timekeeper and Lifegiver caused you to grow up and change into this." Now that was an exciting revelation. I guess it does make sense, though. If Chimera was the first attempt to host the Lightbringer, then it does stand to reason that Lightbringer's afflictions would have side effects. But is that how those first two beasts I saw with victor were created? Or were they imitations of what Lightbringer caused? Whatever it was, this information caused Chimera to stop flailing around for a moment.

"Chimera... hate... YOU..." it yelped before trying to grab onto Shameis's neck with his lobster claw again. This time, Shameis dodged underneath the claw and ran around Chimera until he was near this room's window. That was when I realized what Shameis was doing. He purposely tried to antagonize Chimera into messing up while trying to wear him out. Chimera's strength may be greater than Shameis's, but Shameis had the monster beat when it came to speed.

"Dennis, I know this may be a shock, but you're thirty-seven. Not fifteen. I will make the Lightbringer pay for doing this to you, but you need to calm down! If you don't, I will treat you the same way I handled

294

all those adult monsters." Shameis proclaimed as he balled up his fists and prepared to go on the offensive.

"Liar! CHIMERA... HATE... ILE..." Chimera belted out and swung his right yellow paw as a fist, to which Shameis quickly blocked with his left hand and delivered a blow with his metal fist to Chimera's right elbow. That punch caused the sound of ripping tendons to fill the air as it was quickly followed by the wail of pain escaping past Chimera's insidious grin. I guess the information about Dennis's age caused Shameis to snap into his old habits? No, he did give an ultimatum. No way! I get it now! Shameis wasn't fighting back because he was trying not to cross that line! Shameis won't hurt kids and was giving Dennis the benefit of the doubt because of the gray area. This means that though Shameis was once a ruthless protector, he had a code that he still adheres to! Is that what it means to be a hero? Having the power to do whatever is needed but restraining yourself over what you believe is just? I can get behind that.

"I have not been The Ile in six years!" Shameis shouted to Chimera, snapping me back to their fight. "The same amount of time you have been the Chimera." This bit of information caused a look of confusion to come across Chimera's face.

"But... just saw... Ile..." It muttered.

"What do you mean you just saw The Ile?" Shameis demanded to know while slightly dropping his guard. Seeing this, Chimera then pounced at Shameis while letting out another ferocious roar with the intent of trying to bite Shameis with its massive fangs. This sequence caused Shameis to leap forward. Instead of meeting the Chimera, Shameis did a strange somersault maneuver and rolled across Chimera's spiny back, causing Shameis to land on his feet above the broken glass in the middle of the room. The instant shift in momentum caused Chimera to lose balance and tumble face-first into the window's glass, shattering it. With the window now being open, a strong gust of wind quickly blew past Chimera's massive body as he leaned over the ten-story drop. A blast that strong could only mean that the storm cloud I observed earlier was approaching rapidly. However, Shameis paid no attention to the weather as his sight was fixated on the Chimera with his coat flapping in the wind. At this moment, I realized that the coat's right sleeve began to tear around the shoulder seam, revealing a bit of his metal arm. "I didn't want to hurt you, Dennis," Shameis hollered.

"Chimera, kill you..." It declared as it pulled itself back into the room before slowly charging at Shameis. Once again, Shameis dodged, rolling to Chimera's right before popping back up to his feet. The room wasn't wide, so by the time Chimera had caught itself and had turned around to face Shameis, Shameis had already been within arm's length. Then, before Chimera could react, Shameis leaped into the air and landed a haymaker with his metal fist on the right side of Chimera's jaw. The impact caused the monster to lose its balance and fall backward through this office's oak desk.

"I told you, if you wanted to act like an adult, then I was going to treat you like an adult. I'm sorry that all this bad stuff happened to you because I couldn't save you, but that does not mean you can act like the monster they turned you into. I'll ensure the correct people take care of you." Shameis proclaimed as he walked up to the Chimera's left side and swung a punch from his right arm, intending to knock out the beast, but Chimera quickly caught Shameis's arm with its crab claw.

"You... don't know... Chimera. Chimera... Apex Predator... Chimera... no lose. Chimera... kill doctor... and Ile... Both Ile... Chimera kill... All Heroes!" It shrieked as it quickly rose to its feet while trying to squeeze the claw on Shameis's arm. The sound of straining metal could be heard, but I was surprised that Shameis's arm didn't break. "You... lose arm!" It shrieked as it applied more force onto the arm while driving Shameis a few steps backward past the shattered glass. The expression on Chimera's face first appeared as if he expected to win this transaction, but it quickly changed to an expression of confusion. "What... gives? Why... Not break?"

"Shameis... Is that what I think it is?" I questioned with severe skepticism and amazement.

"It is. Deitanium, the metal of the angels. Apparently, Lightbringer gave a substantial amount of it to Jakelyde when tasked to experiment on the humans. It is one of the chemicals used to alter human DNA into potential hosts. It boosts the candidates that were thought to be close enough. Still, after getting some of the material, Victor decided to have some tools crafted. What are the odds that he would graft such a tool to me? He probably did it for the Lightbringer." Shameis explained.

"Was that also part of the info Zatael gave you while I healed you?" I assumed.

"Bingo!" Shameis agreed.

"Angel... metal?" Chimera interrupted while still trying to break Shameis's arm.

"Stuff you wouldn't understand." Shameis shot down. "It's knowledge me and my imaginary friend share."

"Is that all I am to you?" I giggled, knowing he was joking. "Your imaginary friend?"

"Until we figure out a way to get others to see you, then you'll be much more." Shameis provocative suggested, to which I giggled again. I guess Dennis didn't like what Shameis said since he quickly let out a fierce roar before letting go of Shameis's arm.

"Chimera... am Smart!" Is howled as it swung its limp right arm at Shameis, to which Shameis easily caught underneath his left arm. What followed, I can only describe as peak performance on Shameis's behalf. Within seconds of hooking Chimera's right paw, Shameis firmly grabbed the right elbow, which caused Chimera to yelp. Then, fell backward while twisting to the left. It sounds simple, but the momentum transfer caused Chimera to follow suit and become airborne. Since Chimera was startled to be sent flying, he desperately tried to grab Shameis again but could only latch onto his right sleeve. Since it had begun to tear, all Chimera did was detach the arm from the rest of the coat as he hurtled toward the wall with the window. Between the massive creature's weight and the hole already caused by the window, a gigantic crack and indentation was formed before Chimera fell to the ground.

After laying on the ground for a few seconds, Chimera slowly rose from the ground before stopping in a kneeling position; supporting himself with all his limbs beside his right arm. Judging by how heavily he was breathing, it seemed that he was not used to being beaten like this. So, Chimera turned his head to look at Shameis as Shameis made his way to the creature, and once within reaching distance, Chimera tried to swing its crab claw at Shameis. I guess Shameis anticipated another attack since he met the cretaceous pincer with the fist of his prosthetic arm. The collision filled the room with the sound of a cracking shell followed by more whimpers of pain. "I told you to stop attacking." Shameis reminded Chimera as he stood above the fallen behemoth.

"Chimera... kill you..." Chimera muttered as he pushed himself up onto his knees while trying to grab Shameis with the smaller, injured arms. All Shameis had to do to avoid this was to take a step back, which gave enough space for Chimera to return to its feet. Then, slowly, it pulled its right foot out from underneath itself and prepared to pounce again. I could see in Shameis's eye that he really didn't want to fight anymore, but Chimera just kept coming. Once on his tiger-like paws, Chimera slowly swung his limp yellow paw again. Does it not realize that this arm is all but broken? Or is it willing to endure pain to use the only natural weapons it has? Well, whatever the reason, Shameis again caught Chimera's arm before yanking on it, causing Chimera to stumble forward while yelping. With this, Shameis quickly rammed his shoulder into Chimera's incoming chest and knocked him back into the weakened wall. I swear I saw the whole wall shift as if it was about to topple over.

"This is your last warning." Shameis barked. "Stop attacking. I am not The Ile anymore."

"Then... What... Are you?" Chimera whimpered as it looked toward the ground while leaning against the wall with its guard completely vanished.

"I'm an experiment like you. The Lightbringer wanted me too, but I am here to fight against the Lightbringer. I am Shameis Eli." Shameis answered. "Now, Stay here. I will find someone to take care of you." Upon saying that, Shameis turned toward the new office's still-closed door and attempted to leave, which I started to follow as I kept my eye on Chimera. And I'm glad I did. As soon as Shameis crossed back over the shards of glass, Chimera lifted its head as its reptilian eyes glimmered while opening his heinous grin wide with the intent of biting my partner.

"Shameis! Watch out!" I shouted, which alerted Shameis to spin while throwing a haymaker with his metal fist. The punch then made contact with Chimera's razor-sharp teeth and shattered them. If that was the final result of the blow, I'm sure Chimera would have finally conceded. However, the outcome was so much worse. The force of Shameis's punch caused Chimera to be launched back into the fractured wall for the third time. Unfortunately, this time it wasn't able to catch the creature. As Chimera hurdled through the wall, chunks of wood, drywall, and thick cement bricks followed as the sound of Chimera's howling plummeted to the parking lot below.

Initially, both Shameis and I stood in stunned silence while gazing out of the hole, but we quickly snapped back to reality and rushed over to the new opening after hearing the sound of smashing glass and twisting metal as car alarms blared. Several cars had shattered glass from the falling debris, and one vehicle appeared to be crushed from Chimera's impact, but Chimera was nowhere to be seen. After a few seconds of wondering where Chimera had gone off to, Shameis pointed out a sign in the distance near where the parking lot connected to the main road.

"Of course. We had to be at Cherished Souls General Hospital. Where else would Victor be able to get a near-endless supply of volunteers for his unethical experiments." Shameis let out.

"Cherished Souls General Hospital? Near the outskirts of Chicago, Illinois?" I then questioned as I turned to look at him.

"Yeah..." Shameis let out as he stared out toward the approaching stormcloud, to which I let out a sigh as I too stared at it.

"You said that you knew where we needed to go to?" I questioned awkwardly since I really didn't know how to comfort a situation like the one Shameis just went through.

"Right, we have to go into the city," Shameis answered.

"Why? Shouldn't we stay as far away from the person using your mantle?" I cross-examined. "I mean, I know that we will eventually need to come forth and tell the world that you're a hero. But that won't be until after we beat Victor. If the heroes find you and lock you up for looking differently, then we won't be able to stop Victor or The Lightbringer."

300

"That's my fear too. But Zatael said that the information we seek is in my old bunker." Shameis informed me.

"So we just have to get into downtown Chicago?" I wondered as I turned my attention back to the City. "But if that is Chicago, that has to be seven miles away."

"It is seven miles in a straight line from here. With twists and turns, it'll be more like ten to twelve." He corrected me.

"I am not walking that far," I rejected his implied proposal as I pulled out my scythe.

"Right! I forgot you could open portals!" He retorted as he turned to look at me.

"Yeah, but being in the Void under my own power instead of being *pulled* drains my energy. Seven miles might be a bit too far." I suggested.

"Don't worry, Grim. We'll be able to make it." Shameis responded. Just then, a loud, rhythmic thump sounded from the closed wood door of the office we were standing in.

"This is the Police. Come out with your hands up, or we will enter by force!" A male voice sounded from the other side of the chunk of wood serving as a barrier.

"I guess that wraps up our time here. We need to go! Now!" Shameis suggested, to which I nodded in agreement. So, with my scythe in my right hand, I reached out toward Shameis with my left. Once feeling his metal fingers interlock with my own, I quickly slashed my scythe at the open air just above the parking lot. Instantly, a portal to the Void opened.

Remember, we have to know where we want to go, or the other end won't open and since I don't, you need to keep the image in mind." So I instructed before leading Shameis through the swirling vortex. As we passed through, I could hear the sound of the door bursting open. I'm not sure why they didn't just come through the entrance to the office that

301

we thought to be Victor's since it was still open, but now all I could do is speculate. Humans are weird creatures.

Nevertheless, after Shameis and I stepped into the darkness of the Void, the portal we used to get here closed. Now all we have to do is walk through this darkness until the other end opens. That is if Shameis is thinking of where we need to go. I really hope he was because the heaviness of the Void hit me instantly; like a ton of bricks. And this time, it was heavier than I ever felt. Was this because I was dragging a living body with me. I'm exhausted! It felt as if I was sinking deeper into mud with every step. I tried to focus on my efforts, but it was too much. I quickly lost count.

I don't know how long we walked for. It could've been ten steps or one thousand, but I dredged on. Thankfully, I did see the light of the exit portal appear. However, I lost control of my legs by this point and felt myself begin to collapse. When I did this, Shameis did call out to me, but I couldn't hear what he said. My hearing and vision were beginning to blur. That was when I felt him hoist me up and begin to carry me toward the exit. I knew he wouldn't leave me behind, even though the thought might've crossed my mind. Is this what it's like for humans when they near a natural passing due to old age? They lose all their energy and fade, only to be confronted by an outside force to help lift them again? It was terrifying, but being on the receiving end did make me feel loved and cared for. That is why I always tried to be as friendly as possible, but not many humans are keen on a walking, talking skeleton. I am incredibly grateful for Shameis to help in my time of need, and I am glad that my decision to devote my time and resources to him did not go up in smoke. I guess you could say that I was falling for him.

Chapter Twenty-Five

Over the millennia, I have encountered many souls that had taken their own lives. Each and every encounter resulting from this type of action was saddening, but I felt like there had to be a reason for why this was happening. So, of course, I've pried into their situations and thought processes. Many claimed that their actions were due to loneliness, depression, the loss of another, or even the loss of their material wealth. Yes, those may be a reasonable answer to my inquisition. Still, as this kept occurring and I received more and more perspectives, I've concluded that the true underlying reason is that these souls felt stuck in their position and powerless to free themselves. I will admit, I, too, have struggled with this thought, although my situation was vastly different since I had nowhere else to go.

As I encountered these souls, I wondered how to help the human race and prevent this from happening. I knew I couldn't converse with them before their passing, but there were few occasions when they could be saved and sent back to the earth. If only I knew what I knew now, perhaps I could've enlightened them for the hardships that lay beyond what they understood. If only I could've told them that the angels they wished to be with looked down upon them as humans looked to ants. Then again, if I had known what I knew now, I think the only thing I would tell them is that life on earth is entirely more impactful than what lies beyond.

Still, I understand their need for escape. I have always hated the feeling of being useless and trapped. If Azrael forced me into isolation, my drive to become useful again would never have manifested. I now know that he was only acting on the orders of the Lightbringer and that my only saving grace was the Worldforger, but if these circumstances had never aligned, I wouldn't be here now.

I don't want to beat a dead horse by bringing it up again, but I'm starting to think about it now since those thoughts of uselessness are beginning to flood my brain. Falling limp in the Void was the one thing I've always feared. I've tried to evade the topic for as long as I could, but I can't avoid it forever. So, as much as I sympathize with the souls looking for something better, there is nothing worse than the feeling of falling endlessly in a sea of nothingness. This is the exact reason why I pay no mind to the souls that refuse to come with me. Once the Void has taken as much energy as it can from a soul, then it swallows you. The imaginary floor is the energy draining from the soul. I'm pretty sure that is why this trip was worse than any other; I was feeding it for the both of us. It's moments like where the fact that this place is the river Styx makes sense.

That's how I knew I could trust Lucifer when we met him at the tree or in the Realm of Wrath. Just after my soul was taken and dumped into the Void by Azrael, I was subjected to its harshness. I don't know how long I had fallen, but I was ready to give up. That was when Lucifer swooped in to save me. I'll forever be thankful to that angel, but I am even more grateful for having Shameis at my side. He knew exactly what needed to be done. Instead of letting me fall, he held fast, hoisted me up, and carried me through the exit. I know that this must've been rough since the Void needs to take its chunk of flesh, but I began to recover as soon as Shameis took charge. My vision refocused and my hearing returned, but it wasn't until we left the Void that I felt my strength start to come back.

Although I could feel my energy returning, I knew it would be a while until I was at full strength. But, at least I had enough strength to look around. Instantly, I noted the peculiarity of where Shameis's imagination had led us. I thought he was supposed to be thinking of his bunker. But, instead, we found ourselves exiting into an alleyway between two fifteen-story brick buildings. I was about to inquire why he led us here, but Shameis had other priorities. Immediately after stepping onto the concrete ground, he rushed over one of to the buildings and promptly sat me down. Once in a sitting position with my back propped up against the wall, he then ran to a silver trash can near the other building, lifted its lid, moved the gauze from in front of his mouth, and proceeded to unload whatever contents he had in his stomach. Yep, that was the exact reaction I had after the Void stole my energy for the first time.

I couldn't see what his skin looked like from this distance, and frankly, I didn't want to. I have nothing against how he would look underneath his bandages, as my feelings would remain the same. I've encountered countless burn victims, humans with terrible scarring, people that were ripped apart by shrapnel and other war-time explosives, and those with disabilities that might haunt another person's dreams. They are all just flesh that serves as a temporary vessel until the soul within develops into their true selves. I know Shameis has scarring, and it doesn't bother me. What does, however, is watching a human relieve themselves in whatever way they need to. I know it is natural but I prefer not to see it.

So, as Shameis did what he needed to do, I decided to look around our environment to see what was going on, but there wasn't much. To my left, the two buildings we were between connected to create a dead end. That section of the building wasn't as tall as the rest, maybe only three or four stories, but it was hard to tell since there weren't any windows. Matter of fact, neither of the taller buildings had windows either. I guess it makes sense, though. I don't know a single human that would like to overlook a dingy alley or to look into another person's home... unless they were a creep. With that being said, there were a few doors leading to this alley. One was positioned near the trash can Shameis was hurling into, one was placed next to me and near a stack of boxes and shipping pallets, and the final one was near a green metal dumpster pushed up against the middle of the shorter wall. I don't know why humans need a trash can when a dumpster is less than twenty feet away, but I have seen them do weirder things.

Overall, this was just an ordinary alley. It even had murky puddles of water that never seemed to evaporate. So why would Shameis lead us here instead of to his bunker? Maybe what we needed to go to was across the street from here, and this was just a safe place to open a portal? But, of course, that was just wishful thinking since the entrance to this dead end led out to a four-lane road while a parking garage sat directly across from here. Strangely enough, it seemed that all the lights inside it were off, and the gate was down. Even the sign that would display the pay rate to park there was shut off. As odd as I found this, I found it even weirder that not a single person or car had passed by within the several seconds. If we are in downtown Chicago, the streets should be bustling. Perhaps the ominous cloud that was now blanketing the city had something to do with it? This wasn't sitting right with me.

"Hey Grim, what are you still doing down there?" Shameis called out, causing me to snap my attention back to him. He had recovered from his nausea, but his iris was still greener than it should be.

"I can't move. The Void took a lot of energy from me." I bluntly informed him as he proceeded over to me.

"That must be why I felt the effects of it this time." He then pieced together. "What was the difference between last time and now?"

306

"Distance. I felt the strain last time as well, but we didn't go as far." I answered.

"Ahh. Well, I guess that means I'm going to have to carry you." Shameis joked as he crouched down and grabbed onto my arms before spinning around. He then leaned forward, which caused me to move off the wall and onto his back. Once sure I was correctly positioned, Shameis stood up while holding onto my arms so he could carry me like a backpack. "I would cradle you again, but I'm going to need my arms."

"No, this is fine," I assured him. "How far are we going to have to walk since you didn't take us to your bunker?"

"That's the thing. I did exactly what you said to do. I thought of my bunker for a while, and nothing was happening. But when I thought of this place, the exit portal opened instantly." Shameis explained. "I guess I was just a little too late."

"Seriously, it's fine. At least you were there to catch me." I affirmed, to which he nodded his head and began to walk toward the dead end. "So, how do we need to go?"

"Not far." He answered shortly.

"Okay... Well, is it in one of these buildings?" I followed up.

"Close." He again answered shortly.

"Then where are we heading?" I continued to quiz him.

"We are right where we need to be." He answered as we reached the left side of the dumpster, to which he took off the medallion with his left hand and held it next to it.

"In an alley? What if a passer-by would find it?" I worried as he slid the medallion along the edge and around the dumpster.

"Not possible. The entrance is masked with a perception field provided by Hardrive. She's a heroine on the council, and from my understanding, she is a tech-wiz." He put forth.

"If you have a technomancer on your team, then why was the computer I saw in my vision while in the realm of lust just a hobbled mess?" I inquired.

"The only reason I allowed Gabby to use her skills on the outside of this place was so I could have my bunker hidden, but I tried my best not to rely on the rest of the heroes." He answered as he rounded the second corner and slid the medallion along the right side.

"Gabby?" I followed up.

"Yeah, Gabriella Keen. That's Hardrive's real name." I answered.

"Oh, okay. Then what are you doing now?" I then questioned.

"This is supposed to be a key to unlock the door without using voice commands." He elaborated before walking us to the front side of the dumpster while sliding the necklace into the left pocket of his coat and stepping a few steps away. "Computer. Access Base. Isaac Enderson: I01". He commanded toward the large metal receptacle, but nothing happened. "Computer. Override: Access Base. Ile. Isaac Enderson: CS02," but yet again, nothing happened. "I guess this should be expected." Shameis then muttered.

"Are you sure this is the right alley? Or maybe the new Ile and other heroes decided to move the base?" I questioned while staring at the average-looking trash bin. "I did notice that the power across the street was out. If your base is on the same grid, then maybe the power is out?"

"No, this is the right place. Zatael was adamant about it. And the bunker is powered by a small nuclear reactor, also designed by Hardrive. She said that it is supposed to have the capability to power one thousand homes for eight hundred years before running out of energy. The issue probably stems from the fact that I was missing for six years. The council probably had my credentials wiped from the system so an adversary couldn't gain entry. Smart." Shameis put forth.

308

"I guess that makes sense," I concurred. "Then how are we going to get in?"

"The hard way. Forgive me for this." He apologized preemptively, and before I could respond, he quickly rushed back over to the left side of the dumpster. Once close enough to the corner of the dumpster that met the building, he leaned forward so that I would balance on his back, then placed his left foot onto the building's brick wall and slid the fingers of both his hands into the small crevice between the structures. Just after preparing himself, I felt a slight jerk that nearly knocked me off his back. Thankfully, I could use some of my returned energy to hold on ever so slightly.

So, with that jostle, Shameis strained to separate the dumpster from the building. This was when I got my first real inclination that this alley aligned with Shameis's claim instead of being ordinary. Even with his advanced strength, the bin didn't seem to budge. The sound of straining metal did start to grow, but nothing else was happening. That is until a loud snap boomed down the alley, followed by a second and third. After a few more seconds of pulling, finally, the bin was launched. The shock of the release did cause Shameis to stumble backward while nearly dropping me, but he recovered pretty quickly. Once stable, he turned and saw that the bin had slid down the alleyway and crashed into the pile of discarded boxes I sat beside. From its final resting place, I could see two massive connection points with wires poking out of them on the dumpster's back, so I yanked my head around to examine where it used to sit. There, I saw a set of metal tracks that led into the wall with ripped wires, broken bolts, and destroyed mechanisms that kept it in place with a not-so-noticeable false garage-like door for the dumpster to retract into.

Once that obstacle was out of the way, Shameis then walked onto the grimy, wet concrete that the dumpster sat upon and crouched so he was able to touch the ground. Without hesitation, he punched his

309

metal fist down through the concrete, to which we were greeted with more ear-wrenching sounds of twisting metal. Then, without pulling his hand out, he began to pull up, and much like the trash bin, he struggled to move whatever he was grabbing. Still, I was impressed by his strength as he slowly bent a thick metal floor while the concrete covering began to crumble. He may not have been making much progress, but it was a spectacle to see nonetheless. If Shameis could bend metal that was nearly six inches thick and I could heal the human body within seconds, then I was extremely excited to see what the other heroes could do. And with that wonder, a strange foul odor quickly filled the air.

"It's cool that you're doing this, But won't this set off an alarm?" I shouted.

"Of course it will! But I'm hoping to find what we need before whoever is wearing my costume shows up with back up!" He shouted back but then stopped pulling on the metal shortly after. "It's a good thing I have this arm and that I know how to use it."

"Right! How long do you think it'll take for the new Ile to show up?" I then questioned.

"No idea. If they aren't here, they're either at whatever their day job is or is out taking care of the city." He answered.

"Day job?" I wondered.

"Well, yeah. Heroing doesn't pay the bills." Shameis clarified.

"I guess that makes sense. So, did whatever you did here short circuit a secret entrance or something?" I inquired while knowing precisely what the purpose of this hole was for... but was hoping that wouldn't be the case.

"Come on, Grim. You know we have to go down there." He enforced my worry as he moved close to the hole.

"But it smells..." I let out.

310

"Yep. It's a sewer." He enlightened me as he grabbed my arms tightly before jumping into the hole. We didn't fall far, maybe six feet or so. From what I could see with the bit of light provided from Shameis's opening, I could see that Shameis was not lying when he claimed it was part of the Chicago city sewer system. As one could imagine, we were in a half-circle tunnel made of large gray bricks filled with a truely horrendous smell. At least it seemed that we wouldn't have to go much further since directly in front of us, in line with the dead end of the alley, was a dead end of the sewer. Except there was a solid metal door without a handle built straight into the wall. Behind us was just blackness, so I knew that this door was what we were looking for.

Seeing the door, Shameis reached into his pocket and pulled out the medallion before walking up to and holding the necklace to it. This time, the necklace caused the sound of several metal clanks and gears turning to echo throughout the empty tunnel, symbolizing the door was unlocking. It did take a few seconds to finish this process, but once it did, it ended with a single heavy clank as the door popped open enough to grab onto. I knew I was nervous to see what was on the other side, but Shameis was even more so since his heart began to race racing.

I couldn't tell if he was excited to return to a place he once frequented regularly, nervous about being face to face with the person that took his role, or terrified to break into a hero's bunker while appearing as a monster. Whatever the reason, we were here now, and there was no turning back. Shameis even received divine intervention telling him we needed to be here. So as he pulled open the door and began to walk us into the next space, I knew that I needed to play the role of support, even if I couldn't stand on my own at the moment. I could feel that whatever came next was emotional, so I needed to support the man I had fallen for. I just hope my newfound healing ability translates to emotions as well as it does for the physical.

312

CHIMERA

Chapter Twenty-Six

Based on what I know about modern society, change will always be one of the most difficult challenges a soul will ever encounter. No matter how simple the subject matter in question, the action of deliberately changing one's life is never easy to grasp. It's the fear of the Unknown that causes such resistance, and I know that it takes nerves of steel to be able to jump headfirst into something new. However, once the plunge is taken, the benefits will outweigh the determinants more often than not. On both sides of the coin, I've seen stories about rags to riches and others of riches to rags all due to their unwillingness to change. I can not express how many souls I have collected over the years were placed into my grasp because they refused to change.

On the other hand, not all changes can be good. For example, picking up unhealthy habits like smoking and the overconsumption of alcohol is a massive detriment to human health. An estimated six million and 3 hundred thousand souls pass every year because something in their lives caused these souls to pick up these filthy habits as a coping mechanism. I say this as if I know that admitting change needs to occur and accepting the hinge point is the same. But, no, much like when dealing with grief, the admittance and acceptance of change are two wildly different beasts.

Then there are situations like the one I had to face when taken from my life. The situations forced upon a soul, even when the change is unwarranted, like losing a loved one or being forced to do something a person would never do in the first place. Situations where a soul has no other choice but to dredge forward with the terrible change weighing on their back. Sometimes change is hard to deal with, causing the adaptation of unhealthy coping mechanisms. For example, some people may start to over-eat, while others will stop eating entirely. Then, the deniers refuse to believe something has changed, or the ragers become violent when faced with the ugly truth. Sometimes I feel like Shameis falls between these two options, but at least he sprinkles in some jokes for my sake.

My apologies. I don't mean to speak upon such heavy thoughts. Whenever I am faced with situations that remind me of how I became who I am today, my train of thinking tends to run on darker tracks. So far, Shameis and I had had relatively similar journeys that seemed to nearly mirror each other. First, both of our problems started with the loss of someone we cared for, my loss being my brother and his being Dennis Wayne. Then, we were ripped from our lives and forced into a cloud of blackness while those in control toyed with our well-being. After that, a single benevolent force *pulled* us together until we were finally with each other, which led us into the wondrous adventure I've experienced. It's funny how small changes and unlikely circumstances can lead you to meet the love of your life.

Nevertheless, I am reflecting on our journey because of this door Shameis had opened in the abandoned line of the Chicago city sewer system. On the other side of a now unlocked, handleless door laid the remains of Shameis's former life. From the contrast of lighting, it was nearly impossible to see what was, but the shilloetttes appeared as if the space had been cleaned from what I was in the realm of lust. Was the new Ile using Shameis's setup?

314

Regardless of how the bunker appeared now, I find it fitting that our parallels match in this way. Upon being reborn as the first ferryman of souls, the first place on earth that Azrael made me travel to was my village. Just like Zatael directing Shameis here. At least Shameis can feel and use his surroundings. I was simply forced to watch as all those around me passed on one-by-one until my village evaporated from existence. If there was a single event that led to the breaking of my faith, that was it.

I'm glad Shameis decided to face his past head-on. It is a hard decision to come to grips with. However, it did seem as if he was struggling to push forward. It was as if his nerves were getting to him again, like when he broke down after trashing Victor's operating room. I get it; this is hard. Like I acknowledged earlier, admitting that change has occurred and accepting the outcome are separate beasts. Willingly accepting the change is difficult. If I could move more than my chest up, I would lead him through this, but at least I have his back.

"We should probably go in," I suggested.

"Yeah," He agreed meekly as he nodded his head. Still, hesitantly, he slid the medallion back into his pocket as he slowly creaked the heavy metal door open. Then, once it reached a specific point on the opening arch, the lights illuminated inside the bunker. Finally, I was able to see why the exit rift didn't open form Shameis's initial thought. A majority of this place had changes drastically! The overall layout was similar to what I recalled from the realm of lust, but everything else was different. The dingy gray brick walls were replaced with a smooth material painted with bright white paint, the wall of articles about Victor had been cleared, and there was not a single book or scrap of paper to be seen. It looked as if a piece of glass connected to one of those spinning whiteboard carts was replacing the long gone conspiracy theory board, and the wall of smashed monitors had been replaced with a single massive monitor. Event the table below it was replaced with hight-tech table possessing pieces of equipment built into it. To match the new desk, a sleek and massive black computer chair was tucked into the user's leg space. Even the cabinet that held The Ile's costume had expanded to double the original size with two distinct doors, each outfitted with a two-way mirror that opened away from each other. I know Shameis said that what I observed was outdated, but judging by his wide-eyed expression, all of this was new to him as well.

Another thing I noticed, as soon as we were firmly in the bunker, was the reek of the sewer wholly dissipated. It was as if this room was filtering out the foul smell and replacing it with something sweet, yet hardy. After getting a hint of the fresh scent, I tried to look back at the door we entered through and saw that it had closed behind us, so the smell of the sewer was limited to how it could come in.

We were definitely both overwhelmed by how everything had changed. It was so clean and sterile. With the door wide open and the lights on, Shameis began to stroll inside while trying to take everything in before making his way over to the strange electronic-filled table. Once close enough to see, I could tell that some of the advanced technologies were supposed to be a scanner of some kind, a three-dimensional printer, and a water-cooled computer tower. There was even a keyboard directly in the center of the desk with its keys glowed from a white backlight. In addition, there was a square just below the space bar, which I could only assume was a trackpad to control the computer's tower. The entire display reminded me of something that would be seen in a comic book or a movie.

Once beside the desk, Shameis pulled the wheeled chair out from underneath, wheeled it was in the corner of the room where the wall with the monitor met the wall with the entry door, then turned around and set me into it. It was very thoughtful of him to not put me onto the floor again, even though the floor in here was much cleaner than the cement of

316

the alley above. Now, sitting in the chair stirred up a whole other point of contention that I've never been able to wrap my head around. My curse makes it so I phase through almost every structure made by man, yet I'm able to sit in seats like this and those in vehicles? Maybe the universe thinks a seat is grounded enough to support me? Anyways, without saying a word, he turned back to me to ensure that I was appropriately situated before turning back to the bunker so he could thoroughly investigate it.

"Are you okay?" I questioned as I tried my to watch him.

"Yeah," he muttered as he ambled up to the glass board. "This is just a lot to process."

"I know, but we will get through it together," I assured him as too gazed upon he board. It was covered with scribbles and equations written in white from my perspective. Whoever this new Ile was, he was a man of intelligence. I think I could make out symbols of elements from the periodic table, but it was gibberish to me. Shameis, on the other hand, stood there as if he could understand it. At least, that's what I thought until he reached up to the board and plucked a small piece of paper from the top right corner.

"What is that? I hollered.

"A photograph of me with a boy I used to mentor when I was The Ile. I don't know how this person has this, but they do. At least it seems they're trying to honor the past. That is respectable." Shameis confirmed.

"You used to have a sidekick?" I pried.

"Only for a brief amount of time," Shameis answered as he stuck the photo back onto the board. "It was back when I had the run-ins with those gangs. His parents were civilians that were gunned down during a drive-by shooting while he was away at college, trying to better his life and get away from this city. After learning of his parent's death, he was about to throw everything away to try and get revenge, but I was able to give some guidance and help him before he could do anything drastic."

"Is it possible that your old sidekick is the new Ile?" I inquired while trying to put an identity to the mask.

"I doubt it." He answered while shooting my idea down. "We had a falling out just before I was taken. He wanted to go with me, but I wouldn't allow it because I knew how dangerous it was. And our fight resulted in me taking away his access to the bunker. But based on this place, it seems that some millionaire decided to play the hero in my absence." He then explained as he moved away from the glass board and toward the closet.

"Oh... Well, was there anything on the board that could tell us where Victor is?" I inquired while trying to change the subject.

"No, just scientific equations. It's as if this guy was trying to understand the chemical trail inside something he found or was given, but he really knows his stuff based on that. That's how I know it can't be Shawn. Sure, the kid was smart, but he was studying law. Not Chemistry." He explained as he slowly reached to both the handles for the doors and opened the mirrored wardrobe instead of searching for a light to activate. The cabinet's doors creaked as they gradually revealed two mannequins. The one to the left was decked out in the exact attire I have seen multiple times and know to be Shameis's Ile costume, while the one to the right was bare. Shameis's theory of the New Ile being out and about was spot on, so Shameis really needed to moving. I guess the same thought didn't cross Shameis's mind since he decided to reach out and pull his old helmet off the mannequin.

"I'm sorry that isn't part of your new life, but we don't really have time for this." I muttered, which drew Shameis's attention to me. His iris had become a deep shade of blue due to the sadness he felt.

"Right..." He agreed as he turned back to the helmet before slowly putting it away. "Don't apologize. I understand that there is no going back."

318

"Well, technically, you could. The costume completely covers your face. No one would even know what Victor has done to you." I optimistically realized.

"No, Grim. It is not just about the looks. It's about being just an average person. No superpowers or enhanced limbs. The Ile is supposed to serve as an inspiration. Every person has the right and the ability to protect themselves. This person is already teetering on that border since most people don't have buckets of money to burn." Shameis lectured. I guess that would explain the low tech base Shameis used to use. He is trying to stay humble. Well, with that insight, Shameis proceeded to walk over to the computer desk and proceeded to lean over it. In this position, he reached the keyboard with his left hand while reaching the computer tower with his right. "Alright, let's get Victor's location and get out of here." Shameis proclaimed as the lights in his right arm surged, indicating he was using the arm's ability to control electronics. Oh, man! Between the arm's function to control technology and the knowledge that Zatael gave Shameis, this should be a breeze!

So, white numbers and letters began to fall from the top in a matrix-like pattern from the black surface that the monitor displayed. At first, I assumed this was due to Shameis hacking into the system, but then some symbols began to freeze in place as others continued to pass by. The only characters that were freezing seemed to be in the middle of the screen while more of them began to overlap. Within seconds, a shape of The Ile's logo appeared, but just like everything else, it was updated. Instead of being just the upper half of a skull, the logo was updated to include the lower jaw and a pair of horns. That was just the booting up screen! Once the logo faded, a box labeled 'password' came up over the top of a blurred moving background.

"Alright! Let's see what this thing can do," Shameis let out as the lights on his arm started to pulse. I'm not going to pretend that I know the science of what was happening, so I just watched the screen as asterisk after asterisk appeared in the box until thirteen were present. As soon as the thirteen stars appeared, the textbox and asterisks flashed, causing the display to disappear as the background unfaded to reveal an interface unlike the vanilla layout on a typical computer. Typically, the desktop is supposed to have a stationary background with various icons covering it and a toolbar at the bottom. Instead, this computer showed a live feed of downtown Chicago and the toolbar to its left.

Upon seeing the live feed, Shameis pulled away as we watched in horror. There were tens of thousands of people rioting in the streets, vandalizing buildings, throwing Molotov cocktails, shooting weapons, and killing each other. It was as if all the devils of hell had spilled over to the earth. What was happening? Everyone was acting like animals!

"Well, now we know why The Ile isn't here," Shameis muttered while his eye was glued to the screen.

"What... What's going on?" I inquired in a panic.

"I have no idea...," Shameis responded through a quiver.

"It almost looks as if they're possessed," I suggested.

"Well, whatever it is, we are no help here." Shameis put forth as he reached back to the tower, placed his metal hand onto it, then let the lights on his arm flash. That caused a tab on the left side of the screen to open, replacing the live stream with a looped video of a superheroine flying against a black background.

"Are we going out there to help?" I questioned as I scanned over the page while observing the moving image, realizing that the star emblem on her chest, metallic wristbands, battle skirt, and flowing cape identified this a clip of Starseeker.

320

"The only thing we can do is learn as much as we can, just in case the other heroes are affected by whatever is going on." Shameis answered as he caused his robotic arm to open a tab at the bottom of the clip titled "Strengths and Weaknesses."

"But what about Victor?" I reminded him.

"Im assuming that they are behind all of this." Shameis theorized while turning to look at me. "If whatever they're doing somehow caused the heroes to change, and if they were to somehow turn from the side of justice, then our love will not be enough to stop them." He explained before turning back to the screen.

"Our love?" I muttered to myself in a shock before shaking it off to focus on the task at hand. Reading the screen, I could see that the tab was similar to the login screen, in which it covered the video of Starseeker and blurred it. However, instead of having a box to type, the pop-up was split into two columns with a header and subheader that read "Tower of Siloam Protocol" with "Amber Cotter" underneath it. Seeing the name of Starseeker's true identity finally allowed me to realize that Lilith's sister was the Starseeker. No wonder Lilith was willing to do whatever it would take to get powers. But the proper title seemed peculiar.

"Tower of Siloam? That name sounds familiar." I blurted out.

"As it should. A biblical proverb uses the collapse of this tower and the deaths of eighteen people as a metaphor for why people must repent for their sins. It was chosen as a reminder that we heroes are not above the people we serve." Shameis explained as he turned his head to look at me.

"Right. That makes sense, but why would the new Ile create a list like this? Do they not trust their teammates." I cross-examined.

"They didn't... I did." Shameis admitted while turning away from the screen to look at me out of the corner of his eye. I could see that his iris had begun to change from a pale red back to his standard Hazel.

"Why would you do that?" I questioned in shock.

"Because these people are more powerful than nations," Shameis responded bluntly before turning back to the screen. "The Starseeker could punch a hole through the planet if she wanted to. It's not about the lack of trust. It's about the responsibility of holding them accountable for their actions." When put that way, it makes sense to have this worry. But still, you're supposed to trust your teammates.

"Did you make a list for me?" I questioned meekly as I looked toward my feet.

"No grim. I love you. I trust you more than anyone else, and I know you would never betray me, or Zatael, or our goal to stop the Lightbringer." He answered, causing my attention to whiz up toward him, where I saw that he was still fixated on the screen. He loves me? Not only did he admit there was love between us, but he's telling me that he loves me? Did that just slip out due to the stress of these realizations, or was that intentional? Whatever it was, this was not the time for these bombs to be dropped on me.

"I love you too," I affirmed as I turned from Shameis to the screen. "If this is what we need to do, then I'm with you all the way." So for the lists underneath Starseeker's real name, the left itemized list was labeled as strengths while the right was labeled weaknesses. The list included all the powers in her arsenal for her strengths: flight, superstrength, ice vision, super hearing, and nigh-invincibility. Then, a single bold entry read "No known direct weaknesses" underneath her weaknesses column. However, a few ways to distract her underneath could counter her multiple abilities. These counters ranged from reflective surfaces for her ice vision, loud noises for her super hearing, and heavy objects for her flight. The last listed counter seemed a bit out of place, and thus, was very notable. It informed us to attack her hubris but had a question mark at the end.

Once he was satisfied with the information on this page, he used his arm to pull up Crossfade's bio. It had the same setup as Starseeker's page, except its clip was of Crossfade running. Then, just like Starseeker's page, Shameis activated the Strengths and Weaknesses tab where I saw Starseeker's Identity was replaced with the name "Jonathan Fall." As for Crossfade's powerset, this listed that his only abilities were his speed, his ability to change into a Skeleton while running, and his ability to shoot lightning bolts like projectiles. At least there was an actual weakness for this hero. Here, it stated that extreme colds will slow him down and force him to change out of his secret identity. It also listed that lightning rods are great for subverting lightning. Then, just like Starseeker, a single point suggested attacking him mentally by insulting his pride. So, if I understand this correctly, the most significant way to throw this superwoman and this demon speedster off their game is to incite rage and doubt in their abilities? Why does that seem so familiar?

After Shameis had finished with this page, he reexamined the list of heroes at the left of the screen. He scanned it for a minute before the look of confusion grew in his eye as he changed to a pale blue. "What? What's wrong?" I questioned.

"The person who took up my mantle isn't on this list, but Victor is..." He explained.

"What do you mean Victor is on this list? Why would Victor be on a list of Allies?" I cross-examined.

"I... I don't know..." He replied as he pulled up a clip of Victor standing menacingly with his hands behind his back.

"How could this man be considered an ally? He can't be part of the team!" Shameis proclaimed as he threw his hands up and placed them behind his head while taking a few steps backward.

"And who are you to say who can be on my team?" A deep robotic voice suddenly echoed through the small room. Just then, the monitor and computer system shut themselves off, followed by a majority of the overhead lights. At least this room had emergency lighting. But as the lights went, a creepy ambiance emerged while a slight chill started to fill the air. Due to the drastic change in lighting, everything seemed much darker than it was.

Suddenly, the sound of the door unlocking filled the dark hollow, causing Shameis and me to turn and stare. Something about how slowly the door seemed to unlock just increased the anticipation. We both knew who was coming in, but it was eerie. Then, once all the unlocking mechanisms stopped clanging, the door swung open, and the much brighter outside light accompanied by the stench of the sewer poured in. Because of the drastic contrast of lighting, all I could see was a silhouette walking into the room. With every step, I could hear links of chains clanging together while thumps of heavy metal boots struck the concrete before the door slammed shut and relocked. I'm not sure how Shameis used the persona of The Ile, but between the chains and metal, this person is definitely trying to strike fear in the hearts of all that oppose him. From how Shameis described himself, I always pictured The Ile as a friendly hero who would get serious when needed. This person was the exact opposite of those thoughts, which I guess it is warranted since we are invading his space.

Chapter Twenty-Seven

This has to be similar to what all those souls experienced. All those souls that I had to claim. I can't imagine the terror they felt as their surroundings darkened while watching a silhouette of a cloaked figure emerge from the nothingness to antagonize the accused. I knew this had to be similar since Shameis and I had quickly lost control of the situation, just like those souls. I will admit to having some sort of fear when meeting Chimera, but that was the same sense of dread one would have when seeing a shark in the shallow water of a beach. However, the fear that this version of The Ile evoked was something else. Hearing all the information of this persona from Shameis, I know that this is just a human, but tactics he implemented to get into Shameis's head were what Azrael did to me. There was something about seeing a shadowy figure that caused the mind to lose grip of reality.

How could a simple man bring on such a sense of foreboding? Is this why I see myself as the monster? This has to be the same feeling that my victims felt. Even though I couldn't see the color of Shameis's iris from this position, I could feel the sense of foreboding radiating from him. Frankly, I wasn't scared of whoever this was, but a level of intimidation prevented me from acting or speaking. This is so bizarre since I am the

Grim Reaper! My entire stick down to my appearance screams fear and pressure, and clearly, this version of The Ile was trying to harness the human's interpretation of me to play mind games with his foes.

The sound of chains rattling together and metal pounding onto the cement ground with each step didn't help ease the mood. We have seen angels, demons, a fate, and monsters, but they all have given off such a different energy than this one person. Still, I have long since learned from my travels before this adventure that the human psyche is one of the scariest energies to exist. I can't believe this man would try to mess with a person's mind like this! Did Shameis do this as well?

Although the room was much darker than it had been when Shameis entered, there was still enough light to see the new Ile's costume as he trudged forward. This costume was relatively similar to the original Ile and would be mistaken for the same in minimal light, but there were noticeable differences. For starters, the black leather trench coat was decked out in chains, spikes, and studs that quickly reflected light, in addition to the belts Shameis used. I could also see that the coat sleeves were rolled up to allow the application of metal gauntlets that covered his hands and forearms. Since these were black, it was hard to see them, but it appeared that the gauntlets had tubes connected from the central portion to a rectangular protrusion. This Ile was still wearing the black kevlar pants that Shameis wore, but again, they were accented with chains, spikes, and studs. Then, much like the gauntlets, the boots he wore were constructed of black metal with tubes stretching from a part on his calf to another lower spot.

Besides all that, three other articles of the costume were distinctly different from the original. The first was a light gray shirt underneath the coat that bore the new logo. It was clearly over more armor, but still interesting to see that The Ile tried to hide the armor instead of showing

326

t off. Then, I noticed a distinct bulge on either of his hips. Although I initially was going to dismiss them, a quick movement during his approach revealed a holstered pistol-like tool. It did frighten me that this man was openly carrying that around, but seeing that they were holstered even when an intruder was in his space made me realize they were strictly for 'in case of emergency' use. After the shirt and holsters, the final significant difference had to be the helmet he dawned. Like the gauntlets and boots, the helmet was also constructed chiefly of black metal. However, a piece of black glass stretched across the helmet's face and up to its top, giving it a sleek and aerodynamic design.

On top of that, a glowing purple skull shone through the glass. I credit that skell to be the sole reason for striking fear into the hearts of The Ile's foes. This skull appeared like an ordinary human skull, unlike The Ile's logo, but it seemed to have a digital design. The new Ile was a ghost for a modern age.

"I knew it was only a matter of time before a freak made it into here." The Ile let out through his deep robotic voice as they leaped toward Shameis, colliding with my partner. I'm sure The Ile's intention was to tackle Shameis, but thankfully for his strength, he was able to stand his ground as he shoved The Ile back.

"We are not here to fight," Shameis responded as he raised his fists to defend himself. "We are just looking for answers."

"So it can speak properly. Based on the carnage you left outside, I was expecting you be a bumbling buffoon, but I know how to deal with strength." The Ile patronized before charging and swiping at Shameis's legs. Thankfully, Shameis moved toward and jumped over The Ile before they both returned to a neutral position facing each other. Essentially, they just switched locations. "So, you're fast too. But clearly not as fast as Crossfade."

"Stop! You need to listen to me!" Shameis ordered. "All I need is one thing, and we will let you carry on back to protect the city."

"Sorry, just because you're coherent doesn't mean I have time for this. If you couldn't tell, there is an apocalypse going on outside." The Ile declared as an orange glow began to emit from the bottom of his boots that rapidly became a burst of flames, propelling him toward Shameis at an alarming speed. As he did so, he wound up a punch and tried to strike Shameis, but seeing this and knowing how to react, Shameis threw a quick jab forward with his metal fist. Not only did Shameis counter-attack cancel The Ile's punch, but it caught The Ile on the chin and threw him off balance, causing The Ile to tip backward and to fall onto his back.

"The previous Ile would've been ashamed to know you're using tech that the average person couldn't acquire," Shameis uttered as he looked over the fallen hero.

"Previous Ile... How do you... No one is supposed to know that!" The Ile boomed as the bottoms of his boots, and rectangular protrusions in his gauntlets both ignited with focused flames. They then propelled him backward and upward until he stood on his feet just in front of the computer desk. "So you have three powers: strength, heightened reflexes, and heightened intelligence brought on by some form of schizophrenia.

"You're one for three," Shameis answered as he stood up tall while keeping his fists at his sides. "My reflexes have been honed for years, and I'm not crazy. However, my strength was gifted to me by a higher power."

"There is no higher power than the law! And freaks like you deserve to be behind bars!" The Ile proclaimed as he once again jetted forward. This time, instead of winding up a punch, they flew fist first at Shameis. Again, the attack didn't give Shameis time to react and caught Shameis in the chest, which him to fly backward; nearly missing the glass

328

board and causing him to smack the wall with a sickening thud. After making contact with the wall, Shameis just stood there with his head hung while trying to regain the breath that was knocked out of him.

"How can a person under mind control serve justice of their controller's bidding?" Shameis slowly accused The Ile.

"Me? Mind Controlled? My suit prevents any form of external tampering. It was Developed by Hardrive and Victor Jakelyde. My actions are my own!" The Ile boasted. "I bet you're the one that's behind what's happening to my city!" After making that claim, The Ile propelled himself forward a third time while attempting a similar attack to the first. Again, Shameis outmaneuvered The Ile, but instead of counter-attacking, Shameis simply rolled out of the way. This caused The Ile's right metal gauntlet to punch the wall and leave a small impact mark in the brick.

"I have nothing to do with this!" Shameis shouted back as he tried to push The Ile away, but The Ile countered by deflecting Shameis with his left arm and followed it up with a quick strike to Shameis's abdomen. Even with Shameis's strength, the strike caused him to double-over, which allowed The Ile to follow up with another quick punch to the side of Shameis's head, dropping him onto his stomach.

"You can explain that when you're in custody." The Ile offered to Shameis as he pointed his right gauntlet toward Shameis's head while a small flame emerged.

"I know that outside is a problem, but maybe we can help each other?" Shameis suggested as he slowly tried to get off the ground.

"The only help you'll give is sitting in a cell at Gyle." The Ile declared as the spout of fire transitioned into a full-blown flamethrower. Seeing the flames approaching him, Shameis reached out with his metal hand to protect himself as he made his way to his feet. this caused me to watch in awe as Shameis's hand split the flames while slowly inching forward. If the situation wasn't so tense, I would've taken a moment to admire how the orange flames contrasted with the lightless room. Instead, all I could do was worry about Shameis. Even with the ability to slightly protect himself, I was still worried about him getting burned. So, I sat on the edge of my seat and watched as Shameis finally reached the gauntlet that was throwing the fire, grabbed onto the protrusion, and squeezed it tightly to stop the flame. That was when the sound of crushing metal could be heard before a small explosion lit up the room. The force of the blast then knocked both Shameis and The Ile away from each other while pushing the chair from underneath me.

"Grim!" Shameis shouted as I heard the sound of his rubber soles quickly approaching me.

"I'm fine," I responded as he picked me up off the floor. "I'm getting my strength back, so I was able to inch up to the edge of the seat, but that blast knocked it out from under me."

"Good. I'm glad you're safe." He let out as he placed me onto the chair. This was when I noticed that several sections of his lab coat had holes burned through it while the edges of his gauze had been singed. Then, when I gazed upon his bare torso underneath the coat, I noticed many skin patches showed signs of third-degree burns.

"Oh... Sweetie... Let me heal you." I let out as I meekly laid my hands onto his sculpted abdomen. Instantly, my bony hands started to glow that pale color before the light transferred to all of his wounds. All except that single massive scar that presented itself from Shameis's soul, the one Azrael gave him. While I did this, I peered around the room and noted the blast caused all the glass elements except the monitor to show signs of cracking, and the white paint directly near it had blackened, but overall, the room remained intact.

330

"Thanks, love," Shameis remarked just before The Ile blindsided him by once again driving him into the wall sharing the room's entrance. Seeing how close they were to me, Shameis aggressively shoved The Ile toward the middle of the room and followed up by delivering a heavy right-handed punch to The Ile's faceguard. Unfortunately, the impact caused the glass to shatter as the digital designs stopped displaying and dropped The Ile like a sack of bricks. "I was going to take it easy on you since I don't want to interfere with your duties. But if you don't stop, I'm going to hit you harder." Shameis then warned The Ile.

"You're not walking out of here!" The Ile countered as he used his rocket boots and the gauntlet that was still functioning properly to pick himself off the ground again. However, The Ile decided to take this one step farther and use the momentum to throw a punch. Unfortunately for him, Shameis quickly caught the attack mid air with his left hand and delivered a right-handed punch square in The Ile's chest, all before The Ile could make it to the ground. All this combined together caused The Ile to fly backward and bounce off the brick wall beside the cabinet before stumbling back toward Shameis. Seeing that The Ile was disoriented, Shameis took the opportunity to grab onto The Ile, aggressively spin him around and throw him through the glass board and into the wall behind it, as if The Ile was a living ragdoll.

"Geez," I muttered quietly as I gazed upon The Ile's fallen limp body as an eerie silence fell over the room. From here, I could see that Shameis's metal fist had left a sizable indent on The Ile's chest, but the silence allowed me to hear that his heart was still beating and that he was still breathing. Yes, I was a bit startled by how aggressive Shameis acted, but after seeing how Chimera behaved when Shameis tried to act diplomatically, I understand why Shameis wanted to nip this. However, I do believe Shameis needs to get a better understanding of his strength since the act of throwing The Ile caused the brick wall to crack and cause the glass on costume cabinet's doors to finish spidering and shatter onto the floor.

"Man, you're tough," The Ile then muttered through a failing voice synthesizer while moving from his laying position so he could sit up and lean against the wall.

"And you know how to take a punch." Shameis returned.

"I learned from the best." The Ile confessed as he started to get back up to his feet.

"Right. So, are you going to hear me out?" Shameis then questioned.

"Absolutely not. I don't negotiate with terrorists. Besides, I still have a trick up my sleeve." The Ile responded as purple electricity began to spark around his metal gloves.

"There are so many more important things to worry about right now!" Shameis shouted at The Ile. "Think of the time you are wasting when you could be helping the city! That, and you still haven't wondered about who I even am! My identity will make you regret attacking me, but if this is the road you want to take, I'll gladly teach you a lesson."

"I'll know who you are after you're incarcerated." The Ile barked as he again punched toward Shameis while swinging wildly as the sparks of electricity sizzled through the air. Shameis tried his best to dodge the attacks while trying not to get shocked, but The Ile was able to land a blow every so often. All of this ended up driving Shameis backward toward the desk of electronics, but once Shameis didn't have any space to retreat into, The Ile landed a strike on Shameis's face. Instantly my partner spun around and drape himself onto the desk. At first, I thought that this was just Shameis being sloppy, but as he laid in this compromised position, he touched the computer tower with his right arm. Then, with the flash of the lights in his arm, the monitor lit up.

332

Seeing that Shameis was trying to use his computer again, The Ile tried to smash down onto Shameis, but thankfully he knew this was coming and rolled out of the way. However, since the attack missed its target, the blow contacted the table. As a result, keys from the keyboard flew up as several pieces of equipment were activated because of the electric shock. The Ile paid no mind to his equipment, and instead, The Ile chased Shameis around the small room with more electrified haymakers. I, however, watched as the monitor displayed the input Shameis commanded, and it sorted and searched through its file until it finally finished searching. I guess that Shameis's constant dodging was just him buying time because as soon as Shameis saw that the computer had finished, he quickly grabbed onto a punch The Ile had thrown and promptly redirected the electrified fist into The Ile's shattered helmet.

Upon contact, The Ile quickly stumbled about the room while screaming in agony from electrocuting himself. Seeing The Ile experience life-threatening pain caused Shameis to stretch his metal arm forward and pull the electric fist away from The Ile's helmet. Unfortunately, The electricity from the gauntlets must've caused something in the helmet to short circuit. The Ile's screams didn't stop! To this, Shameis to reach out again and latch onto the helmet before pushing The Ile's head into the exact place on the wall The Ile had smacked before. Seeing this, I was startled while thinking Shameis was now attacking a helpless man, but after making The Ile's head hit the wall, Shameis aggressively pulled away and ripped the helmet in two. Essentially, he used this maneuver to crack the helmet like an egg while grounding the electricity. This, in turn, finally revealed The Ile's true identity as The Ile returned to a sitting position over the top of all the shattered glass. There sat the face of a younger African-American man with short black hair and had a well-groomed style of facial hair. As expected, he had a few bloodied wounds due to several blows to the face.

"Shawn? Shawn Olum?" Shameis questioned as he dropped the section of The Ile's helmet.

"How... How do you know who I am..." The Ile huffed as he tried to catch his breath as he slowly pulled his pistol out of his holster, cocked its hammer, and pointed it toward Shameis's head.

"Oh, Shawn... I'm so disappointed." Shameis muttered as he slowly moved to his left, making it so the monitor was clearly visible to The Ile, revealing the archive of when Shameis was Isaac Enderson.

"Wait. How did that get on the screen? Did you bring that up? How the hell do you know about him?" The Ile barked as his hand started to tremble while letting out a slight cough.

"How do you think?" Shameis responded as he began to slowly approach the sitting Ile.

"Don't come any closer!" Shawn ordered.

"Just tell me where Victor is, and I'll be on my way." Shameis followed up.

"You're not going anywhere until I get some answers!" Shawn ordered as he aggressively pointed the gun at Shameis while shaking it as if he was trying to imply that Shameis wasn't in control.

"After everything you've been through, I thought you, of all people, would've learned that guns do nothing but cause more problems." Shameis sighed as he continued toward Shawn.

"I said don't come any closer!" Shawn barked, but Shameis didn't stop. Instead, Shameis walked up to Shawn's right side, squatted beside him, and placed his robotic hand over the pistol's barrel while looking Shawn directly in the eyes.

"Do you think your parents would be happy that you're using this instead of diplomacy?" Shameis spoke softly, to which Shawn instantly let go of the pistol and dropped his hand to the ground.

334

"Who... Who are you..." Shawn trembled as he watched Shameis return to an upright position and take a few steps backward, so the screen's display and himself were together in Shawn's line of sight. "Isaac?" Shawn then muttered.

"Nice to see you again," Shameis responded softly, to which Shawn mustered all the strength he had left to get to his feet, before ambling ambled over to Shameis and wrapped his arms around him. That was when the muffled sound of soft cries could be heard.

"Where... Where have you been?" Shawn mumbled as he pulled away.

"It's complicated..." Shameis responded. "But... How are you The Ile, and why does your computer say Jakelyde is part of the Council."

"Well, six years ago, Victor came to the Council and said that one of the many monsters we faced had finally gotten the better of you. They were all skeptical of the claim, but he provided info about the monster that did this. Some girl that needed to feed off of souls to live or something like that. I wanted to rejoin the battle when I heard about your death, and that was when Victor offered me this injection that would increase my intelligence. Within a year, I got my law degree, as well as a degree in chemistry, physics, mathematics, and mechanical science. The shot made it so I can retain any and all information presented to me. So, I used all of that to found a fortune five-hundred corporation that produces affordable medicines. Victor helped me evolve The Ile into what it is today, and part team because of the intel he's able to provide." Shawn explained. "But what about you? If you're really Isaac, how can you be here?"

"A monster did get to me, but it wasn't a girl. It was Jakelyde. That night I went to that cemetery, I found him, but he overwhelmed and abducted me. He erased my memories and paired me with Lilith to keep his eyes on me." Shameis returned.

"Lilith Cotter? I thought she finally went straight?" Shawn asked.

"Far from it," Shameis answered.

"But... Why?" Shawn cross-examined. "Victor has been nothing but a stand-up citizen."

"Because Victor is working for something else. Not someone. Something. A super powerful angel that is hellbent on taking the place of The Presence. While wanting to rule over all the realms in the process." Shameis continued to explain.

"Naw, man." Shawn denied as he backed even further away from Shameis. "You're not Isaac. He never believed in that supernatural bullcrap. Isaac was a man of science.

"I used to not, but I have seen way too much to be closed-minded." Shameis countered. "There is way too much that we can't see that is a genuine threat to our existence."

"Naw. I'm tired of this. Take off that gauze mask and show me the face of Isaac Enderson." Shawn demanded while getting in Shameis's face.

"I can't." Shameis returned as he bowed his head.

"Why not? Are you scarred underneath there or something?" Shawn mocked, to which Shameis picked up his head again.

"You have a DNA Scanner, correct? Or maybe a retinal scanner?" Shameis suggested. "As long as you still have the record, we can prove it."

"Yeah, built into the desk," Shawn replied. Hearing this, Shameis turned away from Shawn and walked over to the table of electronics, and as he did so, I could see that he was trying his best to stay poised. Still, even the mose modest of behaviours couldn't hind the hint of blue to his hazel iris. Clearly, he was sad that he was forced into this position. Of course, if Shawn would've complied with the request for Victor's location, we wouldn't be in this situation. At least I could see in Shawn's aura that he was entertaining

336

Shameis's request and wanted to see how a DNA scan would play out.

So, upon reaching the desk, Shameis placed his metal hand onto the computer tower and made the lights in his forearm pulse. Within an instance, the computer monitor changed from Shameis's old profile record to the program Shawn used to scan and interpret DNA. As soon as the screen changed to this program, a single title sat in the center; "preparing to scan." Accompanying the program, a microscope slide ejected for one of the machine's desks. Shameis then pulled the small piece of glass out of the drive before purposely pricking the index finger on his left hand with an exposed point of metal from when Shawn smashed his desk. With the bit of blood beginning to dribble out of the tiny wound, Shameis allowed it to drip onto the slide and inserted it back into the drive. There was a slight process, but once it finished, the image on the screen displayed an old picture of Shameis with '85% match' listed to the right. "Isaac?" Shawn questioned again as his eyes widened.

"I go by Shameis Eli now." Shameis clarified.

"Shameis Eli?" Isaac questioned. "I've heard that name before."

"Yeah. Probably from Jakelyde." Shameis reasoned as he turned back to Shawn. "Jakelyde gave me that name. It's supposed to mock the legacy of The Ile. It's spelled as in Shame is Eli, and Eli is just Ile spelled backward."

"I... I didn't..." Shawn sputtered before Shameis cut him off.

"There is no way you would've known. But now you do, and there is no turning back." Shameis consoled Shawn as he approached the new Ile. "But I need to know where Victor is before he does any more bad."

"Eighty-five percent match," Shawn mumbled as he continued to fixate on the screen.

"Yes. Jakelyde experimented on me. He injected me with a chemical that altered my DNA. He's done that to all his victims, and I'm

337

pretty sure he was able to prove all that info about those monsters you guys fight because he makes them." Shameis explained, pulling Shawn's attention away from the monitor and back to Shameis. "Speaking of which, The child I tried to save is still alive. But now he's a huge, freaky monster. Goes by Chimera now." And that bit of information caused Shawn's eye to widen as if he just had the realization of a lifetime.

"Chimera is Dennis Wayne?" Shawn repeated. "I've had several run-ins with Chimera over the years. I... I didn't know." After that, Shawn raised his hands up and put them behind his head before limping around the room. "Victor did this to you?"

"Well... It's sort of my fault since I did fight back, but this wouldn't have happened if it wasn't for Jakelyde and two of his monsters." Shameis clarified before stopping Shawn while placing a hand on each shoulder and forcing Shawn to look him in the eye. "Where. Is. Victor?"

"Gyles Helmsley. After he joined the team, he requested to be set up there so he could try to treat the inmates." Shawn answered, but another realization struck him that slumped his whole stature. "We gave him access to all those people so he could experiment and torture them... If I would've known..."

"You couldn't have known. Jakelyde is a master manipulator." Shameis consoled again before turning away from Ile and making his way toward me.

"I'm coming with you!" Shawn declared as he followed Shameis while picking up the broken section of his helmet. That statement instantly caused Shameis to spin around and stop Shawn in his tracks.

"No. You need to stay here and take care of the city. I have no idea what is happening, but the people need their hero. We also need to keep up appearances." Shameis suggested as he pointed his metal index

338

inger upward. "If Victor finds out that I'm on my way to him, everything will be thrown off. The actual fate of the world hangs in the balance." With that, Shameis turned back toward me and continued his path while leaving Shawn in the middle of the bunker. Then, once to me, he held out his left hand, to which I used it as support as I struggled to get back to my feet. "I'm glad that you have most of your strength back." He then whispered.

"Me too," I agreed with a smile. "But I don't think I'll be able to use my ability for a while."

"Hey, Isaac... Ehr... Shameis..." Shawn then called out, causing Shameis to turn around. "I understand that Victor did a bad thing to you, but did it cause something to go wrong in your brain? What you're doing right now is kind of weird." To that observation, Shameis let out a sigh.

"Shawn. Victor saying that I died was a half-truth." Shameis admitted. "I wasn't dead for all six years. But I, technically, died after he injected that chemical into me. I had to go through hell and back, but I had some help from the Grim Reaper, and now I can see her."

"The Grim Reaper is a woman? You can see her?" Shawn questioned out of disbelief, to which Shameis turned back to me so he could look me in the eye.

"Yes, a beautiful woman." He elaborated but then turned back to look at Shawn. "Oh, and her name is Cain."

"Dude... Are you in love with the Grim Rea... Did you say Cain? As in Cain and Abel? The first murderer?" Shawn cross-examined with skepticisms now showing in his voice. "Man, Now I know you've lost it."

"Yes I am. I recognize that this all sounds crazy, but it's true." Shameis assured Shawn. "You don't need to believe me."

"Not crazier than a man returning from the dead after six years." Shawn joked as he looked at his messy computer station, up to the proof

339

that Shameis and Isaac were one and the same, then back at Shameis. "But here's the thing. I'm pretty sure that I believe it. If you say the Grim Reaper is in this room, I believe you. I've seen a lot of weird stuff, and everything has exponentially gotten weirder today. So tell Cain I said hi and to be merciful to me when I die."

"I won't be the one taking his soul. I'm not actually a ferryman of souls anymore." I reminded Shameis since Shawn couldn't see or hear me.

"She said hi back," Shameis returned to Shawn as he tried not to start another conversation since we had our heading. With that, we then began to make our way to the exit of the bunker.

"It was good to see you again, Isaa... Shameis." Shawn called out to bid us farewell. "The door's unlocked, and the ramp is down. Please don't break anything else."

"No promises," Shameis retorted as he pushed the heavy door open; allowing an orange twilight glow to pour into the room. I was pleased to see that the concrete-covered metal floor Shameis had ripped a hole in had been converted into a gradual incline leading back to the alley, with no stench to be smelt.

"Oh! One more thing!" Shawn shouted, getting Shameis's attention again. "Take the bike!" To that, Shameis nodded as his iris lit up a bright green, telling me that he was excited about the offer.

"We'll see you soon, Shawn." Shameis let out before leading me up the ramp and into the alley. Everything seemed like it was about to be smooth sailing. That is until we were actually in the alley when I noticed that the orange light I saw was not from the twilight sun. In fact, the dense, ominous clouds had overtaken the city. Instead, the orange I noticed was the flames of the parking structure across the street being engulfed in flames. Besides that sight, I could see maybe one-hundred people rioting in the street just in front of this one alley while the sounds

340

of screams and sirens filled the air.

"Shameis..." I muttered as I squeezed his hand tightly.

"We need to go..." Shameis belted out as he pulled me into a sprint. Thankfully I had enough strength to stay on my feet, but I swear I nearly tripped a few times. So, as I looked ahead to where Shameis was leading, I noticed the 'bike' that Shawn had just mentioned was positioned near the metal trash cans that Shameis had used earlier, with the front of it facing The Ile's bunker. I don't know the exact model, but the bike in question was matte black with aerodynamic plating and was designed so the driver would have to lean toward the handles. The wheels consisted of thick rubber, while its gas tank, gear shaft, and sections covering the tops of both tires were plated in aerodynamic armor. Even though the engine was exposed, it seemed that The Ile tried his best to have this thing as bulletproof as possible.

"I've never been on a motorcycle before!" I informed Shameis as we approached it.

"There is a first time for everything," Shameis responded as he threw his left leg over the seat before flicking the kickstand up and turning over the ignition. Instantly, the engine's roar filled the alley, causing a majority of the crazed people to stare at us. They then slowly began to walk toward us. "Come on, Grim! With this noise, the perception field won't fool them for long!"

"Right!" I agreed as I hiked up my robe to get my leg over and be able to straddle the seat. The seat definitely wasn't designed for two people, but I was able to get on with a tight squeeze. Also, I was forced to lean forward so that my chest was against his back due to the positioning.

"Hold on." He ordered, to which I quickly wrapped my arms around his torso. He didn't have to tell me twice! Then as soon as he felt my embrace, he revved the engine and whipped the bike around. Once facing the exit, Shameis floored the clutch so we could speed out of the alley and through the crowd of people. As we passed by, they did try to jump at us and even in front of us, but Shameis expertly was able to dodge them all. Once again, I was filled with so many emotions. I was elated to hold onto Shameis as he steered this thrill ride, but I was scared for these people since they were acting as if hell had come to earth. Most importantly, I was relieved to know that we were finally on the last leg of this odyssey. We were finally on our way to face Victor Jakelyde. And once he is dealt with, there will no longer be an 'inside human' creating monsters and potential hosts for the Lightbringer.

Part Three: Desiring a Resolution

Chapter
Twenty-Eight

This is not the world I remember. How could such disarray happen so quickly while we've been away? After learning that I'm not the only ferryman of souls, I know that this can't be a result of unwelcome souls being left on Earth. So what caused the humans to act like this? Men, women, children, the elderly, Black, White, Asian, Middle Eastern, Hispanic; no one was spared by what had gripped this city. As we swerved through the hectic streets of downtown Chicago, I watched in horror as every type of person looted, rioted, and fought one another. A multitude of buildings was engulfed in flames while vehicles were smashed into one another as well as other structures as if they performed a demolition derby. Everything was just a chaotic mess of anger and fire. It was as if all of society had collectively chosen to rid love and peace from their lives. This sight is what I would imagine when told to imagine Hell on Earth.

I can only imagine the trauma these souls face to put out such evil. As we swerved past violent fights, mangled heaps of metal, and hundreds of thousands of lifeless bodies, I feared as to why this was happening, but deep down, I knew. Even though we were unwilling participants, I fear Shameis and I caused all this and he darkness of the overhead storm did not help to settle this fear. Due to the chaos surrounding us, the only sources of light that led us through this powerless city were the headlamp of the motorbike, the fires that bellowed from the building fronts, and the flashes of lightning that shot down from overhead. This had to be what Zatael warned us about. We knew this was inevitable. The reason why this feels like Hell on Earth is because this is Hell on Earth. The Vale had fallen.

As we drove through the city, people were drawn to the roar of the motorcycle. More people than I could keep track of tried to jump at us. They were yelling, snarling, and growling as they tried, but thankfully Shameis was skilled enough to maneuver through the masses without being interfered with. The legions of possessed citizens were ravenous, yet Shameis stayed determined as I clung to him. He was dead set on making it to our destination as he gunned the throttle. Through this, there were many times Shameis needed to take evasive maneuvers to avoid blocked streets. Maneuvers like using downed street lamps as bridges, holes in buildings as pathways, and even shortcuts through abandoned alleyways, but thankfully The Ile's bike was built for this kind of punishment.

Within ten minutes of snaking around buildings and through the congested streets, Shameis turned onto an entrance ramp for a bridge like overpass of a highway that ran through the city. The carnage up here was only amplified since it was once a bustling highway while only a few signs remained upright amongst the heaps of wreckage. I was pleased to see that one of the few signs that did stay upright indicated we were heading westbound. I really needed a sense of direction on the near pitch-black roadway. Many fires emitted light as they burned upon indistinguishable vehicles, which helped light our way since there was no electricity running to the overhead street lamps. What made this scene even eerier was all the lifeless bodies lying still in the darkness as

344

blood-soaked and injured zombies continuously limped toward the roar of our transportation. That's the only way I could describe them since that's how these people were acting.

Compared to the roads of downtown Chicago, Shameis had to swerve significantly more as a result of the apparent high impact collisions. There were holes blown in the asphalt, vehicles ingrained in the concrete median and in the side railings, massive gasoline fires, and the bodies. Oh, the bodies. I wanted to pity these poor souls, but the hecticness of this all gave me no time to. That was when Shameis instructed me to hold on as tight as possible. Of course, I peered over his shoulder to see what he was referring to, and there I saw a mountain of semi-trucks and other random vehicles all smashed together. Then, as if it was placed there on purpose, one of those massive green road signs rested against it and served as a ramp to get over it. Shameis intended to use it! So I bunkered down and braced for impact.

Shameis again revved the throttle, causing us to accelerate until we traveled at nearly one-hundred and fifty miles per hour. Within a matter of seconds, Shameis went over the ramp and sent us airborne. Looking below, I could see that the section of road that had passed over a pretty large river had given way, so the intentional ramp was placed to try and get over it. Unfortunately for many souls that tried to escape the madness surrounding us, they met an untimely demise at the bottom of this ravine. It looked like a mass graveyard that was causing the river to dam up. Even Shameis barely made it over the gap! Thankfully he sped up when he did.

After experiencing all this, I was relieved to see that the massive amount of carnage did let up after that gap, but there was still the occasional wreck and car fire. Still, Shameis did not use the calmness to let off the throttle. No, after seeing all of that, we needed to get to our destination. Who knows the chaos that could be enveloping the place where Victor was. That is if he was safe from any of this. As I looked around the blackness, I caught the burning city in one of the rearview mirrors and instantly felt a sadness enter my heart. How could I be a hero if there wasn't anyone left to save? Was this event centralized, or is this happening worldwide? Were the heroes trying their best to help those that are unaffected? With that thought, I felt a raindrop hit my forehead. Great, we were definitely driving into the storm.

"Hey, Shameis. how much longer do we have?" I questioned over the roar of the motor.

"Not long." He shouted back. "This is our exit!" He then belted out as he slightly turned the motorcycle's handles and drifted us into the rightmost lane. As he did this, I could feel our momentum begin to decelerate. Through the light of the motorcycle's headlamp, I watched him drive us down the exit ramp into a heavily forested back road before pulling up to a crossroad and stopping. Surprisingly, there wasn't a single person, car, or incident insight. So, I decided this would be the best time to get something off my chest. I knew I needed to before things went from zero to one hundred again.

"Shameis?" I called to him meekly.

"Yes, Grim?" He responded, trying to turn to me while balancing the motorbike.

"Did you really mean it when you said you loved me?" I questioned meekly.

"Yes. Of course I did." He replied.

"Even after the betrayal that Victor and Lilith caused? I thought they would've broken you." I cross-examined.

"I really think they tried, but they didn't realize that I would be introduced to you because of it." He let out.

346

"But, I'm nothing special. There are an unknown number of souls that do exactly what I did. I am a murderer, and a walking skeleton because of that..." I pointed out before being interrupted by Shameis wrenching himself around and nearly knocking us off the bike.

"We have been over this. Jakelyde is a murderer. The Lightbringer is a murderer. You are not. The only thing you are guilty of is making a mistake. And you are special. Even though others fill the same role as you, you were the first. You are THE Grim Reaper. No one else can take that title from you. You and I are connected in ways no other human will ever experience. We have traveled through time and space to be together. I do love you, Grim. Nothing will stop that." Shameis spilled out, causing tears to come to my eyes.

"Well, I am still a walking skeleton." I followed up as I tried to wipe my tears away.

"Not to me. I'm pretty sure skeletons can't cry." He then pointed out, which was an excellent point. So good that it made me look into one of the mirrors to see my own reflection. The darkness did make it hard, but I could make out the outline of my face. My real face. After seeing it, I quickly looked down at my hands, but they were still skeletal, leaving me in confusion. "If you're still seeing yourself as the embodiment of death, maybe you should stop thinking of yourself as a monster and love yourself in the way I love you." He let out as he turned around to grab onto the handlebars before revving the engine. The jerk of the bike starting to roll caused me to wrap my arms around his muscular torso again.

"I love you too!" I shouted back to him over the once again roaring motor. "Hey, Shameis," I called out again. "What is Gyles-Helmsley? Is it a prison or something?"

"Or Something." He responded as he drove us down the dark wood lined highway. "It's a state penitentiary, an insane asylum. One of a handful in the world dedicated to locking up potentially dangerous and mentally deranged villains the council face off against,"

"Why would he be here? If there were more places like this, why wouldn't he be at another place?" I then pointed out.

"Probably due to its relation to the city. All the others are kept away from any substantial amount of civilians. However, being that he was able to swindle his way into the council, I can only assume that he also paid off the Government officials so they could turn their blind eyes away from him." Shameis theorize.

"Right. Victor must've done something to cause everyone to forget about all those articles I saw while in the Chamber of the Wanting." I continued with his theorizing.

"Exactly," Shameis concurred just before sharply turning left onto a narrow dirt road. Without hesitation, our dark surroundings felt as if it was trying to engulf us as the dense foliage overgrew the path and tree limbs hung too low for comfort. But as I looked up, I noticed that the canopy was thick enough to block the light from the thunderstorm while the sound of precipitation falling through leaves enveloped us. Based on how the greenery grew, I could tell that this single-track road had not received proper maintenance for a reasonably long time.

Thankfully after only a few minutes of traveling this path, the foliage gave way as a bolt of lightning streaked across the sky. The flash of light revealed we were now in a massive clearing. A twelve-foot-tall brick wall was directly ahead of the woodline with an entryway built around the dirt path. As we drove between the two sections of the wall, I noticed it was equipped with a rusted-opened gate and a metal arch with rusted letters spelling "Gyles-Helmsley." Based on this sight, it seemed as if nothing was keeping the inmates from escaping.

348

After we flew past the wall, the path instantly diverted into three. The two tracks to the left and right branched off and hugged the walls as they led around to the backside of a massive mansion. Shameis ended up choosing the middle path that led up to the front of the estate and around a relatively standard decorative fountain. It has a platform with minor sculpture work in its central basin. On top of the platform sat a tier that led to a second basin. For a majority of it, there was nothing remarkable. It seemed like a deteriorating decoration with no water flowing through it. However, the sculpture that stood at its top stood out.

It's common to see a statue of an angel serving as a guard to an institution like this, but it was the state that this angel was in that worried me. First off, it was sculpted to have its arms stretched out in a welcoming gesture, but its right arm had broken off at the shoulder. Then I noticed that its face was demolished as if someone had beaten it with a stone. Finally, It was made to have a set of outstretched wings, but much like the right arm, the right wing was nowhere to be seen. It was as if this statue mirrored what Zatael looked like when possessing Shameis's body. There is no way that could be intentional, right?

Nevertheless, as Shameis pulled us around the fountain, he brought us to a stop, shut off the engine, and parked the motorcycle just in front of a large staircase, which led up to the front door. As for Gyles-Hemsley itself, it was immaculate, although a bit worn down. The building was four stories tall and covered in sprawling vines and greenery. The greenery continued form its face onto two spires serving as the building's corners. Above the building was an oxidized copper of the roof nearly matched all the vines. I couldn't speak for all of them, but several windows that were not overtaken by the greenery had been cracked or shattered in one way or another.

I wish I would've been allowed more time to enjoy the structure, but I was only given a few seconds before Shameis hopped off the bike, turning to me and hoisting me back to the ground. Then, as soon as both of us were freed from our steed, Shameis made a b-line up the grand staircase. As I followed him, I was expecting to be greeted by a massive wooden entryway, but was saddened by this section of the architecture. It was modified to have a glass door. It made sense because this mansion was changed to be a modern-day home for the mentally insane, and the receptionist of such an organization should see who was approaching. However, I was still heartbroken to see such disregard for the grandeur of this place.

Shameis, on the other hand, gave no thought to it whatsoever. Clearly, there was now only one thing on his mind. So, once at the glass door, he reached out for the handle and tried to pull it open. There was a slight shift before the clank of the deadbolt rattled the frame. This noise caught the attention of a person who seemed to be a teen boy sitting behind an oak desk on the other side of a small white room. After the locking mechanism denied us entry, Shameis pulled again with more of his strength. This caused the locking mechanism to rip through the frame and to fill the silent air filled with the sounds of twisting metal. I was surprised to see that the pane of glass decided to remain intact.

Seeing us barging in, the teenager quickly hopped up from his seat and rounded the desk to try and confront us. "What the Hell man? The door was locked for a reason. If you want to check yourself in, you'll have to wait for…" He started berating Shameis before interrupting himself by doubling over in pain. This reaction caused Shameis and I to freeze, and after a few seconds, the boy looked up to Shameis as if he needed help.

350

Unfortunately for the boy, Shameis stood motionless since he had no idea what was happening, nor could he alert any other staff members. So, we watched as this person's irises changed from a baby blue into a crimson red, while the whites of his eyes turned yellow as his groans of pain transformed into an unholy screech. Almost as suddenly as this transformation occurred, the young man lunged toward us, but Shameis instinctively threw a right hook and caught our assailant on the jaw. Almost instantly, his body fell limply to the floor. His heartbeat was slowed, but it was still existent. I did scan the room to see if anyone else was around to help, but it was empty. It was just us, thirty black waiting room chairs with gray cushions that lined the white walls and the reception desk.

"What was that?" I questioned after looking back at the boy's unconscious body.

"No Idea," Shameis coldly responded as he stepped over the body toward an oak door that sat to the right of the desk. "We probably just witnessed a possession, like what was happening in the city."

"But, Zatael said that only a few humans were capable of hosting souls from the other realms." I tried to recall as I followed closely behind.

"He also said that Victor was making it possible so some people could eventually hold them." Shameis reminded me. "The last time I saw Shawn, he could barely afford the one degree he was working on, but in less than six years, Shawn became the founder of a fortune five-hundred company that produces medicine. This proves that Victor some how manipulated everything." Shameis then explained just before reaching the door.

"You really think so? Geez, how much money does this guy have?" I cross-examined, causing Shameis to turn his attention to me.

"Millions. I don't know how Jakelyde has so much, but you can't afford a secret base under a cemetary without having too much." Shameis breezed by as he turned back to the door, grabbed onto the doorknob, and opened the door without having to break it. "Besides, he's always had the backing of the United States government."

"I can see that," I agreed as I followed Shameis out the blindingly white lobby and into a dark corridor with periodic low-hanging light fixtures that projected light to the ground below. As I gazed through the darkness, I could see that these pools of light appeared in small diameters and were spaced drastically apart. Each lights revealed small portions of the walls and two doors, each on either side of the hall. Contrasting the vibrant white color of this waiting room, the sections of the hall revealed by the lights were made of neutral gray bricks.

As we passed through the first light, I noticed these doors had rectangular nameplates to indicate who used the space behind each barrier, like the hospital doors. As I looked to the door on the left, the placard labeled this room as 'Interrogation room #1' in gold text on a black background. As for the door on our right, I could only assume it was an office space since it was labeled 'Dr. Antonio Palevski'. I concluded that Shameis knew this hall was where the office spaces were held. With that, I assumed that if we were to find Victor here, he would be behind a door with his name. Again, I could only think that he was here based on what was happening outside, but we also assumed Victor was back at the hospital.

Well, seeing that neither of these light-colored wooden doors had the correct name, we pushed on into the darkness towards the next light and set of doors, which was only twenty feet or so. The next also didn not have what we were looking for, so we nonverbally decided to quickly blew past each set that didn't have his name. However, after passing five sets of lights and doors, we finally came upon an island of light much larger than the rest. Accompanying this cylindrical island of light were two sets of double gunmetal gray doors opposite of each other in the hall.

352

To our right, a set of doors serving as a large entrance had a plaque on each door inscribed with the same title 'Infirmary.' A place where the sick can rest to become better. I'm sure for a place like this, this refers to the physically injured instead of the unwell since everyone here is mentally unwell. Then, to our left sat a second, smaller hallway with a set of doors with windows emitting a blueish glow.

Seeing this, I let go of Shameis so I could have a look at what was on the other side, which caused him to stop rushing for a second to join me. Through the one of the windows, I observed a massive four-story room with walkways wrapping around the room at each level. There were thin metal stairs that connected one level to the next. Down the middle of the room was a giant open space, making it so any person on any landing could see where another person was, and each of these landings was fitted with waist-high metal railings to prevent anyone from falling over. There seemed to be little cubby-like areas built into the walls on all four levels of this room, and each one was paired with a tiny keypad and a glass wall that served as a cell door; separating the interior from the rest of the room. These glass walls seemed to be split in half, with the right portion protruding past the left. At the bottom of this pit was a cafeteria-like floor with several hexagon-shaped tables and a stool attached to each side. There was no soul in sight, so I assumed they were all in their cages. Then the ceiling consisted of a skylight with several lights circling around it spaced out evenly.

"It makes you think, doesn't it?" Shameis spoke up.

"Think about what?" I questioned back.

"Of all these people locked away in here. Many of them we put in here simply because of their abilities or because of how they looked as a result of getting them. These people have been deemed a menace to society and were locked away. After going to Hell and back in their shoes, I'm starting to rethink as to why they are here." He explained.

"Does that mean you're going to let them out once this is all over?" I asked hopefully, to which he chuckled in response.

"Not all of them. There are murderers, arsonists, thieves, and many other people who have done heinous things in here. There is no way I could let them all out with a good conscience, but I would want to reevaluate which people should actually be here and who shouldn't." Shameis countered.

"But from what we've seen from Chicago, every single person is acting like that. So I don't see the reason why people should be locked up if everyone in the adjacent city is doing the exact same thing." I cross-examined his argument.

"That is a fair point, but I'm hoping a solution to that comes when we finally put an end to Victor and the Lightbringer. However, many of these people have been here for much longer than any of that hysteria. If we were to let these people loose and then fix the regular people, then the heroes would need to recapture all the bad ones." Shameis uttered before falling silent for a bit. "Let's put a pin in this topic. We have way too much on our plate that needs to be taken care of first." Shameis let out as he took my hand before leading me away from the windows.

"Right. Let's go take care of Victor," I concurred as I followed him back toward the main corridor. I was expecting to rush down the hall once we turned the corner, but, instead, both Shameis and I froze in our tracks. Down at the end of the hall that we needed to get to, I could see a figure standing motionlessly while draped in dramatic shadows underneath the fifth light away. I was startled since that person had not been present before, but that quickly subsided when I realized who that was. The fiery red hair was a dead giveaway, but something was off. It appeared as if the bounce in her hair had flattened while its vibrance faded. It almost looked stringy. And that was when a familiar foul stench rolled past us.

354

"Lil... Lilith? Is that you?" Shameis stuttered as he took a few paces forward without leaving the puddle of light we were in.

"In somma my flesh." She responded in a raspy and weak voice that sounded nothing like the shrill Bostonian accent I've come to expect from her. After acknowledging Shameis, she slowly began to turn toward us. The sound of her bones creaking echoed throughout the hall. This wasn't right at all. What... What happened to her? She used to be so full of life, but now her skin was grayed, and she seemed to barely walk straight. This is what I was afraid of. I can't even imagine what Victor had to do to keep her body alive while her soul was in the other realms. But as she proceeded toward us, that smell grew exponentially. It was awful. I remember smelling something like this before. It was worse than the stench of the sewer, and I have become accustomed to the stench of death. This was terrible. It even caused Shameis to plug his nose even though his gauze mask should filter most smells out. Finally, when Lilith crossed the patch of darkness into the fourth puddle of light, I was able to see her more clearly, and I finally realized what I recognized that stench from. It was the odor of decaying flesh.

THE ILE

Chapter
Twenty-Nine

I guess this is something that I will have to get used to. First those two monsters, then Chimera, followed by the City, and finally Lilith. I need to get used to the fact that everything Victor Jakelyde touched will be corrupted. I can't believe that one human would achieve such villainous goals or that an angel would guide someone to do something like this. Yet, even with my disbelief, this is the life that I have chosen to pursue. I can only hope that the portion of Zatael's soul within me would provide the same strength Shameis displays when facing these monsters. Yet, I still have the drive to push forward, even when my heart weighs me down.

Well, I can only speak for myself in these matters. Especially now, as Lilith's corpse-like body is ambling its way toward us. Even if Shameis never was a fan of Lilith, one would have to assume that he would be terrified to see Victor's handiwork. We were led to believe that she would serve a critical role in this story, and I took that to mean that she might change sides and help us. Yet, finding her here, in this state of being, I know that she was meant to serve as a roadblock to our end goal. So, unfortunately, we allowed a roadblock to stand by bringing her back up, and clearly, she was not meant to.

So, Shameis and I stood silent as the heavy thwomp of her steps echoed through the empty hall as she made her way across a puddle of light four fixtures away. This was surreal. A month is too long to try and keep a soulless body alive. I know Victor has the impulse to play creator and has the backing of a nigh-almighty being, but this should never have happened. This is unnatural. Perhaps Victor was attempting to recreate what happened to Shameis, since his body was the only one in existence to be exempt for the natural order. I don't care what Lucifer said about Lilith needing to play a more significant role. Clearly, Lilith was meant to die and stay dead. This can't be a way someone is supposed to live. I know I don't know the most about keeping someone alive, but there has to be a way to keep someone's heart pumping once it stops... right? There is no reason to allow decay if you're expecting a soul to come back. Unless... Unless Victor wasn't aware that Lilith's soul was going to come back.

That has to be the reason for this. Lilith's body became Victor's most recent experiment! Just like those soulless beasts that Victor used to pin Lilith to the table and caused Shameis to lose his arm and face! Only in Lilith's case, her soul came back. So, the next question would be, "what was the goal of this"? If the Lightbringer didn't inform Victor of Lilith's return, then what was Victor's endgame? Was he going to try and study Lilith's genetics to figure out why she wasn't turned into a hero, but Amber was? On top of that, Why would the Lightbringer want Lilith's soul to come back if his lackey wasn't informed? Whatever the reason, was this really the cost?

"What's tha matta? Stunned by my gorgeous looks?" Lilith suggested in her hoarse tone of voice as she passed through the darkness between the fourth and third light fixtures before entering the next closest puddle of light.

358

"What... What happened to you?" Shameis inquired hesitantly as he took a back toward the middle of the light we shared.

"Whatcha think happened? I may have had ta go ta Hell and back, but the Doc gave me supa powas. Just like he promised. " Lilith enlightened us as she crossed the third puddle of light. "It woulda been betta if that one didn't send me there in tha first place!"

"That one? Wait, can you see me?" I called out.

"Of course I can. What happened to your skin, cutie? Ya look tha exact same as when ya sent me ta Hell." Lilith affirmed as she left the light of the third lamp. This revelation caused me to sharply turn toward Shameis, and he, in turn looked to me.

"She can see me..." I muttered.

"She can see you..." He echoed equally as shocked.

"Does that mean that any soul that comes from the other realms will be able to see me too?" I questioned as I turned back toward Lilith's direction, but she was still in the darkness between the third and second lights. This was massive news that nearly shifted my entire worldview. So it's possible for ordinary souls can see and hear me! That isn't reserved for just the angels and Shameis. I can't believe it took a living zombie to figure this out; as if the angels would've shared this information with us.

"Ya really thought that your boy toy would be tha only one ta see ya?" She mocked as she stepped into the second spot of light while using the wall to our left as a support. I guess she was not strong enough to support her weight for very long in this deteriorated state, but as she dragged herself agains the wall, every spot on the brick wall start cracking, which could've been a sign that the building had a weak point. I nearly brushed that fact off, but as she slid off the brick and onto the left wooden door under the second light, every part of the wood she touched decayed instantly.

"Shameis..." I uttered without looking away from Lilith.

"I see... " He responded quickly.

"Ya like my new powa. The Doc truly is a man of his word." Lilith fluttered as she rolled off the decaying door and onto the brick wall again before slinking into the darkness just before our section of light.

"Lilith. We are not going to get into this with you." Shameis informed her. "Lucifer said that you were meant to play a bigger role. So just let us know what we need to do, and we can help you find what you are meant for."

"Isn't it obvious that my job has been done?" Lilith's heinous voice sneered from the darkness.

"What are you talking about?" Shameis inquired.

"I broke the Vale." She then cackled.

"What do you mean by that?" I then inquired as I took a few steps toward her.

"The Lightbringa said he needed me ta break the borda so he could come ova. You guys opened the door for yourself, but I opened it for everyone." She admitted as she entered the final section of light. Finally, I got a good enough look here, and I was instantly repulsed. Yes, the smell of rotting flesh was coming from her, but not all of her. I slowly stepped back to Shameis's side once seeing the true scope of her condition. First off, she was wearing the exact same red shirt and blue jeans she had died in, except they were now severely tattered. Then her skin was covered in stitches and scars that were held together with various chunks of flesh that obviously belonged to multiple different people. The skin tones and skin colors were all over the place! Even though she has new skin, there were still bits that were rotting away.

"Lilith! Stay there!" Shameis barked as he brought up his fists in an attempt to ready himself for an ensuing conflict.

360

"Oh, Shamey... There is no stoppin' what is ta come." She muttered as she entered the final stretch of darkness. "Also, Just like how the Doc gave ya that name, the Doc gave me a new name too! One ta match my new powas!" She continued before falling silent.

"Please don't tell me you want us to start calling you Sammie again." Shameis let out nervously as we waited for her to enter our patch of light.

"No way, I've got a betta name. Necrosis!" She then screeched as she lunged out of the shadows as if she was a zombie on the prowl. Instinctually, Shameis grabbed onto me and forced himself and me away from her grasp, causing us both to slam up against the infirmary doors. Seeing us move, Lilith tried to reach out toward either of us, but her weakened state caused her to trip over herself and fall into the darkness behind us. The sound of her decaying body smacking the ground was not a pleasant sound to hear.

"Necrosis, that's on point." Shameis remarked as we both returned to the center of the light while the sound of Lilith struggling to get off the ground echoed down the hall. "Was this really worth it? Your years of dedication to Jakelyde and the Lightbringer? Was it worth becoming a living corpse?" Shameis then questioned as Lilith stumbled into our puddle of light.

"I have supa powas now." She answered. "I can demand tha respect I deserve!" Lilith shouted as she tried to swipe at us, to which we were able to quickly step out of the way.

"Can you even control it?" I then questioned.

"Not yet, but the doc promised ta make me a special supa suit out of a special metal if I can separate Shamey's soul from his body," Lilith explained as a sinister grin formed on her face while continuing to reach out. She was very close too. The hall wasn't vast, so there were minimal opportunities to evade her plague-infested hands. Hearing this, Shameis reached out to her with his metal hand grabbed onto Lilith's wrist so he could push her backward. Being so weak, the little force Shameis used caused her to stumble out of the light again.

"How did you know that would work?" I questioned as I looked at his hand, to which I saw no sign of corrosion.

"She said she was going to get a suit made out of a special metal, and there is no metal more special than dietanuim," Shameis answered quietly to me while also looking at his hand before looking into the darkness. "So Jakelyde knows we are coming?"

"Of course he does. I was tha one that updated him on tha Lightbringa's plan." Lilith answered as she slowly re-entered the light, now with her arms down at her side and a wicked gleam in her clouded eyes. "All tha lightbringa needs is you, then his plan will be complete."

"He can't have either of us." Shameis barked as he raised his fist in preparation for a fight.

"Don't ya realize that ya already lost? I broke tha Vale! Tha demons of Hell have already possessed all the people ya care about." Lilith pointed out.

"If the Lightbringer can bring them here, then the Worldforger can send them back!" I added in, to which Lilith cackled.

"We don't have time for this!" Shameis then let out before stepping up to her and landing a punch with his metal square in her chest, which launched Lilith backward. What followed was the sound of Lilith's rotting body smacking the ground again just before silence fell.

"Was that necessary?" I questioned as I turned to him.

"Grim, heroes fight monsters. She is a monster, just like Dennis." He responded as he took a few steps forward without leaving the light.

"She is in this position because of us!" I defied.

362

"We are in this position because of her!" He then reminded me as he turned to look at me. "She's the one that took away my mundane life by handing me over to Victor! Besides, I'm pretty sure she is already dead." To that second point, I paused our conversation and focused on the ground so I could listen to the heartbeats; to which there was only one. So either Shameis was right, or he stopped her heart in one punch. So I looked back up to him to confirm his observation, but my attention was caught by the slight glimmer of two reflective eyes peering out from the darkness.

"Look out!" I shouted as I quickly pushed Shameis out of the way. To this, Lilith's rotten body re-entered the light with a lunge, but because I pushed Shameis out of the way, Lilith and I were now on a collision course. The only reason I pushed Shameis out of the way was that I didn't want her to touch Shameis's flesh. I could possibly heal it, but I don't know if there would be any other adverse effects. For all I knew, her newfound ability of decay wouldn't be able to recover from. The other reason I put myself in harm's way over Shameis was that I thought she would pass right through me. After all, I am just a spirit bound to Shameis though the tether of our fractured Seraph. Instead, to my surprise, Lilith instantly wrapped her arms around me as if she was trying to give me a bear hug. Yes, it was surprising that she touched me, but I was even more surprised that her embrace was accompanied by horrendous pain.

"I wasn't expectin' ta go toe-ta-toe with someone who was more dead than me, but I'll rot a skeleton if I have ta." Lilith cackled over my screams of agony. It felt as if all the parts she touched were instantly set ablaze.

"Let go of her!" Shameis then barked as he pulled me away by the back of my robe, and as soon as I was free, the burning instantly stopped. Out of disbelief, all I could do was look at her.

"Aww, What's tha matta? Can the Grim Reapa not take a little pain?" Lilith let out as she tried to lunge at me again, but Shameis quickly batted her away with his metal arm. This, in turn, caused her to tumble until she smacked into the infirmary doors, to which she caught herself by placing both of her hands up them. Instantaneously, the door began to rust where she touched, leaving a set of handprints behind as she turned back to us. "You can hit me as much as you want. I can't feel pain. I can't feel anything!" Lilith then informed us through her sadistic cackle while approaching once again. "Oh, I can't wait ta have a suit made outta the metal your arm is. Life will be so great once tha Lightbringa has you."

"You really think The Lightbringer is going to keep you around if he gets his way?" I aggressively cross-examined.

"No, he'll keep me around. He promised." Lilith denied.

"Not even the angels care about humans. So why do you think that the super angel that is trying to take The Presence's place would care about you." Shameis chimed in, which only made Lilith laugh even harder.

"Either way, at least everyone will know that I helped make this all happen." She let out just before she was within arm's length.

"I will not let you touch him!" I then barked as I stepped up to her.

"Grim! What are you doing?" Shameis shouted as I reached out to Lilith with both hands and grabbed onto her head.

"Ending this!" I responded as I stared directly into Lilith's eyes. Yes, the burning sensation instantly returned, but I assumed that the damage wouldn't be more than just the pain since I was still standing after her first embrace.

"Whatcha gonna do. Give me a penance stare? Make me see all my sins?" Lilith mocked as she placed her hands over mine so I couldn't back away. Once she did that, my eyes started the water from the torturous sensation as I felt the urge to scream, but I needed to stay focused.

364

"Grim! You're hurting yourself!" Shameis worried as he tried to grab onto me and pull me away.

"I know what I'm doing!" I forced out through gritted teeth.

"Ya wish ya did. But, I'm telling ya, no one can stop Necrosis. With my help, tha Lightbringa will…" Lilith gloated before falling limp and slipping out of my grasp and onto the floor. That was when I turned back to Shameis and saw that he was staring at Lilith's unconscious body.

"What just happened?" Shameis questioned.

"The temple is a very soft place with a lot of nerves. Even though she couldn't feel anything, the nerve endings didn't just go away. So, press them long enough, and the recipient will fall unconscious." I explained.

"Huh…", Shameis shrugged as he looked back up to me. "And she is still alive?"

"You and I both know that is a matter of opinion." I joked as I looked over my shoulder to her before turning back to Shameis and holding out my left hand to him. "We should probably get going before she wakes up." That was when I froze as I felt my eyes widen while I stared at it. My hand! I can see my hand! Not just the bones from my curse, but my actual olive-colored flesh! My curse, has it finally been broken?

"Let's get going," Shameis agreed as he latched onto my hand and broke my shock in the process. I nodded in agreement before we both briskly stepped out of the light so we could hurry down the rest of the hall. To be honest, I wouldn't be surprised if he wasn't here. Being a short and stocky man with a distinct look seems pretty elusive. So, I won't lie when I claim that my hope diminished with every door we passed that didn't have his name. There are several of these institutions across the United States, so maybe he was somewhere else. Perhaps Shawn and Shameis had some outdated information? I was just about to suggest that, but then we found it.

Finally! Victor's office was at the very end of the hall, kind of like the operation room we escaped from. Whoa... Wait... I'm starting to get a horrible feeling about this. Upon reaching the door, I looked around the corridor as everything in my mind began to spiral. I knew that we had to go in there, but it just seemed a little odd. It was as if everything we had experienced thus far was in rewind and in negative. A dark hall full of rooms that leads to a space owned by Victor Jakelyde. And we know we don't even have the upper hand.

"Grim, is something wrong?" Shameis worried as he turned me so I could look at him.

"We can't go in there!" I let out.

"We have to," He responded. "There is nothing else we can do. The world is ending outside, and we are the only ones that can fix it. There is no way the other heroes will be able to stop the Lightbringer."

"No, something doesn't feel right about this." I continued to freak out. "We really, really shouldn't go in there."

"Grim. I understand your concern, but we have to." Shameis reiterated. "As of now, the whole world is in their pockets. We are the only heroes that can do this, and if the heroes won't fight for what's right, then who will?"

"I love your inspiration." I let out as I walked up to him, grabbed onto the tattered lab coat he was wearing, and pulled him in close so I could kiss him passionately. I know that there was a layer of gauze in between our lips, and although it did feel a bit strange, I had this weird feeling in my gut that I wouldn't get a chance to do this for a long time. "Alright," I then agreed softly after unwantedly pulling away, to which I saw that his hazel iris had become a bright pink.. "I trust you more than anything else.

366

"I love you, Grim. We will get through this together." Shameis then let out just before the pink in his iris transitioned into a blazing red as he turned and reached out to the door handle. This is it, the moment of no return. The moment we are on the other side of this door and facing Victor, we will be waging war against the Lightbringer. Not like we have another choice since the world is ending. At least I know that Shameis and I are the heroes this world needs. To the other powerful beings, Shameis and I are the only ones willing to stand up to this corrupting evil. So, ready or not, Victor Jakelyde, here we come.

LILITH COTTER (NECROSIS)

Chapter Thirty

So this is it. The only thing that stands between us and the end of this leg of our journey is a single chunk of wood. Although my adrenaline is spiking while emotions are running high, it is sobering to think about how far we have come. Even still, when we draw near to the end of this leg, our plot continues to thicken. We knew that there is much to do after dealing with Victor Jakelyde, but the bombshell Lilith dropped on us only cemented the realization that we still don't have the whole picture.

I'm torn. It's been said that when one door closes, another will open, but still, that feeling deep inside me is warning me that this might not be the best path of action. We don't even have a plan. Although I trust Shameis with all my being, I was still worried about what he planned. There is no proper recourse that we can go through since there is an apocalypse raging outside these walls, so do we just lock him up until something better comes along?

But what if he manages to escape or be let free? What if all of this was for naught? Lilith told us that Victor knew we were coming, so does that mean he is prepared to face us? We still don't even know what Victor gets out of this. Was the Lightbringer planning on sparing him once the Vale was broken? We still haven't figured out how and why Zatael would expect two ordinary souls to face off against a crazed deity. If we were to win, would Shameis and I be able to stay together? No, I can't think about all that right now. I need to focus on what is just ahead. I need to push these uneasy feelings aside and have faith that this must be done. After all, if there was no one left on Earth that could make a host for the Lightbringer and Shameis won't surrender his body, then perhaps our conflict with the Lightbringer could be avoidable.

Nevertheless, I could hear Shameis's heart beating rapidly at this very moment. It was as if his heart wanted to burst through his chest, even though he stood motionless while staring at his metal hand on the doorknob. I wasn't sure why he was hesitating since he was the one who encouraged me to go forth, but I still had to stand here and wait. Perhaps it was because he was as nervous as me. Everything weve been through has been building up to this moment. So, I reached out with my left hand to nudge him a bit, to which he glanced over to me before looking back at the doorknob. Perhaps he hasn't opened it yet because it was locked? Of all the doors we had to break through, this is the one that should be, even though he has the strenght bypass it. but after that nudge, Shameis proceeded to twist the knob and pop on the door with barely a squeak of its hinges.

Once open, we walked into our final destination, to which I was instantly greeted with a severe case of déjà vu. Everything about this place was identical to the room Shameis was forced to endure by himself in the realm of lust. The lighting, morgue drawers, cabinetry, holding cell, and operating tables. Even the dark gray bricks were identical. The only difference was that one of the operating tables was now caked in dried blood and covered in rust, indicating that this was where Victor was holding Lilith's body when she was reanimated. That, and Victor stood near his computer with his hand behind his back as he watched us enter. He looked exactly the same as when I last saw him. White dress shirt, red

370

tie, black slacks, dress shoes, white lab coat, thick circular glasses, and heavy gray beard. From the moment I saw him on that cruise ship, I knew he was going to be a thorn in my side.

"I don't know how you caused my Necrosis to collapse without touching her, but I was fairly certain you were going to best her," Victor let out in his confident and smug German accent.

"You were watching?" Shameis questioned softly as the door closed behind us.

"He can't see me." I added in.

"Of course, I was watching. Do you think I don't have cameras planted in my own places of operation?" Victor cross-examined. "My only question is, how did it feel to meet the one child you failed to save?" To that, Shameis let out a deep breath as he began to march toward Victor. "Oh, did I strike a nerve? Frankly, I was surprised to see you heal from the blow Chimera gave you. I didn't think healing would manifest from the serum I gave. Speaking of which, why couldn't the Lightbringer attach himself to your body once your soul left?"

"Because he also needs a soul, and my soul is spoken for!" Shameis barked without stopping his progression.

"Surely you don't believe that I am supposed to know what that means, do you?" Victor responded.

"It means that I already have a Seraph attached to me!" Shameis answered as he was finally within arm's length of Victor. Once there, he grabbed onto the collar of Victor's shirt with his left hand and wound up a punch with his right. With quick succession, Shameis threw the fist toward Victor's head while Victor stood confidently and unflinching.

"ELI protocol Omicron," Victor muttered as the incoming attack reached the halfway point, which caused the arm to abruptly jet left and hit Shameis's left arm and making Shameis release the doctor.

371

"What the Hell?" Shameis let out through clenched teeth as he shook his left arm to get rid of the pain.

"I know you saw the functions of my mechanical arm you're sporting. Did you really think that it wasn't pre-programmed with commands?" Victor questioned as he stood still. "Now, did you say that your soul was already connected to a Seraph?"

"You don't deserve answers!" Shameis shouted back as he tried to swing a punch with his left hand.

"ELI protocol Sigma." Victor let out in response. This command caused Shameis's metal arm to fling backward and stretch toward me with a high velocity. Knowing that the prosthetic is made out of Deitanium and that I can touch it, I quickly jumped out of the way instead of letting it phase through me. Thankfully I did, because within half a second after I was out of the way, the hand smacked the brick wall behind me and imbedded its fingertips into the brick. "Interesting, that protocol was designed to attack beings other than myself. I intended for it to simply cause you to miss me again, but this just raises even more questions." Victor explained as the extended arm started to reel itself in, pulling Shameis away from Victor. Shameis was trying his best to hold his ground but was sliding across the slick tile floor.

"I swear if you hurt her, I will rip you in half," Shameis threatened as Victor proceeded to approach my helpless partner.

"I thought that my serum might have caused you to lose your mind like so many before, but now I see that you can actually see someone else." Victor realized as he stroked his thick gray beard. "Tell me, Isaac. Who can you see?" To this, Shameis stared silently at Victor as he struggled to keep his position. "Oh, it's no matter. Once the Lightbringer finally comes to Earth, I'm sure he'll let me experiment on your friend."

372

"No. You. Won't!" Shameis grunted as he pulled on his outstretched arm, causing the wall around the hand's firm grasp to start to break.

"Do you have feelings for this invisible woman? After what I forced Lilith to do to you, you were still able to find love?" Victor continued to question without noticing what was happening to the wall. But, of course, Shameis continued to pull instead of answering. "Tell me, Isaac. What does this invisible woman offer that no other person can?"

"Death itself." Shameis then muttered as the wall broke away. With this, Shameis swung the extended arm at Victor while it rapidly returned to its standard length. Based on Victor's expression, he clearly didn't recognize that it wasn't just the arm that was giving Shameis his super-strength. I can see why Victor would be surprised, since, from his vantage point, Shameis was using the arm for everything. I guess that's the benefit of being right-hand dominant and having that same appendage replaced. So, as Shameis swung the arm at Victor, he finally was able to land a blow. I guess Victor was just as surprised as I was since Shameis used the large chunk of the wall he pulled free and used the brick to hit Victor square in the torso. The impact's force must have been dispersed a bit since I didn't hear any bones break, but it launched Victor into the cabinet, knocking his glasses off in the process. "This ends here, Victor." Shameis then let out as he dropped the chunk of brick before approaching the mad scientist.

"You're really going to break that rule you set so long ago?" Victor questioned through mild wheezing and coughing as he slinked off the countertop.

"What rule?" I cross-examined as I followed Shameis toward Victor.

"He's implying I have to kill him," Shameis answered as he reached Victor's position and grabbed him by the collar of the lab coat and lifted the doctor into the air.

"You've always been so smart, Shameis. And now that you have another partner, you've become so strong." Victor admitted. "Too bad the strength of my intellect will always be stronger. ELI Protocol Gamma." Once the arm received that command, Shameis instantly dropped the Doctor Then, Shameis dropped to his knees while letting out scream of pains as he used his left hand to grab onto the metal plating over his right pectoral.

"Shameis!" I shouted as I knelt next to him while watching his masked expression show actual signs of agony.

"Whoever you are, watch as your hero crumbles," Victor spoke to me as he crouched so Shameis and himself were eye-to-eye. "ELI Protocol Gamma." Victor then repeated, causing Shameis to stop shouting. "Now, Shameis, if you would like to avoid more of that pain, I suggest you surrender your soul to the Lightbringer."

"I'd... rather...die..." Shameis forced out as he breathed heavily. I don't know what Victor was doing, but it did cause a small stream of blood to trickle out from underneath Shameis's metal plating.

"Oh, Isaac. Don't you see? We will be able to manufacture a suitable host for the Lightbringer." Victor boasted as he returned to a standing position. "As we will use your perfect D.N.A. to do it. Once you're dead, of course."

"I'm not the one... that's going to die today...." Shameis responded as he tried to get up while using me as support.

"I'm sure you've pieced it together that I'm using Deitanium to create potential hosts for the Lightbringer, but have you figured out how I've been able to produce so much?" Victor questioned while watching Shameis return to his feet.

"Because the Lightbringer gave it to you," Shameis answered.

374

"Only the initial sample. But after receiving it, I quickly learned that overexposure to the purest form of Deitanium will convert other metals it touches into more Deitanium." Victor enlightened us before calling out the name of the protocol gamma for the third time and causing Shameis to drop back to his knees and start screaming again. "The process is long, but as more are introduced to the system, the more painful the process. The bit I initially injected into you was only enough to unlock your hidden potential while trying to keep you docile. I'm not sure what caused the negation, but the metal is still in you. So this should be enough to produce more. Last chance. Surrender."

"No!" I shouted in response as I quickly slid my left hand into the opening of the tattered lab coat Shameis was wearing and onto his bare torso. I wasn't sure if my healing ability would counteract the surges of Deitanium being injected from his prosthetic, but I knew I had to do something. So, just like last time, I imagined the opposite of what could possibly be going on, but his screaming made it seem like my healing wouldn't work. Yes, I was hoping this would work, but I also felt way out of my depths. That is until Shameis suddenly stopped screaming and fell limp. "No!" I shouted again.

"No!" Victor echoed as he crouched down and lifted Shameis's head. "This is not good. The Lightbringer will not be pleased."

"Then maybe you shouldn't have failed him." Shameis then let out as he opened his eye, revealing that his iris was now glowing the pale light of Zatael instead of the blazing red I saw outside of this room.

"What... How are you..." Victor sputtered just before Shameis forcefully grabbed him by the throat with his metal hand as the two of them rose up to their feet. I, too, got off the floor and watched as the glowing blue lights in Shameis's forearm transitioned into the same pale glow that was in his iris. "ELI... Protocol... Alpha..." Victor forced out.

"No! No more protocols! The arm is mine!" Shameis barked before tossing Victor at his computer desk, knocking everything off in the process.

"How is this possible?" Victor demanded to know as he slowly rolled off the desk and into a standing position. It was at this moment that I could see the twinge of fear crept onto his face and into his pitch-black aura.

"My friend that you can't see. She is THE GRIM REAPER! She controls when I die! And now is not the time!" Shameis shouted as he began to approach Victor.

"ELI Protocol Omega!" Victor quickly shouted before Shameis stretched a punch at Victor that connected with his chest, causing him to fall back onto the desk as he writhed in pain. This time, I definitely heard a distinct snap.

"Shameis!" I shouted to him as I quickly ran up to and got in front of him before he could reach the injured Victor Jakelyde "What do you think you are doing?"

"He already told us the only way to stop them. We need to put an end to this!" He answered as he tried to move me out of the way.

"No! I won't let you do this. I won't let you become a murderer!" I shouted at him. "If we can't fix this apocalypse and there are no more humans, I won't let you become the last murderer. I already have to wear the burden of being the first."

"If not me... Then who?" He questioned aggressively as the pale light in his iris faded into the raging red we came in with. Strangely enough, the lights in his arm did not go back to the light blue they used to be. Although I was interested in that phenomenon, I turned away to look at Victor, who was now rolling back off the desk into a standing position. I could see a bit of blood leaking out of Victor's mouth now, meaning this man had some definite internal bleeding.

376

"A soul is a soul," I muttered as I stared at the dazed Victor Jakelyde. With that, I reached into my robe and *pulled* out my scythe. Before Shameis could react or respond, I swung my blade and planted the point of my blade into Victor's chest, right where his heart would be. Did I expect anything to come from this? No, and yes. I now know that I can not be seen, heard by, or touch anyone that hasn't been to the other realms. However, after recalling what Zatael mentioned before disappearing, I thought that maybe this wretched man has been exposed to enough Deitanium that perhaps I could have some effect on his life. I will not let Shameis become a murderer!

So, I just stood there waiting to see if anything would happen. Being that my scythe, like me, is not originally of the human world, the blade went right through Victor's flesh without an entry wound. I wasn't expecting anything to happen, but I held out hope while Shameis stood frozen behind me. As I stared at Victor's face, I could see Shameis standing motionlessly in the reflection of my blade. Is this because he realizes the sacrifice I am offering to ensure his safety? This is the sacrifice that I should've offered to my brother such a long time ago. It's funny how one simple choice can change every outcome. I guess my risk paid off. After a few seconds of standing with my scythe in his chest, Victor finally started to react. His eyes widened as he slowly looked down to his chest before looking back up and staring directly into my eyes. He was terrified, and his aura attested to such, as the hints of yellow slowly started to engulf his blackness.

"Tell the Lightbringer that we are coming," I whispered to Victor as I slowly pulled my blade out of his chest and allowed his lifeless body to collapse.

"Grim. Did you... How?" Shameis questioned, causing me to turn to him.

"A soul is a soul..." I repeated while slightly traumatized from taking another life. At least this one was not innocent. I guess Shameis could see it in my face that I was off since he slowly walked up to me and pulled me into a hug. "I didn't want you to go through the same punishment I did," I explained to him while resting my head against his chest.

"I wouldn't have. We are far beyond the point of needing another ferryman." Shameis theorized softly as he caressed my head. "How did you know that would work?"

"I didn't." I let out as my voice quivered and a tear rolled down my cheek. "I guessed based on what Victor and Lilith said and what we saw for ourselves. But this confirms everything. The other realms really can reach Earth." After saying this, I pulled away from Shameis to look him in the eye. "Why would they do all of this? Everything used to be so calm."

"Relatively." He rebutted softly as the rage in his iris faded into a somber blue. "Much calmer than now, that's for sure."

"Are you the slightest bit worried about all the people you care about?" I followed up, to which he looked away from me.

"I don't have anyone else. Victor killed my parents a long time ago as part of that mass murder he committed, which, in hindsight, was an attempt to mass produce Deitanium." Shameis answered before looking back at me. He, too, had tears in his eye. "That was the defining reason I became The Ile. I had no one left. Now all I have is you and Shawn, but with Hardrive's and Jakelyde's tech, I'm sure he will be able to be just fine."

"Oh... I'm sorry... You're all I have too." I comforted him, to which he nodded. "So, what do we do now?"

"We do exactly what you told Victor," Shameis answered as he took my hands and held them. "We go for the Lightbringer."

378

"But how?" I then questioned as Shameis started leading me toward the exit.

"I'm not sure, but I know it's not here," He answered. "If we had to go through the seven realms of sin to get back to earth, then maybe we need to go to Heaven or Hell to find him." He then suggested.

"Yeah!" I agreed energetically as I wiped the tears from my face. And with that, we were on our way to the next leg of our adventure, even though we had no idea how we were supposed to accomplish it. At least we thought we were, but I guess fate had a different plan. The moment we reached the halfway point between Victor's lifeless body and the door we entered through, everything inside the room that wasn't bolted down or built into the walls began to rattle. It was as if a freak earthquake decided to strike, even though an earthquake of this magnitude would be impossible to experience here. Still, the shaking caused us to stop and look around as the cabinet doors swung open and some of the equipment and materials inside started to spill out. Thankfully it only lasted for a second before stopping, so I turned to Shameis and saw that his iris was engulfed in yellow.

"Shit..." He let out quietly as he continued to scan the room. He swore! He has not said a single curse word through all this, so something terrible was happening.

"What is it? Was that Protocol Omega?" I questioned just before the wall above the computer desk exploded violently, causing pieces of brick, concrete, and smoke to instantly fill the room. The suddenness of the blast caused Shameis to turn away while trying to protect himself from any oncoming debris while I stood firm, knowing that the incoming projectiles would pass right through me. So instead, I just watched as the debris field quickly dissipated to reveal a gaping hole in the wall. There, floating outside the reach of the light illuminating this room, was a pair of glowing blue circles.

"No, That's..." He started to answer before being interrupted as the pair of glowing blue eyes zoomed toward us. Whatever this was, it was moving faster than anything I've ever experienced, besides Zatael and Raphael racing on in the realm of greed. It simply looked like a pale blue blur as it approached, and before I knew it, Shameis and I were both whisked out through the newly formed hole and into the darkness of the storm-covered night. It was so dark, and we were moving so fast that I couldn't recognize anything around us. All I knew was that I was being dragged by the collar of my robes and that I couldn't touch the ground. This means two things for sure. One, we were somewhere in the air. Two, whoever was doing this had to have been to the other realms. No doubt coming across after the Vale fell. Through this, I could hear Shameis struggling beside me as his metal arm pounded on something that sounded soft, which I assumed to be the flesh of whoever grabbed us. So they are fast, strong, and have been to the other realms? As a last resort to figure out who this was, I decided to use my ability to see if this thing had an aura. Instantly, I was blinded by the color of the aura. No shade, just a pale-yellow light.

"No, This can't be..." I let out upon realizing what type of soul had snatched us.

"I told you this wasn't over." A female voice spoke out just as I finally felt us stop moving. Then, almost as if it was planned, a bolt of lightning streaked across the sky and illuminated everything around. The flash of light revealed that our captor had her dark brown hair done up in a ponytail while her eyes continued to glow that bright blue. Her uniform was a skin-tight latex suit consisting of a bright blue sleeveless singlet wrapped around her voluptuous body tucked into a royal blue skirt. The materials were separated by a golden belt that rounded her hips and reached a point. Matching the belt was a pair of golden bracelet cuffs

380

wrapped around her muscular forearms, a golden star that sprawled across the middle of her chest, and a long golden cape connected to the singlet's collar bone through smallish golden trapezoids. As for her footwear, it seemed as if she was wearing a pair of royal blue calf-high combat boots accented by golden laces and soles. So this was the Starseeker. It would've been nice to meet her, but she, unfortunately, started this off by dangling Shameis and me ten stories over the ground.

What does she mean by that? That phrase implies that we had an unfinished experience, but this was the first time we have ever been in the same place. We haven't even spoken before. I wanted to follow up on her statement, but before I could, she cackled before violently smashing Shameis and my skulls together. Instinctually, I closed my eyes, and boy, that wallop hurt! Well, at least it wasn't as bad as the burning sensation that I felt when Lilith grabbed me. Then, after I opened my eyes, I found myself standing in a strange void and no longer being suspended by my robes. Although everything was pitch black, I could feel that this wasn't the Void between realms.

Perhaps I could have been released by Starseeker and was now standing behind the penitentiary? No, that couldn't be right. There wasn't any lightning, nor lights from any potential windows. There wasn't even any noise. I was definitely in a Void, just not the one I know and loathe. This was odd... Very, very bizarre. So, I looked around for a bit at nothing, trying to figure out what I should do. I swear I spun in a circle at least five times, but then I finally came across Shameis. He was motionless and facing away from me. This was not a good sign, but I knew I would need to interact with this vision. I needed to get some answers.

YGGDRASIL, EARTH, AND THE REALMS

Chapter Thirty-One

I take solace in knowing that an ending is never truly an end. On the contrary, I know from experience that something much more significant is afoot once a finale approaches. Most humans spend their lives searching for a greater purpose, only to meet it in life beyond what they know. Thankfully, Shameis and I are two of the lucky few who can continue the good fight on earth after seeing the other side. Indeed, I am gracious for the opportunities I have been given on this journey. With that, it's strange how my indenturement has led to so many beautiful experiences. I've explored the world, watched humanity evolve, and met the one person who can literally be named my soulmate. On top of all that, I learned that I am half of the one all-powerful angel who's willing to devote themself to the safety of the souls on earth. I just wish all those lives didn't have to hang by a thread while we ventured to the climax of this war.

Still, everything has led to this point. Through Zatael, I restored Shameis's memories, traveled through various realms, best the might of angels, fought against demons, returned to earth, found love, and defeated genuine monsters. My life has been nothing but exciting since meeting Shameis, and I can feel that it is far from over. Shameis and I still need to face off against the Lightbringer or die in the process! And I am willing to give my life to ensure the safety of the human race, even if a chunk of them are murderers and thieves. However, before we can get to that point, I still need to figure out where I am. I'm completely surrounded by nothing, with the only clue as to what I should do is Shameis standing motionless in front of me. At least he was here with me, even though he felt off.

"Shameis?" I questioned to the back of his gauze-covered head as I started to approach him. "I know what it looks like, but I promise that I did not bring us to the Void." I then let out to try to bounce an idea off of him, but he did not respond or turn to look at me. "Hey, can you hear me?" I continued As I reached an arms-length away before reaching out and trying to grab onto his shoulder. "You're starting to worry me," I mumbled as I touched him, which finally caused him to react.

"Fear not, my child. All is as it should be." A deep, booming voice sounded from the other side of Shameis.

"Shameis?" I questioned again as I pulled my hand away, and as I did, Shameis then turned toward me. As I've seen multiple times, his iris was glowing that bright pale-yellow color, but the light streams in his arm were inactive. "Zatael?" I then inquired as he continued to stare blankly.

"Yes," the voice boomed again.

"Zatael, It is good to see you! I thought I wouldn't ever see you again since Shameis saw you for the second time." I exclaimed as I hugged Shameis's body quickly before backing away.

"This is now the second time you have seen me and will be the last." Zatael's voice let out.

"Right, but why? Where are we? Where is Shameis?" I inquired as I looked around the darkness again.

384

"Your tether to the mortal plane is through Shameis's consciousness. Although your souls are in tandem, he must remain in a state of awareness for you to be present." Zatael explained.

"So we are in Shameis's mind, and whatever Starseeker did knocked him out." I pieced together.

"Precisely," Zatael agreed as I returned my attention to him.

"So, now that the Vale between realms has fallen, does that mean you intend to reclaim us?" I asked timidly.

"No, my fight will be on a different front." He answered vaguely.

"Right..." I let out since I could tell that Zatael was vague on purpose. "So, if you are not trying to take command of our souls, why are you here?"

"Simply to inform you that all is as it should be. There are many questions aloft and many experiences that will seem unright. I need you to know that all is as it should be." Zatael informed me.

"Thank you, Zatael. Thank you so much for everything you've done for us." I let out to show my gratitude.

"You are very welcome." The Seraph responded as he raised his right hand as if he was about to snap his fingers.

"Wait." I pleaded as I jumped toward him while trying to stop him. "Will you please tell me how we are supposed to find the Lightbringer without you?"

"All is as it should be." He repeated as he snapped his fingers, causing a whirlwind to whip up.

"But, how do you expect us to face him?" I questioned over the howl of the wind as I felt myself being lifted off my feet.

"All is as it should be." He echoed again as I was whisked away, and he vanished from sight. I was a bit frightened about what was happening, but within the blink of an eye, I found myself within a large rectangular room lined with twin-sized beds, several of which were occupied by people being held against their will. The room was well lit and revealed that the walls were concrete bricks painted a nasty beige color. The space was so neglected that various smudges and handprints littered the paint while sections of beige had chipped or peeled away. The floor was covered in darker beige tiles that were so only they began to crack from the gradual wear and tear. Based on everything around me, I assumed I knew where I was, but the set of two gunmetal grey metal doors with rust spots in the shape of handprints at the far end of the room sealed the realization. This place was the infirmary at Gyles-Helmsley. And with that, I knew that Shameis had been captured, and I needed to find him.

So, I started to walk around the room as I scanned for my partner. Much like the city, the people in this room were of various races and genders. Some were sleeping, some were lying peacefully, and others were actively trying to shake free from their beds, but all were restrained to the rickety metal bedframes and tucked into their light beige linens. Just as I suspected while in that main hall, every one of these people seemed battered and bruised. However, I was intrigued to see that not a single one of them had been inflicted by what was happening outside the compound's walls. I would've wondered how Victor managed to pull that off, but the thick metal collars each of these people wore was the obvious answer.

I had no idea how the technology inside those things worked, but I had a feeling that they somehow were negating the Deitanium in their systems. That has to be the reasoning, right? What else would prevent them from using their powers and escaping? But that doesn't explain why these people were unaffected by the possessions when the people of Chicago were. Nevertheless, as I looked upon these people, I noticed that they were outfitted in matching attires and the metal collar strapped around their necks. These pieces of machinery were in turn equipped

386

with a small screen that displayed their name and heartbeats while a rectangular light positioned just beneath the chin flashed one of two colors. On all of the sleeping patients and some of the awake ones, these lights were lighting up red, but I could get a glimpse of one changing to green as prisoners tried to escape from their restraints. How strange.

After a few minutes of searching, I finally found my partner lying in the bed closest to the giant metal doors on the right side of the room. I was relieved to see him stirring, but then I instantly tensed up again as I noticed he was restrained to the bed while wearing one of those collars, although his restraints were done differently. Unlike all the other people here, who were kept here with standard handcuffs, Shameis was tucked entirely into his linens. Then, two large leather straps stretched across his body over top of all his bedding. He was also still wearing the gauze around his face, but it seemed whiter than I remember. As for the collar he was wearing, his light was lit up a constant green instead of flashing between red and green.

"I'm so happy to see that you're okay! Are you still hurt? How's your head? I questioned as I ran up to and kneeled at his left side so that I would be at his eye level.

"Where... Where am I?" He asked as he hazily looked around.

"We're still in Gyles-Helmsley," I answered. "Starseeker grabbed us and used each other to knock you out."

"This is not good." He sighed while slightly overlapping my explanation before throwing his head back into his pillow. That was when the pair of double doors busted open as six men wearing dark blue guard uniforms that had "Gyles-Helmsley" printed on the right arm entered the room while escorting a tall, slender woman. These men were armed with assault rifles, pistols, tasers, handcuffs, and bulletproof vests over their uniforms. As for the woman, she looked older and had silverish gray hair that was slicked back into a ponytail and wore a black wool turtleneck, khakis slacks, a pair of circular glasses similar to Victor, and a couple of slip-on canvas shoes. Besides her apparel, she carried an inactive handheld electronic tablet in her left hand. As I stared at her, I noted that something seemed so familiar about her facial features. It was as if I'd seen her before.

"Hello," She greeted Shameis with a german-accented voice. "My name is Victoria Jakelyde, and I am the warden of this establishment." And thus, the shoe dropped as to why she seemed so familiar.

"Victoria Jakelyde? Well, that's original?" Shameis quipped as he stared intently at the woman.

"Make your jokes. It does not change that I'll be keeping you here until you decide to cooperate." She stated matter of factly.

"So you work for the Lightbringer too?" Shameis questioned.

"I do not work for a made-up being." She protested aggressively. "I loved my brother and would do anything for him. Before you came, he wished that I subdue you if anything bad were to happen to him. And now he is dead."

"Oh, I didn't kill him. It was... natural causes. So I was spared from the title of murderer." Shameis informed her, which is technically accurate.

"Victor had twelve broken ribs and a cracked sternum." She argued. "Starseeker confirmed it."

"I am a hero, and he was a villain. It is not my fault he decided to stand up against a powered individual of his own creation." Shameis barked as he leaned forward as far as his restraints would allow.

"You are a menace to society! You are directly responsible for everything that has happened around us!" She let out as she leaned over the end of Shameis's bed toward him and fell silent. The two of them stayed in this position for a few seconds as they stared intently at each other, but then Shameis relented and laid back.

"Why have none of you been affected by the apocalypse?" Shameis finally inquired.

"Only those with my brother's metal in their system are affected." She informed us as she too stood up tall.

"Are you implying that all the people of Chicago have Deitanium in them?" Shameis cross-examined skeptically.

"Trace amounts, but not enough to become similar to your peers in my Penitentiary," Victoria affirmed as she started to stroll past a few of the other beds. "Olum Industries quickly became one of the most influential distributors of medical ingredients due to their effectiveness. I assumed this was because of my brother's 'magic' metal. But now, all those people are starting to do such awful things ever since my brother told me that you were coming."

"Shawn's company distributed the catalyst? Shawn is the cause of why the city is in ruins?" Shameis continued to interrogate as he tried to sit up in his bed again.

"I'm sure it is not The Ile's fault. After all, he left my brother to produce the chemicals." Victoria denied as she returned to Shameis's bed. "But Olum Industries distributes worldwide."

"So the Lightbringer's plan to take over the world is well into effect." Shameis then muttered.

"I'm not going to pretend like I know what that means, but yes. It seems that the world is coming to an end. And you killed the only person that could fix this." Victoria accused through a thickening German accent.

"I'm the one who is supposed to fix this!" Shameis shouted back.

"Not from inside your cell!" She returned before pointing at Shameis. "Guards! Grab him!" With that command, four of the six armed men broke their formation and enclosed Shameis. These four guards stood so that two were on each side of the bed. In this grouping,

389

one guard was at each shoulder, and one was at each ankle. They then proceeded to unbuckle the restraints and remove the linens, revealing that Shameis had been changed into a pair of bright orange sweatpants and a white t-shirt. This also showed that his legs and left arm were handcuffed to the bed while his metal arm was missing.

"Shameis, your arm!" I then let out through the chaos of these guards trying to handle my frantic partner as they pulled him to the left side of his mattress.

"My arm! Where is my arm?" Shameis shouted while fighting off the armed men as they lifted him to his feet.

"We have it," Victoria responded. "My brother also informed me to ensure you have access to it once you decide to comply, but no tools or weapons are permitted in the cell. And I'm glad to see that your inhibitor is functioning properly. Still, I'm surprised to see that the light is constantly green. Only those with the strongest abilities make that thing constantly green."

"Well, I don't need my superstrength to get out of here!" Shameis declared once on his feet. He then proceeded to slip the guard's grasp and throw a punch with his left hand across the bed. Shameis's fist contacted with the guard to his right's face and did bloody his nose, but within a second, the guard to his left pulled out a taser and zapped him, causing Shameis to drop to his knees. That was when Victoria walked up to Shameis and stood over him.

"I think you best save your energy. You might need it for the pit." She provoked before stepping away and turning toward the doors.

"Shameis, it is okay. Zatael told me that everything is as it should be." I tried to console him while he was being lifted to his feet and dragged out of the room. As I followed, group brought Shameis into the hall and down the subsection that led to the holding cells

390

"You won't... hold me... for long..." Shameis let out just as Victoria opened the doors, letting the roar of the inmates pour into the quiet hall.

"And what makes you say that?" Victoria inquired as she stopped the group and turned to face Shameis.

"My powers... were given from... an angel." Shameis spewed out, to which Victoria laughed maliciously before turning back around and leading everyone into the main cell blocks.

"Have you not realized? According to my brother, they all have been graced by angels!" Victoria then let out as she displayed the room to us. Instantly, I rushed over to the banister and looked over the sea of inmates. Just as the infirmary showed, this room was filled with various people ranging in age, gender, and ethnicity. However, this room was indeed a madhouse. Inmates were scattered around the lower level as they interacted with each other. Some were eating, playing board games, coloring, but many were acting heinously. Some people were screaming, others were fighting, but I could pick out two or three people in this crowd that was violating another. It was grotesque and I was horrified. Even if these people weren't affected by Deitanium, I think they should be locked up here.

Unless... Unless these people are acting like this because of the Lightbringer? Victoria's declaration clarifies everything! The Deitanium acts as a binding agent so the Lightbringer can latch onto an imperfect host! So when the Lightbringer tried to inhabit these people, the Deitanium activated and gave them powers while he transferred some of his madness. The Timekeeper's and the Lifegiver's madness wasn't only poisoning the Lightbringer, but it was also poisoning all these people! That must also be how the heroes on the council got their powers too! But, how have they not gone insane like all these people?

There is still a disconnect that I am missing. I needed time to wrap my head around this, but the screaming would not cease. This room was so much louder than that cruise ship. Why were the guards just standing and disregarding the chaos?

After gazing over the crowd for a few moments, Victoria proceeded to her left, leading us down the walkway before stopping in front of an open and empty cell. Once here, the pack of guards ushered Shameis toward the opening so the guard that Shameis injured could unlock Shameis's cuffs. Then, the same guard forcefully pushed Shameis inside, causing him to trip and fall. As he tried to get up, Victoria tapped the tablet screen she was carrying. Unfortunately, this action caused the glass wall to ceil Shameis in. Seeing this, Shameis scrambled to his feet but could not move fast enough to stop the cell from closing.

"I will get out of this!" Shameis shouted as he pounded on the glass with his left hand.

"Unlikely," Victoria replied as she led the guards away, leaving me to walk through the glass wall into Shameis's new room. There wasn't much to see in here. There was a sink with a mirror above it and a strange metal toilet to its left on one wall. On the opposite wall were two beds positioned in a bunk-like style. Not much at all. Upon seeing everything, I turned to Shameis and watched as pressed his head against the glass and sulked for a bit.

"I know this isn't ideal, but we will get out of this. Zatael said that everything is as it should be." I let out as I tried to cheer him up, but he did not respond. Instead, he just stood there while staring through the glass. Then, a few more aggressive inmates made their way up to examine Shameis while making a few threats. At least their hand gestures made them seem like they were threatening Shameis, but their voices were heavily muffled by the glass. Seeing these men trying to antagonize him,

392

Shameis let out a long sigh and stepped away from the glass before walking past me and sitting on the lower bunk of the bed. And all I could do is continue to watch and I pitied my now powerless love. "It'll be alright."

"Grim? I really hope you're still here." He let out with a sigh.

"Of course I am! I would never leave your side..." I let out as I quickly came closer to him and squatted down to his level, but he didn't look up at me. Instead, he just hung his head as he rested his left arm on his knee.

"If you are still here, please don't leave me," he muttered.

"I'm still here! I'm not going anywhere! I love you!" I then let out as I tried to caress his cheek, but I ended up phasing right through him. It took me a minute to process, but as soon as I realized the scope of what that collar was doing, I quickly got up and backed away from him. "Can you not see me anymore?" I questioned, but he did not respond. No! No! This can't be happening! We can't be back to square one! This isn't fair! How could they take away the one thing I genuinely care about? How is this the way things are supposed to be? Zatael, why did you not warn me?

I'm livid. I'm scared. Once again, I'm alone, and it feels as if the whole world is against me. No, Grim. It's okay. If something terrible was going to happen, Zatael would've told you. The world may be against us, and they may have separated you from your love, but apparently, everything is as it should be. Take a deep breath, calm yourself down. We will figure out a way to get that collar off of Shameis so we can be together again. If everything was out of place, Zatael would've told you. All we need to do is bunker down and hold fast. I'll stay by his side, just as he asked. We will figure something out. Besides, It's not only us two hanging in the balance. Zatael cannot exist without us. He wouldn't willingly allow himself to become an Ever-Lost Immortal... Would he?

CPSIA information can be obtained
at www.ICGtesting.com
Printed in the USA
LVHW011308180522
719075LV00015B/1547